'With rich writing and plenty of wit, _The_
Scottish history into a thrilling time-trav.....
Sophie Cameron, author of _Out of the Blue_ and _Last Bus to Neverland_

'With magical mysteries, secret societies and a wise-cracking best
mate, _The Rebel of Time_ is an exhilarating adventure through time and
space. A rich world with relatable characters, I devoured this novel'
Claire McFall, award-winning author of _Ferryman_

'An ambitious and inventive romp through time, rich in themes of
friendship, family and forging your own destiny'
Darren Simpson, author of _Scavengers_

'This opening volume lays the groundwork for what I believe will
be one of Scotland's great fantasy series. Craig Andrew Mooney is a
formidable storyteller and _The Rebel of Time_ is easily one of the best
books I've read this year'
Kenny Boyle, author of _The Tick and the Tock of the Crocodile Clock_

'A modern, fantastical adventure through time'
Pierre Novellie, award-winning comedian and writer

'A pacy, pictish/Celtic-inspired fantasy adventure story full of dangers
and intrigue, with a strong, touching and enduring friendship at its
core'
Janis Mackay, author of _The Accidental Time-Traveller_

'A wonderful debut novel. This writer is one to watch'
Kevin McLeod, author of _The Viking's Apprentice_ series

A compelling and unusual twist on the coming-of-age story with a rare
focus on positive male friendships'
Alan Bissett, author of _Boyracers_

Published in 2023
by Lightning Books
Imprint of Eye Books Ltd
29A Barrow Street
Much Wenlock
Shropshire
TF13 6EN

www.lightning-books.com

ISBN: 9781785633423

Cover by Nell Wood

Typeset in Adobe Jenson Pro, Cinzel and Cinzel Decorative
Printed and bound by CPI Group (UK) Ltd, Croydon, CR0 4YY

British Library Cataloguing in Publication Data
A catalogue record for this book is available from the British Library.

THE
REBEL
OF
TIME

CRAIG ANDREW MOONEY

Lightning Books

1

DESTINY CALLS

He's not coming. That's what the letter had said. For decades they had waited and there it was, in black and white. The boy was to be kept away from the dangers bound to his name, protected by ignorance.

The decision, once shared, would surely mean war. It was hard to envision any other outcome. Clutching the declaration was a professor, suffocated by tweed and sodden with sweat. Ianto Everie scuttled along a narrow corridor, his pristine Oxford shoes scuffing the velvet carpet.

Nonsense. Utter nonsense. Being asked to personally convey the news, like some errand boy. A doctorate in languages and yet, here he was, running around like Tobias' lapdog. The man had become drunk with power. That was it. He had been in charge too long.

Ianto's grip tightened around the letter. How many more

years of this would he be able to stand? Perhaps it was finally time to move on. Cambridge would surely jump at the chance to employ a linguist of his prestige.

The professor paused for a moment to catch his breath. His hand danced across his chest. There was that twinge again. It was happening more and more. Stress – that's what the doctor had said. But Ianto knew better. He'd seen too many of his own kind fall prey to similar conditions once they reached a certain age. You couldn't expect to wield power usually reserved for gods without a few side effects.

His knuckles brushed against the door. If he made light enough contact, he could simply turn around and get back to work. *Sorry, I must have missed you, Tobias. Avoiding you? Never.*

A silky-smooth voice came from inside. 'Enter.'

Damn.

Trying to rid himself of every last crease, Ianto smoothed his jacket and trousers. Only when the final crinkle had been dispatched did the door creak open.

Tobias Blue was hunched over his desk, scribbling furiously, his broad frame concealing his work. The minute he saw who was before him, the pen fell from his hand.

'Well?'

'His mother replied,' Ianto said, irked by the crack in his voice.

'His mother?'

'Yes. She…eh…well…'

'Oh, spit it out will you, Everie?'

Ianto started and his hand hovered over his chest again. 'She…she said that the boy is completely normal and is to be left alone.'

'Completely normal? A West?'

Ianto could almost taste the scepticism. 'It's not so outlandish an idea. His grandfather, for example?'

'But that was a chance in a thousand,' Tobias said. 'Let's not forget the boy's father.'

'A cautionary tale, yes.'

'And precisely why the boy must be trained.'

Ianto frowned. 'You mean to say, you wish the boy to come?'

'And why would I not?' Tobias said. 'Shouldn't any loyal Eternalisium member wish it?' His tone was amiable but his eyes flashed with the predatory gaze of a coiled snake. Ianto fought back a shudder.

A likely story, Ianto thought. He cleared his throat. 'But if the boy possesses no trace of—'

'I'm inclined to disbelieve the boy's mother. I think we should keep a very close eye on him over the coming year. If he shows no signs after that, then we can assume he is indeed as ordinary as his dear grandfather. But if not…then the safest place for him would be here.'

Ianto pulled himself up to full height, which wasn't at all impressive, and fixed his gaze on Tobias. 'And how exactly do you plan on keeping him safe?'

The linguist immediately regretted his boldness, as Tobias disappeared from his chair at such an impossible speed it was as if a trap door had opened beneath him. He left a spark of electric-green lightning in his wake and before Ianto could even finish his blink, Tobias was inches from him. While Ianto would have needed a small stepladder even to reach Tobias' shoulders, he stood his ground.

When Tobias spoke, his voice was low and soft but had the hiss to match his gaze. 'You appear to have woken up with an uncharacteristic amount of backbone this morning, Professor Everie,' he said. 'My loyalty is – and has always been – to this society and its preservation. And, of course, to those who require its sanctuary. Now in the interest of the boy's…*safety*…I ask that we keep an eye on him, just to make sure his mother isn't being foolish.'

Tobias grew closer still, his hot breath tickling Ianto's ear. 'And if he does exhibit any traces of his heritage, then I want him here. You will bring him to me. You will bring me Doran West.'

2

THE FOREST OF LINNTEAN

Doran West charged through the overgrown grass and hurdled over fence after fence. These were his fields, his home. He had the advantage.

Time was running out and he ignored the prickly sweat forming in his hair and on his face. The main road was in sight; he was almost there.

He vaulted over a crumbling drystone wall and stopped, taking in the cloudless sky. Catching his breath, he closed his eyes, the June sun warming his face.

And that's when he heard the school bus drive past him.

Great.

Following a swift kick at the gravel, he noticed Mrs Angus, the semi-professional gossip who spent her retirement glued to her living room window. He provided the customary smile and wave his mum had taught him to the old busybody and trudged in the direction of his school. After all, what choice did he have? One more missed day and his mum was sure to be called in. Then he would be subjected to a meeting with a bunch of sour-faced adults taking it in turns to outline their disappointment in him. Or better yet, utter the six words every teacher seemed programmed to say: 'We expect much more from you.' There was nothing for it. A hike it must be.

The walk to school, while long, was described by many a tourist as 'unbelievably picturesque'. And Doran supposed that was true. Objectively speaking. He imagined outsiders would be enchanted by such a view. The arrogant trio of mountains with their perfectly pointed snow-topped peaks. Who did they think they were? And then there was the winding 'devastatingly blue' loch, to quote another enthralled passer-by. A stretch of hydrogen and oxygen molecules that got lucky. That's all it was.

Doran reached a white sign which stated in big bold letters, 'YOU ARE NOW LEAVING LINNTEAN THANK YOU FOR VISITING'. He paused for a moment, as he always did, and glared at the black letters. Were they taunting him?

The village of Linntean was located in the Scottish Highlands, with nothing but remote islands to the west. The sort of places where puffins outnumber humans by about five to one. The village itself consisted of one main road winding around the houses, and various local businesses, clinging to the one place commercialism hadn't yet found.

The village didn't have enough people to warrant its own high school, which meant that those of age from the surrounding villages had to get the bus to a central academy. Five miles and two throbbing feet later, Doran reached this school's large, rusted gates and hobbled to the main entrance.

Glenmoral Academy was split into two large box-shaped

buildings, connected by a cylindrical red structure. The building had been painted that colour to mask its overwhelming dullness and to try to hide its need for renovation.

Doran arrived at the front door and pressed the buzzer for reception. He met the familiar gaze of Mrs Hunter, the head of the school office, whose beady eyes had seen multiple generations of the community pass through the school. According to Doran's mum, her 'winning' personality was nothing new. The pair performed what had become their habitual greeting for one another: Mrs Hunter raising a thin, wispy eyebrow at him, Doran replying with a small shrug and the slightest of smiles before being allowed to enter.

Mrs Hunter wrenched open the reception window. 'You're late, Doran West.'

'Mrs Hunter, how are we this morning?' Doran said, resting his elbows on the counter.

'You would think by sixteen years of age you'd have learnt to keep time,' Mrs Hunter said. 'This is the tenth time this year you have shown up whenever it has suited you.'

'The bus was early. You would think that by fifty, Jack would be starting to slow down.'

Mrs Hunter narrowed her eyes. 'Just like your father; always a quick answer.'

Doran fought to keep his face neutral. 'Yeah, well I wouldn't know, would I?' he said before tapping the counter. 'Be a pal and sign me in.'

It was 10:40, which meant he should be in History with Mr Bishop, a young, newly qualified teacher with an inordinate amount of enthusiasm. Doran reached the open classroom door and all thirty sets of eyes fell on him. It was always a downside to being late. The attention. A few extra minutes in bed didn't seem a fair exchange for their judgemental stares.

'Ah, Doran. Nice of you to join us,' Mr Bishop said, not a trace of sarcasm in his voice. 'Take a seat, take a seat. We are just about to learn about some local history.'

A collective groan rumbled through the classroom.

'Now, now,' Mr Bishop said, ever the showman trying to placate his audience. 'Remember, history isn't just about world wars and bubonic plagues. We are all here as a result of history and some very interesting things might have happened right on your doorstep.'

'Only thing on my doorstep is what my dog had for lunch, sir,' came the cocky voice of Kieran McDowall from the back of the room.

This provoked some laughter from the class, a few only joining in out of fear of reprisal from the school's current alpha male. Doran remained quiet, settling into his seat and trying to blend into the desk and chair.

'Yes, very amusing, Kieran,' Mr Bishop said when the laughter died down. 'But I'm talking about something which is unique to this area and this area alone. I'm talking about why Linntean celebrates *Latha an Siubhailadair*. Does anyone know why Linntean celebrates *Latha an Siubhailadair?*'

A small, mousy-haired boy raised a timid hand. 'Isn't it to do with Pictish times?'

'Close,' Mr Bishop said. 'Anyone have anything to add?'

A girl at the back of the class shot her hand into the air. 'Sir? Is it not about remembering people going missing back in olden times and those weird Jedi kinda people you see folk dressing up like?'

'You're both dancing around the answer,' Mr Bishop said with a smile. He turned to the whiteboard and began writing while he explained. *'Latha an Siubhailadair* or "Traveller's Day" traces its origins to Pictish times, around the same era that the Romans began to invade Britain. Now the Picts would use such a day to remember those of their tribe who had gone missing throughout the past year. Some people believe these disappearances were due to the Romans stealing people away in the night. Perhaps to ship back to Rome as slaves or for some other nefarious purposes. Though this is widely accepted, there is another more mystical and mythological story that I am sure most of you remember drawing pictures about in primary school. It is said that...'

Mr Bishop continued to drone on but Doran's attention drifted out of the window to the PE lesson outside. He had noticed his best friend, Zander Munro, staggering around the faded running track, panting like a thirsty dog. A smile spread across Doran's face, knowing exactly what Zander would be thinking at that moment. Firstly, how to successfully get away with killing their PE teacher, Mr Urquhart, and secondly, how to make light of his distinct lack of ability. Zander had always been short for his age and, with little need for persuasion, had taken on the role of the year's jokester.

Sure enough, as he approached the finish line, he slowed down, raising his arms in the air like a rock star trying to get the audience to make some noise. The rest of his class, who had finished a full minute ago, began clapping and whooping, much to the annoyance of Mr Urquhart. Zander came to a complete stop, cupping his hand behind his ear. The class grew louder and more animated, and he nodded in appreciation of their response. He feigned a run-up, then dashed to the finish line, performing a dive forward roll and ending in a seated position. He raised his arms as a gymnast might to indicate the completion of their routine, waiting humbly for the applause. It came in floods, and he stood and bowed, shaking a few hands before coming to a stop in front of Mr Urquhart. Zander also grabbed his hand and shook it firmly, patting his teacher on the arm. It was then that Doran finally let out the snort of laughter he had been trying so hard to suppress.

'Something funny about pagan sacrifice, Doran?' Mr Bishop said.

Doran's attention snapped back to where it should be. Once again, all eyes were on him. 'No sir. Sorry,' he said, sinking even further into his chair.

Not soon enough, the school bell rang and Doran sprang from his seat. Swinging his bag over his shoulder, he made a beeline for the exit. He had to escape before...

'Doran, would you mind waiting behind for a second?' Mr Bishop called after him.

So close. He hovered by the doorway while his peers bustled around him as though he were a troublesome rock in a fast-flowing river. Only when they had all gone, did he turn around to see the familiar concerned smile on his teacher's face.

'Everything all right?' Mr Bishop asked.

'Sir?' Doran replied, shuffling on the spot.

'Late again – and may I say you seem distracted. I'm just wondering if you're all right?'

'Fine, sir,' Doran said, one eye on the exit. 'Can I go?'

Mr Bishop sighed, sitting on the edge of his desk in an apparent attempt to seem relatable and understanding. A classic ploy from the teacher handbook. 'You're a bright boy, Doran. But you seem rather disengaged in my class. Local history bore you, does it?'

Doran didn't answer, suddenly finding his shoe laces very

interesting.

'It's all right,' Mr Bishop said with a chuckle. 'I know it's not everyone's cup of tea. I have the advantage of not being from Linntean. So for me, your village's history is all new and fascinating. Whereas I imagine you have had it drummed into you your whole life.'

Doran nodded and managed to tear his gaze away from his feet. Mr Bishop reached behind his back and pulled out a small textbook. The teacher gave it a loving look that lasted a fraction too long.

'This was given to me by my old professor,' Mr Bishop said. 'It's what got me so interested in this subject in the first place. I'd like you to hold onto it for me.'

'What?'

'Just for a couple of weeks. Have a read and see if it piques your interest.'

Doran outstretched his hand and accepted the book. As he did so, he felt a small tingle in his fingers, like a static electric shock from a balloon. With a start, he dropped the book and it hit the floor. 'Sorry, I…' he said, bending down and gathering up the book.

'It's all right, it's all right; don't worry about it.'

Doran stared at the book in his hands. When he had felt the shock, he could have sworn he had seen a short-lived green spark. He looked at Mr Bishop, whose expression had not changed. He didn't appear to have seen anything.

The book was faded and battered; the spine worn. Doran ran his hands across the cover, its texture like sandpaper. It had no attractive artwork – merely gold writing which read: *Ancient Myths of the Pictish People by Oswald MacAlpine*.

'It's a good read. Chapters ten through eighteen are all about the lesser-known tribes of this area, including Linntean.'

'Thank you, sir.'

'History made us all. It's important to learn where we come from. It helps us discover who we are.'

Doran nodded again. *What?* Brandishing the book, he gave an awkward smile and hurried out of the classroom.

Once in the freedom of the corridor, he stared at the book again, wishing Mr Bishop was as cynical and apathetic as the other teachers in the school. Why did he have to care? Did he not have a life?

Doran stuffed the book into his school bag and headed toward his locker.

The corridor was crowded, every class emptying and moving to its next destination. Doran wove in and out of the bodies to reach his locker, delighted to see Zander was already at his, putting away his PE kit.

'Quite the performance,' Doran said.

Zander spun around, the curls of his mousy-brown hair bouncing. 'Yeah. Coach says I should make the track team this year,' he said in a convincing American accent. 'If I can get my eight hundred metres time under ten minutes that is,' he added, in his natural Scottish twang.

'Sport's Day will be a breeze I'm sure,' Doran said, grinning.

'What time did you make it in today then?' Zander asked. 'Maybe you should buy a rooster?'

'I notice you didn't ask Jack to stop the bus for me.'

'No fun in that.'

Doran laughed. 'Not like it's my first time.'

'Mrs Hunter give you much stick?'

'No more than usual. You think she'll ever retire?'

'Doubt it. My theory is that she might have died about ten

years ago but didn't realise. Now she's just haunting the place in between filing… You coming tonight?'

Doran had been waiting for this question. 'Do I have a choice?'

'Not really, no.' Zander jabbed him on the arm. 'Come on, we've finally started to get invited to these things. You've got to come. Be a person, you know?'

Doran rubbed his arm, his eyes narrowed. '*You're* invited.'

'And you're my plus one,' Zander said. 'I tell you something. Taking drama was the best thing I've ever done. Those girls are the people to know in this school.'

'Not to mention it's a place where you can finally fulfil your incurable desire to show off,' Doran added.

Zander grinned and shook him by the shoulder. 'There he is,' he said. 'Have you asked your mum yet?'

'What do you think?' Doran asked, eyebrow raised. 'Any tips?'

Zander scoffed. 'Doubt my dad would even notice I was out. I don't plan on telling him either.'

Doran nodded, regretting the question. Parents had always been a sensitive subject with Zander. When he was eight his mum had walked out on his dad and left Linntean without warning. Neither had spoken to her since. Since then, his dad had spent more time drinking than being with his son. Zander had basically lived with Doran during their final primary school years.

'Besides,' Zander continued, 'your mum won't mind, surely?'

'You've met her, right?'

'Fair,' Zander said. 'Well, don't let me down. I'm such a shy, anxious young man without you.'

'Is that right?'

'Rendered mute, I assure you,' Zander said, trying and failing to look as serious as possible. 'Right, I'll see you at lunch.' He flounced away but paused to call back, ensuring the whole corridor could hear. 'We can talk through our outfits for tonight. Make sure they don't clash.'

He smirked before darting out of sight, leaving Doran to roll his eyes. He considered his friend's pep talk as he shuffled along the grimy linoleum floor. While Zander's words had provided some much-needed confidence, he hoped the evening wouldn't be as bad as he was envisioning.

Doran passed the two lacklustre apple trees outside his home and traipsed up the front garden path. The plot of land on which the house stood had been in the West family since the 1700s. Doran had been entertained as a child with stories of his ancestor, Jonathan West, an English soldier who fell in love with a Scottish woman. He eventually defected to the Jacobite side during the War of the British Succession and fought alongside his adopted Scottish brethren at the Battle of Culloden. As Doran recalled, the story did not have a happy ending. Their son, Douglas West, managed to survive and built the first house on this land in the late eighteenth century. The current version was the third incarnation, a sturdy two-bedroom bungalow. Doran's parents had built it themselves with help from local contractors.

The house and the plot of land would one day be his to do with as he pleased. As much as he hated Linntean, he knew he could never sell it. Though he also didn't want to stay. The plan since beginning secondary school had been to do enough to escape this close-minded, small village. At eighteen, he could leave and go to university, perhaps in a city like Edinburgh, or even London. He thought of all those people, bustling around, going about their day. All the traffic; people rushing. Rushing to get somewhere. Imagine! Doran heard a rustling inside the house and his momentary glee faded. That must be his reason to stay.

He opened the front door to see his mum, Kate West, moving around the narrow hallway at record speed. 'Doran, thank God. Help me find my keys, would you?' she said, lifting a small wicker basket in the air.

Doran strode to the array of coats hanging up and put his hand in one of the pockets, immediately bringing up a set of jingling keys. His mum smacked her palm against her forehead. She took the keys and smiled, brushing his cheek. 'Thank you, Dory,' she said. 'What would I do without you?'

Doran shrugged away from her. 'Don't you think it's time we retired the Dory nickname?'

His mum laughed and resumed her chaotic bustling. 'Not a chance. She was your favourite character as a kid and it matches your name. It's too perfect.'

'I was three, Mum. Let it go.'

'And you always will be,' Kate said, giving him a playful tap on the nose.

Doran couldn't help but grin. 'You're a lot sometimes, you know that?'

'Ooh so sassy today,' Kate said. 'Let me guess – girl trouble?'

'I'm leaving,' Doran said, spinning on his heels and aiming for his room at the back of the house.

Kate giggled. 'I saw Rufus this morning,' she called as she was putting the keys in the door.

'Please tell me you didn't feed him this time?'

Rufus was a scruffy, one-antlered deer who lived near the West family's plot of land. He would regularly hop over the fence and explore their garden. Doran's mum had begun leaving leftover food for him to scavenge.

'I think he's starting to know who I am,' she replied, with a worrying level of excitement.

'You can't have a deer as a pet,' Doran said. 'It's bad enough that you've named him.'

'That's so unfair,' Kate whined in an all-too-familiar tone.

'Fantastic impersonation,' Doran said, pouting. 'Do you have any more? Perhaps we can get you on *The Highlands Have Talent* next year.'

Kate giggled again and threw open the front door.

Doran chucked his school bag onto his bed with a thud. He was about to unpack when his mum spoke again. 'OK, I'm late for my shift. Dinner is in the oven. Should be ready in five minutes. Now, remember I'm on the night shift this week so I won't be back until tomorrow afternoon.'

Doran popped his head back into the hallway. 'Wait. Before you go...'

'What's up?'

'There's a party in the woods tonight,' Doran continued, considering the order of every word. 'I thought I might go?'

Kate's face fell. 'OK. Be careful.'

'Just like that? I can go?' He hadn't been expecting that response. His mum had always been overly cautious with him – overprotective at times. He had never known why, or what triggered this behaviour. She could be so relaxed about certain things, almost closer to a big sister. Yet there were times this was definitely not the case and she would put her foot down quite forcibly.

'Yes, just like that,' Kate said, with an evenness he found very suspicious. 'As you said, you're not three any more and it would be hypocritical of me to say no. I mean, it's not like I didn't do that at your age. In fact, your dad and I...'

She caught herself mid-sentence and a pregnant pause filled the air. In the silence, Doran's thoughts of escape only minutes before returned, accompanied by a fresh wave of guilt. Doran's father had died when he was very young. He had only known one parent in his life and was fully aware of the sacrifices she had made for him. A single mother, working long hours to make sure he had a decent life. Could he really repay that sacrifice by abandoning her at the earliest opportunity?

His mum appeared to recover, and smiled, though only with the lower half of her face. 'Have fun and—'

'Stay away from the top of the waterfall. I know.'

She gave a less forced smile and nodded as she closed the door behind her.

Doran hovered in the doorway of his room until a sharp *beep* from the oven punctured the silence and he hurried to the kitchen to retrieve his dinner.

He carried the plate of steaming lasagne to his bedroom and laid it on his desk. As he wrestled some books from his bag, the smallest one slid from the pile, knocking his plate onto the floor.

Doran swore loudly and scooped up his plate, returning it to the desk. *That's going to leave a stain*, he thought, as he inexpertly rubbed the mess into the carpet with a nearby towel.

Resting on his knees, he sighed and rounded on the source of the carnage.

Mr Bishop's book lay open beside the stain. Several black and white pictures, labelled as Pictish symbols were dotted across the page. Doran glanced at the chapter title – Chapter Eleven – *The Legend of Garnaith* – before slamming the book shut and stuffing it back into his bag.

After salvaging what was left of his dinner, he scanned his schoolbooks. His shoulders slumped as he tapped his pen on his unfinished homework. The tapping grew louder and louder until it started to sound like a knock at the door, which jolted him back to consciousness. The pen fell, hitting the paper with a dull thud.

He pulled himself out of the chair and paced beside his bed, ruffling his hair with his fingers. Eventually, he threw open the wardrobe. The first problem to overcome: he had to decide what to wear that night.

The marble pools of Linntean were famous around the world. The ancient waterfalls had gradually eroded the rock to create deep basins that had grown more popular with every passing year. Tourists would flock from far and wide to marvel at the majestic views and swim in the emerald and cerulean tarns. But those who had grown up there knew more than the visitors to their village.

The woods of Linntean were home to many secrets. The majority had been transformed into myths and bedtime stories, which had been a staple of Doran's childhood. The trees stretched across and up the area's largest mountain, and, if you knew the way, you might happen upon a clearing no tourist had ever visited.

Doran emerged from the trees and looked up at the largest waterfall Linntean had to offer. The water cascaded down the rocks a full fifteen metres before crashing into the deep marble pool at the bottom. Daylight was fading fast, but the sun and the blue sky were still reflecting, creating a shade of water more associated with the Mediterranean. Despite Doran's downer on his home, he had to admit that few other places could boast such a view.

As he ambled over the small ridge, the sound of the waterfall was increasingly overwhelmed by music and youthful cheering. Gathered by the pool at the bottom of the waterfall were the majority of the senior pupils at Glenmoral Academy. From where Doran was standing, they looked like giant bees, packed together in a tight swarm. Zander had been right. Everyone was indeed there.

He reached the bottom of the path and waded through the various dancing bodies, providing an awkward nod hello to those who spotted him.

Wham. A set of short arms wrapped themselves around his waist and tried to wrestle him to the ground. Doran only just managed to stay on his feet, shoving off his attacker.

'You made it,' Zander cried, with a level of gusto Doran hadn't quite been expecting. He grasped him by both shoulders, holding him at arms-length as a parent might to check if their child was presentable. 'You clean up well. I'm glad I didn't wear my two-year-old black shirt.'

'Shut it,' Doran said, shoving him. 'I know my look.'

Zander laughed. 'Goth kids are off doing pagan rituals in the woods if you want to join them.'

Doran gave a forced chuckle. 'Hilarious. You should save all that wit for your drama girls.'

'Funny you should mention that…'

Doran's eyes narrowed as he searched his friend's face for the rest of the sentence. 'What have you done?'

Zander's jaw clenched and he swung his arm around Doran, ushering him to walk and talk with him. 'Well, you know how me and Georgia Mackay have been messaging after school and stuff?'

He seemed reluctant to get to the point and Doran knew he wasn't going to like the final destination of this conversation.

'Uhuh.'

'Well, it turns out Hanna has just broken up with her boyfriend and Georgia's saying she needs to spend time with her tonight. But I know if I can just get her alone for a bit then I might stand a chance of getting beyond "friend" status.'

Doran decided to raise an eyebrow rather than respond.

'So, I was wondering if you could speak to Hanna and... distract her? Maybe flash a bit of that winning personality?'

Doran glanced over Zander's shoulder to see Hanna Williams, the school's head girl. She was twisting that perfect wavy hair of hers into a bun and laughing with Georgia. The two were sitting on a nearby rock, swinging their legs and chatting. Doran was momentarily mesmerised by the water trickling down Hanna's olive arms before he remembered why he was looking at her in the first place.

His face must have betrayed everything he was thinking but he decided to hammer his point home. 'You want me to talk to Hanna Williams? As in pretty, popular, Hanna Williams? Hanna Williams, who has never so much as looked in my direction? Hanna Williams, who is the recent ex-girlfriend of Kieran McDowall? The school's resident gorilla and all-round nutcase?'

'Basically, yes. Exactly.'

'I hate you,' Doran said, and part of him almost meant it.

'No you don't. I'm far too adorable,' Zander said. 'Please mate, this could be my one shot with Georgia.'

Doran watched as Zander fell to his knees. Like a sinner asking for forgiveness, he clasped his hands together in prayer, batting his eyes for added effect. Doran was in no mood for granting absolution and hauled his friend to his feet. 'Get up, will you?' he said, craning his neck to see if anyone was watching them. 'Fine. I'll do it.'

Zander gave him a swift hug. 'I owe you one.'

'You can start by not messing around, and behaving like a normal human.'

'You got it, captain,' Zander said, saluting.

Doran grinned. 'You're an idiot.'

'Damn right,' Zander replied, wiggling his eyebrows. 'Let's go.'

With every step, Doran felt a fresh wave of panic. What was he even supposed to say? Did he open with a joke? Should he play it cool? Should he scream that there was a bear behind them and run away? That last option became more and more tempting as he and Zander reached the two girls.

His experience with girls was limited to say the least. He had kissed Danielle Hutton at his fifth birthday party, where both parties had found the whole ordeal rather gross. Somehow, he didn't feel that was going to cut it.

Before he knew it, Zander was giving him a supportive pat on the shoulder and hurrying off with Georgia. This left Doran standing in front of an incredibly indifferent Hanna, who seemed affronted by her friend's decision to leave.

The silence seemed to stretch on forever. Doran's mind kept tussling between complete blankness and loud yelling. He reached to every corner of his brain, rummaging for anything useful to say. Hell; two or three coherent words would do. Bonus points on offer if they made sense one after the other.

'Nice night…'

'What's that?'

Doran shook his head. 'Just a rubbish way of opening a conversation.'

Hanna's mouth twitched and her face softened a little. 'Zander put you up to this I take it?'

'No, I regularly look for ways to make myself feel as uncomfortable as possible.'

Hanna laughed. 'Well, I'm sorry you've been forced to come over here. Helping those two get loved up probably wasn't your idea of a party.'

Doran nodded, smiling. He gestured to the open space on the rock beside Hanna. She allowed him to sit and he did so, crossing his legs, then uncrossing them. *Which was more natural? How did human beings sit again?* 'To tell you the truth, I wouldn't know. This is my first real party.'

'No way!' Hanna said, mouth agape. 'Well, you're talking to a girl so that's a good start.'

'Feels amazing,' Doran said. He may as well poke fun at his gawkiness.

Hanna laughed again. That was twice now. 'You're doing just fine. And talking to *me*, Hanna Williams and all,' she said, smirking.

'I think bravery points should be awarded, yes.'

'Well, you're funny. Don't lose that.'

Her fingertips grazed his arm and Doran tried to keep his face as neutral as possible. *Come on*, he thought. *Act like pretty girls touch your arm all the time. Just like any other night as far as you're concerned.* Her face then contorted as if she had seen something she couldn't quite comprehend. 'You also have really nice eyes. What colour is that?'

Between the touch and the fact that her ocean-blue gaze was now fixed on him, Doran momentarily felt his brain freeze over again. 'Oh that,' he said, realising she meant the jagged ring of bright green which circled his chestnut-brown eyes. 'That's nothing. My mum said it's a family trait.'

'It's different. Something else you've got going for you.'

She was being nice. More than that, could she possibly be *enjoying* talking to him?'You know, you aren't what I expected.'

Hanna grinned.'Yeah, I've grown up in the last few months. Getting to the end of high school does that to you. Soon I'll be out of this place. Off to a whole new adventure. I'll leave all these people behind and won't look back.' She nodded to Kieran McDowall who Doran noticed was chancing glances in their direction. Hanna sighed and looked up at the now dark sky as she continued.'It'll be nice not to be Hanna Williams. Head girl. Popular. "*All should fear her*". I'll get to just be…me again, you know?'

'I think I do, yeah,' Doran murmured, settling on a bright star in a glittering display.'Can I come too?'

Hanna laughed again, this time more loudly and Kieran's attention fell completely upon them.'You'll be out of here in a couple of years too, hopefully. Big old world out there. Got to see it.'

'Yeah.'

A red plastic cup arced through the air and collided with Doran's head. The fizzy liquid exploded over him, soaking his dark hair. Both he and Hanna leapt to their feet and before he knew what was happening, he felt himself being grabbed and pushed against a nearby tree.

'What you trying here then?' came the arrogant voice of Kieran McDowall through the froth.

Doran blinked away the liquid on his face to see his assailant more clearly. Hanna appeared next to Kieran and grabbed his arm.'Get off, Kieran!' she yelled.'He wasn't trying anything.'

'Like hell he wasn't,' Kieran said, thrusting him against the tree again.

'Now, now, Kieran, let's be gentlemen about this,' Doran

said between winces. In these situations he knew flippancy was rarely recommended, particularly when the adversary's fists were quicker than his brain. But he couldn't help himself.

'Someone doesn't know the law of the jungle,' Kieran said. 'That's my girl you were talking to.'

'I am not,' Hanna said, still trying to pull Kieran away. 'We broke up, you moron.'

Kieran didn't appear to like that last comment because he dropped Doran as though he were a book with no pictures. 'What did you call me?' he said, advancing towards Hanna.

Doran coughed. '"Law of the jungle?"' he said. '*Seriously?*' he added to Hanna.

Flippancy may well be ill-advised, but antagonising is near-suicidal. Though it had the desired effect. Kieran turned back to face him instead, which let Hanna slip away to find her friends. She glanced back at him, biting her lip, but Doran nodded for her to carry on.

'What makes you think she'd be interested in you?' Kieran asked with a sneer.

'Well, she went out with you, so surely even a shaved gorilla would have a chance.'

Kieran swung a leg and booted Doran in the stomach, delivering him to the dirt. 'You just don't know when to shut up, do you?'

'It's a sickness,' Doran said, choking on his words.

Kieran shook his head and was gearing himself up for another kick when a familiar voice yelled, 'Hey, Kieran!'

He paused, confused by the interruption. Doran's eyes refocused to see Zander emerging from the bushes, Georgia slightly behind.

'Who are you?' Kieran demanded.

'I'm Zander Munro,' Zander said, as though introducing himself at a friendly dinner party. 'I sit behind you in English. You've got a fantastic undercut. Who did that for you?'

For a moment, Kieran resembled a curious infant, mouthing back the words he had just heard.

'I was just wondering if you could keep the noise down a bit – you're kind of spoiling the mood if you know what I mean?' Zander said with a wink, prompting Georgia to hit him with mild disgust. 'Ow. Was that necessary?'

Once Georgia had marched off and was out of earshot, Zander leant towards Kieran. 'We totally made out,' he said in a stage whisper, cupping his hand beside his mouth.

Doran grinned and crawled on his hands and knees behind the tree before slipping into the forest. He'd have to thank his friend in the morning for his excellent distraction.

As soon as Zander's voice began to fade, Doran broke into a run. He charged through the spiky bushes and wove in and out of the trees.

'After him!' he heard Kieran call to his friends in the distance.

It wasn't the most ideal of head starts but it would have to do. If he could just make it to…

'He's heading for Garnaith's Path!' Doran heard Kieran yell. 'Cut him off, McCart.'

Doran swore under his breath. Of all the times Kieran could have picked to have more than one brain cell. Garnaith's Path was the closest way out of the woods and the nearest to his house. He'd have to find another way.

'There!' McCart said.

They were gaining on him. He ran even harder, desperate to stay ahead.

Chest burning, he made a snap decision and scurried to the

right, bashing into a low, protruding branch. As he stumbled, he heard the boys' voices getting louder and closer. Where could he go? How could he get away?

He kept weaving and changing direction until even he wasn't sure where he was headed. Eventually, a low rumbling sound crept into his eardrums and gave him pause. It couldn't be. How had he ended up there?

Doran felt a squelch underfoot as he scaled the steep hill. He could no longer hear his hunters so he caught his breath while he had the chance. Edging his way to where the ground stopped, he peered over the side to see the same waterfall at whose base he had been a short while ago.

As he stared at the raging avalanche of water, a thought struck him that he quickly dismissed as crazy. He couldn't? Could he? If he didn't die from the fall, his mum would surely kill him. There had to be an easier way to escape. A safer way. But he couldn't think of a direction to go at this point where at least one of the boys wouldn't catch him.

He peered over the side again. The idea was becoming both crazier and more necessary by the moment. Doran edged towards the precipice. The forest floor ran out, and before he could stop himself, he did what any right-minded person tells you not to do in such a situation: he looked down.

His legs wobbled and, with the poorest of timing, he heard Kieran's voice once again. It had an unmistakable sense of glee. 'I've got him lads! He's over there!'

Doran stumbled backwards away from the waterfall. He tripped over a large root and fell, crashing onto the ground and rolling back down the hill, unable to stop himself. Rocks and tree stumps battered into him, piercing his skin.

He thought he would never stop falling – until he clattered

into something solid. His head bobbed lazily, the trees and the rage of the rushing water interspersed with quiet darkness.

His eyes tried to focus on what he had crashed into. Some large rock?

No. A rock implied no thought or placement. Doran didn't understand why the thought had crossed his mind but it was as if this piece of stone was *meant* to be here. It stood waiting, covered in moss, forgotten.

Doran slammed his hand against the stone, trying to use it to get to his feet. As he fought to stay conscious, his hand slipped down the jagged, uneven surface.

Ouch. Doran retracted his fingers. It was hot; more than that: boiling.

As he looked closer, he thought he could see carvings underneath the thinner moss – and he suddenly realised they were like the black and white drawings he'd glimpsed in Mr Bishop's book. *Pictish?* But these were no pictures. The carvings were glowing, growing a brighter shade of green with every moment that passed.

Doran found his hands floating of their own accord towards the glowing symbols. He felt a tingle in his fingertips. It was the same sensation he had felt in Mr Bishop's classroom. His hands were hovering just above the enchanting light when a low whistle cut through the air.

Darkness threatened to overwhelm Doran as he turned in search of the sound. He wrestled it back, desperate to stay awake and find the source of the noise.

It was then he saw a man, cloaked in shadow, standing up where Doran had fallen from minutes before. A fleeting spell of blackness overcame him. When he regained his senses the man had vanished.

'Where did he go?' Doran heard Kieran ask his friends.

'He must have turned back and tried to make a break for the path again,' one of the boys replied.

Kieran growled. 'Come on,' he said and he charged off, the two boys in hot pursuit.

Doran lay very still, clinging to the stone. What if they saw the glowing light? He may as well have sent up a flare.

'What's that?' he heard Kieran call.

'He's over here!'

Doran heard the rustling leaves crunch louder with every step. The darkness continued to tempt with its warm embrace. It would be so easy just to give in.

They were going to find him, and he could do nothing to stop them. Why did Zander have to bring him to this party? At school, Kieran and his goons wouldn't dream of touching him. They at least had that much sense. But out in the woods anything could happen and be chalked up to an unfortunate accident. For once he longed to be within earshot of a teacher.

The tingling sensation had returned to his fingertips, and as he blinked in and out of consciousness he was sure he saw bright green sparks again, flashing in the darkness all around him.

The last thing he heard was an unmistakably triumphant cackle from Kieran as he finally gave in to the nothingness.

3

TRAVELLER'S DAY

'*DORAN…*'

Doran's eyes flickered open, an unknown voice and the faintest trace of the whistling sound ringing in his ears. Above was the clear blue sky; beneath, dewy grass that tickled his palms.

He wasn't sure how long he remained still, unfazed by the damp seeping into his clothes, or the mild morning breeze that made his hairs stand on end.

It was morning.

Doran sat bolt upright. Blinking, he tried to adjust to his new surroundings. He wasn't sure how he knew he was no longer in the forest, but perhaps the aroma of freshly cut grass gave it away.

He swivelled himself around and gaped at the sight of a familiar, ugly red cylinder. He was at school. How could he possibly be at school? While the forests of Linntean were vast and stretched all around the area, the waterfall would still have to be at least five miles away.

Images of the previous night flashed in his mind and he jerked his head around, ignoring the burning pressure from behind his eyelids. But there was no sign of his pursuers. There was no sign of anyone.

Doran pulled out his phone: 7:35am. So, it was indeed the next morning. But that still didn't explain how he had managed to get there. He pressed his temples as if trying to squeeze the memories out of his head. More images flashed in his mind but quickly faded, forever lost, like a dream dwelt on for too long.

The last distinct memory he could muster was those green sparks dancing all around him. He had clearly hit his head rather hard. Perhaps he had been seeing stars. His hand danced across the back of his head, feeling a grape-sized lump underneath his hair.

Choices limited, Doran limped towards the main entrance of the school. He tugged on the front door but it remained shut. Through the glass, he saw Mrs Hunter gawping at him, as if he was a wildcat that had wandered in from the forest.

Mrs Hunter slowly reached under her desk and the door clicked open. Her eyes didn't leave him as he staggered towards her, resting his elbows on the counter just as he had done the previous morning. He frowned. Had it really been a whole day since then?

Mrs Hunter's lips were not twisted into her usual grimace. For the first time in all the years Doran had appeared outside her office, she looked concerned.

'What on earth has happened to you, young man?'

Doran wished he knew the answer, searching every corner of his brain. He was about to respond when he realised how dry his mouth was. He glanced inside to see a group of pupils sitting eating toast and jabbering to one another. 'Breakfast club,' he said, thinking on his feet. His voice sounded like he smoked ten packs of cigarettes a day.

'Well, I'm glad you're finally starting to make an effort to arrive at school on time,' Mrs Hunter said. 'But I must admit this seems a little excessive. Did your mother kick you out of the house this morning?'

'Yeah… She had an early shift,' Doran said, continuing to invent wildly.

'While I commend her for it, she has allowed you to come to school in quite frankly a horrid state. You look as though you've been up all night. Where's your tie? And are your trousers torn?'

Doran looked down at his outfit from the party. There was indeed a gaping hole in the left knee of his jeans. 'Got dressed in the dark.'

'Clearly. You're not coming in looking like that. Mrs Scrimgeour would have a fit. There are spare uniforms in lost property. Go and find something your size. I'll want it back on Monday, mind you.'

Where usually a sarcastic comment would have escaped his lips, Doran couldn't seem to find the words. Instead, he meandered into the school and found a passable shirt, tie and pair of trousers. Before he knew it, he was sitting in the dining hall, having a staring contest with an uninviting piece of soggy toast.

His attention drifted to two of his teachers, who were rushing to put up a banner before the bell rang. It read 'LATHA AN SIUBHAILADAIR' with the helpful translation of 'TRAVELLER'S DAY' underneath in bright, multi-coloured letters. Doran found himself drawn to the luminous green of the first 'E'. The letter seemed to be leaping at him, like he was staring at it through a pair of 3D glasses.

The chatter of his peers seemed distant and muffled as the unnerving whistling sound invaded Doran's mind once again. Goosebumps arose across his arms as that unknown voice also returned, calling to him, whispering in his ear. 'Doran... Doran... DORAN...'

'Doran?'

He snapped to attention to see Mr Bishop standing before him. There was that concerned smile again. Did he ever have a day off?

'Come with me.'

Doran was in such a malleable state he complied instantly, gliding after Mr Bishop and leaving his untouched piece of mushy toast behind.

'Take a seat,' Mr Bishop said as they entered his classroom. 'Are you all right? You look a bit peaky.'

'Fine,' Doran mumbled.

'Has anything happened?' Mr Bishop asked. 'Anything you want to talk about?'

Doran shook his head, forcing his face to look as nonchalant as possible. Inside, he was still searching for any memory of his missing chunk of time.

'All right,' Mr Bishop said, though Doran doubted he had given up his enquiry. 'Did you have a chance to read the book I lent you yet?'

Doran shook his head. *Books? Really?* He had far more pressing concerns than some old textbook.

'I'm sure you'll get around to it,' Mr Bishop said. 'It's got quite a few interesting theories about Traveller's Day, actually.' He gestured to the title on his whiteboard which read, 'HAPPY

TRAVELLER'S DAY!' in big black letters. The handwriting seemed to mirror Mr Bishop's frustratingly sunny disposition. 'Some of the symbols in the book refer to it.'

'Symbols?' Doran said, finally meeting Mr Bishop's gaze.

Curiosity flashed in his teacher's eyes. 'Yes…'

'I saw some.'

'In the book?'

'Yes…but also…'

'Also? Also where, Doran?'

The school bell cut through the corridors.

'Ugh. You'd best get to assembly. As must I as a matter of fact,' Mr Bishop said, glancing out of the classroom. He seemed disappointed at their conversation being cut short. Doran hoped that didn't mean he'd try to find him later for a further catch-up. There should be a daily limit on chats with teachers.

'Assembly?'

'Of course. It's the Traveller's Day assembly today, remember?' Mr Bishop said, with an eagerness Doran had no intention of matching.

'Right… Of course,' Doran said, rising dreamily to his feet and wandering out of the classroom to be carried off by the procession of people outside.

He surfed the wave of his peers into the assembly hall and sat down, watching the remainder of the school file in. Doran caught a glimpse of Kieran McDowall and his cronies. Their mouths hung open, staring at him as if he had just performed some incredible magic trick. Clearly, they too had no idea how he had eluded them the previous night.

'Well look who survived,' Zander said, plonking himself down next to Doran. 'You managed to get home then?'

His grin fell away the moment he caught sight of Doran.

'Oh my god. Look at the state of you. Mate, I'm so sorry. I should have come after you. I thought you'd have had enough of a head start to get to Garnaith's Path. They've given you a right seeing to, haven't they?' Zander examined him, inspecting all the scratches and bumps on his face and neck.

'They didn't.'

'What do you mean?' Zander asked. 'You certainly look as if you've taken a beating.'

'Thanks.'

'I'm only saying if Kieran didn't do this to you, then what happened?'

'That's just it – I don't know,' Doran said as Mrs Scrimgeour, the headteacher, walked across the small stage to begin her address. 'One minute I'm running for my life, the next I fall and smack my head on some old stone statue.'

'And then what?' Zander whispered, completely ignoring Mrs Scrimgeour's demand for silence.

'I was completely out of it,' Doran said. 'Hearing strange voices and sounds, seeing things. A weird glow, a man…'

'What man?'

'It was only for a second. Probably just the knock to my head playing tricks on me.'

'Did your mum freak?'

'Not seen her yet. She's on nights this week and besides…' Doran paused, unsure whether to go on. Would Zander think he had gone mad?

'What?'

'I woke up here.'

'*Here?*' Zander said, a little too loudly, and a few eyes fell on them. Doran saw Mrs Hunter give them a reproachful look and they huddled closer, speaking out of the corner of their mouths.

'What do you mean here?'

'In the school grounds.'

'How on earth did you end up here?'

'No idea. The last thing I remember, I was about to pass out in the woods. Kieran and his fellow Neanderthals had found me – and then I woke up here.'

'So, you blacked out?'

'Must have done,' Doran said, though a small part of him was struggling to believe it. How could he possibly have made it all the way to the school grounds, injured, potentially concussed, and with three determined bullies chasing him? It made no sense. But that must have been what happened. Right?

The boys fell into a thoughtful silence, turning to watch what was unfolding on stage. As per tradition, a local amateur dramatics group had come from Inverness to put on a short play about the history of Traveller's Day. It was exclusively dull and appealed to the audience as much as the *Antiques Roadshow*. Doran noticed a few heads in front of him bobbing.

'That's your future,' Doran said to Zander, gesturing to the overacting performers on stage.

Zander smirked. 'Shut it. West End for me, mate. I'm going to be a star.'

'West End of Glasgow you mean?' Doran said and both boys chortled, only stopping when they heard a sharp shushing sound from one of the teachers.

It felt good to be cracking jokes again and the laughter soothed Doran's soul somewhat. He even began to push away thoughts of the previous night's ordeal and tuned into the performance.

'And so, the Romans began a craftier venture,' one of the actor's voices boomed. 'Some say that because they couldn't strike fear on the battlefield, they resorted to stealing away people in the night. But is that the whole story? What of the legends and tales of old, passed down from generation to generation? Could these stories be the true history of the Travellers?'

Another actor stepped forward as the rest of the cast began constructing a contraption behind him. 'Some say the people of this land simply vanished, without a trace. But there are legends throughout history of lost souls reappearing, sometimes generations later, as if no time had passed, and returning to the place they once called home. The tribes would call this a miracle and a feast would be thrown every year to celebrate those who had returned and remember those who were still lost.'

The other actors raised a black cloth in front of one of the women. With a white flash and a *crack*, the black cloth fell and the woman had vanished. The black cloth was raised again and with another *crack*, she had reappeared at the other side of the stage, an over-the-top look of bewilderment on her face.

The same process happened a few times, the other cast members all taking a turn. With every *crack*, Doran began to feel more and more queasy, his fingernails digging into his palms. The flashes seemed to be growing brighter and on the last one, he found himself standing, as though the flash itself had willed it. Only Zander and a few others around him seemed to notice his apparent premature ovation to the performance.

Doran could feel Zander tugging at his shirt, trying to coax him back to his chair. But he was unable to take his eyes off the stage. 'Not feeling well,' he mumbled and staggered out of the hall, a few chairs screeching in his wake.

He broke into a run, charging into the boys' toilet. After a swift glimpse of his ghostly white complexion, he grabbed the sides of the basin and vomited into the sink, his knuckles matching the colour of his face.

Once his breathing had returned to normal, and no further retching occurred, he sank to the floor. Perhaps he did have a concussion, but he couldn't ask Mrs Hunter to phone his mum. Not only would she never allow him out of the house again, he would also be dragging her away from her work. No. He would ride out the rest of the day and hope he didn't get any worse.

Nevertheless, what he had just seen on stage had disturbed him. Could the impossibility of what had happened to him last night only be explained by something completely absurd?

'*Get a grip*,' he told himself, shuddering.

Gingerly, he got to his feet. As he left the bathroom, he thought back to what Mr Bishop had said. The book currently in his possession had information about Traveller's Day and the mysterious Pictish symbols he had seen the previous night. He would have to wait a few hours but certainly some of the answers he sought could lie within that old textbook. Mr Bishop had finally got his wish. He was beginning to find local history incredibly interesting.

Doran arrived home to find the house still empty. As the day had progressed, a degree of normality had returned to him and he managed to make it to half-past three. It appeared his ordeal had only left him with a small lump on the head and no lasting damage.

Tired as he was, he grabbed the copy of *Ancient Myths of the Pictish People*. The writing was so small that he almost needed a magnifying glass. Oswald MacAlpine was painstakingly thorough.

Yawn after yawn interrupted his reading. He couldn't remember ever feeling so tired. It was as though he hadn't slept at all.

Perhaps you didn't, came a small voice inside his head.

Doran cleared his throat, interrupting this unwelcome topic of conversation. *How well would you have slept if you'd been clambering through the forest all night?*

Another yawn. There was no denying he was exhausted, and this drily written book was not helping. Perhaps he would have more chance of taking in the densely typed text after a brief nap?

He was about to stop reading when the word 'glowing' sprang from the page. He peered at the paragraph containing the word, his nose risking a paper cut. 'One such myth is the six standing stones. While there is proof of the existence of the stones themselves, marked by their remnants in the surrounding forest, the mythology surrounding these standing stones is much less clear. It is said that the stones possessed magical properties, reacting to those blessed by the Traveller's gift. In popular folk tales, some have suggested the rocks themselves change temperature. Other depictions show the stone glowing as shown in diagram 3.2.'

Doran frantically turned the pages of the book, looking for the drawing. He finally found a black and white sketch – at the sight of which the book fell from his hands, landing on the floor with a dull thud. It couldn't be. But there it was. Despite its lack of colour, the drawing resembled exactly the same stone he had seen before passing out.

What on earth was going on? Magical stones weren't real. Were they? The fact he was even asking himself that question gave him pause. One thing he did know: he wasn't going to get any clarity sitting in his room. He had to go back to the stone. He had to work out what had happened.

As if she had known what he was planning, at that moment the front door opened and he heard his mum's weary greeting.

He would have to go later. Setting an alarm on his phone, he flopped onto his bed. Perhaps it was for the best. He could rest now and sneak out when his mum was asleep. Instantly, his brain shut down as if someone had flicked off a light switch.

Somewhat rested and refreshed, Doran set off in the dead of night, heading up Garnaith's Path into the forest. Using his phone as a torch, he ventured deeper into the trees, trekking through the overgrown wilderness.

Soon he could hear the familiar whooshing of the waterfall, and breathed in the crisp air around it. With considerably greater care than the previous night, he clambered down the steep hill. He had nearly made it to the bottom when the leaves slipped from under him and he rolled over his ankle, landing on his back. *Another injury to add to the list.*

Limping on, he finally saw the hunk of stone again. With the aid of his torch he could see it in its entirety – or what was left of it.

It was obvious that the monolith was far from its former glory, with jagged chunks missing from it. It was also much shorter than in the drawing. The entire top section looked as if it had been sliced away, beheaded by a sharp blade.

He could make out the symbols that matched the ones in his textbook. Oswald MacAlpine had claimed that they translated as 'green fire'.

It was different this time. As far as he was aware, he was in possession of all his faculties. The stone seemed quiet: just a regular piece of forgotten history.

Suddenly, an invisible force swirled around Doran and he felt himself being dragged forwards with a powerful tug. He dug his heels into the earth, dislodging leaves and dirt as he continued to be reeled in, but he couldn't resist the power that compelled him to touch the stone, press his skin against it. Every sense screamed at him that this was impossible, and he felt his eyes widen as the symbols began to glow.

His fingertips were hovering just above the illuminated surface when a prolonged, piercing, ringing sound hit his eardrums. The noise grew louder and more painful until he was forced to drop to his knees, clasping his head in his hands. His eardrums felt as though they were about to burst, the agony spreading to his jaw and down his neck.

There was a flash of electric-green light and Doran was suddenly thrown backwards. The pain lessened enough for him to remove his hands and squint at the source of this madness.

A few metres from him was a man on his hands and knees, panting and showing the same symptoms as Doran. The man's face was heavily scarred and had cuts from his forehead to his chin. His clothes were smoking. Doran thought he looked in his mid to late thirties but his eyes seemed older. As he inspected the man's eyes further, Doran thought he saw a speck of green in the moonlight.

The man peered at him and then at the rock, which had returned to normal. 'I made it,' he muttered to himself.

Run, Doran thought. *Why are you just standing here? Run!* But he couldn't move. And even if he could, he knew his ankle wouldn't get him anywhere fast. He had no option.

'W-who are you? What's going on?'

The man stared at him and staggered to his feet, wincing. He ran his hands through his dark hair. His mouth twisted into an agonised grimace. 'I don't have a lot of time. He'll be here soon. You have to listen to me very carefully, Doran.'

'How do you know my name? Who's coming?' Doran's voice

shook but he managed to find a bit more volume.

'Samael. Samael is coming for you and I can't stop him. No one can. Only you. You have to find a way this time. You have to change it. I failed, but you don't have to.'

None of what the man was saying was making any sense. Who was Samael? Why did he want him?

Doran's face must have said everything he was thinking because the man's features softened, and Doran suddenly felt an unexpected rush of warmth, as though everything was going to be all right.

'I know you don't have a clue what I'm talking about,' the man said. 'But I don't have time to explain everything to you. I'm sorry. He'll be here soon – and then everything begins.'

'I-I don't understand. What does? Who are you?'

The man smiled, though Doran couldn't find any trace of happiness in his features. 'You'll find out, and one day I hope you can understand,' he said. He reached into a pocket and brought out a small metal object. He tossed it to Doran, who caught it deftly, despite his shaking hands.

It appeared to be an old fob watch. He had read about them during 'Technology through the Ages', a topic in Mr Bishop's class earlier that term. It was the only thing he had found interesting in school so far that year. They had been popular timepieces in the Victorian era, worn on waistcoats or kept in pockets.

But this watch was different. There were no numbers. In their place were symbols, not unlike the ones carved into the stone behind him. Doran peered at each one in turn through the watch's clear casing. Every symbol was gold in colour, as was the circular rim around the watch. Doran had never seen a more elegant timepiece. At the side of the watch was a small button that he noticed was glowing the same colour that had blinded him minutes before. He looked up at the man who was smiling at the wonder on his face.

Suddenly, in the distance, there was another flash of light. The man spun around to face it, then back to Doran, his face grave once again.

'He's here,' he said in a low, solemn voice. Doran felt the pain from before beginning to bubble to the surface again. He looked up to see the man was experiencing a similar sensation of discomfort. 'And I'm out of time.' The man clutched his right ear briefly but he blinked away the pain and looked at Doran, now stern. 'You need to get far away from here. He's coming. It's up to you now. The watch will get you started. All you need to do is think of where you want to go and press the button.'

'What are you talking about?' Doran said. The man was a lunatic. 'What do you mean where I want to go?'

The man slumped to his knees, clutching his head as though it might explode at any moment. Doran could see his nose was bleeding and his face was panic-stricken. They stared at each other for a prolonged moment. Doran noticed a single tear running down the man's cheek. The speck of green surrounding the man's iris began to glow ever so slightly until it resembled the electric-green that had preceded his arrival. He smiled that sad smile again before his face gained a sense of purpose. 'Good luck…Doran West.'

The light in the stranger's eyes faded and he collapsed to the ground.

Doran went rigid. Was he *dead*? He couldn't be, could he? The man was very still, and his eyes had closed.

The forest seemed to have been robbed of all sound. Doran could no longer feel any pain in his ears. Then, cutting through the darkness, he heard that now familiar, melodic whistling sound. He spun around, searching for it. It grew louder and clearer, accompanied this time by the echoing snap of broken twigs. Someone was coming.

Doran didn't want to wait to find out who, and began moving as quickly as his injured body would allow. He glanced over his shoulder and saw, to his horror, a tall, slender figure emerge from the bushes. The figure's face remained shrouded in the darkness but Doran was sure he was the source of the whistling.

Floundering now, Doran staggered through the trees, sweat drenching him. Both his hands were balled into fists, his knuckles white. His right hand clutched the watch, his thumb pressing on the button. He had to escape. He had to get away from the terrifying figure behind him. What had possessed him to go there that night? Why couldn't he just have stayed at home?

It was then he felt it. As if someone had attached jump leads to his brain and shot a wave of electricity through his veins. His entire body vibrated, his hands tingling and trembling as though something was fighting to escape from his fingertips.

Electric-green sparks erupted from every inch of his body, becoming a large ball of light that engulfed him. As he shielded his eyes, he could still hear the whistling; it deafened him until nothing else existed. With a whoosh, a rush of air smacked into him with such force that he was amazed he remained on his feet. The tornado swept around him, knocking the air from his lungs. Gasping for breath, he slammed his hands against his ears, which still, impossibly, were filled with the shrill whistling sound. Each high note stabbed his eardrums. When would it stop? Why didn't it end?

He felt his stomach drop as though he had been yanked into the sky by an invisible bungee cord. There was an almighty lurch and then…silence.

After a moment, Doran opened one eye, then the other. Not only had the whistling stopped, but the raging wind that had threatened to tear him to shreds had also ceased.

It took a second for his eyes to adjust. His tongue tasted something very rough. Was that…his mum's air freshener? This wasn't the woods. This was…his bedroom. He was lying on his bedroom floor. There was the recently added lasagne stain.

Doran sprang to his feet, yelping. He had forgotten his injuries. He glanced out of his window, doing a double take as he saw it was daytime again. The sun was shining. He stared at the world outside and then at the watch still clutched in his hand.

His eyes rolled back into his head and he fainted, falling to the floor again.

4

THE WATERFALL

Doran hammered his fist on the front door of a worn-down cottage across the street from his home. As soon as he regained consciousness, he had sneaked past his sleeping mother and out of his house. She had been slumped in her armchair in the living room, still in full nurse's uniform. It appeared she had been too tired even to make it along the corridor to her bed.

She had been working long hours recently. Perhaps he should talk to her about it, let her know he could pick up a summer job to help with the bills. Then again, he knew better than to bring up the subject. He knew his mum loved her job and believed in the work she was doing. Hopefully one day he would feel the same about whatever he decided to do with his life.

Doran continued to pound the door until a voice from within called, 'All right, all right, I'm coming!' The door swung open to reveal Zander, half asleep. He yawned, stretching his arms behind his back, the penguins dotted upon his navy-blue pyjamas elongating with the material. Pushing his bushy hair out of his eyes, he squinted to see who had disturbed him at such an unearthly hour.

'Zander! Zander, it's morning!'

Zander stared at Doran as though he were a stranger. He peered at the blue sky above before his eyes settled on his friend once more. 'I see you got a rooster then,' he said and made to close the door.

Doran slammed his hand on the hard wood, stopping Zander in his tracks. 'Will you keep it down?' he said. 'Are you trying to make my dad want to kill me before breakfast?'

'No, sorry. It's just…something insane happened.'

'Yeah, you're standing on my doorstep at six in the morning,' Zander said. 'And why do you look as if you've been up all night again?'

Doran hesitated. How on earth could he explain it? 'Because for me, last night is like ten minutes ago. There was this man, and he gave me one of those old fob watches, and then this other guy came out of nowhere and started chasing me and then I must have pressed the button on the side of the watch 'cause in a flash it was morning and I was in my bedroom…'

Doran cut himself off as he heard how crazy he must be sounding. Sure enough, Zander was gawping at him with an expression that reminded Doran of how his mum had looked at his grandfather when he had started wandering to the shops in his dressing gown.

'Did you get your mum to have a look at the lump on your head?' Zander said. 'What are you talking about? What man? What watch?'

Doran rummaged around in his pocket and pulled out the

fob watch, brandishing it in Zander's face. 'Look. It's got Pictish symbols on it.'

Zander reached out, unsure, and accepted the watch. He examined it for a moment and then clicked the button with his thumb.

'Don't touch that!'

But Doran needn't have shouted. There was no flash of light, no storm whisking Zander away. Nothing whatsoever out of the ordinary happened. Zander looked at him again, showing signs of impatience.

'Zander, who is that? Is that Doran? What the hell is going on?' came the voice of Zander's dad from upstairs.

'Now you've done it.' Zander glared at him before calling back to his father. 'Nothing, Dad. Doran's just had a bit of a rough night. He got...locked out of his house.'

'Well, can he go and bother his mum at six in the morning and not me? Does he not know it's Saturday?' Zander's dad replied.

Zander turned back to Doran. 'Surprised *he* knows it's Saturday,' he muttered. 'Right, give me five minutes. I need to change and tidy up Dad's bottles from last night. I'll meet you out here with the bikes and you can explain what happened.'

The boys rode towards the forest. Doran had been reluctant at first to return to the scene so quickly. What if the dead body was still there? What if the police had been called? Would he be in trouble for not reporting the incident?

Then again, if he were to explain to a police officer what he had seen the previous night, he was likely to be carted off in a straitjacket. Maybe it would be wise to do nothing until after revisiting the scene.

Zander was more than happy to accompany him, still clearly

sceptical and concerned by his friend's ramblings. He had made it abundantly clear he wasn't going to believe anything until he saw it for himself.

After a short trek, the boys reached the stone, still wrapped in the blanket of moss. 'You see? I told you it was here,' Doran said.

'The fact there's a big rock with some carvings on it is not the part I'm struggling with, mate,' Zander said. 'It's everything else I'm not coping with.'

'Right,' Doran said. He had to organise his thoughts if he was going to make sense of all of this and convince both Zander and – if he were being truthful – himself. Like a lawyer conducting his opening argument, he paced back and forth, the forest floor his courtroom, Zander his jury. 'So, the night of the party I fall here and hit my head.'

'I still think you should have that looked at.'

'There's nothing wrong with my head,' Doran snapped, instantly regretting his choice of tone. It did nothing for his intended presentation as a sane person. He hadn't imagined all this. He couldn't have. He felt the cold metal of the fob watch against his palm. 'If none of this happened then how did I get the watch?'

'You maybe found it?' Zander said. 'Come on man, think of this from my perspective. What you're saying is…is…'

'Crazy – I know!' Doran's shoulders slumped. Why was he yelling? 'But look,' he said, marching across to the stone. He thrust his hand at the jagged rock, waiting for it to burn at his touch and for the symbols to light up.

Nothing.

Just like when Zander had touched the button, the symbols remained lifeless; not a trace of the greenish glow. Doran glared at the stone. Why hadn't it worked? He pressed again, then again, harder. *Come on you stupid rock.* Finally, cheeks flushed, he punched it.

With a yell and a string of words that could have made even the trees blush, Doran collapsed onto a nearby stump, rubbing his knuckles and trying to ignore the jolts pinging up and down his arm. The seat was surprisingly comfortable and he once again appreciated just how tired he was.

He could feel Zander's eyes on him but had no desire to see the concern on his friend's face again.

'So, you're saying the tall, whistling man came from where? Those bushes?' Zander asked in a calm manner.

'What are you doing?' Doran said, examining his knuckles, which were now red and raw. 'You obviously don't believe me.'

'Of course not,' Zander said. 'But you're my friend and you say something happened to you. So let's imagine for a second that it did.'

Doran's mouth twitched into a smile. His facial muscles actually felt stiff at moving in such a way. When was the last time he had smiled?

'Yeah, those ones there.'

Zander wandered over to them and bent down. 'Looks like they've been trampled on... So, where's the body of this other guy? The one you say gave you the watch?'

Doran had been waiting for this question as soon as they had arrived and found no dead body. But the man had died, right there in front of him. Hadn't he?

'I don't know. Maybe the other man took him away?'

Zander continued to look thoughtful. 'Let's go up to the waterfall.'

The boys clambered up the sharp incline and then down to a sheltered ledge that was safe from the pounding water. They had spent countless summer days playing in the area as children, despite Doran's mother's warnings to stay away.

Their legs dangling, they sat, breathing in the cool air emanating from the waterfall. Doran twirled the fob watch in his hand, contemplating his own sanity. He had never needed to do this before. Which he supposed was a good thing. Was this what a breakdown felt like? If so, he would like to know what had caused it. It was hardly the time. Could it be years of bottling up emotions? Or perhaps a latent reaction to some past trauma his mind had made him forget?

His game of *'What had finally caused Doran to snap?'* ended when Zander nudged him. 'You remember the time we played Peter Pan here?'

Doran thought for a moment and the corner of his mouth twitched into a small smile. 'Yeah. You were Captain Hook. You had the end of an old coat hanger sticking out of your sleeve. Then you slipped and knocked your last two baby teeth out on that rock.'

'We had to tell my dad that you accidentally knocked me in the face with your baseball bat.'

'Why didn't we come up with something better than me being a careless idiot?'

'We were nine,' Zander said. 'I'm surprised we didn't just cry and come clean.'

"Cause we knew how much trouble we'd be in if my mum found out I was up here.'

Zander nodded, thinking. 'Yeah, I mean you can't really blame her for banning us from coming up here. You know…after what happened…'

'Yeah, I guess,' Doran said. As a young girl, his mum had been playing in the same spot and nearly fallen to her death, only to be saved by a couple of passing teenagers. 'Didn't listen though, did we?'

'When do we ever?'

The boys smirked and stared at the deep marble pool below. Doran was about to return to twiddling the fob watch when Zander let out a sigh that didn't suit him. It would have better matched an under-pressure business owner or perhaps their art teacher, Mr Harrington, when he'd been locked in his store cupboard for the fifth time in a week.

'I know this last year's been kind of difficult for you,' Zander said. 'The parties, less time hanging out together and mucking around like we used to.'

Doran's head whipped around. 'What are you trying to say?'

Zander paused, searching for the right words. 'Like…we're getting older, growing up. We've stopped coming up here and playing Peter Pan or being superheroes. Now life is about parties, girls, and I think you're finding it hard to…I don't know…move on.'

'So you think I'm what? Trying to relive the glory days?'

Zander shuffled on the spot as if the ledge had suddenly become very uncomfortable. 'Maybe,' he said. 'What happened last night, mate? Really?'

Doran resumed his fiddling. 'I don't know… I know that I was scared. The most scared I've ever been. My heart was pounding. I was sweating. It felt like all my senses were on fire. And this man…when he was chasing me… I don't know… I really thought I wasn't going to make it out of there. And then…'

'You time-travelled?' Zander finished. 'I didn't realise how into yesterday's assembly you were.'

'But what if what they say about Traveller's Day is true? What if those people really did disappear and then turn up again one day with no idea how they got there?'

At Zander's dubious look, Doran flung his hands in the air. 'I know it sounds insane – like I'm losing my mind.'

'Well, yes but…' Zander's voice died. 'Doran… What's that?'

Doran followed the direction of his friend's gaze to see the button glowing. He shot to his feet. 'That's it,' he said as the glow faded. 'It's not just the device. It's…me.'

'What?'

'What if last night wasn't the first time I did this?'

'How do you mean?'

'I blacked out… I blacked out after hitting my head the night of the party. What if I did it then too?' Doran said, his brain buzzing. 'I ended up in the school grounds, five miles away, right? I wasn't cold from a night in the woods. I have no memory of how I got there. Kieran and his pals seemed baffled as to how I escaped them. And I was scared then too. I didn't know what they were going to do if they found me. I was praying for a way out, a way to escape—'

'Slow down,' Zander said, clutching his forehead. 'Are you now saying this has happened twice?'

'It must have happened while I was losing consciousness. I remember seeing those green sparks as I was passing out. The next thing I know I'm on the school grounds. What if I never properly passed out? What if I…*appeared* there?' Another thought struck him. 'The man. The man who gave me the watch. He had the same weird thing with his eyes that I do, and before he collapsed, the green part glowed, just like the button. And both were exactly the same colour as the symbols on the stone. But when he arrived, he wasn't holding the watch. He pulled it out of his pocket.'

'So…?'

'He didn't need the device to travel. He said, "The watch will get you started." Maybe this watch is like…like a set of stabilisers that you put on a bike when you're learning. But I didn't use the watch that first night. I could still travel without it. What if the watch helps control what's inside *me*? What if I'm like those Travellers from the stories?'

Zander gaped. 'It's a great theory,' he said. 'But how, might I ask, are you planning on testing it?'

'Well, there is one way...'

'Why don't I like where this conversation is heading?'

'The device worked when I was scared, fearing for my life. My heart rate must have been through the roof. And when I was in that state, I thought of where I wanted to be – home – and that's where I ended up. Just now, when I was reliving it, the watch glowed again. That must be the state I need to be in to use it.'

'Doran,' Zander said. 'Listen to yourself. I know I said I would support you here but what you're saying is like something out of a sci-fi film that you see at the mobile cinema when it comes to the village.'

'You're not going to believe me without proof so there's only one thing for it… I jump.'

Zander stared. 'I believe you,' he said hurriedly. 'I believe you. Course I do.'

'I'm doing this.'

'But it's fifteen feet, if you hit something you aren't supposed to, you're done for.'

'I know. That's why this is perfect. Genuine risk means genuine fear. It'll get my heart going enough for me and the watch to work.'

'I won't let you. I'll…I'll phone your mum.'

Doran raised an eyebrow. 'You'll phone my mum?'

'No,' Zander muttered. 'Are you sure you want to do this?'

'No. And that's the point. You're going to see. Then once you believe me, we can work out what to do about all this. And if I'm wrong, I'll hopefully only get a bit wet and we can laugh about it at school on Monday.'

Zander nodded but he resumed wringing his hands. 'You'd better be a wizard,' he said.

Doran replied with a small nod and shuffled to the edge. His legs trembled as he eyed the deep marble pool below. *I'd better be a wizard*, he thought, and stepped forwards.

He felt the air attack him, saw the fast-approaching water beneath him. From this height, it resembled a flat layer of tarpaulin, covering the potential dangers beneath. He looked at the watch gripped in his hand and stared at the button, willing it to turn green.

But it didn't.

He braced for impact, hammering the button and hoping this wasn't the last thing he'd see. The water drew closer and closer and Doran continued to hit the button frantically. *Turn green!* he screamed inside his head. *Turn green!*

Smack. Doran hit the sheet of water. His limp body sank like a boulder down into the depths of the pool. Bubbles floated from his mouth and his eyes sprang open, the icy water plunging into his throat.

His head pierced the surface and he lapped up as much air as he could in each breath. Flapping his arms and legs, he eventually managed to gain enough rhythm to swim to the nearest rock.

He called upon every available muscle to haul himself onto it and flopped onto his back, still gasping. As he tried to calm himself, an unsettling prickling sensation spread up the back of his neck and forehead. He had failed. It hadn't worked. Why hadn't it worked?

'Oh my god,' came the panicked voice of Zander. 'Oh my god, oh my god.'

Great. Now he'll definitely think I'm crazy, Doran thought. He forced himself to sit up, ready to appeal to his friend to let him try again. 'I'm fine,' he said. 'My side hurts but everything else is good. I...' He trailed off. Zander's face was chalk-white and his mouth was hanging open. 'What is it? I said I'm fine.'

Zander closed his mouth with a gulp. 'Mate,' he said. 'Mate, look around you...'

Doran frowned. *What's he on about?* He looked up. The sky. It was dull. But it had been sunny before. It was also later – much later.

'Wait...' And Doran suddenly realised. 'How did you get down here so fast? And why are your clothes wet?'

'I ran down as soon as you didn't come back up to the surface. I thought you'd hit your head or something, so I dived in. But you weren't there. You weren't there.'

'How long was I gone?'

'Three hours...'

Doran's chest heaved again, though this time it was nothing to do with his dive into the water. A small chuckle erupted from his mouth. It grew until he was rolling around on the rock, beside himself with laughter. When he finally stopped, he stuck both arms and legs in the air in triumph. 'I'm a wizard!' he yelled, his voice echoing around the pool and nearby trees.

'Doran West, get up now!' came a stern voice.

Doran froze, knowing the owner of that voice all too well. He needed a lot more will power to sit up this time. Next to Zander was the furious figure of Kate West, her lip quivering.

Zander no longer seemed able to look at him. 'I phoned your mum...' he said.

5

THE WEST FAMILY SECRET

The front door of the West household slammed shut. Kate had driven the boys back in silence, only speaking to ask Zander to go home.

Doran remained on the doormat, his mind racing. *What was she going to do? Was she going to scream? Was she going to lock him in his room?* She'd never done that before but, then again, they were in uncharted territory. Perhaps a short prison sentence in his room would be seen as a just punishment for breaking her golden rule.

His mum's handbag fell from her arm and landed on the floor with a thud. Without a word, she strode into the living room.

Should he follow her? Should he run to Zander's and barricade the door? He had seen his mother angry many times but never like this. The silence was new.

It was as he was trying to make his choice that he began to

hear soft sobbing coming from the living room. The sound was enough to unstick his feet and he drifted through to the living room.

'Mum?'

Kate sat hunched in her armchair, cradling her face in her hands. At the sound of her son's voice, she froze, just as still as he had been moments before.

'Sit down,' she said. Her voice was hoarse, her eyes fixed on a chair opposite her own. Doran edged towards the empty seat and sat down with the care of a man three times his age. Only then did his mother finally look at him. Blood-red blotches had invaded the whites of her eyes. He had expected to see fury or disappointment but found neither. His mum was scared.

'I hoped never to have this conversation with you,' Kate began before her voice broke. She gave a single shake of the head, apparently trying to suppress further weeping. 'Zander didn't say much, but he told me about today and what happened in the woods. Was last night the first time?'

Had he not already been sitting down, that question most certainly would have seen to it. His mum appeared to believe everything already. She didn't seem to have any doubt that he had indeed travelled in time. Doran attempted to respond but found he couldn't form the words, so instead merely nodded.

'Now under normal circumstances, I would be giving you a piece of my mind. You know how I feel about you being up at that waterfall. Or did you forget that I nearly died up there? That place is dangerous and you decide to jump...'

Kate halted what would have turned into a furious lecture and rested her hands on her lap. 'When you were born your father did warn me that because you had the *teine uaine* there was a strong chance, but I guess I just felt more comfortable living in denial.'

Doran found his voice this time to reply. '*Teine uaine?*'

'It means the green fire,' Kate answered, sniffing. 'The jagged ring that's part of your iris. Your dad had it too. He said it's the genetic marker of a Traveller.'

Doran frowned. How did his mum know so much about this? Had his dad been like him?

One question kept coming to the forefront of his mind, and as it did, his face hardened. 'Why haven't you told me this before?'

'How could I? How could I even begin to explain all this?'

'You could have tried. How could you have known all this time and said nothing? I thought I was losing my mind. I really was beginning to think I'd snapped and made the whole thing up.'

'I know, I know. But you have to understand I was just trying to protect you.'

'Protect me?'

'Yes,' Kate said. 'Everything I've ever done has been for you; you must know that?'

Doran paused. He did know that. But how could she have kept something like this from him? 'I need you to tell me everything you know about whatever is happening to me. No more lies. Leave nothing out. You tell me everything.'

His mum stared at him, clearly debating his demands. With a sniff, she gave a swift jerk of her head in agreement. 'OK... I suppose we have to go back to when I first met your dad.' She paused again, considering her next words carefully. 'Arlen was the most gifted man I ever knew. Far too good for this place. Always smarter than everyone in the room, a bit of a show-off to tell you the truth. When we were at school, I didn't think much of him. We both happened to be going to the same university in Edinburgh. I was studying nursing and he was doing engineering but would take extra classes in biology. That's how we got talking. He sat behind me in one of those classes and well… He was just so different. Calmer and measured. And he was funny; so quick. He could make me laugh with just the simple raising of an eyebrow.'

Doran held his breath. This was already more than she'd *ever* revealed about his father. 'When did you find out about him?'

Kate blinked from her reverie and for a moment looked at him as though she had forgotten he was there. 'Not until much later. I think he tried to tell me many times but couldn't go through with it. I can't blame him, to be honest. I don't know how you could explain any of this without people thinking you're certifiable.'

'Tell me about it.'

'Your dad then did a master's degree in bioengineering while I did my nursing placements. He started to become distant. He would spend all night in his lab. I wouldn't see him for days until eventually I'd had enough and turned up at his office to confront him. It was then he finally crumbled and told me everything. He phrased it like he was ill, like he had a degenerative disorder. The reason he had been working so hard, and even why he'd specialised in this field, was all to find a cure.'

'A cure?'

Kate's eyes glistened. 'I hoped you'd be like me. You'd shown no signs. Not even when you turned sixteen. Arlen said it manifests when you reach adulthood, or what was classed as adulthood in the past.'

'Wait, wait. Slow down.'

'You're right, I'm sorry,' Kate said, acknowledging the volume of information she was giving him. 'Arlen said that it was a

West family trait. His father had been lucky and it had skipped a generation but Arlen inherited the condition. He became obsessed with trying to find a cure. He said he couldn't bear to leave me behind and he wanted to have a normal life with me and not let our children…'

Kate's voice broke and she descended into sobs once again. Doran's instinct was to go over and comfort her but he knew he had to remain still and not let his mother stop. He had to know everything.

After a few watery gulps, Kate managed to compose herself enough to continue. 'I said I didn't care and that we would make the most of the time we had, still not fully realising the nature of his condition.'

'Why do you keep saying it like that? What's wrong with me?'

Every feature of his mum's face sprang to attention. 'Nothing, sweetheart. Nothing is wrong with you,' she said, but he could tell this was an automatic motherly reaction.

'Then tell me. Tell me what's happening to me,' Doran said, his nails digging into the sides of the armchair.

Kate gave a heavy sigh. 'OK,' she began. 'Now, I won't be able to explain this as well as your dad but I will try. Arlen said that this…ability of yours is linked to your biology. It's a part of you. The less in control of your emotions you are, the less control you have over it.'

'So that's why when I was scared and my heart was pounding I…time-travelled,' Doran said. It had just occurred to him that this was the first time he was saying it out loud.

Kate nodded. 'Your dad said that if at any point he lost control of his emotions, got too angry or upset, then he might disappear to a random time and have no guarantee of getting back. So, when we found out we were having you, he became even more obsessed and threw himself back into his work. He would spend days and nights in the garage, attempting to devise a solution. Most of his work is still locked in his trunk. You always used to try to get inside it when you were little, do you remember?' The memory offered a weak smile but it was brief and sadness washed over her face once more. 'He was desperate to find some – any – way to rid himself of his abilities, and hopefully, if it came to it, yours as well.'

Doran reached into his pocket and pulled out the fob watch. 'You mean, like this?'

Kate leapt to her feet. 'Where – where did you get that?' Her voice was quiet but her eyes burned.

'From the man in the woods,' he said, as though saying the wrong thing could cause his mum to explode.

'What man?'

'I don't know,' Doran said. 'He was all battered and bruised. He had dark hair and eyes just like mine.'

Kate's eyes now looked positively wild. 'Did he say anything?'

'What?' Doran said, still confused. 'Mum, what's going on?'

'Give me the watch, Doran,' Kate said, advancing towards him.

Doran shielded the fob watch from her. 'Wait, what? No. Why?'

'Give it to me!'

Kate grabbed his arm. The pair wrestled over the watch until it fell to the floor. Without a second thought, Kate stamped hard on its casing. The glass smashed, along with the dials and cogs inside. There was a small puff of pink mist, which quickly rose and evaporated.

'What...?' Doran said, his entire body numb. He blinked furiously as if doing so would somehow change the scene before his eyes. But the watch remained broken. He fought back the flood of tears threatening to escape. 'Why?'

His mum appeared equally upset. 'That…*thing* is what caused your father's accident. He kept tinkering with it and tinkering with it, pumping it with those chemicals he kept making, until one day…he was gone.'

Doran couldn't speak. *She'd destroyed it.* 'Wait… What do you mean, gone? You mean dead, right?' Kate simply stared back at him. 'You mean dead, right?' he asked again, not wanting to believe what his mother's silence was telling him.

'Fifteen years ago, Arlen was in his workshop when there was this flash of green light. When I went to check on him, he was gone. Only an outline of grey dust where he had been standing.'

'So, he could still be out there? He might not be dead?'

'I… I don't know.'

Doran blinked, trying yet again to change the scene before his eyes. 'All this time? All this time and you never told me?'

'You were a child. How could I explain that to a child? You have to understand, I never knew if he would come back or if he'd even survived that night. I had to tell you something and that was the best thing for you.'

'You don't get to decide that!'

'Yes, I do! I am your mother! It was better that you – that *we* – believed he was dead. So that you wouldn't spend the rest of your childhood, the rest of your life even, wondering whether your dad was going to miraculously walk through that door.'

A tear burned Doran's cheek as a rage brewed inside him. *How could she? How could she have kept this from him?*

His fingers tingled just as they had done when he was running through the woods. It was happening again. He was about to time-travel. He looked up at his mum, fear now etched all over his face.

'No… No, Dory,' she said, horrified. 'Doran, stop. You have to stop. Calm down. Take deep breaths.'

'I can't,' Doran cried. 'I don't know how.'

'You have to try,' Kate said, pleading with him. 'You have to try and calm down; it's the only way.'

Doran felt as though his breathing was being controlled by someone else. His hands shook violently, beginning to blur before his eyes. 'I can't!'

'You must! I'm not losing you too.' She flung her arms out and pulled him into a tight embrace. 'If you go, I go with you.'

Doran clutched his mum, returning her hug. He could see the green sparks flickering and felt a rush of air surrounding them. He closed his eyes and tried to feel nothing else except the warm grip of his mother. His breathing slowed and, as he opened his eyes, he saw the sparks fizzle away and the air settle. The tingle in his hands had faded and he balled them into fists to check they were once again steady.

Slowly, he and his mum parted and stared at one another. It had stopped. They were still there. Both parties gave a deep sigh of relief and Kate dragged Doran back to her for another hug. He allowed it to happen but quickly shrugged her off. His mum looked as if he had just slapped her.

'Dory,' she began softly.

'Don't call me that,' he snapped. 'This changes nothing. You still lied. You still kept all of this from me. And I hate you for it.'

The words hung in the air. Doran scooped up the remaining fragments of the fob watch and charged out of the room. He slammed the door shut behind him, leaving his mother crying once more.

6

THE TRUNK

At one in the morning, Doran was still fully dressed, staring up at the ceiling as if it held some great secret. The unanswered questions continued to torment him, coupled with a nagging voice within that had been continually chastising him about how he had left things with his mother.

But she had lied to him his whole life, right? Why should he feel guilty? He had every right to be angry. To hate her, surely?

Then again, he knew his mum. He knew that every choice she had made would have been with his best interests in mind. He should apologise.

But why should he apologise? She had broken the watch. She had lied about his father. Surely, she should be asking *him* for forgiveness.

Doran flung himself onto his side. *Enough.* His eyes fell upon the broken pieces of the fob watch, which lay in a pile on his bedside table. Had this really been what had taken his dad away from him? But if so, how had it come into his possession?

He had been wrestling with an idea since the fight with his mum. And it was crazier than any of the insane things that had happened to him in the last forty-eight hours. The man who had given him the watch shared the same eyes, the same nose as his own and Doran remembered feeling instantly safe in his presence. Could this man have been his father?

Doran flopped onto his back. '*Stop it*,' he told himself. He had made it sixteen years without a dad and didn't need one now. He was nearly an adult, a man in his own right. He was no longer some sad four-year-old watching the other children play with their fathers in the park. His mum had coped just fine, thank you very much.

And he'd just told her he hated her.

He grabbed his pillow and smothered his face, screaming into it. After hurling it across the room, he looked back at the watch fragments. His eyes weren't the only thing he had inherited from his father.

Doran scooped up the remains of the fob watch and crept to the bedroom door. Gently, he pulled the handle and, on tiptoes, snuck out of the room.

Every uneven or creaky floorboard was known to him, even in the dark, and with the grace of a ballerina he danced on his toes along the quiet pieces of wood. He was just about to hop across the threshold of the kitchen when something in the corner of his eye gave him pause.

On the wall where the hall met the kitchen hung a framed picture. He suddenly felt compelled to stare at the usually ignored image. It was an etching of the West family's coat of arms, drawn by his grandfather. A black knight bordered a jagged shape of the same colour. When he was younger, his mum used to lift him up so he could look and tell him a story based on the image about a knight watching over a river. Apparently, it was a story passed down from generation to generation. Although remaining cagey about his father, his mum had always tried to tell him as much as she knew about the Wests, despite only becoming one through marriage. She had wanted him to feel a connection, however small, to his name.

His brow furrowed. Why did he have to say what he had to her? When she got home from her shift the following night he would apologise, make her dinner maybe. He might not have forgiven her for lying but she hadn't deserved what he'd said. For now, though, he had a watch to repair.

Through the back garden of the West family home was a side entrance to the garage; a chipped blue door with a rusty latch. Doran tugged the handle, wincing as it creaked, and slipped inside.

Reaching blindly into the darkness, he pulled on a cord. The lights flickered and revealed what had once been a workshop. Boxes and old possessions littered the place, covering the central workstation.

Doran placed the fob watch fragments on a handy shelf and began removing all the pieces of junk. Once he had hauled away a last forgotten lawnmower, the workstation was clear and ready for use. Doran ran his finger along the solid, metallic surface and inspected the dust that stuck to it. Had it really been that long?

His eyes were drawn to a black trunk, which he dragged out from underneath an old shelving unit and heaved onto the countertop.

Doran gazed at the trunk. How he had wondered as a young child about the secrets held within that casing. Perhaps a piece of a fallen meteorite or a dinosaur egg? But this had been a child's fantasy, a game. In recent years, he'd forgotten it even existed.

He grabbed the toolbox and found a set of bolt cutters, slicing the lock in two and watching as it fell to the floor with a sharp clang. His hand hovered over where the padlock had been, but at first it refused to go any further. It might not be a dinosaur egg, but there was something inside. With luck it would be something to help him fix the watch or, better yet, hold clues to his abilities – and his father's disappearance.

When he finally lifted the lid, he found piles of paper, some crumpled, some still smooth. There were also spare parts that looked awfully like what he had just placed on the shelf behind him. There was also a set of tools that he had only ever seen online. Everything from the precision screwdrivers to the soldering irons had a sleek design, the light from the bulb above bouncing off their shiny surfaces.

While Doran's attitude towards school was indifferent at best, this did not mean he had low aptitude or lacked a desire to learn. On the contrary, he had simply spent the ten years of his schooling mired in boredom, terminally uninterested by his teachers' lessons.

For as long as he could remember, he had craved to understand how things worked. He would spend long afternoons taking apart his toys and other household items before putting them back together again. When he was seven, his mum had walked into the living room to find him sitting surrounded by the deconstructed pieces of the family laptop. His toolkit had been hidden for a month after this incident.

Doran grabbed a few bits of paper which were clearly notes and other musings. He stared at them for a second, realising this was the first time he had seen his father's handwriting. It was not unlike his own – chaotic and lacking grace.

It was clear to him that his mum had stuffed these into the trunk without a second thought, as nothing was in any kind of order. He removed all of the scribblings from the trunk, finally finding a series of schematics tucked away at the bottom of the heap. He grinned to himself. These would do nicely.

Doran spread the diagrams out across the workspace, eager to examine them. It seemed the watch itself was not unlike a normal fob watch, with the cogs and coils all in their customary places. But his eyes rested on the part of the drawing which had been extrapolated and enlarged. It showed a small cylindrical tube that appeared to be connected to the spring, which was in turn connected to the button. Underneath the button itself, he spotted some kind of inbuilt sensor. There was another larger, similar sensor at the back of the watch. As he studied it more closely, he found himself being reminded of the time he had taken apart and rebuilt the heart monitor in the school gym. As he recalled, Mr Urquhart had given him a whole week of lunchtime detentions and a letter home to his mother. Doran had conveniently forgotten to give it to her.

'So, it's some kind of hi-tech heart monitor?' Doran muttered to himself. That would explain why the light only flashed when his heart was pounding. It also made sense, given what he had just learned about the link between his emotions and his ability. On the path to finding a cure for his 'condition', his father's logical first step would have to be to find a way to control his abilities. Therefore, knowing when you were losing control would be important.

So what happened when the button was pushed?

He scanned the diagram, following the connections from the button to the device itself. The button appeared to trigger a release valve to the cylindrical tube.

Doran gathered the components of his watch from the shelf behind him. Laying them out neatly on the worktop, he tried his best to follow the plans and place them roughly where they should end up being. For some elements of the watch's design he turned to his father's scribbled instructions for assistance with placing them. The watch was badly damaged and many of the pieces were now useless. Nevertheless, even from these fragments, he was able to work out the various networks that allowed the watch to function.

On his father's second diagram he had scrawled something inside the cylindrical tube. 'VAL2.1/IU 0.4g'. Next to this was the word, 'Inhalant!!'

Doran frowned. His mum had mentioned something about a chemical. Perhaps that was the pink puff of smoke that had disappeared when the watch broke. He skimmed the various pieces of paper, some of which were charred and torn. One word appeared over and over again, 'Valerian'. Doran knew he recognised that word from somewhere. Near the back of the pile of notes was also a drawing of a flower, labelled with various scribbles.

The flower must be part of the chemical somehow, he thought.

Taking another look inside the trunk, he noticed a small black bag. It looked like one of the bags his mum used for work. Sure enough, it was indeed a medical bag, filled with empty vials – except for one which contained a bright pink liquid.

Doran peered at it closely in the light, then put it down and reached back into the bag, pulling out a wilted flower that resembled his father's drawing.

'Valerian…'

He organised the notes, realising that most of them detailed equations for whatever was inside that vial. But there were no instructions on how to create the formula from scratch, and the notes that did exist were beyond his current level of understanding. Still, he had a prepared sample. All he needed to do was rebuild the watch. The idea of doing this provoked a pleasant tingling sensation across his entire body that had absolutely nothing to do with his powers.

Doran picked up two warped cogs and examined them, smiling to himself. It was time to get to work.

7

THE TEST RUN

'OK, take me through it one more time,' Zander said, closing his eyes in concentration.

Doran was almost starting to empathise with his teachers. This would be the fourth time he had explained it. 'Right. So the watch itself is merely a calming agent. It monitors my heart rate and then activates. I press the button and it releases the chemical inside into the air as an inhalant, which calms me down enough to control where I go.'

'I'm starting to regret being so mean to Miss Duncan in first-year biology,' Zander said, rubbing his temples. With a sharp intake of breath, his eyes fluttered open. 'My brain still hurts but hey, you're the genius-slash-mutant here.'

Doran scowled. 'I told you not to call me that.'

'Don't be modest. You are a genius.'

Doran's narrowed eyes remained but his mouth had contorted

into a begrudging smirk. 'You know, it's at times like this I forget why we're friends.'

Zander bounded forwards and swung his arm around his companion. 'Best friends,' he corrected with a toothy smile. 'And don't be daft; you love me,' he added, ever confident. 'Now, are we going to do this or what?'

After Doran had spent all night repairing the parts and rebuilding the watch, he had immediately called Zander, and the two boys had headed for a more open area of the woods. The plan was to test Doran's handiwork and see if he had followed his father's schematics correctly. He now stood before a long, fairly even stretch of dirt, clutching a diagram to which he had been adding his own notes. Had he missed anything? More important, what would happen if he had?

'I still feel like there's a better idea to be had here,' he said, stuffing the schematic into his pocket.

'Says the boy who jumped off a waterfall.'

'Fair point,' Doran said, swinging his leg over the saddle of his bike. 'OK, OK, let's do this,' he added, more to himself than to Zander.

'Try not to make me wait for three hours this time,' Zander said, patting him on the head and backing away.

Doran shot him a disapproving look, then settled his attention on the path ahead of him. Path was perhaps too grand a word for it. Ahead of him lay twenty metres of bumpy forest floor, leading to a sharp, steep drop to what used to be the main exit out of Linntean. A newer, safer route had replaced this old road, which was now overcome by a green and brown jungle of undergrowth. On the other side, across the ravine, was dense woodland. No one could hope to make it across from one side to the other; a perfect location for attempting to defy death.

Doran fixed his gaze on the destination ahead and lifted his foot off the ground. The fob watch was pressed against the right handlebar as he pedalled, his thumb hovering over the button. He could already feel his heart stirring.

Trying to ignore this, he leant over the handlebars, fixing his eyes on his target. His legs burned as he powered on, pushing his feet down harder and faster.

The edge of the forest grew closer and closer and he felt the bike begin to wobble on the uneven surface beneath. His heart pounded while doubts grew inside his head. Was he about to do something unimaginably stupid?

Eyes wide, he suddenly saw the open space just in front of him and, on instinct, he braked hard. At first the bike skidded and swivelled as though he had performed some impressive turn, before its wheels slipped out from under it, clattering it onto its side, with Doran joining it in the dirt. He lay sprawled on top of the bike, as its back wheel dangled right over the precipice.

His face the shade of magenta, he clambered off the frame and got back to his feet, dusting himself off. This time felt different from the waterfall. Before, he knew the device would work. Now, it was *his* engineering skills he was putting to the test. He had to admit his confidence had wavered.

He trudged back to his starting point. Now was not the time to lose his bottle. He gave Zander the quickest of looks then turned back to stare down the ravine once more. 'Not a word,' he warned his friend, his face still scarlet.

Zander merely held his hands up and mimed zipping his mouth shut.

Refusing to waste another moment overthinking, Doran kicked off and hurtled towards the open air before him. He felt the wind rush past his face and smelled the familiar scent of pinewood. The bike wobbled but he pressed on, not allowing reason to take over this time. He snapped his eyes shut as his heart hammered in his ears. The bike soared into the air, Doran clutching the handlebars as though they were the key to life itself.

With what felt like a great physical effort, he prised his eyes open to see himself flying across the ravine. He glanced down to drive home the sense of danger. The drop was substantial; nothing but spiky bushes and moss to break his fall. None of that mattered. He wasn't going to land there. He pictured where he had started, sitting on the bike next to Zander. He reached out to the image, attaching a timestamp to it, and the button glowed. Pressing his thumb down hard onto it, he felt a rush of air and before he could blink, he felt himself landing on the ground with a small thud. He felt a sharp pain shoot into his stomach as though he'd been punched in the gut. Slowly, he looked down to see the black rubber seat still clutched between his thighs. He was still sitting on the bike.

'Ha, ha!' Doran heard Zander exclaim with delight as he patted him on the back. 'You're not dead.'

'I'm not dead,' Doran agreed with a grin. He hopped off the bike and clutched his knees, letting the cool breeze fill his lungs.

'Half an hour,' Zander said, and Doran's face fell. 'What's wrong?'

'I was aiming for five minutes.'

'Will you quit being such a perfectionist?' Zander said, punching him on the arm. 'Doran, it worked. You time-travelled. Smile, for God's sake.'

Doran feigned a smile. But once he had, it became genuine and jubilant. 'I time-travelled.' He shoved Zander. 'This is insane!'

'You're telling me,' Zander said. 'Now, my first question is this,' he added, nodding towards Doran's bike. 'If you can take a bike with you, what else can you take?'

'Take you with me?'

'Not yet, obviously,' Zander said. 'I'm not a madman. Let's see if you can get a better handle on this first. No pun intended. I would like to make it to my seventeenth birthday.'

'A fair request. But are you sure? There's not exactly a safe way to test the theory.'

Zander shrugged. 'Well, you're the brains of the operation – you figure it out. Remember you said this watch was like a set of stabilisers, so maybe once you've mastered it, you'll be able to find a less risky way to travel. Then we can go party like it's nineteen ninety-nine.'

'What?'

'Something I heard on TV,' Zander said, looking thoughtful. 'What was so special about nineteen ninety-nine?'

'Suppose we can find out,' Doran said with a grin. For the first time, he was feeling a sense of possibility about the whole situation. Perhaps it didn't have to be all doom and gloom. There was so much opportunity. So much to see. He hadn't even begun to wonder about how far he could go. 'Where would you go, Zander?' he asked. 'Like, if you could go anywhere, where would you go?'

The question appeared to stump Zander for a moment. 'I don't know,' he said after a few seconds. 'Mr Bishop always made the nineteen twenties sound so exciting. The world was changing so much and it was the birth of talking pictures. We watched some of those films in drama class; they looked so cool to be a part of. I'd love to go see that, maybe?'

'Did I just hear you get excited about something you learnt in school?'

'Shut up,' Zander said. 'You are mistaken, sir!' he added in an indignant, posh English accent.

Doran laughed. 'You'd probably try and get a starring role in one of those films if we went back.'

'You know it,' Zander said. 'What about you? Where would you go?'

'Well, da Vinci was the best inventor of all time, so I'd maybe like to go back and meet him,' Doran said. 'Plus, I've never been to Italy. Or outside of Scotland for that matter.'

'Me neither,' Zander said, sighing. 'One day, right?'

A silence fell. Glancing at Zander, Doran could tell by the distant look in his friend's eye that the desire to escape was a feeling they shared. Zander nodded towards the watch. 'Better get practising then.'

These words reinvigorated Doran. 'Let's try and beat a twenty-five-minute difference.'

'By all means,' Zander said. 'It gets boring at my end. I've already checked my phone three times.'

The next hour, at least from Zander's perspective, consisted of Doran doing jump after jump, trying to get closer to the timestamp in his head. His second attempt was seventeen minutes out. His third, twelve minutes. On his fourth try, he reverted to thirty-five minutes.

'You're just tired,' Zander said, after Doran threw the bike to the ground. 'No big deal. Maybe we should call it a day and come back tomorrow?'

Doran stared out across the ravine. 'One more.'

'You sure?' Zander asked. 'You said on the third one you were only inches from a spiky demise.'

'So what?'

'So, maybe you're losing the fear a bit? What if the button doesn't turn green and we end up having a Doran-shaped hole in the ground?' He put his phone to his ear, pretending to make a call. '"Yeah, hi Kate, Zander here, you know, Doran's wildly more charismatic friend? Well, I'm afraid Doran now resembles a pancake and won't be making it home for dinner tonight."'

'Hilarious,' Doran said, though part of him had been thinking the same thing. The button was flashing green later with every jump. But that didn't stop him from picking up his bike from the dirt. 'One more,' he said. 'Then I'm done for the day, I swear.'

Zander raised his phone above his head. 'Just checking I've got signal.'

Doran pedalled to his starting point and stopped. His pulse was racing again but this time, he realised, it wasn't only through fear. Enjoyment was also there. He had begun to relish this part of the process. This feeling also brought with it an overwhelming sense of self. He could feel every erect hair on his arms and legs. He could understand every thump of his heart, as though they were notes from a musical instrument he was an expert in playing.

Perhaps this had been what his father had meant when he gave him the watch. The watch had got him started but control over his emotions would ultimately lead to control over his ability. At this thought, he winced. Why was he so eager to label the stranger in the forest as his father?

He pedalled harder but the night he received the watch plagued his mind. He felt the chill he had experienced when the second flash had occurred, bringing with it the terrifying, slender man who had pursued him. He tried to shake the feeling but couldn't, the whistling noise competing with the thump of his heart. It grew louder until Doran could no longer hear anything else.

Suddenly, a rustling cut through the chaos of sounds and Doran saw movement in the bushes in the distance. It was the man. It had to be. He even saw a dark leg extend and a set of beady eyes peering out at him. He was here. He was back. He had to warn Zander.

The rustling increased and the bike wobbled, Doran nearly toppling from it. A figure emerged from the bushes. Its outline was hard to make out but he was sure it was the nightmarish man who had chased him.

The bushes burst open to reveal not a man, but a stag. A stag with one antler and a terrified look in its eye.

Rufus? Doran thought and the realisation seemed to wipe his mind clear. He stared at the stag for a second longer than he should have and survival instinct kicked in. He braked, but this time he was too late. The bike swerved sideways, taking him with it over the edge of the ravine.

The bike slipped from under him as his hands clawed at the air, searching for anything to latch on to. They found a protruding tree root and Doran dug in his nails, hearing his bike crash into the undergrowth below.

His arms burned as he hauled himself up the root, trying to gain a better grip. Willing his muscles to keep working, he caught sight of something shimmering to his left. The watch was teetering on a nearby ledge. It was going to fall. It was going to disappear forever into the spiky undergrowth.

A mound of earth flew past him and he looked up to see Zander flat on his stomach, gaping at him over the precipice. 'Hold on!' he called.

'Not got much choice,' Doran said in a strained voice, gesturing to the watch with his head.

'OK, let me think,' Zander said, leaping up again to scan the area for something – anything – that could help.

'I can't hold on much longer!'

'I have an idea, but you're not going to like it.'

If Doran didn't require both hands, he might have swung a fist at him. 'Does it beat dying a horrible death?'

Zander nodded. 'Good point... OK, you've got to reach for the watch. When you've got it, grab my arm and I'll pull you up.'

'You what?'

'Just trust me,' Zander said, already extending his arm.

Doran looked across at the ledge and the watch. He reached out once but brought his hand back to the branch. 'I can't!'

'Yes you can,' Zander coaxed. 'OK, grab my arm first and let me get you closer.'

Doran didn't particularly like the sound of that either but he didn't know how much longer he could hold on. Taking a deep breath, he flung one hand up and dug his fingernails into Zander's forearm. Zander's entire body pressed into the ground above as he took Doran's weight, grasping his arm with both hands.

'On three,' Zander called, his voice shaking. 'One, two, *three!*'

He suddenly swung Doran towards the ledge with what seemed his last sliver of energy. At the same time, Doran dug his heels into the side of the ravine and pushed off. Still clinging to Zander with one hand, he swiped the air with the other, making a grab for the watch.

But Doran's weight proved too much and Zander cried out as he was pulled over the edge of the ravine by the momentum of Doran's movement, and both boys were suddenly plummeting towards the bracken below, bodies entwined. The cold metal of the timepiece tickled Doran's hand and he squeezed his eyes shut, pressing down hard on the button.

8

THE SPY

Some hours previously, the corridors of Glenmoral Academy had been filled with excited chatter and lively feet scuffing its freshly buffed floors. Now it was deathly quiet and should have remained so, were it not for a flash of light that suddenly illuminated the cobalt blue of the lockers.

Professor Ianto Everie's footsteps echoed through the corridors as he followed the route he'd committed to memory. Every other step he glanced over his shoulder – something that had become common practice in recent months. He wasn't sure whether he actually expected to see someone there following him, but he could never rule it out as a possibility.

Finally, he reached a sign that said 'History Department' with a crude drawing of a cartoon man in a suit of armour. Ianto rolled his eyes and pushed through the swing doors, which closed behind him with a horrid squeak.

The noise made his heart twinge and he grasped his chest. After another furtive glance, he took out a damp handkerchief and mopped his brow. He briefly held up the cloth to inspect its moistness. He had lately acquired the habit of measuring his emotional state by how much perspiration had seeped into the cloth.

Get a hold of yourself man, he thought, stuffing the handkerchief back into his breast pocket. Tobias couldn't possibly know he had come here.

Or could he? The man's reach had continued to grow rapidly in recent years. The Vigils had quickly fallen into line, spying for him and acting as his private army. Even the Seers had begun to do his bidding – and they were usually a law unto themselves.

Shaking off any misgivings regarding his decision to go to the school, Ianto rounded the final corner and entered the only lit classroom in the building. Sitting at his desk was Ewan Bishop, examining a piece of paper, a pile of unmarked essays sitting lopsidedly in front of him. Ianto thought it looked a bit like the Leaning Tower of Pisa, but it was seemingly less stable than the Tower: as he watched, the papers fell, covering the desk and floor.

Bishop sighed and rubbed his eyes. He was about to scoop up the essays when he looked up. He gave Ianto a warm smile. 'Professor. Good to see you.'

'Hello, Ewan,' Ianto said. 'May I?' he asked, gesturing to the mess.

'By all means,' Bishop said.

As though lifting off an invisible cloth, Ianto waved his hand carelessly. The papers jumped from the ground as if attached by a hidden piece of string. One by one, they reverted to their place in the pile, the first page to fall landing delicately back on the top.

'Thank you,' Bishop said, neatening the stack of papers to prevent another avalanche. He rose from his desk and strode over to Ianto, pulling him into a hug.

For the first time since he had left his quarters, Ianto felt able to relax. 'It's good to see you too,' he said, holding Bishop at arm's length as though checking him for cuts and scrapes. 'You're looking well. Teaching suits you.'

Bishop grinned. 'I had a good role model.'

'I don't know about that,' Ianto said, chuckling. 'And the Highland air doing you some good I hope?'

'It's wonderful. Quite the contrast to London I must say,' Bishop said. 'How are things down there?'

Ianto sighed. 'The same... Worse in fact. I'll be honest; I've considered leaving.'

'You can't do that,' Bishop said, horrified. 'You're one of the few teachers left willing to stand up to him. And he still trusts you.'

Ianto raised an eyebrow. 'Personally, I feel Tobias thinks I'm simply not a threat. But you are right about the staff. Xavier's given up and Victoria is far too inclined to accept authoritarian rule, as you well know.'

'What about Professor Harlequin?'

'Dead,' Ianto whispered.

'What?'

'Heart attack, they say,' Ianto said, his lip curling into a dejected smile. 'They found him lying in an alleyway in Berlin. But the man was only forty, and had the body of a Greek god I might add. Best anthropologist we ever had.'

'You think Tobias...' Bishop began but appeared too disturbed to continue.

'It wouldn't surprise me at this point. That's all I'll say,' Ianto said. 'The Society is becoming unrecognisable. We need an intervention and we need it fast. Now, I entrusted you with this task because I knew you'd be up to it. How is the boy?'

'A little closed-off, not unlike his father. A brilliant mind, possibly to rival his father. But he hides it. Either that or he disregards what doesn't interest him—'

'Is he what we need?' Ianto interrupted, raising a hand. He wasn't interested in a full school report.

'He's not ready.'

'But will he be?' Ianto said. 'Tobias wants him brought into the Society *now*. I think he means either to bend him to his will or eliminate him as a rival.'

'With training…' Bishop said, a distant look in his eye. 'Yes. I think he could be extraordinary. And his fresh perspective could be exactly what the Eternalisium needs.'

'What about his mother?' Ianto said. 'I tried, but Tobias didn't believe her response. I've been told to bring the boy in the moment there's any sign of manifestation.'

'I don't imagine she'll let him go without a fight,' Bishop said. 'But I have worse news I'm afraid.'

Ianto felt the need to clutch his chest again. 'What?'

Bishop's young face seemed suddenly withered. 'Why do you think I called you? Doran hasn't been to school in a week.'

9

TRESPASSERS IN TIME

Doran and Zander landed with a hard thud on parched ground.
Dust kicked up, concealing them in a cloud of dirt. It wasn't until
their bodies adjusted, and their senses began to return, that they
felt the heat of the ground beneath them. Gasping, both boys
sprang to their feet and Doran inspected his clothes. They were
burning hot, as if he had been lit on fire. Shielding his face, he
looked up at the glowing sun above.

'Did we…?' Zander began in a raspy voice. He didn't manage
to complete the question.

Doran simply nodded in reply, prompting Zander to turn
and vomit into a nearby wicker basket.

They had time-travelled. And Doran knew immediately they
had gone a lot further than he had gone before. The buildings
surrounding them were old, at least by his contemporary
standards. They were also tall; taller than any building he had

ever seen. Yet the biggest indication was the heat. This was a temperature he had never experienced. Even the wind was warm. One thing was certain. They were not in Scotland any more.

Zander pulled himself away from the unfortunate wicker basket and gave Doran a swift nod. His face was pale but he looked more himself again. His eyes had started to take in his surroundings and he pulled out his phone. 'No signal,' he said, and the level of glee this gave him concerned Doran greatly. 'No internet. Nothing. So we're definitely in the past. Wow…a time before the internet…' He shuddered but still seemed positively giddy at the prospect of where they might be.

Doran could tell his friend was already thinking of all the possibilities and fun to be had from their current predicament. 'Don't even start,' he said. 'We are going back right now.'

Zander looked like he was hoping he hadn't heard him correctly. 'You can't be serious? Mate, we've time-travelled. And let's face it, not only that, we must be in a completely different country. Are you seriously telling me you want to go back now? Without even exploring a little?'

Doran didn't have an immediate answer. Zander wasn't wrong. He did want to explore – more than anything. But that didn't quieten the nagging, responsible voice in his head that told him it wasn't a good idea. 'We don't know where we are,' he said. 'It could be the Middle Ages out there. Plus, if we are in a different country, what if they don't speak English? We could get into some deep trouble here. And what if we do something that messes with history? What if we step on something that then leads to…? I don't know… Hitler winning World War Two or something?'

Zander raised an eyebrow and grasped him by the shoulders. 'I love you, man,' he said. 'But sometimes you can be a real fun sponge.'

He gave Doran a sharp tap on the arm as though to hammer home his point and walked away, leaving Doran standing rooted to the spot.

'I am not,' he called after Zander.

Zander kept walking. 'Let's go help the Germans win then.' He looked back with an impish grin.

While Doran despaired at Zander's dark attempt at humour, he decided to ignore the nagging voice in his head. 'OK, let's go have a look around,' he said. 'But not for long, and we have to be super careful we don't mess with anything.'

Zander raised three fingers in the air. 'Scout's honour.'

'You were kicked out of the Scouts.'

'It was a mutual decision.'

Doran smirked but his smile soon faded as he cast an eye over himself and Zander. 'OK, first things first. We can't be seen like this. Not when we don't know what century it is. We have to find some clothes.'

'A costume. Now we're talking,' Zander said, rubbing his hands together. 'But what if we steal Hitler's father's trousers and then Hitler wins the Second World War?'

'Shut up,' Doran said. He glanced upwards to see a web of washing lines reaching up into the sky. Dangling on the lowest of the lines, among an assortment of monochrome clothes, were two hooded cloaks. 'They look big enough to hide most of our clothes for now. Then we can try and find something better later on if we need to.'

'You've gone from "let's leave" to committing a crime very quickly,' Zander said. 'Can I just say I'm loving Holiday Doran?'

'Just get on my shoulders before someone sees.'

As it turned out, the cloaks only covered the boys' upper halves but they didn't fancy sticking around to pick out something else.

They edged towards the end of the small side street, a window into their new world. They pressed their bodies up against the stone wall, trying their best to stay hidden in whatever shade they could find. But any attempt to stay in the shadows was abandoned when they saw what was in front of them.

It was one of the most beautiful buildings Doran had ever seen. A giant, sun-kissed red dome which, from their current vantage point, was blocking out the sun. Attached to it was a long, tunnel-shaped structure leading to a grand façade, though he could tell this was still unfinished.

'I think we're definitely in the past,' Zander said. He was no longer looking at the building – rather at the people walking in the street.

There was an array of outfits on display, ranging from flamboyant hats and coats in a rainbow of colours to basic brown rags, torn and caked in mud.

Zander chuckled. 'I'd love to see you in that.' He pointed at a man who was wearing a pair of emerald green tights, and a cloak that looked like a murder of crows stitched together.

Doran grinned. 'Maybe something more inconspicuous. Right, come on, let's wander around a bit and hope no one takes too much notice.'

Pulling their cloaks over their heads, the boys emerged into the open square, slipping into the crowd of people. For a while they followed the man in the green tights and someone they assumed was his wife, trying to listen in on their conversation. The couple definitely weren't speaking English but Doran found it difficult to work out anything further. This wasn't helped by the fact that they spoke in brief, sharp sentences followed by lengthy pauses.

'You getting anything?' Doran asked Zander.

'Only that their marriage is clearly in trouble.'

They veered away from the couple and noticed a group of girls huddled in the corner of the square. At first, Doran thought they resembled Hanna Williams and her friends, engaged in an animated conversation and checking over their shoulders to see if anyone of note was watching. But as he continued to look at them, he realised that one of the girls, who seemed a little older than the others, seemed to be giving some kind of instructions. She had the lean frame of someone unable to count on her next meal and keen, hungry eyes that never settled anywhere. She gave the slightest of head nods and the group of girls dispersed like a flock of birds, flitting off in different directions.

Doran continued to watch as the smallest of the group, a raven-haired girl no taller than Doran's waist, ducked and wove among the passers by. Seemingly unseen by all, she danced her way around the square until she was back at the group's ring leader, who opened a small sack. The raven-haired girl dropped in an assortment of shiny trinkets, looking incredibly pleased with herself.

'Maybe we should get them to steal us some clothes,' Doran heard Zander beside him.

'Come on,' Doran said as they moved on.

Their next target was a jaunty man playing the lute, with whom Zander was particularly taken. The boys followed him for a while, listening to his songs and watching his music bring a smile to the faces of those he passed.

'Doran,' Zander said, as they followed the singing man onto a cobbled street filled with stalls and workshops, 'I know what I want for my birthday.'

'Just don't come round mine to practise.'

Zander stopped. The spell of the lute player finally appeared to have been broken. 'Where are we?'

'I was just about to ask the same thing,' Doran said, watching the locals go from stall to stall. It was as if the whole city had descended onto this one street, the spaces between shoppers growing ever smaller.

The boys joined in with the excited crowd, seeing men hammering metal, an older woman spinning silk and a young boy trying to convince passers-by to purchase some meat. Doran and Zander stared at the meat for a few seconds but agreed its origin was doubtful at best.

Towards the end of the bustling street was a large workshop, filled with cloth in every colour. Three men were working behind a wooden workbench. One cut, one sewed and one was currently charming a wealthy-looking young woman into buying the dress he was fitting for her.

Doran noticed that when the third man wasn't happy, he threw the garment he'd been handed to the ground and screamed at the other two men. A woman with dark skin, wearing rags, then scurried in to scoop up the rejected clothes. As she did so, the furious fitter also yelled at her, though Doran was unsure what exactly it was she'd done wrong. She cowered as spit propelled from the man's mouth, then dashed through a gap in a curtain at the back of the workshop. The man then turned back to his customer with a plastered smile, as if this sort of exchange happened all the time, and resumed his charm offensive. The wealthy woman didn't seem perturbed by his outburst at all. In fact, she seemed to consider the man's behaviour perfectly justified.

The boys turned to each other, and Zander raised his

eyebrows. Doran knew exactly what his friend was thinking.

Slowly, they slipped round to the back of the workshop, only a thick curtain separating them from the people inside. There, in a pile, was an assortment of rejected clothes, ready to be torn apart and reused. Casting wary glances over their shoulders, they crept towards the pile and cautiously began to investigate its contents. After a few moments of digging, Doran managed to find a brown tunic and hat which looked roughly his size. He scooped them into his arms, while Zander admired a bright red tunic and shoulder cape.

'Inconspicuous, remember,' Doran whispered.

Zander shrugged. 'I just thought it would suit me.'

Doran pulled a grey tunic and hat from the bottom of the pile. 'Here.'

'Ugh! It smells like rotten fish,' Zander said, holding it at arm's length.

Doran shushed him as they heard movement from the other side of the curtain.

The dark-skinned woman came back through, carrying more clothes. When their eyes met, she froze.

Doran dropped the tunic and hat, holding up his hands in a calming manner. They may not speak the same language but he would just have to hope the woman would show kindness.

She craned her neck, looking from the shop back to the two of them. No one spoke and Doran pressed his palms together, silently pleading with her not to alert anyone while Zander mimed their desperation for the clothes.

Her face softened, and to his relief she dropped the rags she was carrying onto the pile and went back into the workshop as if nothing had happened.

'Let's go,' Doran murmured, scooping up his brown tunic

and hat again and running with Zander behind him deeper into the city.

After donning their new clothes and rubbing their trainers with dirt and dust to hide any trace of modern shine, the boys began to walk around the city with a bit more freedom.

Zander, in particular, was loving their escapade, inhabiting the role of a local peasant boy. 'So, any theories about where we are yet?' he asked, while mouthing and gesturing pleas for money to those who passed.

Doran yanked him to his side. 'Will you stop?'

'Sorry.'

'Not much. But wherever we are, it seems like it's pretty far back in the past.'

'Yeah, I mean, look,' Zander said, gesturing to a haggard old woman pulling a cart of blackened vegetables. She smiled at them as she tottered past, revealing an equally black set of depleted teeth. 'No cars, no supermarkets, apparently no chance of a yearly dental check-up.'

'It's somewhere hot,' Doran added, pointing up at the sky. 'Maybe somewhere in Europe?'

'Most likely. All the buildings look old. Why don't we try and get up high for a better view of the city? Maybe that will give us some clues.'

'Not a bad idea – for you.'

'Why thank you,' Zander said, doffing his cap and bowing low to the ground. They heard a giggle and noticed they had attracted a fleeting glance from a couple of young women in matching lilac gowns. 'Are you sure we can't interact with *anyone?*'

Doran dragged him onward. 'Wherever we are it beats Linntean.'

'I've been meaning to ask you, actually. What happened on that last bike ride? How did you end up falling?'

'I… I thought I saw that man again.'

In the moment, he had been convinced the suited man had found him. But he had been wrong, and now, because of his stupidity, they were in an unknown foreign country in the distant past.

Zander, who had been mimicking the rigid strides of an ostentatiously dressed man in front of them, finally seemed to give Doran his full attention. 'You mean the man who chased you the other night?'

'Yeah,' Doran murmured. 'But it was only Rufus—'

'Rufus? Your mum's deer? She's still feeding that thing?'

'Bigger picture, Zander.'

'Yeah, sorry,' Zander said. 'Well, you went through some crazy stuff that night. Maybe you're just not quite over it yet? I mean we weren't that far away from where it happened. Don't worry, it'll pass.'

Doran nodded. 'Yeah…maybe.'

Zander gave him a pat on the back. 'Hey, race you up that hill.' And without further warning, he darted ahead up the steeply rising street, leading to what looked like the highest point in the city.

'You'll need that head start!' Doran called after him.

Laughing, all thoughts of the man from the woods temporarily forgotten, they scampered to the summit, heading for a small open esplanade at the top of the hill bordered by a low wall.

Doran reached out and touched the wall a fraction of a second ahead of Zander. He raised his arms in triumph and Zander gave a sarcastic clap in response.

The clapping died when Zander looked over the wall. 'Wow.'

Doran followed his gaze and both fell into a stunned silence. The entire city lay stretched out in front of them. They could see every landmark, every side street. The sun-baked red of the big dome was clearly visible, rising above a sea of rooftops in this same signature reddish shade.

It was too much to take in, yet Doran felt he had to try to memorise every detail. His sweat-covered hair clung to his face. He ran his hands through it, sweeping the wet strands back so they could no longer impede his vision. Drips spattered the dry ground and he licked his lips, realising just how thirsty he was.

'Beats Mr Stow's cow field any day.'

'Yeah...'

'I knew sitting next to you that day in nursery was the best decision I ever made.'

'You just wanted my Play-Doh.'

'You had the green one; it's like the best one.'

Doran kept finding something new each time he glanced in a different direction. As the wave of excitement faded, more sobering thoughts arose. 'What if we can't get back?' He felt Zander's eyes on him but fixed his gaze ahead. What if they were stuck? What if he had dragged his best friend to the distant past and didn't have the skills to get them back again? What if they could never get back to their own time and kept jumping around, aimlessly trying to find their way home?

Zander gave him another encouraging pat. 'You'll get us back,' he said. 'And if not, then as long as you don't take us to the Ice Age, I'll be happy wherever we end up. I don't fancy my chances against a sabre-tooth tiger.'

Doran snorted and gave Zander a thankful smile. He was about to open his mouth to respond when a sudden great gust of wind blew at them. As one, they stepped backwards, shielding their eyes.

At first it was a welcome chilling breeze, as though someone had switched on the air conditioning. The cold air tickled Doran's bare skin and goosebumps spread down his arms.

But then, through the gaps in his fingers, he saw a flash of white light and removed his hands to see a tall, slender man, strolling toward them.

It was him. It was the man from the forest. He was there. How had he found them?

The man continued to walk towards them and Doran noticed he had begun to throw in a jaunty step every few paces. With any other person, this would have been seen as amusing or indicating a happy disposition. In this case, it simply added to the man's overwhelming eeriness.

As he neared, Doran began to hear the whistling again. It was the same tune as he had heard in the forest. For the first time, their eyes met. Electric-green coloured the entirety of the man's iris, glowing as the symbols on the stone had done.

Doran felt Zander grab his arm, trying to haul him into action. The two boys broke into a run – the kind of running that only occurs in times of mortal danger. It was the same way Doran had run in the forest – and he knew what had happened next.

He pulled out the watch and grabbed Zander, making sure they were connected. The button began to flash green and he readied his thumb. He looked over his shoulder to see that the man was following them as though out for a pleasant wander around the town. He remained in sight, but apparently in no hurry to catch them. Unblinking, unwavering, his cold eyes were still fixed on Doran. They had to escape; to leave. Doran turned back to look at the watch, sliding his thumb towards the button.

Suddenly, there was another flash and he felt as if someone had booted him squarely in the chest. A rush of air knocked both boys clean off their feet. The watch left Doran's hand as his head bounced off the dusty earth. He looked up to see a woman standing over them. She appeared to be in her early twenties, certainly older than Doran but still with a youthful spark in her eyes. This spark was accompanied by a jagged green circle within her iris, just like Doran's. Waves of thick, blood-red hair were tied into a bun, with the locks that could not be contained cascading over her shoulders and down her back. She tossed any rebellious strands back from her light-brown face and reached behind her back, pulling out a long, thin samurai sword. Doran's vision was still hazy, but he thought he could see symbols like the ones on the fob watch etched into the blade.

The woman looked down at him for what seemed like an eternity, then back to the still-approaching suited man. 'Right then, Doran. I've got this. Time to run,' she said.

10

LEONARDO

'Come on, didn't you hear me? Run!' the woman shouted at them both. Doran had indeed heard her but neither he nor Zander appeared able to move.

She seemed to grow tired of their lack of urgency and tugged them to their feet. 'Both of you need to get out of here, now.' She locked her hazel eyes onto Doran. 'Jump if you have to; just get out of here.'

'What about you?' Doran said.

The woman raised her eyebrow and gave a cocky half-smile. 'I'll be fine. It's *him* you should be worried about,' she said, indicating the suited man who was now only metres away.

Confidence radiated from her and Doran didn't feel any further need to argue. He picked up the watch and they ran past her, not stopping until they reached a small archway.

'What are you doing?' Zander asked.

'We can't just leave her. What if she needs help?'

The boys turned around to see the woman and suited man now in full combat. The suited man was dodging every swing of the sword with ease, as if he knew exactly where the blade would strike next. But as Doran continued to watch, he began to realise this was not exactly the case. Rather, the man was moving so fast that, to him, the blade would be moving in slow motion.

After a short while the woman, apparently disenchanted by her failure to slice the man in two, sheathed her sword and decided to engage him in hand-to-hand combat.

Hands still clasped behind his back, the suited man ducked and wove around her, seemingly uninterested in trying to land a blow himself. The woman leapt backwards and twisted her hand as though turning a dial anti-clockwise. The suited man repeated his impressive moves in reverse order and then began walking backwards, retracing the same casual footsteps he had taken to reach the woman. It was like watching something being rewound on an old VHS tape. A hint of a smile appeared on the man's face. He seemed impressed.

'I think she's got this,' Zander said. 'Let's go!'

With one last look, Doran followed Zander, and the two boys sprinted down a narrow passageway between two buildings. They continued until they emerged into an open square. People were still going about their day, some carrying large baskets and pots above their heads.

Where should they go next? Doran thought. The decision was very quickly made for them as they spotted three men dressed in soldiers' uniforms charging towards them.

With a fleeting glance at each other, the boys darted across the square, hearing the soldiers yelling and drawing their swords.

Threading their way between the passers-by, they narrowly

avoided knocking over a woman with leathery skin, who was carrying a vase three times the size of her head.

Other unknown words were thrown their way as they charged on into a compact market street, with foodstalls lining one side.

'Why are they chasing us?' Zander asked as they tore past the food stands, narrowly avoiding all manner of barrels and buckets and pots that were strewn around on the ground.

Doran didn't answer. *Why indeed?* Had the woman from the workshop told on them after all? It seemed unlikely. Whatever the reason, it wasn't their most pressing concern. Doran could feel his heart pounding. He was in danger of 'jumping', as the mysterious woman had called it. He threw a look over his shoulder to see the soldiers were a good distance behind, navigating themselves over the barrels and other obstacles in their heavy armour.

The boys came to the end of the street and found they had arrived at a hilltop. Below them was nothing but slum huts, mud and hay.

'She did say to "jump", Zander said, staring at the drop before them.

Doran raised an eyebrow. 'I don't think she meant literally.'

'We haven't much choice, seeing as you've still got your L plates,' Zander said, nodding towards the watch.

Doran glanced back at the ever-advancing soldiers and closed his eyes, calming himself enough to get a clear picture in his head. *I want to take us home.* The thought repeated and grew louder in his head. His eyes burst open and he grabbed Zander, preparing to drag them both over the brink.

Suddenly, Doran felt as though a hook had been attached to his collar and he was yanked backwards. He crumpled onto the dusty ground, Zander at his side.

Rubbing their backs, both boys glanced upwards to see a huge figure towering over them. His muscular legs were barely contained by a pair of maroon trousers. Ruffled sleeves, the same shade as the rooftops of the city, stuck out from an armoured chest plate with a large cross etched into the metal. A long, thin blade resembling a fencing sword hung low from his waist, inches from the dirt.

The soldier was so huge he was blotting out the sun as he leaned over them. But this didn't unsettle Doran nearly as much as when the soldier's thick brow softened and his lips curled into a warm smile as if he were looking upon an old friend.

This did not stop him from drawing out a long, broad stick from behind his back. To Doran, it looked like a police baton, with the added possibility of giving its victim a splinter. Still smiling genially at them, the man raised the baton and, with a sharp thrust, struck Zander hard on the head. Doran saw his friend's head hit the ground, just before another hefty blow delivered him, too, into darkness.

Doran awoke from his enforced sleep heavy-headed. As his senses gradually returned, his first thought was that the world had somehow shrunk. The darkness appeared to have followed him into his waking world and he jerked his head in every direction, trying to find any trace of light, any sign he was not alone in the blackness. He could feel a coarse material scratching his forehead and cheeks and found his hands were bound behind him.

Don't panic, he told himself. *Stay in control.*

He tried to call out to Zander but heard only a muffled growl as he felt the rag tied across his mouth.

Another equally muffled howl erupted from beside him.

Zander was clearly in a similar state, no more than a metre away.

So, the world hasn't shrunk after all, Doran thought, focusing all his efforts on staying calm. After a few moments, he felt the material clinging to his face brush up his nose and he was welcomed back into a world of sharp, blinding light. Squinting, his eyes adjusted to the bright sunlight that was gleaming through the windows all around him.

Windows. So, they were inside. But where had they been taken?

As his eyes gradually came back into focus, he started to process his new surroundings.

Before him was a large, square room crammed with work tables. These in turn were laden with a disorderly-looking clutter of models, drawings and paintings.

Dotted around the room amid the rest of the chaos were an array of extraordinary whirring contraptions of every shape and size. Each appeared to move in a way independent from the rest, each seemingly with its own unique but unknown purpose.

Moving up and down the centre of the room was a cart, not unlike the one the toothless old woman had been pulling. But this cart appeared to need no person or horse to pull it. It made a low clicking sound as it moved in a straight line to one end of the room before reversing as a train might after reaching the end of the line. There was a rhythm to its jaunts up and down the room which mesmerised Doran for some time. It had a simple elegance to it and he couldn't help feeling he had seen a very similar machine somewhere once before.

The most imposing piece in this collection of wonders was a large circular object resembling a Ferris wheel. It rotated slowly in the corner of the room, its wooden panels creaking round and round and disappearing momentarily through a small gap in the ceiling.

Doran was trying to work out the wheel's function when he glimpsed a taut rope attached to the stone wall. His eyes followed the rope towards the ceiling and he gaped.

Overseeing the workshop was an enormous eagle. At least, that was what it looked like at first glance. Yet as Doran peered closer he could see the bird was made completely of wood, its wings and tail layered with a thick brownish cloth.

Where the bird's underbelly should be, there was an open cylindrical tunnel that contained ropes attached to the wings at the front and what resembled bicycle pedals at the back. As he looked, realisation slowly dawned about where he had seen both the cart and the wooden bird. It had been another part of the 'Technology Through the Ages' history topic.

'Da Vinci…' Doran said through his gag.

Zander's muffled moan brought him out of his reverie. He glanced over his shoulder to see Zander with a brown sack over his head, his hands also bound behind his chair.

A dark hand reached out of the shadows to tug the sack from Zander's head. He winced as his eyes adjusted and Doran witnessed what he presumed his own face had looked like some moments before. Finally, their eyes met and they engaged in a wordless conversation, checking both were all right.

The owner of the dark hand came into full view, revealing himself as the soldier who had knocked them unconscious. Once again, he wore that same affable grin as he untied the gags around their mouths.

'*Scusatemi, amici miei, ma era l'unico modo per sfuggire agli altri soldati,*' he said.

Doran and Zander stared. The man had spoken as if certain they would understand him. There was a look in his eye again, as there had been in the moments before he had so rudely knocked them out. It was clearer than ever that this man inexplicably seemed to *know* them.

'*Va tutto bene?*' the man asked, now curious about their apparent lack of recognition.

'*Non credo che ti capiscano, amico mio,*' a raspier voice came from the other side of the room. Then, for the apparent benefit of the two blank faces in the room, this voice added in perfect contemporary English, 'I do not think they understand you, old friend.' There was a pause as footsteps echoed around the room and an older man came into view. 'The question is, why?'

The man had long, thick silvery hair that was woven into his matching beard. He peered at them with dark, beady eyes which never rested, analysing every aspect of them. His appearance matched another picture Doran had seen many times as he pored over book after book in Mr Bishop's class. The resemblance was striking, even down to the grey robes from the image. It was Leonardo da Vinci.

Doran blinked. It was him. It was really him. According to his history textbooks, that put them in the Renaissance period. But why had they travelled there? He cast his mind back to the woods. Before his ill-fated jump on the bike, he had mentioned wanting to meet da Vinci to Zander. Had his subconscious somehow brought them there?

'How can they not know?' the soldier asked in a manner that made it sound like speaking English caused him a great deal of pain.

'Well…' da Vinci said. 'It is possible they are pretending?'

'W-We, eh, Mr da Vinci, sir,' Doran began.

'Aha! So you do know who I am?' da Vinci said.

'Of course,' Doran said. 'But not because we've met before.'

Da Vinci inspected him again. 'You said those very words the first time we met.'

'You know us?' Zander asked.

It was Zander's turn to behold da Vinci's piercing stare. This time he said nothing, now looking as if he had been given a particularly challenging equation to solve.

'Leonardo,' the soldier said. 'Their faces look much the same as they did in our last encounter but' – he gave Zander a rough thump on the shoulder with his calloused hands – 'this one rivalled my height when last we met.'

'I did?' Zander asked, eyeing the soldier, and Doran could tell he was trying to measure him by sight alone. 'Good to know...'

'You are right, Raffaello,' da Vinci said, ignoring Zander. 'They seem close in age to our last meeting. But that would mean...' His voice trailed off and he sprang towards the nearest workstation at a speed that did not match his frail-looking body.

'What does it mean?' Zander called.

Da Vinci, who was now hunting through piles of parchment, did not answer. Finally, his frenzy ceased, and he stood ashen-faced, staring at something hidden by the pile of useless papers. 'I need you to be honest now, Doran,' he said.

Doran and Zander stared at each other, their faces matching the colour of da Vinci's.

'You know my name?'

'I know far more than your name,' da Vinci said. 'Now tell me, from your perspective, is this the first time we have met?'

'Yes,' Doran said, dumbfounded by the question.

Da Vinci bowed his head and he didn't speak for several moments. 'Untie them, Raffaello.'

'Are you sure?' Raffaello said, and Doran could have sworn the burly soldier gave him an apprehensive glance.

This expression was even more perplexing than the soldier's kindly smile. Why on earth would a man as physically imposing as this have any level of fear towards a stringy sixteen-year-old?

'Use your logic, Raffaello,' da Vinci said. 'If they do not know us, then for them the events of our last meeting have not happened yet. They do not have it.'

'Have what?' Doran asked, gulping at the sight of da Vinci's fiery stare.

Once more, da Vinci seemed to be doing multiple maths problems in his head before answering. 'You and I have met many times,' da Vinci said. 'We were friends once. We taught each other many things. How do you think I know your native tongue? In fact, a few of these designs came from our many conversations,' he added, waving a hand at the nearest workstation.

'We're…friends?' Doran asked, his brain on fire. Da Vinci *knew* him. Not only that, he seemed to know about his powers.

'*Were* friends,' da Vinci said with an icy tone. 'You may not have experienced our last meeting yet but I have. Two years ago – well, two years ago from my perspective – you stole something from me during our last meeting. Something of great importance.'

'Your beard trimmer?' Zander asked.

Da Vinci ignored him again, although Doran wasn't sure whether this was out of ignorance or annoyance.

'What did I steal?'

'I'm afraid, due to *your* rules, I am forbidden to say.'

'My rules?'

'Yes. As I said we have met many times, though not always in chronological order. One of us always tends to be older than the other.' Da Vinci drew closer, a wistful look in his eye. 'I've known you most of my life, Doran West. But eventually time makes fools of us all, does it not?' He gestured at his silvery locks.

Raffaello began loosening their bonds, but still stared at Doran as though he were a landmine that could go off at any minute.

'Why did you bring us here?' Zander asked, massaging his wrists. 'And what happened to the soldiers who were chasing us?'

'You made a few enemies on your last visit here. But Raffaello is a high-ranking soldier,' da Vinci said, tearing his nostalgic gaze away from Doran. 'I do not get along well with the soldiers in the city but Raffaello has been my friend for most of my many years in Florence.'

Doran and Zander glanced at each other. So that's where they were.

'We have also met before,' Raffaello said to them. 'He then pointed to a small gash on his cheek and grinned at Zander. 'In fact, you gave me quite a bit of trouble on your last trip.'

Zander stared at the scar. 'I did that?' he asked, and Doran was unsure whether his tone was horrified or awestruck.

'Best swordsman I ever—'

'Quiet, Raffaello,' da Vinci snapped. 'We've already said too much. The point is that Raffaello managed to placate the other soldiers and pretend he was arresting you himself.'

'But why did you bring us here?' Doran asked.

'Raffaello was under strict instructions that if either of you ever showed your faces in Florence again, he was to bring you straight to me.' He gave a weary sigh. 'I had *hoped* it would be a version of you subsequent to the theft, but apparently it's not.'

'So what now?' Zander asked. 'Can we have a go on the flying machine?'

Da Vinci turned his alert gaze on him this time. 'It has been some time, but I do not recall you being this maddening.'

'Why thank you,' Zander said, putting his hand on his chest as if these words were somehow humbling.

Raffaello's mouth twitched but before this could turn into a grin there was a loud banging on the door. In one swift movement, he was at the window, hand clasped on the hilt of his sword.

'Soldiers,' he said. 'They must have tracked us here.'

'How?' da Vinci said, joining him at the window.

'They must have grown suspicious when they realised I hadn't taken the prisoners to the dungeons.'

There was a loud crunch and the sound of a dozen voices bellowing under their feet.

Da Vinci's eyes widened. 'They are inside,' he said. 'We have to get them out of here,' he added, gesturing at Doran and Zander. 'If they are arrested or killed now, then our entire history together will vanish.'

Doran frowned. 'But I thought you said we were no longer friends.'

Da Vinci hurried over and knelt before him. 'That may be,' he said. 'But friends we were. And I wouldn't change our story for the world. Now you have to go.'

'Go? Go where? How?'

'You must use your powers.'

'I can't, I don't have that kind of control yet. I need – I need to feel like my life is in danger.'

'News flash, Doran: I think our lives *are* in danger,' Zander said as the clink of armour and pounding footsteps echoed from the stone stairs leading to the door. Raffaello jogged across and pulled out his sword, readying himself for the onslaught to come.

Doran stood up from his chair and pulled Zander to him. He listened to the sound of the approaching soldiers, trying to let the fear and adrenaline take over. His pulse racing, he pulled out the fob watch, all the while staring into the dark eyes of da Vinci.

'Goodbye,' Doran said. There were so many questions he wanted to ask him. His historical hero was standing right there before his eyes and he already had to leave.

'Until we meet again,' da Vinci said, and for the first time, he smiled. Yet, there was a twinge of sadness to it. 'While that is certain for you, I do hope it is for me as well,' he added, twiddling a strand of his silvery beard.

Doran closed his eyes and pressed down hard on the button, awaiting the rush of air and spontaneous sparks.

Neither came. Nor did the tingle in his fingertips. He could still hear the advancing soldiers, yelling in Italian as they marched.

One at a time, he opened his eyes. Da Vinci was still staring at him, though now all sadness had been replaced with concern. 'What's wrong?'

'I-I can't do it. It's not working.'

The door burst open and, two by two, a squadron of soldiers began pouring into the room. Raffaello sliced and whirled his sword through the air as smoothly as if it was cutting through water, and dispatched the first two through the door with ease. His burly exterior gave way to a well-honed finesse that Doran would never have expected.

Upon seeing the number he faced, Raffaello quickly changed tack. Dropping his sword, he sprang upwards and grasped the top of the door frame. He swung his huge body through the air and kicked out, each leg colliding with one of the next two soldiers through the door. They fell backwards, crashing into the men behind them. Like a series of dominos, they all fell into each other, rolling down the staircase.

'Go!' Raffaello yelled, picking up his sword and readying himself for his foes' return.

'I can't,' Doran pleaded to da Vinci. 'It's not working.'

'Is there any other way out of here?' Zander asked.

Da Vinci shook his head. 'Only the roof,' he said. 'But there's nothing up there apart from the most recent model of the flying machine,' he added, waving his hand.

The boys glanced at each other, Doran feeling his mouth dry up, Zander looking as if Christmas had come early.

'That'll work,' they both said.

'Absolutely not,' da Vinci said, as they heard the guttural yells of Raffaello from the stairwell.

'But it's our only way out of here,' Zander said.

Da Vinci appeared to being weighing up the value of the flying machine against their lives, taking an uncomfortable amount of time to answer. He nodded, though his head barely moved. 'Come with me.'

The three of them hurried through another door at the far end of the workshop where a very precarious-looking rope ladder hung from a trap door in the ceiling.

One by one they climbed, swinging on the frayed rungs as they did so.

They emerged onto the rooftop of da Vinci's workshop, with the city of Florence stretched out below them, although for Doran the view may as well have been a landscape of identical, beige office blocks, given what was perched beside them.

A wooden bird, like the one hanging in da Vinci's workshop only much larger, sat primed, its makeshift beak facing down a wooden ramp. The ramp looked like something out of a skate park, curving up at the end of the roof.

Doran peered closer at the body of the bird and could see

its framework also matched the model. At the front of the now much larger open cylindrical tunnel hung four ropes with loops, two attached to each wing via a pulley system. But it was the rear of the tunnel that captured his attention. It was as if someone had taken the handlebars and pedals from a bike and grafted them on to the wood. The parts looked very out of place and Doran felt the strangest desire to rip them off the bird with his bare hands. *They weren't right. They didn't belong.*

This curious sensation didn't last long, as he was hurried forwards by da Vinci. 'It will take the two of you to keep it in the air. One of you must use these ropes' – he tugged on the loops of the four ropes and the wings shuddered slightly – 'to control direction.'

'Shotgun,' Zander said, bounding headfirst into the front of the cylindrical tunnel and taking the ropes from da Vinci.

'What is shotgun?' da Vinci asked Doran before shaking his head. 'Never mind. Doran, you must use your feet to propel forwards.' He indicated the pedal mechanism. 'And with your hands, do the same action on these levers.' He put one of his wrinkled hands onto the thick metal handlebars and pushed down on one side so that it began to rotate in a similar fashion to the pedals. 'This will help you gain height.'

'Did you invent these?' Doran asked, gesturing to the pedals and handlebars. Despite their current predicament he had to know.

Da Vinci flashed him the oddest smile and he too appeared for a moment to forget their plight. 'I had a little help,' he said with a twinkle. 'Perhaps this was why.'

Doran dwelled on the words as he clambered into the cylinder, unsure if he had done so of his own free will or if da Vinci had pushed him inside. All his limbs were stretched to their fullest extent as he grasped the handlebars and put a foot on each pedal.

Once in position, he realised he was suspended in mid-air facing down the ramp, his nose mirroring that of the bird's beak. It felt as if all the blood in his body had rushed to his head, leaving nothing to support him from the neck down.

In front of him, Zander had stretched into a similar position. He had dug his feet into two carved out footholds and wrapped both ropes around his hands.

'You crash her, and I won't have Raffaello bring you in alive next time,' da Vinci said.

Doran didn't trust himself to move his head to check if the inventor was joking or not. His legs were trembling so violently he was scared they might shake themselves free from the pedals. This was madness. Utter madness. There had to be another way. There just had to be. Why couldn't he simply have used his powers in da Vinci's workshop? Why had he brought them here in the first place?

Doran, unsure whether vomit or words would come out, opened his mouth to voice his concerns when there was a loud crash from below. It appeared the soldiers had reached the ladder.

'*Arrivederci*,' da Vinci said and, in a flash, he had whipped a small knife from his robes and slashed the ropes holding the flying machine in place.

Doran and Zander shot forwards as the flying machine hurtled down the ramp. Doran experienced every groove, every bump along the way until, with a great lurch, the bird soared off the end of the ramp and up into the Tuscan sky.

11

TOBIAS TORMENTED

'What do you mean, there's no trace of him?' Tobias Blue thundered.

'There is a black cloud surrounding the boy,' a tall, thin woman with pursed lips replied. She wore a long, cream-coloured dress and stood so rigidly it was as if she were constantly needing to balance her head on her neck.

'A black cloud?' Ianto asked, adopting a politer tone.

'Yes. Something is blocking our ability to place him.'

'What could possibly do that?'

'It could be a number of things,' the woman said tetchily. 'A large anomaly? Someone shielding him from us? It could even be the boy himself.'

'He couldn't possibly have that kind of power yet,' Tobias said, though it pleased Ianto greatly to detect the tiniest hint of fear in his voice.

'It's possible. He is a West after all,' the woman said.

'Indeed,' Tobias said tersely. 'Well, do keep trying. Call for Victoria if you have to. I'm sure she'd be glad to help.'

The woman nodded, though she didn't appear at all happy with that suggestion. She glided away to a group of similarly dressed individuals and joined them in a meditative circle.

The moment her gaze left them Ianto felt Tobias grasping him by the collar, and dragging him out into the corridor.

'Would you care to explain exactly how you lost him?' Tobias hissed, the words echoing throughout the narrow passageway.

Ianto fought back a whimper. 'The boy's powers didn't appear to have manifested—'

'I asked you to tell me if he started showing any – *any* – trace of his potential,' Tobias said, snaking back and forth along the corridor, the heels of his shoes barely making a sound. 'And now you're telling me that he's travelled!'

'We don't know for sure yet what has happened.'

Tobias' slinking movements ceased, as his eyes burned darkly at Ianto. 'While your optimism is touching,' he said, 'all the evidence seems to suggest that your useless former student has failed in keeping an eye on him. Where else could the boy have gone? On his summer holidays?'

Ianto's cheeks flushed. '*If* the boy has travelled then surely the Seers would have sensed it? You've clearly had them tracking the boy long before now?'

Tobias leered at him momentarily, before resuming his silent pacing. 'You seem to be very aware of what I've been up to, don't you, Everie?' he said, as though asking about his plans for the weekend. Ianto felt his hand begin to tremble at the sudden change in Tobias' tone. 'Why so interested?'

'I-I—'

'It's almost as if you're…checking up on me?'

'N-no, of course not, I just—'

'You know what I've been finding as I get older?' Tobias pressed on. 'It's that I'm becoming increasingly clumsy. The odd missed step on the staircase, poorer grip and reflexes… I'm worried that one day in the training room my hand might just…'

It all happened within a single breath. Tobias pulled a shiny object from his trouser pocket and flung it directly at Ianto's head. Green sparks flickered all around Tobias' arm as if it were caught in the middle of a localised lightning storm. He darted forwards and seized the shiny metal projectile, the razor-sharp blade inches from the end of Ianto's nose.

Ianto stared open-mouthed at the thin penknife, which was so close to his lips he could almost taste the tangy metal.

'…slip,' Tobias finished. 'At our age, we're so accident-prone, aren't we?' he added, still in the manner of a friendly chat between colleagues.

Ianto's legs were threatening to give way at any moment, but he stood firm and mustered the courage to maintain Tobias' gaze. 'Quite,' he said, mouth dry. 'I find that myself.'

Tobias' eyes danced with menace. 'You leave me no choice. I had hoped the boy would come to us willingly but he evidently has other ideas. As we speak, he is using his powers unsafely and without training. For the sake of the timeline, we must find him. Quickly.'

Realisation dawned on Ianto's sweaty brow. Surely he couldn't mean… 'Don't you think that's a little excessive?' he said. 'The boy is just confused. He doesn't know our ways.'

'He can thank his overbearing mother for that,' Tobias said. 'You and your spy have had your chance. The Seers will find the boy soon and when they do, we will send in the Vigils.'

12

FATE AND FORESIGHT

It was at least a full minute into the flight before Doran opened his eyes. Until then, he had settled for pedalling as hard as his legs would allow and hoping Zander was a natural navigator.

A scream from Zander to pedal faster finally forced his eyes open, just in time to see his friend yank hard on his leftmost rope. Doran's stomach gave another unwelcome lurch as the flying machine's left wing dipped towards the ground.

The bird became vertical, the right wing pointing at the clouds above. It took every ounce of Doran's strength to hang onto the handlebars and avoid slipping downwards. He was about to give Zander a piece of his mind when he realised why his friend had performed such a dangerous manoeuvre.

The flying machine was gliding past the great dome, its undercarriage scuffing its terracotta roof tiles.

With a yelp, Zander pulled hard on the opposite rope and the right wing swung down level once more.

'We have to get higher!' Doran called to him.

'You think?' Zander shouted. 'Pedal faster; I'm going to try something.'

He tugged hard on all four ropes at once. The flying machine jerked upwards and then started to climb, leaving a much more comfortable gap between the unexpected aeronauts and the buildings.

The wind pounded into Doran's face. If Zander planned on firing any more instructions his way, he hadn't a hope of hearing them. The relentless air rushed past his ears, drowning him in an unbearable whooshing sound. He wouldn't be able to pedal through this much longer.

His prayers were quickly answered, though not in the manner he would have liked. There was a different kind of *whoosh*, followed by a soft *pop*, and the flying cylinder suddenly wobbled. Another *whoosh* and *pop* and the machine seemed to be sinking.

Forcing his head up to look at the wings he saw sunlight poking through a series of small holes. *Whoosh*. Something thin and pointed whistled past his ear. At first, he thought it was a small bird but then realised, to his horror, that an arrow had flown past him and pierced the right wing.

They were being shot at. The Florentine guards obviously didn't take kindly to an unknown object soaring through their skies.

The flying machine plummeted towards the ground. Zander abandoned the ropes and instead clung to the bars of their pod for dear life.

There was nothing for it; Doran had to save them. He was the only one who could. He took one hand off the handlebar, clinging to the other pedals with his other three limbs. He thrust his hand into his pocket and pulled out the fob watch, which he saw was already glowing at his touch.

Taking a deep breath, he released himself from the remaining pedals and fell, arms outstretched, towards Zander, smashing into him as da Vinci's flying machine continued to hurtle towards the ground. The boys hugged each other tight; it was now or never. A fiery death or a time jump into the unknown.

The last thing Doran heard was the sound of the beak colliding with the ground, and then…silence.

A flicker of lighting appeared a few metres above a frosted side street. Luckily, it was ten o'clock at night and the main road ahead was bustling with tourists and locals trying to find a good place to socialise.

So no one noticed two teenage boys falling face-first and landing in an empty skip.

'I think your next target should be to master your superhero landing,' Zander mumbled, his cheek pressed against the cold steel. With a groan, he raised his head and looked around. 'Good thing it's bin day.'

'Agreed,' Doran said. 'Are we in a skip?'

'I think we might be, yes.'

'I can't work out if that's an improvement or not.'

Both boys staggered to their feet, clutching their sides. Sighing with relief, they embraced each other as tight as they had been when seemingly careering towards their deaths. Doran was unsure for a moment whether Zander would ever let him go.

'It really smells in here,' he said, patting him on the back.

'I thought that was you.'

Grinning, both boys broke apart and clambered out of the

skip. They shivered as they staggered towards the lively main road. Wherever they were, the temperature certainly felt a little more like home. But Doran had the sinking feeling they were still a long way from there. 'Where do you think we are?'

'No idea.'

The Tuscan sun already a distant memory, they emerged from the alleyway and realised the weather was not the only contrast with their previous location.

Each of Doran's senses seemed to be taking it in turns to be the most offended. Wherever he turned, light blinded him. Every building was lit up with neon signs or gigantic television screens.

Then the sounds of the city hit his ears. Chatter, buses and live music all seemed desperate to make their presence known.

'So we're not in the past any more,' Zander said, taking time over every word. He gestured to the largest of the screens. The adverts being played were recognisable, as were some of the shops making up the street. 'But also not in Linntean,' Doran added, his fears confirmed. They still hadn't made it home. He had got it wrong again.

'I feel like I've swallowed a mouthful of pool water,' Zander said, scratching at his throat.

Doran frowned and drew in a deep breath, stifling a cough. 'I know what you mean. It's like someone has tried to cover up the smell of petrol with disinfectant.'

Zander nodded. 'Where do you think we are?'

'No idea.'

'Something about it feels familiar,' Zander said. 'Do you think there's a signal this time?' He pulled out his phone to investigate.

Doran whipped out his own. 'Good thinking. You find out where we are. I'm going to see if I can phone my mum. She'll be worried sick.'

Doran walked a little away from Zander and passers-by funnelled around him. No one seemed to pay him any attention – they were merely irked that his presence had required them to make a slight detour. He was about to dial his mum's number when he felt a hand grasp his shoulder and Zander wheeled him around. 'We're in the future!'

Zander thrust the phone in his face and he squinted at the date on the screen. It was true. They were nearly three years in the future. At least he wasn't that far off.

'This is Leicester Square,' Zander continued, tapping his screen, and he whacked Doran on the chest. 'We're in London! What should we do first?'

'Wow, wow. Slow down. Are you not forgetting we nearly died a minute ago? Not to mention the suited psychopath who appears to be chasing us?'

'He's busy in the past, fighting that badass samurai woman,' Zander said, as though that settled the matter. 'Mate, we're in the home of the West End. Musicals, five-star plays, you name it!'

Doran stared. Zander's lack of perspective never failed to astound him. 'It doesn't matter where he is if he can travel in time like me. He could pop up five minutes from now for all we know. If he found us once, he can find us again.'

Zander's face fell. 'What do we do then?'

'I don't know. We don't even know why he's after me, or who that woman was.' Doran paused, noticing people beginning to glance in their direction as they hurried by. He wondered why for a second, then looked down at his outfit. 'But right now, we have to get rid of these clothes.' He opened his tunic to reveal his present-day clothes underneath. 'We may have been sweating buckets in Florence but I'm glad we kept these on.'

They threw the Florentine attire into the skip and instantly felt more at home. They could now walk inconspicuously in the crowd and begin taking in the sights of London. It was only when they were passing a fast-food chain that Doran felt his stomach growling for attention. Luckily, Zander had brought his wallet to the woods so they had enough to buy a burger and chips each, wolfing it down as though they hadn't eaten for days.

Stomach monsters appeased, they began to explore London. Zander had taken charge and used his phone to find their way to a street with a gigantic, glittering billboard for *Singin' in the Rain* illuminating one theatre. Zander danced up the steps to stand at the entrance and burst into a tap routine dedicated solely to Doran. He might have gone on forever if a bouncer hadn't come out of the door with eyebrows raised. Zander cackled and leapt down the steps, calling over his shoulder in an American accent. 'Gotta dance!'

The boys laughed and strolled along the pavement, and Zander pointed to various other billboards on display. 'And I want to see that. Oh, and that. This is so awesome. Let's just drop out of school and move here.'

Zander's enthusiasm was infectious, and Doran almost forgot about their predicament. At that moment, he was simply a teenager in the big city for the first time. He was just beginning to enjoy himself when both their phones began to ping incessantly. It appeared the devices had finally fully adjusted to being back in a time with technology.

Doran's eyes widened as he saw multiple texts from his mum, as well as numerous notifications for missed calls. 'It's my mum,' he murmured. 'There's messages here from years ago – our present. She's wondering where I am...'

Zander frowned at his phone and showed Doran his screen. It was filled with notifications from various social media sites of posts from people from their school.

Doran began to scroll down his own phone and saw the same. The boys clicked on one and saw a long paragraph that had been shared by nearly everyone they knew. After they had read the paragraph in its entirety, they looked at each other, horror-struck.

'We're missing,' Zander said.

Doran felt the realisation cut through him. 'Of course. To everyone else, that day in the woods would be the last time anyone saw us. We've been missing for years.'

They pored through all the messages and social media comments on Zander's phone. It was filled with police statements, emotional tributes and pleas for information. One particular post gave them pause and Zander pressed play on a video.

On the screen was Kate West, sitting at a desk beside a man in a suit with police officers standing behind her. The post was dated two weeks after the day they had fallen over the ridge in the Linntean woods. Doran held his breath as his mum's voice came from the phone.

'...We just want the boys back. Whatever has happened. If someone has them or they've just run away and don't think they can come home. We just want the boys back.'

She broke down in tears but refused the comfort of the police detective beside her.

'Doran... Doran, if you're out there... I'm sorry. I'm so sorry. Please. Please just come back. I love you. Please...please just come back...'

The video clip ended, and Doran felt a tear trickle down his cheek. He brushed it away before Zander could see and stared at the image of his mum. 'The last thing I said to her was that I hated her,' he murmured. He could feel Zander's gaze but didn't look away from the screen. 'We have to go back.'

He waited for some sign of agreement, but it never came. Instead, he saw his friend trudge over to a nearby fountain and sit down. 'Zander?'

There was no reply. Zander was scrolling through his phone, his thumb attacking the screen harder with every tap. With a guttural yell, he leapt to his feet and hurled the phone into the fountain. It cracked off the marble centrepiece and landed in pieces in the water.

'Zander?' Doran said, rushing towards him. 'Zander, what's wrong?'

Zander didn't seem able to speak. He looked as if he had just run for miles, his shoulders rising and falling. Eventually, his body sagged. 'He didn't even call.'

'Who didn't?'

He turned abruptly and Doran could see his eyes were glistening. 'My dad,' Zander spat. 'He didn't call, he didn't make an appeal video. All I got was one lousy text message the day we vanished, asking me if I was bringing in dinner.'

Doran's tongue remained fastened to the bottom of his mouth, unsure of how to respond. 'Maybe he couldn't. Maybe something happened. We don't know—'

'I know!' Zander yelled, before his voice became quiet. 'I know. He never gave a damn about me. Not since Mum…not since she left. I'm nothing to him. Just some kid who lives in his house and looks like the woman who ditched him.'

'That's not true,' Doran said, though it was more of an automatic response than how he really felt. He was perfectly aware of how neglectful Zander's father had been.

'I'm not going back,' Zander said, rubbing his eyes with his sleeve. 'It's good he thinks I'm gone. I should just stay here and start my life again.'

'Zander we have to go back,' Doran said. 'The world thinks we've disappeared. We have to go back and put things right.'

Zander shook his head. 'No. No, I'm staying. There's nothing for me back there anyway. This is where I belong.'

'There's me.'

'Then stay,' Zander said. 'Just stay. Or take us somewhere new. You have the whole of time at your fingertips. Let's just keep travelling. We don't have to go back. Maybe…maybe this is what we're meant to do? You heard da Vinci. He said we've met him many times. That must mean we keep travelling, that we have tons of adventures still to come. The world thinks we're dead so why don't we let them? We could just keep going. See the world. See it all.'

Doran stared at his friend. Da Vinci's words had troubled him too. Was he indeed meant to keep travelling? But how could he, after seeing his mum's tearful appeal?

'I can't,' he said, though it required all the conviction he could muster to say it. 'You saw my mum. I can't let that happen to her. I can't let her think I'm gone, and that I left hating her.'

'Phone her then. Let her know you're all right before we carry on.'

'If I phone her now, it won't matter. To her, it'll still be three years after I left. I need to go back so I can stop this future from ever happening, so we don't ever go missing at all.'

'Then go,' Zander said. 'Leave me here. I'll be fine.'

'You don't know that,' Doran said. 'Come on mate, stop this. Let's go. When we get back this will never happen.'

'But *I'll* still remember,' Zander said, and his eyes had a feral look about them. 'I'll still know what he really thinks of me. You don't get it. You had a mum who would do anything for you. You're lucky. You never had a dad.'

Doran stepped back and his face hardened.

'Doran...' Zander began, reaching out a hand as though trying to claw his words back.

'No, you're right, you should stay,' Doran said, cheeks flushed. 'Maybe you'll get your big break on the West End and everything will be wonderful.'

'Maybe I will,' Zander responded, his willingness to apologise gone. 'Bye then. Have a good life finishing school in the middle of nowhere. Look me up when you eventually get here the slow way. Maybe if I'm not too famous I'll give you a call!'

'Famous?' Doran cried, followed by a cackle even he didn't recognise. 'Don't make me laugh. You think because you've played Seymour in a school production of *Little Shop of Horrors* that you're going to be this big movie star? You were just the only boy in our year dumb enough to audition.'

'You don't mean that.'

'It's the truth.'

'Just go.' Zander spun on his heels and marched away.

'Fine!'

'Fine!'

'Where are you going?'

Zander turned around and flapped his arms in a shrug. 'To get a drink. Technically, I'm over eighteen now, right?'

And with that, he stomped out of sight. Doran watched him for a moment and then did the same, in the opposite direction.

Doran charged through the streets of London, barging into every passer-by who dared to get in his way. He moved at a formidable pace for someone who didn't have a clue where they were going.

The London air seemed to cling to him. Linntean air didn't feel anything like it. Who would want to stay in this place? He couldn't believe how selfish Zander was being. Not to mention how stupid. How would he survive? He wasn't thinking clearly.

But, would you be? If you were him?

No, another part of Doran's brain countered. *But I wouldn't know, would I? Zander made that perfectly clear. I never had a dad.*

Doran finished his argument with himself and stopped. He needed a plan. He pulled out his phone. There may not be any marble pools to dive into but surely there was a bridge nearby, so he could launch himself towards the Thames.

Waterloo Bridge seems the closest, he thought as he tapped the screen to get an idea of his surroundings. *A decent height as well.* He looked up from his phone. *How is this my life now?*

Following the directions on the app, he found his way to the bridge. Cyclists flew past him and Doran wondered how they could stand the chill in the air as he reached the centre of the bridge.

The dank smell of the Thames below invaded his nostrils – quite the contrast to the spring waters of home. Doran glanced over the side and saw the dark water beneath. It was closer than the pictures on his phone had suggested, but it would have to do.

Picking his spot, he clambered over the parapet and leant back on the railing to steady himself. His toes poked over the edge as his hair was blown back by another blast of the chilling wind. But as he pulled the watch from his pocket, the view caught his eye.

London was quite different to the sun-warmed world of Florence, but no less spectacular. Perhaps he had been a little harsh. The scene before him was a tourist's dream. There were the Houses of Parliament and Big Ben, lit up in a warm glow. There was the London Eye, currently dressed in a radiant pink. Every building in sight sparkled in the moonlight, although so many manmade stars prevented him from seeing the real ones. For a moment, Doran thought of Zander, out there somewhere. He would have loved this view.

Stop it. He was going home. He had to get back to his mum. If Zander wanted to stay, then so be it.

He took out his phone and quickly found the image of his mother's face in the police press conference. The din of traffic echoed all around him, getting louder inside his head.

Doran closed his eyes, trying to block it all out. He thought of Linntean. The mountains. The sparkling blue lochs. The forests. The marble pools.

He saw his house. His mum smiling at him. All the surrounding background noise softened as if someone had turned the volume down and he focused on nothing except the feeling of his heart, beating rhythmically in his chest.

As he continued to imagine his home, memories emerged. Each one contained one of two people. Either his mum or Zander.

Zander's face became more frequent and Doran's brow furrowed.

'Kid! Hey kid! What are you doing?' a voice came from behind him.

All the background noise of London returned in an instant, unmuted. He wobbled and, on instinct, reached with his nearest hand for the railing. But this hand contained his phone, which it reflexively dropped. As Doran wrapped his fingers around the railing to steady himself, he watched the phone falling into the dark waters of the Thames with a pitiful plop.

Brilliant. Just brilliant.

He turned his head to see who had disturbed him and saw a worried-looking police officer. 'I said, what are you doing?'

Doran gaped at him, then at the watch. He knew what he had to do. 'Nothing,' he answered. 'Sorry.' He clambered back over the parapet and hopped down to the safety of the pavement.

The police officer looked as if he was about to question him further when a drunken yell from further down the road stole his attention.

Doran seized his chance and sprinted back the way he had come, pocketing the watch once more. Now wasn't the time to go back. He had to find his friend first.

The downside of storming off is that it can be very difficult to find your way back.

Every street seemed the same as Doran desperately sought to find his way back to where he had left Zander. Had he passed that alleyway already? He had just stepped over a fallen dustbin when something – or rather, someone – caught his eye.

A man was hovering at the end of the alleyway. He somehow seemed a little out of place. Dressed in a full black suit and trench coat, he was also sporting a hooded cloak not unlike the one Doran had donned in Florence. It wrapped around his upper torso and cast a shadow over his face. A decidedly odd fashion choice for London: might it be the suited man in some new guise? Had Doran been tracked down again?

No. This man was shorter and had several well-maintained muscles, seemingly ready to burst out of his tight-fitting suit. Nevertheless, every instinct in Doran's body was telling him to go no further. He turned on the spot and was about to head back the way he had come when he froze. The same man was now standing at the other end of the side street, sparks flickering around him. Doran glimpsed a chapped set of lips curling beneath the shadowy hood.

'What do you want?'

The man didn't answer, the chapped lips twisting into a grin.

'You're like me, aren't you?' Doran said. 'Why are you here?'

'You're to come with us, Doran West,' the hooded man said.

Us? Doran thought. There was a flash of light above his head and another man was standing at the top of a nearby fire escape. He too was shrouded in black, his blue eyes fixed on Doran, shining in the darkness.

Doran motioned to the currently unguarded exit. 'I'm actually on the way to find my friend, so…'

As one, the two men vanished and reappeared a few metres in front of him. 'You are to come with us…' the first hooded man said.

'…It is foretold,' the blue-eyed man added, as if finishing his partner's thought.

'Fantastic,' Doran said, edging backwards. 'Great news. Let me just…'

He darted out of the side street and into what he was relieved to find was a busy main road. He smacked into a group of young women, one of whom had a 'Bride' sash draped over her.

'Does your mummy know you're out this late?' one said.

'Aw look, he's cute,' another chimed in.

They all cackled as Doran looked back into the side street.

Nothing. The men were either hiding in the darkness or had vanished once again.

'Sorry,' Doran mumbled and thrust his hands into his pockets, striding along the main road. One quick glance over his shoulder showed him his pursuers were still on his track; there they were, marching side by side a few paces behind him.

They're not using their powers, he thought. So there must be a degree of secrecy to their work. He had to keep them out in the open. That was his only hope.

Quickening his pace, he scanned his surroundings, seeking any means of escape. Should he try to find a police station? Good luck explaining his predicament. *Sorry, officer, can you stop the two time-travelling creeps from chasing me?* He'd be carted off in a straitjacket.

He settled on aiming for a crowded square. He wove in and out of late-night shoppers, trying to lose himself among them.

His pursuers knew his name. Why did they want him? Perhaps he had broken some kind of time law on his trip to Florence. Which made the cloaked figures…what? Time police? Had they come to arrest him?

The crowd swallowed him, and for a moment he hoped he had thrown off his two hunters. He charged forward, trying to make it to the far edge of the sea of people. He had to get back to Zander, and get the two of them out of London.

The bodies before him parted and Doran froze. The cloaked figures were once again standing and waiting, passers-by gliding around them as if they were another of London's monuments.

Doran broke into a run, darting around a corner and into the narrow gap between two theatre buildings. He could hear the thump of the musical ensemble inside one of them. The melody, he noticed, was keeping time with the beat of his heart, thumping with what felt like the same force. He drew air into his lungs, breathing out slowly. He had to remain in control. The worst thing would be for him to jump now and risk not being able to find his way back to get Zander. If the men chasing him knew his name, what else did they know? Did they know about Zander? Would they hunt him next?

Doran was about to edge out of the gap to check whether he could make a break for it when he was yanked backwards. He swung his elbow, ready to lash out, ready to fight off the shadow men with everything he had.

He was thrust against the opposite wall and a hand covered his mouth. Doran was about to scream when his aggressor's face moved into the only shred of light in the passageway.

Doran's whole body went limp. It was neither of the two men pursuing him, but rather the last person he would have expected to see.

'Mr Bishop?' Doran said through his history teacher's fingers.

'Hello, Doran,' Mr Bishop said. 'You've been missing a lot of school lately. Is everything all right?'

'What the h—' Doran began, but Mr Bishop pulled him further into the shadows. He touched his finger to his lips, the corner of his eye checking the main road beyond the passageway. Sure enough, the two hunters passed by, their cloaks billowing behind them. Once they were out of sight, both Doran and Mr Bishop dared to breathe.

'This way,' Mr Bishop said, and he pushed Doran in front of him, ushering him further down the already cramped passageway.

'But I don't understand,' Doran said, resisting his teacher's shoves. 'What's going on? What are you doing here?'

Mr Bishop pushed a little harder and Doran stumbled forward. 'There's no time,' he said. 'The Vigils won't give up now they've found you. I've got to bring you in.'

Too many questions were forming within Doran's mind, each one fighting to be the first out of his mouth. 'Vigils?' he asked.

It seemed the most pressing concern. 'What are Vigils? Is that who's been chasing me?'

'Yes,' Mr Bishop said, checking over both shoulders. 'They are a militant faction. Generations ago they were soldiers – protectors – but nowadays they are essentially Tobias Blue's private army.' Everything Mr Bishop said seemed to create more questions. 'I've got to get you across town to my contact. Come on.'

He tried to usher Doran forward again but Doran shrugged him off. 'What do you mean, your *contact*? You're – you're my history teacher. Not freaking James Bond. I'm not taking another step until you tell me who you really are and what the hell is happening.'

Mr Bishop arched an eyebrow and for a moment Doran felt like he was back in the classroom. Had he really just spoken to a teacher like that?

His history teacher groaned. 'Fine,' he said, and to Doran's astonishment he reached up to his eyes and plucked out a pair of contact lenses. His hands dropped to reveal not the dark brown that Doran was familiar with but a pair of amber eyes with the jagged *teine uaine* carved upon them. 'My name *is* Ewan Bishop. I'm a Traveller, like you. I tracked you here from our present. I'm part of a secret organisation called the Eternalisium, also colloquially referred to as the Society. At sixteen, every Traveller is inducted into the Eternalisium. You are taught to control your gifts, find your discipline, and can study in a variety of fields. I was sent to observe you, to see if you had any abilities and to bring you in if they manifested. But I…momentarily lost you. Now I've got to get you back to the present and to the Eternalisium before the Vigils and Tobias Blue get to you first.'

'What happens if they do?' Doran said, his mouth dry.

'They'll bring you in instead.'

'Wait. What?' Doran said. 'So, you're saying those creepy ninjas are also part of this Eternalisium? And this Tobias Blue person?'

Mr Bishop's lips became very thin. 'Unfortunately…yes, they are. But there's no time to explain all that now. What you need to know is that Tobias Blue doesn't have your best interests at heart, despite what he might say.'

'And you do?'

'Of course.'

'And how can I know that?'

'You can't. You'll just have to trust me.'

It was Doran's turn to arch an eyebrow. 'I'm finding that a little difficult for some reason.'

'That's fair,' Mr Bishop said, holding his hands up. 'But I'm not the one who's sent "creepy ninjas" after you.'

'Also fair,' Doran said. Did he have a choice? Perhaps at this point, Mr Bishop was his only hope. 'OK, let's go and find Zander and then get out of here.'

Mr Bishop's face drained of colour. 'Zan… As in Zander Munro? The school thought he must just be ill. He's the curly-haired boy who loves to talk through my lessons, right? Are you telling me you brought a passenger along with you?'

'Yes…?'

'Then that means…' Mr Bishop began, but he never got to finish his sentence. Doran felt goosebumps spread across his arms, sounding the alarm that they were no longer alone. Sure enough, blocking their exit from the passageway stood the two Vigils.

The shorter of the two smirked at Mr Bishop. 'They'll exile you for this, Ewan,' he said.

'Doran West is to be brought in under my protection, Crum,'

Mr Bishop said, but Doran could see his hands were shaking.

'I see,' the Vigil named Crum said. 'And you think you can protect him, do you? The man whose stopping powers are so weak he could barely halt the buzzing of a fly's wings?'

The blue-eyed Vigil gave Mr Bishop the same glass-eyed stare he had given Doran in the alleyway. 'The boy will come with us. Events are unfolding.'

For some reason, these words seemed to unsettle Mr Bishop even more. 'That won't prevent me from trying,' he said, drawing himself up to full height.

'Then you're a fool,' the blue-eyed Vigil said. 'Take the boy, Crum.'

'Run, Doran!' Mr Bishop yelled, and he shoved Doran out of the passageway.

Doran stumbled out into a side street. A car screeched and swerved around him, the sound of the horn blaring.

Heart racing, Doran looked back into the passageway to see Mr Bishop had raised a hand, as if ready to push the two Vigils back by sheer force of will. Doran could see the vein in his forehead pulsating. Whatever he was trying to do clearly wasn't working. Crum simply laughed at him and grabbed the history teacher's fingers. A crack echoed from the passageway, followed by Mr Bishop's screams.

'Let me show you real power,' Crum said. In a flash, both he and Mr Bishop had vanished. A flicker of sparks danced high above Doran's head and Crum and Mr Bishop returned, hanging in the air. Crum let go of Mr Bishop who plummeted to the ground with a shriek. His legs hit the concrete first and his ankles snapped. With a yelp of agony, he collapsed, smacking his face on the road.

Before gravity could take hold of Crum he vanished in a storm of lightning and reappeared on the ground. He strolled towards the contorted body of Mr Bishop, who gave a soft moan. He was still alive but Doran wasn't sure if Crum had intended him to be.

Crum bent down, his lips close to Mr Bishop's ear. 'Would you like another go?'

'No!' Doran said, and to his surprise, Crum sprang to his feet as though his words had given the man some kind of electric shock. He didn't have quite the same level of wariness that Doran had seen in Raffaello's eyes but Crum did appear cautious for the first time. Why were all these grown men looking at him that way?

'I'll go with you,' Doran said. 'Just leave him alone.'

'No, Doran,' Mr Bishop said with a wheeze.

The blue-eyed Vigil glided out from the passageway to join Crum. He had the air of someone who was exactly where he needed to be. 'Events have unfolded,' he said, his voice as light as the breeze wafting in his cloak.

'Very well,' Crum said to Doran. 'Take my arm.'

Doran checked on Mr Bishop, who was still muttering pleas for him not to go with them. His face was cut and it looked as if his nose was broken.

Crum hauled Mr Bishop to his feet and both he and the other Vigil propped him upright. Crum clasped his hand on Mr Bishop's shoulder and squeezed. 'He may have saved your life, but you'll still have to answer to Tobias.' He then motioned for Doran to grab his free arm.

With a final glance back the way he had come, Doran wondered where Zander might be. Was he lost, like him? Was he just as scared?

I'll come back for you, he thought, and he dug his nails into Crum's muscular forearm.

13

THE ETERNALISIUM

Doran stood at the edge of a stone archway. The two Vigils hovered behind him, still propping up Mr Bishop. His eyes drifted to a battered street sign on the cobbled wall. 'Glenmoral Row'. The street shared the same name as his school. The coincidence struck him as odd and he was about to ask Mr Bishop about it when Crum nudged them both in the back, shepherding them onwards.

Doran was unsure where they going. There was nothing through the gate except a large patch of unmown grass and some equally overgrown flower borders. Yet with every step he took a thought grew louder and louder. He had the overwhelming desire to look away from the area before him, to turn around and march straight back through the archway. The others drew level with him and he checked to see if they were also experiencing this same feeling. But it was quite the opposite. The three men were in fact all staring up at something, taking in a view Doran apparently couldn't see.

'Don't look away,' Mr Bishop said, sensing his confusion. 'It's your first time so it'll take a moment for your brain to accept it. But you're a Traveller; *this* is your home.'

Doran nodded, though he wasn't sure why. He hadn't exactly understood Mr Bishop but the words had somehow made sense and muffled the small voice inside trying to make him avert his gaze.

The view before him wobbled. Reality seemed to bend as though someone was trying to claw away the empty space behind the grassed square. It happened again, this time for longer and Doran caught a glimpse of a gigantic mansion that his brain told him had no right to be there. In a blink, it was gone but its presence was now known to Doran and Doran to it. It was as if the building wanted to be seen, to show off its existence to him, and it continued to shimmer behind the mirage of mundanity. Longer and longer, it stayed, calling to him, begging him to see it.

It was like stepping inside an invisible bubble, and Doran felt the hair on his arms stand to attention. The mansion finally became fully visible to him and the shimmering ceased.

They had found each other.

Mouth agape, Doran stared at a colossal red-brick building. Countless chimneys lined the rooftop, suggesting a great many fireplaces in a great many rooms. A whole world concealed.

A lot of care seemed to have been taken with the front of the mansion. Decorative marble carvings lined the impeccable brickwork and trimmed the symmetrical outline of the building. Rising from the centre of the mansion was a tower topped by a faded green dome that reminded Doran of an observatory. Below this, facing towards the square was a large clock with golden hands and numbers.

The building's broad frontage was flanked at either end by two identical tall square towers that seemed to stretch far up towards the heavens. Their great height made them appear out of proportion with the rest of the mansion, while the more functional, rugged architecture of their crenellated tops – more like church towers or parts of a castle – seemed out of tune with its elegant grandeur. Doran had the impression that they had been built with a specific purpose in mind, rather than simply to impress, or even to dominate. He half-expected to see a solider or guard patrolling the battlements. Nevertheless, the architect clearly couldn't resist adding a touch of flamboyance to their sombre forms, for golden finials sprouted incongruously from their corners.

Though he winced in the attempt, Mr Bishop smiled at him. 'I had the same look on my face when I first arrived here,' he said. 'Just wait until you see the inside.'

'Enjoy it while you can,' Crum said.

'You don't have to do this,' Mr Bishop said. 'It's not too late for me to be the one to bring him in.'

Crum dragged the young teacher forward. 'Keep moving.'

'The Vigils of the past would be ashamed of what their order has become.'

'The Vigils of the past were built for war,' Crum said, and he displayed a set of yellowing teeth. 'This is peace time.'

Mr Bishop scoffed. 'You think so?' he said. 'I think war just has a new face.'

The arched emerald-green front door was adorned with a gold embossed letter 'E' with symbols surrounding it, not unlike the ones on Doran's fob watch. The door opened silently as the visitors scaled the steps of the mansion. Doran forced his reluctant legs to carry him over the threshold. He felt the need to be brave, to show no fear.

The mansion was dark and quiet, yet Doran halted immediately as though a hundred voices had commanded it. Before him, was a vast open ground floor, almost the size of a football pitch.

It was as if he were looking at a painting. What was before him couldn't possibly be real. He could see all the way to the back of the mansion, with countless rooms opening off on either side of the great hall. The first thing that fully focused his attention was a gigantic emerald-green banner, hanging in front of an arched glass window. Another gold 'E' was embossed upon it in the centre of a pentagon, with five emblems surrounding the letter. A hand, an eye, a clock with numbers in reverse order, what looked like someone running at speed, and finally a shadowy figure with its hand on the shoulder of another figure. Doran glanced at Crum, who had gripped Mr Bishop's shoulder in the same way before they had all time-travelled there. Could those emblems be for the different disciplines his teacher had mentioned?

Below the banner was the foot of a large switchback staircase, which seemed to go only as far as the next floor. Doran wasn't sure how many floors the mansion contained but he felt a sudden keen desire to explore every inch of all of them.

The only opening he could see in the far corner of the ground floor was the entrance to what was without a doubt the biggest library Doran had ever seen. There didn't appear to be a door; the entrance was simply a large gap in the wall. Even in the dim light, he could make out an almost infinite-seeming expanse of books. The shelves stretched well out of sight, all of them fully stocked.

It took Doran a while to realise that Mr Bishop was staring at him, smiling as if to say, 'I told you'. Surprising even himself, Doran smiled back, but the moment didn't last long as Crum's hand squeezed Mr Bishop's shoulder again. They both disappeared with a flash of sparks, the memory of Mr Bishop's grin etched so deep that Doran could still see it when he blinked.

'Where has he taken him?' Doran asked the blue-eyed Vigil, who had lowered his hood to reveal a dark buzzcut. He was a lot younger than Doran had expected, his face free of lines, perhaps in his mid-twenties.

'To have his injuries reversed,' the blue-eyed Vigil said, in that sickening, airy voice.

Doran frowned. It was an odd choice of word. 'What do you mean, reversed? Like healed? By a doctor?'

The Vigil gave a knowing smirk. 'Not quite.'

'And then what?'

'He will stand trial in due course.'

Doran's nostrils flared. 'He was only trying to help me. Where's the crime in that?'

The blue-eyed Vigil didn't answer and his demeanour suggested that he took pleasure in this refusal. He gestured to the switchback staircase, which somehow didn't feel quite as inviting any more.

'And what makes you think I'll go anywhere with you?'

The Vigil surveyed him, a modicum of a grin dancing across his face. 'Intuition,' he said, and strolled towards the staircase. 'I'm Malloch by the way,' he added. He didn't appear at all concerned about leaving Doran unattended.

Doran stared after him. The more time he spent in the Vigil's presence the odder the young man became. What had he said before? *Events are unfolding.* Was that why he was so assured? Did he somehow *know* what was going to happen?

Doran's attention returned to the crest above; this time he was drawn to the emblem of the eye. It cast its gaze across the mansion and he imagined it would follow him no matter where he went. An all-seeing eye. Was this another discipline?

He glanced back at the emerald-green doors – the world he knew lay out on the other side of them, blissfully unaware of the impossibility hiding within these walls. One thing was for sure: the answers to all his questions did not lie out there. He would have to climb those stairs.

Reaching the top step, he found Malloch waiting for him, looking almost unbearably smug. Seeing him almost made Doran change his mind but his curiosity won out. 'Where are we?'

'The Eternalisium,' Malloch said, as though he had asked a ridiculous question.

'I know that. I mean *where* are we? Are we still in London?'

'Yes. London. Present day. Near Greenwich Park. You can see the whole city from the top floor. Best view in the country if you ask me.'

Doran frowned. So he was back in his own time. But Zander wasn't with him and he was still hundreds of miles away from home. He joined Malloch and the two of them wandered down a long, thin corridor. 'Where is everyone?'

'Term time is over,' Malloch said. 'Most students have returned home for the summer. The professors are either sleeping or on holiday.'

It had been the most normal sentence the Vigil had spoken. Wonderfully ordinary. 'So…so you can leave, then?' The notion seemed quite alien to how Doran currently felt.

Malloch seemed to find the question highly amusing. 'Of course,' he said through a chuckle. 'This isn't a prison. The Eternalisium is essentially a university with a few...extra-curricular activities.' And to Doran's surprise, he *winked* at him. 'You spend your first couple of years learning to control whatever abilities you may have, while taking a general array of subjects. Then in your third and fourth year, you can specialise. You can do a degree of some kind which you can use in the outside world or train to serve the Eternalisium in a particular field.'

'Like being a Vigil?'

'Like being a Vigil.'

A thought struck Doran. 'So, you're telling me there are people just walking around out in the world who can time-travel?'

'It's not like it's every other person you pass in the street,' the Vigil said. 'But yes. Those who do degrees and choose to live in the outside world tend to be Travellers whose abilities aren't particularly strong. Like your teacher friend.'

Doran thought back to Mr Bishop, desperate to perform some kind of feat in the passageway. 'And they can just...use their powers?' Doran asked, thinking about his time in Florence. 'What if they mess with history?'

'You're asking an awful lot of questions.'

'Wouldn't you?'

'In fact, I did,' the Vigil said, his eyes glassing over, a memory apparently playing back in his mind. He was quite different now from the person who had been chasing Doran through the streets of London. No longer a shadowy hunter, but rather, simply a young soldier asked to do a job.

'That's what a Vigil is for,' he continued. 'Or at least, that's one of our jobs. We keep full members of the Society in check and bring in anyone who is found to have been careless with their abilities.'

So Doran had been right about his 'time police' description. 'So why bring me in?' he said. 'I'm not a full member of your society.'

'But you have been careless,' Malloch said, tutting. 'Advanced for your age, I must say. Most people at manifestation can't so much as time-jump two feet.'

Doran's hand drifted to the pocket where his watch was hidden. Did the Eternalisium know about his father's work?

'Then again, you are a West, after all,' Malloch added.

'What difference does that make?'

Malloch's eyes widened, all smugness dissolved. It was clear he had said something he shouldn't. Maybe he wasn't as all-seeing as he appeared. He stopped outside a door at the end of the corridor. Embossed on a gold-plated sign were the words, 'Head of Discipline Categorisation'.

'Tobias will see you now.'

Doran's eyes darted from Malloch to the carved letters on the door. So he was about to meet Tobias Blue. He wasn't sure what to expect. Mr Bishop had spoken of him with such contempt, and as Malloch disappeared back down the narrow corridor a thought popped into his head. Why had this man been so desperate to bring him in that he had sent trained soldiers – a right usually only reserved for adult rule-breakers? What was so special about him? There had to be a reason, and Doran vowed to remember that as he turned the handle and entered the office.

14

THE SERPENT

A broad-shouldered man stood gazing out of a large window overlooking the mansion's grounds. The morning sun was shining into the room, bouncing off his gleaming, slicked-back hair. Upon hearing Doran enter, he turned to face him with a smoothness surprising for a man of his stature. His lips curled into a thin smile and he skated across the room as though it were a sheet of ice, holding out his hand to Doran.

'Tobias Blue.'

'Doran West.'

'It is a pleasure to meet you, Doran,' Tobias said and Doran felt a slight squeeze as he withdrew his hand. 'An absolute pleasure. Please, sit, sit.'

He gestured in the direction of a circular leather chair in front of the desk. Doran felt his feet move before his brain had fully agreed to it while Tobias paraded around the desk, arm still outstretched. He reminded Doran of the time his mum had taken him to the circus. Like a ring master gesturing to a crowd, his every movement was carefully timed, part of the act, and Doran wondered who exactly the performance was for.

'Welcome…' Tobias said, and he actually paused for dramatic effect, '…to the Eternalisium. I'm sure you must have a thousand questions and I will do my best to answer each and every one. But first, can I get you anything? A glass of water? A stiff brandy after the little adventure you've had I'd bet!'

He gave a deep chuckle and Doran forced out a small sniff of laughter. Tobias Blue wasn't the only one who could put on a show. 'I'm fine, thank you.'

Tobias bowed his head and clasped his hands together. 'Then let's get to it, shall we?'

'Let's,' Doran said, though what they were 'getting to' he had no idea.

Tobias pulled out a stack of papers from the top drawer of his desk and selected an expensive-looking fountain pen from a neatly laid-out collection. 'Name?' he said, and his hand floated across the paper. 'Well, we know that. Date of birth? We know that too. Many happy returns on your manifestation day. Address? Number twelve, Linntean. How quaint to live in a village with only one street.'

Doran stared as the pen continued to flurry down the first page. This wasn't a simple gathering of information. This was a display of power. Tobias was letting him know just how carefully they had been watching him. Was this down to Mr Bishop? Despite any noble intentions he may have had, he was still part of the Eternalisium and he must have passed on some of this information.

'Parents,' Tobias continued. 'Mother. Kate West. Non-

Traveller.' For the first time, he paused, choosing this moment to look Doran in the eye. 'Father. Arlen West. Traveller. Outlier. *Deceased.*'

The pen pressed into the paper, the ink setting into a perfect point. Tobias rested the fountain pen back in its place and clasped his hands together again, elbows resting on the desk.

'You appear to know an awful lot, Mr Blue,' Doran said, forcing his eyes away from the word 'deceased' written in beautiful penmanship.

'Dr Blue,' Tobias corrected.

'Of what, if you don't mind me asking?'

The thin lips curved. 'Many things.'

'What's an outlier?' Doran said. He had a suspicion Tobias had intended for him to ask this but he didn't care.

'Someone in a family line who displays no travelling abilities, or a Traveller who rejects the Eternalisium entirely. Your father was the latter. He shunned the Society when he was only a little older than you. As I recall, he wanted a "normal life".'

'He rejected you?'

'It's rare,' Tobias said, and Doran was unsure of the last time he had seen him blink. 'But some people over the centuries have refused the sanctuary and training the Eternalisium offers. If they remain harmless, we leave them alone. Though there has never been an outlier who hasn't met a sticky end. Your father was no exception, as I imagine you know. My condolences, by the way.'

Doran didn't detect a trace of sincerity but he accepted the condolences with a gracious nod of the head, despite having to dig his nails into his leg to do so. Did Tobias and the Eternalisium really believe his father to be dead, or did they also know that there was a chance, however small, that he was lost in time?

'Now we know all about you so it is only fair you get to know us,' Tobias said. 'I am the head of discipline categorisation here at the Eternalisium and what that means is that I assess new students upon their arrival to place them in their discipline. Your discipline is like your family within the Society. You train together, sleep in the same dormitory, and are assigned a tutor with the same gift as yourself. For a lot of our students, it's like having siblings or friends for the first time. Some Eternalisium students are part of dynasties – generations of Travellers who can trace their lineage back for centuries. I myself can trace my family tree back to the very beginnings of the Society.'

He seemed to take great pride in this fact, as if it gave him some kind of status, and Doran fought back a grimace.

'But there are others, not unlike yourself, who have no idea of their heritage, or are a genetic anomaly with Traveller DNA that could have been lying in wait for generations. The Eternalisium gives them a sense of belonging – of family, as I said. That is what we can offer you, Doran. Friends, a family. A purpose.'

Doran reflected on Tobias' words. A family? He already had that, thank you very much, and she was currently worried sick about him. Not only that, the person he considered a brother was stuck in this very city a few years in the future. He had to get back to them both. That was more than enough purpose to be going on with.

'Why have you brought me here?'

Tobias raised a perfectly plucked eyebrow. 'You're a prospective student. I—'

'No. Why have *you* brought me here? It's my understanding that Mr Bishop was sent to spy on me and bring me in. So why send in your foot soldiers?'

Tobias looked almost impressed. 'Managed to have a little

chat with young Ewan, did you?' he said. 'Let me explain. In cases such as yours when you have been raised in the dark—'

'Raised in the dark?'

Tobias' eye twitched. 'Certainly. We've tried to get in contact with you, Doran. We sent letters. Many, in fact. They were largely ignored until, finally, we got a response.' He reached into his desk drawer again and spread out a carefully folded letter. 'Your mother informed us that you were to be left alone, displayed no travelling abilities, and that even if you did you would not be permitted to come.'

Doran scanned the letter. It was definitely his mum's handwriting and confirmed what Tobias had said. She really had wished him to be normal. Why did that sting so much?

'Now, as a precaution, we sent Ewan Bishop up to your school to keep an eye on you. But not to spy on you. No, no, no. Purely for your protection.'

'My protection?'

'Of course. In case your mother was mistaken or – forgive me – not being entirely truthful. And we were right of course. You do possess abilities and have travelled. In a matter of days, you used your abilities unsafely and without training. You could have done irreparable damage to the timeline. You could have severely injured yourself. I had no choice. I had to send in the Vigils to bring you in. I have only your best interests at heart.'

And there it was. The very thing Mr Bishop had warned him about.

Doran used all the facial muscles he possessed to piece together a smile. 'I understand.'

'Excellent,' Tobias said and he tapped the desk in his exuberance. 'Now, would you like a tour? I can answer any questions you may have along the way.'

'Sounds perfect,' Doran said. Perhaps he could scope out an escape route.

Tobias led Doran through the mansion, stopping occasionally to deliver a longwinded story about a painting on the wall or a personal anecdote of his time as a student. Doran was doing his best impression of someone giving their undivided attention, *oohing* and *aahing* in all the right places. Whenever Tobias was particularly lost in his own yarn, Doran would scan his surroundings, trying to memorise every door, every room he was shown, and most importantly the location of every set of stairs.

'And this wing was the last to be rebuilt after the Second World War. A bomb destroyed the entire street, including the mansion. Luckily our Seers predicted the attack was coming and were able to evacuate all members before it happened. The Society used this as an opportunity to use our extensive fortune acquired over the years to buy the entire street and make the mansion and surrounding grounds a second out of sync with time. Now only Travellers can see the mansion. To the outside world, this street is a protected green space in a polluted city. A wise move, given the way the world has modernised. Secrecy is paramount to the Eternalisium's continued survival. Can you imagine if the world knew what we could do?'

Doran nodded, counting the number of steps to the nearest staircase. 'How do you make an entire building a second out of sync from the rest of time?'

'With great difficulty,' Tobias said. He stopped and cast his gaze over Doran. 'We can teach you things beyond your wildest dreams. What you have discovered so far is only the beginning. You are capable of so much more.'

Doran wasn't quite sure how to respond. Tobias was still

examining him, looking for a reaction to this invitation. Doran had the distinct impression he was currently taking some kind of test. 'I just want to learn how to control these abilities so I can go home.'

Another searching look. 'Naturally,' Tobias said after a moment. 'Many students feel this way when they first arrive here, particularly those like yourself who have been raised without any knowledge of the Eternalisium. But this place does become home for a lot of people.'

The words of Mr Bishop echoed inside Doran's mind. 'You're a traveller, this is your home...'

'I already have a home.'

'Of course,' Tobias said. 'I only meant—'

'And what sort of home is this exactly?' Doran asked, unable to stop the words from tumbling out of his mouth. 'Where you arrest people and make them stand trial?'

'If you're referring to Ewan Bishop, he will be tried fairly in front of his peers for disobeying orders. I'm sure justice will be served.'

Doran's eyes narrowed. He wasn't entirely sure what Tobias considered justice. 'Where is he? Can I see him?'

'I'm not sure that would be wise. But if you're concerned about how your teacher is being treated you needn't worry.' He gestured down the corridor. 'He is quite comfortable right here, in a dormitory room.'

Doran peered around Tobias to see Crum pacing outside a closed door. Doran raised an eyebrow. 'Under guard?'

'A precaution; nothing more,' Tobias said and he gestured to the stairs with what Doran felt was an excessive amount of flourish. 'Why don't I show you the grounds? They are quite lovely at this time of year.'

His tone was light-hearted but it was clear this wasn't a request and with a final look towards Mr Bishop's makeshift prison cell, Doran trudged back down the grand staircase.

Once back on the ground floor they stepped outside through a set of glass doors so clean that Doran had thought there was an open gap in the wall.

The grounds stretched out before him, beginning with a well-kept garden teeming with flowers. Sculptures of men in various poses were dotted around the garden. Doran passed a curious one of a man facing the mansion and reaching up to the heavens. A lot of the clay seemed to have gone into capturing the man's moustache, which dominated the lower half of his face and framed a set of pursed lips. It was difficult, but he tried to look past the moustache and into the man's eyes. As it was a sculpture, the artist had made an effort to capture the *teine uaine*. But there was something about the shape of his eyes, not to mention the high cheekbones, that seemed familiar, as if Doran had met him before.

'Who's that?'

Tobias gave the briefest of glances at the sculpture. 'A once-great leader. Long dead now.'

Doran craned his neck to take one last look. So, they couldn't have met before.

As they walked through a maze of perfectly trimmed hedges, Doran came across another sculpture, then another. The first was kneeling, head facing down and arms outstretched as if trying to push away an oncoming force from both sides. Doran side-stepped away from Tobias to sneak a peek at the man's face. Again, there were those same eyes and cheekbones. But this sculpture was even older than the last, moss covering it from head to finely crafted toe. This wasn't the same man as the previous sculpture; he had no facial hair and his face showed numerous scars. He had wanted his battle wounds captured.

The other sculpture was at the centre of an array of bushes, clipped to look like various sea creatures. This was by far the oldest of the three, the man captured in an old soldier's tunic and kilt. The outline of a sword had faded into the man's leg, its definition gone. The soldier stood, stoic, water cascading over his head in a rainbow arc. His eyes had also lost their soul, now just an outline. Yet the resemblance to the previous two sculptures Doran had passed remained, which meant one of two things. Either all the sculptors carved in the same way or, more likely, all these immortalised men were related.

Tobias had quickened his pace and was already beyond the final sculpture. Hurrying to keep up, Doran joined him at the edge of the garden.

Beyond the final hedge and down a set of brick steps was an open grassed area, bordered by towering trees. There would certainly be no escape in that direction. Who needed barbed wire and attack dogs when you had Mother Nature and a bit of time on your side?

It appeared those who had not left the mansion for the holidays were outside enjoying the sunshine. Doran watched as two men dressed in the same attire as Crum and Malloch sparred with bamboo staffs. They leapt at each other, twirling the poles around their bodies. One of the fighters then launched himself backwards with a flip that would have made an Olympic gymnast proud. He disappeared as though one with the molecules of the air, then rematerialised on the other side of his opponent. Legs outstretched, he collided with the other fighter's back, knocking him to the ground. The triumphant Vigil landed, barely making an imprint on the grass and thrusting his bamboo staff towards his opponent's face. The staff stopped inches before the fallen Vigil's nose and the pair stared at one another, both panting. A begrudging smirk spread across the defeated Vigil's face and he knocked the staff away with his hand. He sprang to his feet and the pair embraced, patting each other on the back. Arms around each other's shoulders, they walked off together and Doran noticed the victorious Vigil seemed to be providing a set of instructions, or perhaps tips for the future.

'Impressive, aren't they?' Tobias said.

'Yeah,' Doran said, and he meant it. He didn't feel quite as bad about being caught any more. What chance would he have stood against that?

He scanned the rest of the grounds and noticed a group of older men and women who seemed to be having an intense discussion under an oak tree. They were seated on a picnic blanket spread with an array of sandwiches.

Near them a very odd-looking group of people, dressed in flowing cream robes, seemed to be in some kind of meditative circle. At that very moment, a woman with the longest neck Doran had ever seen opened her eyes and stared at him. He saw her mouth move and everyone in the circle turned as one to look at him. Each murmured something which he couldn't quite hear but whatever it was seemed to grab the attention of the scholars under the tree and the two Vigils. They all ceased their activities and joined the new group endeavour, which was apparently to creep out Doran as much as humanly possible.

What on earth was going on? He felt like some kind of celebrity, only he wasn't sure what he was supposed to be famous for. Why did they all seem so interested in his arrival? Surely it couldn't be that noteworthy for a prospective student to be taking a tour?

Doran glanced at Tobias, who was also surveying them all. Perhaps they were gossiping about his misdeeds in Florence and London. Had Tobias been spreading rumours about the elusive Doran West?

'Oh my,' came a shaky voice from behind them.

Doran turned to see a short, balding man dressed in a tweed suit despite the warm midday sun. His poor outfit choice already seemed to be taking its toll as he mopped his forehead with a white handkerchief.

'Doran,' Tobias began. But for the first time, his assuredness had slipped, as if part of his perfectly choreographed show wasn't quite going to plan. 'This is Professor Ianto Everie. He teaches languages and linguistics.'

Doran outstretched a hand and the professor started as if he had pulled a gun on him. Slowly, Professor Everie extended a shaking hand. It was as sweaty as his forehead and Doran fought back a grimace as he took it in his own.

They shook – and continued to shake. In fact, it became what Doran believed to be the longest handshake of his life. Professor Everie appeared transfixed by him, the *teine uaine* around his grey eyes expanding and retracting.

'That will do, Everie,' Tobias hissed, and Professor Everie released Doran, who gave his hand a subtle rub on his jeans.

'Nice to meet you, Professor Everie,' Doran said. 'I'm Doran West.'

'Of course you are,' Professor Everie replied, as though he couldn't say the words quickly enough. 'You're here; you're actually here.' A horrified expression passed across the professor's face. 'My goodness, where are my manners?' And then he did the oddest thing of all. He *bowed*.

'That will do, Everie,' Tobias said again, a faint hint of panic in his voice. 'Why don't you go and join your colleagues?' he added, in an attempt to regain composure. 'I'm filling in young Mr West on everything he needs to know.'

Professor Everie's back stiffened and he and Tobias locked eyes. For a moment they had a wordless conversation that Doran was not privy to. But the outcome was clear. Professor Everie gave a swift nod and a final fascinated glance at Doran before shuffling away down the bricked steps.

'Don't worry about him,' Tobias said. 'He's a little eccentric.'

That's an understatement, Doran thought. But Professor Everie had only been marginally odder than the companions he was now joining on the grass.

Tobias led Doran back inside, away from all the prying eyes. He was no longer attempting to regale Doran with tales of old and barely said a word during their return to his office. Eccentricities aside, the interaction with Professor Everie had irked him.

When they returned to the office, Crum and Malloch were waiting for them, guarding the office door. Tobias strode past, ignoring them, and sat behind his desk. Doran hovered near the door, the corner of his eye on Crum, who was looming behind him.

Tobias clasped his hands together and a smile stretched across his face. 'Well, I hope you enjoyed your tour. But you must be tired after the adventure you've had. Get some rest and we can talk more about your enrolment tomorrow.'

'And what makes you think I want to enrol?'

The smile remained. 'Sleep on it. That's all I ask. Destiny calls, Doran West. It is up to you whether you answer. You are a Traveller and have a place in this society. All I can do is hope that you make the right decision.'

Crum and Malloch moved as one to stand on either side of him. After looking over both shoulders, Doran raised an eyebrow at Tobias. 'And will these two be joining me? I'll be honest: I'm not used to sharing a room.'

'Crum and Malloch will escort you to your quarters and stand guard.'

'As a precaution?'

'As a precaution.'

There was a short pause as they locked eyes. 'Am I a prisoner, Dr Blue?'

'That, Doran West, is your choice.'

15

THE FROZEN RAIN

Doran sat on the edge of a single bed, twirling the fob watch between his fingers. His dad must have had a very good reason to go to such lengths to avoid becoming part of the Eternalisium. He had died or disappeared in the quest to be independent of this society – an outlier as Tobias had put it. Not to mention his mum, who had hidden its existence from him all those years, who had rejected the Eternalisium's advances on his behalf. It can't have been just out of a desire for him to be normal. Yes, the thought had crossed his mind, but he knew his mum. She would love him no matter what.

There had to be more.

His dad must have warned her about the Eternalisium and told her to keep Doran far away from it. The question was, why? Doran would be lying if the thought of staying wasn't tempting. Here, he could learn about his abilities and how to control them.

And after that, Malloch had said, he could leave and have a normal life. But that had been what his father had wanted, right? Tobias had said so himself. If that option was on the table, then why hadn't his father taken it? Why had he tried so hard to rid himself and Doran of their powers? And why were there guards outside Doran's room? If leaving was a possibility, then why have two highly-skilled fighters tasked with keeping an eye on him?

There was more going on than met the eye and he felt the need to find a way back to Zander and his mum. If that made him an outlier, then an outlier he would be.

Doran closed his eyes, trying to recall every inch of the mansion he had just been shown. He knew he was on the first floor – and that he needed to get up to the top of one of the outer towers.

The only option he could think of was to leap from there and jump forward three years to Zander in the future. Doran's mouth almost twitched into a grin. It was weird how something so insane as leaping from the top of a tower had now become a logical decision in his mind.

After internally visualising every corridor, every door, he opened his eyes, with the route clear inside him. He needed to go up one floor to the wing where Mr Bishop was being held. From there, to his great relief, he had spied, at the far end of the hall, the foot of a spiral staircase, which was presumably starting its ascent of one of the towers. At the very least, it would surely get him closer. It was a gamble, but one he would have to take.

He rose from the bed and glanced at the door. There was just one problem with his plan: how to get past the Vigils? He certainly couldn't fight his way out. He'd have to be smarter than that.

'Hello?' Doran called. No answer. 'Hello?' he tried again, a little louder.

The door swung open to reveal a disgruntled-looking Crum. 'What is it?'

Doran noticed Malloch hovering behind him, also interested in what he wanted. Did he know what he was planning? Would he be able to predict it? He was still a little vague on how Malloch's discipline worked. The Vigil certainly wasn't infallible; Doran had noticed that. And as far as he was aware, Malloch's powers didn't include reading minds, so perhaps there was a chance Doran's plan would be unknown to him.

'I haven't eaten all day,' Doran said. 'Can I go make a sandwich or something?'

'Tobias has told us you're to stay in your room until the morning.'

'Well then, could you go and make me something?' Doran asked. 'I'm starving.'

Crum's jaw clenched. 'Giving orders now, are we? You don't seem to understand the situation you're in.'

Doran held up his hands. 'I'm just hungry. I'm sure you are as well, after chasing me around London. Feel free to make yourself something too.'

Crum looked ready to charge at him but Malloch put a hand on his colleague's shoulder. 'He shouldn't starve, Crum. Why don't you go down to the kitchens and make us all something? It's going to be a long night.'

'Fine,' Crum said through gritted teeth, but he locked eyes with Doran before he left. 'Don't make this a habit, mind.'

'Wouldn't dream of it.'

Crum sneered and stomped out of the room. *One down, one to go*, Doran thought.

Malloch didn't move an inch, staring at him as if he were

trying to burn a hole into his skull. Was he sure the Vigil couldn't read minds?

'Can I help you?' Doran asked, mainly to try to break Malloch's penetrating gaze.

'Time is in flux,' Malloch murmured, though Doran was unsure whether he had realised he had said it out loud. 'You have a choice to make, Doran West... And so do I...'

'What do you mean?'

'Events are unfolding.'

After his cryptic remark, Malloch remained silent, so Doran bided time. A few minutes later, the sound of footsteps echoed from outside the room. Crum appeared, carrying a plate of sandwiches. 'Here,' he said, thrusting the plate into Doran's chest.

As Doran reached out to take a mouldy ham sandwich, a *thump* broke the silence. For a moment, Crum froze with a stupid expression on his face. Then he crumpled to the ground and the platter clanged as it hit the floor.

Malloch stood over him, the hilt of his sword hovering where Crum's head had been.

Doran imagined his face was not too dissimilar from how Crum's had been, seconds before. 'What?' Malloch tore his gaze away from Crum's limp body. 'I don't understand. Are you helping me? I thought you worked for Tobias.'

'A Vigil serves the Eternalisium,' Malloch said. 'Not the whims of Tobias Blue.' He glanced back to Crum. 'Though most of our order have forgotten that.'

'But why help me? I'm not part of the Eternalisium.'

Malloch didn't answer right away, taking him in. 'Things are more complicated than you know. Tobias is making a power grab for full control of the Society. I don't know when and I don't know how but his plan must involve you somehow. Which means this place isn't safe. Not until you're ready to challenge him. You have to go. You have to run.'

Nothing Malloch was saying was making any sense. 'Challenge him? What are you talking about?'

A stifled groan came from the floor. 'There's no time,' Malloch said. 'Go. Now.'

'What about you?'

Malloch handed him his sword. 'You displayed powers we didn't know you had and surprised us, knocking us both unconscious.'

Doran gaped at the blade, then at Malloch. 'I can't do that.'

'One quick thrust to the back of the head is all it takes,' Malloch said, turning around. 'It's easy.'

'For you maybe,' Doran said. He gripped the hilt of the blade. Was he really doing this? 'Thank you.' It was all he could think of to say.

'Thank me by surviving. Now get on with it.'

Doran drew in a breath and raised the hilt above his head. *One quick thrust, Doran. It's easy. Come on.* He squeezed his eyes shut and hammered the back of Malloch's head with all his might. A shock pinged up his arm and he heard another *thump*.

Opening his eyes cautiously, Doran saw Malloch flat out in front of him. He dropped the sword, the blade ringing as it hit the platter, then leapt over Malloch's prone body and out of the open door, making for the stairs. The second floor would lead him to those spiral steps.

Reaching the curved staircase, he froze. *Keep going. What are you doing? Keep going.* His eyes drifted to the door he had seen during his tour with Tobias. Would Mr Bishop still be in there? What if there were more Vigils on the other side? Doran wasn't sure how many of them shared a worldview with Malloch. But Mr Bishop had risked his safety and freedom to save him. Surely, he should return the favour.

Doran growled. 'I must be stupid,' he said to himself as he turned away from the staircase to potential freedom to enter Mr Bishop's room.

Inside he found his teacher lying on a bed, a book entitled *The Rise of Robert the Bruce* wedged between his fingers. He was reading. He was facing a trial and exile and he was *reading*.

'Doran?' Mr Bishop said, sitting up. 'How did you—'.

Doran stared at his teacher's ankles. They seemed perfectly fine; no trace of a break. 'You're OK,' he said. 'How?'

'Some highly skilled members in our society have certain gifts that allow them to reverse more minor injuries – breakages and the like,' Mr Bishop said, as if this was a perfectly normal sentence. 'But enough about me. What are you doing here?'

'We've got to go. Now.'

'Go? What do you mean go?'

'I have a way out but you have to come with me – now.'

'Slow down,' Mr Bishop said, shuffling off the bed. 'We can't just leave.'

Doran reached into his pocket and pulled out the fob watch. 'I can take us. I took Zander to Florence and the future. I can take you too.'

'What is that thing?'

'Something my dad designed to help control our powers. I rebuilt it.' He grabbed Mr Bishop's arm. 'Now *come on*.'

Doran yanked hard but Mr Bishop didn't move. 'You built this?' he said, still staring at the fob watch. 'Doran... Do you have any idea what this means? What this could mean for the Society? This...' he reached out towards the watch, 'this is revolutionary.'

Doran lunged backwards, releasing Mr Bishop. Why on earth was he talking about the Society? They were about to put him on trial. Didn't he care? 'Mr Bishop, *please*, we don't have time for this. We have to go.'

'Why do we have to go?' Mr Bishop asked. The history teacher didn't seem to grasp their predicament at all.

'Don't you want to leave?' Doran asked in exasperation. 'They've got you locked up in here. You're a prisoner; why would you want to stay?'

'There are no longer any guards on my door. I'm free to move around as I please. Tomorrow I shall stand trial and I'm confident the truth will out.'

'Tobias won't let that happen,' Doran said. Why wouldn't Mr Bishop understand?

'Tobias will state his case and I will state mine,' Mr Bishop said. 'I will be tried fairly by the system I have pledged my allegiance to and I will respect their judgement.'

Doran was beginning to regret not taking the stairs. 'Even if they exile you?'

'If I come with you, I will be exiled. If I remain here to stand trial, I have a chance.'

'Well, I'm not prepared to stick around to find out,' Doran said. 'I'm leaving – now – with or without you.'

Mr Bishop grasped his shoulders and nodded to the fob watch. 'What you've created here is exactly why you need to stay. I was right; you're exactly what the Eternalisium needs.'

'I'm not,' Doran said, his lip trembling. 'I have people waiting for me. I won't leave them. Not for this.'

'Your destiny is bigger than any of them,' Mr Bishop said. 'I'm sorry, I truly am, but you're far more important than you realise.'

Doran shrugged him off and stepped back towards the door. 'No,' he said. 'I can't.' And with one last look at his teacher, he left the room, Mr Bishop's pleas following him.

He began to run up the spiral staircase, two steps at a time. On and on it twisted its way aloft, rising up through the dark cavern of the tower's interior. The higher he climbed, the darker and more difficult it became as he groped his way upwards. His steps grew slower and slower as his legs ached more and more, but eventually he began to feel fresher air, and to see more light coming down to meet him. Glancing up, he could see daylight streaming in around the frame of a door somewhere above him.

At last, he was pushing the door open and emerging out onto the roof space enclosed within the tower's low crenellated wall. He had made it.

Pausing to catch his breath for a few moments, he filled his lungs with the air of the summer evening. Finally recovered enough to move, he staggered over to the parapet, clambered up into one of the crenellations, and looked out. The evening sky greeted him and he beheld the outside world for the first time in what felt like years. There it was, waiting for him. London's skyline stretched far into the distance, as if nothing other than this infinite city existed, a vast mosaic of light. He pictured the fountain where he had last seen Zander, and his friend's phone shattering as it collided with it. He thought of Zander walking away, disappearing out of sight.

Squeezing the watch in the palm of his hand, he took a deep breath and closed his eyes. With a giant leap out into space, he slammed his thumb onto the flashing green button as he soared through the evening air.

Sparks reflected in the pool around the fountain. Doran tumbled out of a small local tempest of lightning down onto the hard street below, rolling until he collided with something solid.

Panting with shock, but also relief, he looked up to see water cascading above him. With the remainder of his strength, he pulled himself up enough to flop forward over the fountain's basin. There, still bobbing in the water, he could see the fragments of Zander's phone. He had made it.

Despite his body's protests, he rose to his feet. Zander had stormed off straight ahead, down a neon-infested side street. Hopefully his friend hadn't ventured too far.

After a few minutes, Doran found himself among a series of bars and clubs, all competing with each other noisily with different types of music.

He squinted at each dazzling sign until one caught his attention. 'Little Bar of Horrors' shone in bright green lights above him. The window display had a large prop of a Venus flytrap and a menu stuck to the glass. Seeing the drink names based on songs from the *Little Shop of Horrors* reminded him of his argument with Zander and a comment he wished he hadn't made. It seemed exactly the kind of place Zander might have gone to.

Doran showed the bouncer his ID, which now stated a legal drinking age, and was allowed entry. He made his way to the bar.

'What can I get you?' the bartender asked with a cheery smile. 'We've got an offer on "I've Ginning you Sunshine".'

'What? No, I'm looking for my friend. I was wondering if he came in here. It wouldn't have been that long ago. He might even still be here. Light-brown hair, blue eyes, probably showed an outrageous amount of confidence.'

Perhaps he hadn't fully forgiven Zander just yet.

The bartender nodded. 'Yeah, he was in here. Left about ten

minutes ago. Had a couple of drinks then belted out "Suddenly Seymour" on the karaoke. He played both parts. It was enchanting, if a little aggressive at times.'

'He's a bit upset,' Doran said. 'Did he say where he was going at all?'

'After his song, he just walked out and shouted something about showing some guy named Doran he was better than those West End hacks. Didn't even pay his tab.'

'Yep, that's him,' Doran said. 'Thanks,' he added, as he ran back out of the bar.

'Hey! Is anyone going to pay for his drinks?' he heard the bartender shout.

Doran marched on. Based on the bartender's account he had a good idea of where Zander might go next, so he headed back towards the theatre district. A light drizzle dusted him as he stopped to plan his next move. London was a far cry from Linntean and its one country road. Who knew where Zander might end up if he didn't track him down that night?

Through the droplets, he saw the sign for *Little Shop of Horrors* glaring at him. Knowing Zander, he would have been as good as his word and tried to show off his skills there.

Sure enough, as he neared the theatre, he saw a small crowd gathered in a circle with a familiar face at its centre.

Zander Munro was in full performance mode, waving his arms around and midway through a Shakespearian monologue.

'I hope he sings again,' Doran heard a woman whisper to the man beside her.

Doran watched as various people dropped coins and notes into a hat that lay on the pavement. Zander must have gone back to rescue the Florentine cap from the skip.

The rain grew heavier, clattering on Zander's captive audience, which began to disperse, much to his dismay. Regretfully, he gathered his cap and bowed to those still clapping. 'Thank you, ladies and gentlemen. That's my time. I'll see you soon.'

He waved off his patrons with a broad grin, which soon fell away when he spotted Doran. Without a word, he spun on his heels and strode in the opposite direction.

Great, Doran thought as he chased after him.

Zander turned a corner into a street very different from the bustling open square he had come from. Doran hovered at the mouth of the alleyway; his friend didn't appear to be slowing down.

'You know how long it's taken me to find you!' Doran called. 'The least you can do is talk to me!'

Zander froze, still clutching his cap full of cash. Slowly, he turned, his face cold, and the two became locked in a staring match, the London nightlife sounding all around them and the rain battering them.

'Thought you'd have gone,' Zander said. 'Or did you, and this is some "future you" coming to check up on me? You always wear the same clothes so it's hard to tell, you see.'

Doran was about to tell him what had happened when there was a clanking of bottles and a group of four young men in tracksuits came swaggering in from the other end of the alleyway.

'You two lost?' the leader of the group asked. Not in a helpful-sounding way.

'No, just visiting,' Zander said. 'Heard this alleyway scored highly on "Outing Guru".'

Doran closed his eyes, steeling himself.

The gang laughed. 'Funny,' the leader said. 'We've got a comedian here, lads. What you got there, mate?' He nodded to the cap of cash.

'Nothing,' Zander said, and Doran saw his grip tighten around the cap.

'Looks like you've had a good night,' the leader said. 'You want me to count that for you?'

'Nah. You're all right,' Zander said, now edging back towards Doran. 'Got my A in maths. I'll manage.'

'I insist.'

The other three men grabbed Zander, holding his arms tight. The leader snatched the cap, the coins spilling onto the ground.

'Hey!' Zander shouted, struggling against his captors. He managed to land a kick on the leader's leg, muddying his tracksuit bottoms. 'That's mine. Get off me!'

The leader threw a punch at Zander's stomach and he doubled over. The other three threw him to the ground. And the brutal kicking began.

Doran's heart raced. He made a grab for one of the men but was quickly thrown backwards.

He slammed into the wall, the force knocking him onto his front – and the air from his lungs. The thugs were still kicking Zander, hooting gleefully. They weren't going to stop. They would go on until they killed him.

Watching in horror, Doran began to feel a tingle in his fingertips and, propelled forward by what could only be described as instinct, he leapt to his feet, raised his hand and yelled, 'STOP!'

And they did. Though not through choice. Everything had come to a complete standstill. Doran goggled at his surroundings, trying to make sense of what had just happened.

The first thing that occurred to him was that he no longer felt the pelting rain on his head. But the downpour couldn't possibly have stopped that quickly.

Peering in front of him, his suspicions were confirmed. The rain had not disappeared. Rather, it had *frozen*. The thick droplets hung in the air like in a photograph. Slowly, Doran raised his index finger and touched one. The sensation was hard to place, cold and uninviting. Perhaps the feeling of a ghost floating through a living soul. There was a small ripple effect, like a stone skimming across a lake, and then the raindrop returned to its former state.

Time had stopped. Doran couldn't believe it. *He* had done this. Did this mean Travellers could have more than one discipline? He had presumed himself like Crum, someone who could take passengers through time. But this was another power, another feeling entirely. Doran thought back to the crest in the Eternalisium. The hand. The commanding hand which his eyes had been drawn to first. Just what else was he capable of?

The moment of wonder faded as he beheld the frozen tableau of violence before him. With a glance at his friend's pain-stricken face, he sprang into action.

Carefully he manoeuvred and positioned each member of the gang so that they were facing each other, like football players seconds away from taking a free kick. Happy with his work, he then turned to Zander, hauling his prone body upright. He then returned to his starting position and raised his hand again. He forced his eyes shut, trying to feel something. Anything. Reaching out to try to find some kind of connection.

The tingle returned, as well as a feeling Doran couldn't quite comprehend yet. His mind interpreted it as a button that he needed to press. He reached out and pressed the imaginary button and instantly felt the rain battering his head again as though someone had chucked a bucket of water over him.

He opened his eyes to see the men landing hefty kicks on each other before falling to the ground in agony.

Not wasting any time, Doran forced the stunned Zander into a run. The two of them hurried away from the scene but almost immediately he heard the furious yells and the thunder of the gang's steps as they gave chase once more.

Doran's heart was pounding, and he could feel a familiar sensation arising inside him. He put his hand into his pocket, his fingers hunting for the cool metal of the watch.

But the pocket was empty.

Where was it? He patted every inch of himself as they ran. The watch must have fallen out of his pocket when he'd been thrown against the wall.

He could hear the gang gaining on them. Sparks flickered into life around his fingers. There was no time to mourn the watch now. It was about to happen. He knew it was inevitable. Though this time he had no stabilisers to help him. Doran grabbed Zander and shut his eyes, readying himself for the infinite unknown.

Just anywhere without dinosaurs, please.

16

THE SLAVE

Finlay Robertson waded through the overgrown grass, his chest heaving. The world was beginning to blur before his eyes but he pressed on as quickly as his legs would carry him. His feet had seemed to grow heavier with every step and now, after numerous miles, they felt as though a blacksmith had dipped them in the densest of metal.

He had to make it to his kin. There he would be safe. There he could be hidden.

It had taken every ounce of strength and cunning for him to break free from his captors and escape into the night. Capture now meant certain death, but Finlay didn't care. He had learned something that could not go unshared. Something which could change the future of his nation. To have stayed would have meant a lifetime of subservience and obedience, which in itself was no life at all. Better to die doing something noble than live the rest of his days as nothing more than a slave. This belief had kept him going those long, gruelling miles, and had finally brought him home.

Finlay stopped for the first time in a day, his legs buckling at the sudden change of pace. He smelled the unmistakable scent of the heather that grew on the outskirts of his town. A memory that no amount of time away could rob him of.

He reached the hilltop overlooking his town. Jedburgh. How he had missed her. The familiarity caused an unexpected lump in his throat and he clasped his hand over his mouth, feeling the tears trickle down his face and over his fingers. He had wondered if he would ever see his home again.

His nostalgia didn't last long as he remembered his mission. He needed to find a willing supporter to carry his message onwards. Failing that, he would travel all the way to Annandale himself if God demanded it of him.

He was beginning to make his way down the hillside when he saw a flicker of green light before his eyes. The sight jerked him to a halt. There was a flash, not unlike when God hurled his rage from the sky, and suddenly two young men, only slightly younger than Finlay himself, appeared as if from nowhere, one propping the other up.

Finlay rubbed his eyes as though trying to correct his clearly faulty vision. His weariness had him conjuring nonsense. Yet, the nearer the young men drew to him, the more solid they became, wearing the oddest garments Finlay had ever seen. He was about to call over to the strangers when he heard neighing in the distance. They were coming.

Finlay staggered towards the strangers, hoping they weren't on the same side as his pursuers. 'Who are ye?'

'My friend, my friend; he's hurt,' the uninjured young man

said.

He had a broad Scottish accent, which in Finlay's mind increased the odds that he wasn't part of the faction currently gaining on him. He looked at the other stranger, who was conscious but clearly in a great deal of pain, and without a second thought allowed him to put his other arm around his shoulder. The three began walking in the direction of the town, Finlay trying to keep the pace needed to stay ahead of the horses.

'My name is Finlay of clan Robertson. Who are you both and where did you come fay?'

'I'm Doran and this is Zander.'

'Doran? Is that Irish? You do not sound like you are fay there.'

'No, we're both Scottish.'

'And are ye on the side of Wallace? I do not mean to be blunt, but we find ourselves in a troubling situation.'

'What do you mean?'

Finlay raised an eyebrow at them both. 'Do ye fight for Scotland or Edward? Ye are both of fighting age, aren't ye?'

The young man named Doran seemed confused. 'What do you mean Edward? Wait, as in *King* Edward? Which one?'

Finlay had never heard anything so ludicrous. '*Which* one? Are you soft in the heed lad? There has only been one King Edward. He is the first of his name. Longshanks. Hammer of the Scots.'

'Longshanks,' Doran mumbled. His eyes widened. 'When is it? Are we before or after Bannockburn?' He then stopped himself, as though he had said something he shouldn't have. That didn't stop Finlay from hearing him mutter away to himself once more. 'Was Edward the First before or after Bannockburn? Dammit, why didn't I pay more attention to that topic with Mr Bishop?'

'Bannock what?' Finlay asked. 'Ye mean the village near

Stirling? What is so important about such a place?' His mind finally caught up with the rest of the lad's strange ramblings. 'What do ye mean, when is it? What a streenge question. It is thirteen hundred and five. Wallace has fallen and the English are heading back south, pillaging and regaining full control along their way. The war is lost. But I have information that could turn the tide and give hope again.'

'What information is that?'

'I cannot tell,' Finlay said. 'I can only pass this on to Robert the Bruce himself, or someone I know is loyal to the cause. I do not know you from the English swine who were keeping me as their servant.'

Another neigh came from behind them. It was so clear now that Finlay even recognised to which horse it belonged. He had spent enough time mucking out the beasts for their owners.

He swore under his breath. 'I knew I shouldn't have helped ye,' he spat. 'I would have made it to Jedburgh by now without having to carry this lump.'

'Still conscious you know,' the lump said. 'My name is Zander of clan Munro. Now, could you at least tell us who is chasing you?'

Finlay didn't fully pick up on the injured stranger's wryness. 'It's Sir Richard West and his soldiers. They must have followed my trail. Quickly now, we have to make it to the town.'

'Did you say Sir Richard *West*?' Doran asked, exchanging a curious look with his fellow.

'Yes? Why, haven't you heard of him lad?'

'Should I have?'

'Everyone in Jedburgh and the entire Borders has heard of Sir Richard West,' Finlay said, his face grave. 'Now move yerselves!'

But it was to no avail. One final, gut-wrenchingly close

whinny came from behind them and the thunder of galloping horses echoed in Finlay's ears.

'There is nowhere to hide,' Finlay said, stopping and searching the area. He studied the two young men for a moment, the terrible decision dawning on him. Perhaps they would be spared. They weren't prisoners after all. 'All right. We don't have much time, so listen carefully and then go as fast as you can. I will hold them off.'

'What? I—' Doran began.

'Listen!' Finlay said. 'I was a servant in King Edward's army. They stormed Jedburgh a year ago and took some of the younger ones with them as slaves. I was one of them. I was bringing water to the king when I overheard the healer in his tent. Edward is dying. He has little more than a year to live, only a little longer if he returns South. The healer said he won't survive a winter here. Edward is leaving and so is his army. In a year or so he will be dead and his son will take his place. Everyone with ears knows his son is less than half the man his father is. We could not defeat Longshanks but perhaps we can defeat his son. You must pass this message on to anyone who can help or get to Annandale, to the Bruce's lands, and tell him first-hand. Bruce is the noblest of us all. He will lead us now Wallace is gone. Promise me. Promise me you will tell him.'

Both Doran and Zander stared at him, bewildered, but they nodded in unison.

Finlay gave them a kind smile. 'For our land,' he said, placing a fist over his heart. 'Now, go!'

He let go of the injured Zander and pushed them onwards. They made their way down the hill, Finlay watching them go. Once he was sure they were far enough away, he turned back to see the familiar armour of English soldiers racing towards him. They each rode a formidable black stallion, the largest of all leading the charge. Upon this steed sat a man, his piercing blue eyes fixed on Finlay.

Reaching Finlay, the horse reared up, its hooves threatening to strike his face as they fell back to earth. Refusing to break his pursuer's gaze, Finlay raised his arm, his fist punching the air.

He stared, defiant, into the soul of the man – and thought he could see a flicker of green, much like the colour preceding his encounter with the two strange boys, sprinkled around the soldier's dark pupils. The same eyes then appeared to sparkle with glee as Finlay felt the man's sword piercing his chest.

It seemed to take him an age to fall, his defiant fist last of all. He felt the grass welcome him and he lay on his side, Jedburgh in his sight. He would gaze at it until the end. Slowly, the town began to blur as though someone had placed a thick sheet of glass in front of his eyes. It was over.

17

SIR RICHARD WEST

Doran and Zander entered the town of Jedburgh unaware of the fate of Finlay Robertson. Doran had tried to engage Zander in conversation as they stumbled down the hill but he had remained stony-faced and refused even to turn his head in Doran's direction.

The boys had fought before of course, as any old friends do. But this seemed different. This wasn't squabbling, aged eight, over who got to be which comic book character on a sunny summer afternoon. This was more than that. This was their first grown-up argument.

'You can be mad at me all you like but I don't care,' Doran said, his voice firmer than he actually felt. 'If I hadn't come back, you'd have been beaten to death in that alleyway.'

Zander still didn't engage, simply grunting or wincing in pain every few steps. They kept hobbling along, absorbing the confused and intrigued stares of the locals. Eventually, they stopped outside a small hut, where they could see strips of fabric and half-made clothes hanging up through a window-shaped hole.

'We have to change again,' Doran said. 'These clothes are already drawing attention. When the English soldiers arrive, we won't exactly be hard to find.'

'Then get us out of here,' Zander said, his tone feeling like a punch to the gut.

'I can't.'

'What do you mean, you can't?'

'The watch. It's…gone,' Doran said, feeling stupid. 'It fell out of my pocket in London.'

'It what?' Zander said, wincing again. 'How did you manage that?'

'When I was saving you, you prat.'

Zander pushed him away and staggered to steady himself. 'I never asked you to.'

Doran barely restrained the urge to shove Zander back. Was he really not grateful that Doran had rescued him? 'Oh yeah, 'cause you'd have been absolutely fine without me.'

'At least I'd still be in a time when toilets have been invented!' Zander shouted, waving his arms in the air before his face contorted in pain. 'It's not that you can't take us back. It's that you won't.'

A few locals had now stopped their daily routines and were peering at them like they were a travelling show that had come to town. But neither boy cared, their attention fixed on each other.

'That's not true.'

'Isn't it? 'Cause you seemed pretty keen on getting back to your mum last time I checked.'

Doran's nostrils flared. 'If I try and jump now, who knows where we could end up,' he said. 'This...*ability* isn't a light switch I can just turn on and off. I don't know if I'll ever be able to control it. So yeah, maybe I am saying I won't take us back this second. *Sorry.* I just don't want to accidentally transport me and my best friend to before civilisation began or before there was even a planet Earth in the first place. We got lucky this time. At least it's Scotland. At least there's people.'

'I wouldn't call this lucky,' Zander said. 'You heard that guy. It's not exactly the best time to be Scottish in Scotland.'

'Well, we're going to have to get used to it.'

Zander stared at him as though Doran had decided to shove him after all. 'What? What do you mean we have to get used to it? How long are you planning on us staying here?'

Doran inspected his shoes. They were caked in a fresh coat of mud, little trace of the natural whiteness left. 'Not forever,' he said, and he gained the courage to look his friend in the eye again. 'Look, the watch was just a set of stabilisers, remember? If I practise enough, work out how this ability works, maybe I can do it on my own and take us back.'

'And how long will that take?'

'I don't know,' Doran said. He was getting tired of saying those three words. 'And there's more.'

'Of course there is.'

'Look, quit it, will you? This is important. After you left—'

Doran was about to tell Zander all about his kidnapping by the Eternalisium when both boys became aware of something in the distance, something coming towards them at a formidable pace.

Riding into town were a small troop of soldiers on horseback. One rider carried a large pole with an English flag billowing in the wind. At the front sat a man the sight of whom made the townspeople scurry away like ants, resuming their tasks or retreating inside.

The soldiers pressed on along the main street until they came to a stop in front of Doran and Zander. Doran closed his eyes as if in silent prayer; Finlay was not with the soldiers.

'Gentlemen,' the leader of the troupe said. Doran immediately picked up on the coldness in the man's eyes, as well as the now very familiar electric-green bordering his pupils. 'I am in pursuit of two young men around your age and description. I am looking to ask them some questions concerning an interaction they may or may not have had on their way into town.' His voice was crisp and distinctly southern English, his demeanour full of a sense of entitlement. He reminded Doran of a bald eagle, with the proud fierceness of his dark pupils and his hooked nose. This was a man who came from a long line of similarly inclined men. Soldiers. Leaders. Men of power and high standing in society.

Looking more closely, he noticed the man's neck was badly burnt. The wound crept up towards his face, resembling, Doran thought, a large oak tree with snaking branches.

'We wouldn't know anything about that, sir,' Doran replied, his voice barely above a whisper.

'Manners from a Scot, wonders never do cease,' the man said, causing his three underlings to titter as he himself chuckled a bit more loudly than they dared to do. 'My name is Sir Richard West, of King Edward's Army. I suppose you have heard of me?'

Doran could feel Zander's eyes burrowing into his skull but he managed to resist the temptation to glance back. They were sharing the same thought. What had Finlay said about Sir Richard?

'The whole of Jedburgh has heard of you, sir.'

'Yes, I imagine they have,' Sir Richard said, his lip curling into a half-smile. 'The other towns will no doubt be passing on the message of our triumph and consequent journey back towards…' – he paused, sneering at his surroundings for a moment – '… *civilisation*.'

Doran could feel Zander's burning desire to knock the man from his horse. It was a desire he shared. However, they both stood very still. The less they said, the more chance they had of avoiding suspicion.

This strategy amounted to little unfortunately as, in the silence, Sir Richard finally processed their modern clothes. He then inspected Doran even more closely.

'I think you both need to come with us,' Sir Richard said, his eyes lingering on Doran for a moment before directing an instruction to his soldiers. 'Find a dwelling with a secure cellar.'

One of the men shifted uneasily upon his horse. 'My lord, shouldn't we take them up to the castle?'

In a split second, Sir Richard West had swivelled around on his horse and swung his shield, striking his subordinate across the face. The soldier toppled from his horse, the clang of his armour ringing through the town. The other horses whinnied with distress.

The soldier who had just been unseated writhed around on the ground and stared up at Sir Richard with a pathetic, blood-soaked face.

'Never question my orders again,' Sir Richard said. His voice had a quiet fury, which terrified Doran more than if he had yelled at the top of his lungs. Not wishing to meet the same fate as his compatriot, one of the other soldiers reared his horse and set off on a search through the town.

Doran noticed the black coat of arms on the shield which

was now splattered with blood, and his eyes narrowed. It was his own family's crest. It matched the one in his house in nearly every way. There was the black knight watching over his jagged river. But it was the centre of the crest that grabbed his attention: a small sun dial, bordered by a green twelve-point star. That was new. Or old, he supposed. All this jumping around wasn't getting any less confusing.

Nevertheless, Sir Richard did seem to be linked to Doran – and not just in name. Could he be his ancestor? Did the two of them share the same gifts?

Sir Richard, once satisfied that his message had left both a physical and mental imprint, turned back to face the boys again. 'Seize them.'

18

'HELLO, DORAN'

Doran and Zander were thrown into an empty cellar beneath what Doran believed to be the local blacksmith's. One of the English soldiers dusted off his gloved hands and slammed the rusty bars shut behind them.

Sir Richard emerged from the shadows, looking down his hooked nose as though the boys were dirt on his boot. 'I am a fair man. I will give you one night to think about where your loyalties lie and to confess any information you may have,' he said with a cold smile. As if wishing to impart a delectable secret, he leaned in, wrapping a leather-gloved hand around one of the bars with a *crunch*. 'Rest assured, when the sun rises you will tell me what you know. One way or another.'

With a glint in his eyes, Sir Richard led the other soldiers up a set of stone steps and through a small wooden door. Doran listened to their footsteps until the sound faded. Only then did he turn to Zander, who shot him a dark look and retreated to the corner of the cellar. He slumped to the ground, brought his knees to his chest, and rested his head upon them. His body was rigid, as though Doran had frozen him like he had done to the rain in London. It reminded Doran of the time Zander had got into trouble in primary school for doing a stunningly accurate impression of their teacher. The then six-year-old Zander had retreated to the fringes of the classroom after his severe telling off and refused to move until lunchtime, and that was only because they were serving chocolate brownies for pudding.

While the behaviour was the same, Doran doubted a freshly made dessert would be enough to coax Zander out this time. The problem was, he was unsure what would. He couldn't recall Zander ever having been so angry with him.

No brilliant idea came, so Doran circled around the cellar, in quest of the perfect spot to sleep. Choice was limited: only darkness and dankness wherever he glanced. A small beam of moonlight had broken through a crack in the wall, providing just enough light in the room to see.

When he had made himself comfortable, in the broadest sense of the word, he stared again at the hunched figure in the corner. Only the rise and fall of Zander's breath gave any indication of life.

Doran inhaled deeply, readying himself, then broke the silence. 'Based on the way things are going for us, if this is our last night on earth, there's one thing you should know... Your Seymour in *Little Shop of Horrors* was the best Linntean has ever seen.'

Zander remained still for a moment then began to shake as if he were having a mild fit. Finally he looked up, a toothy smile on his face. Then he shook his head, apparently annoyed at himself for laughing. 'Not fair. I'm supposed to be mad at you.'

'I know, it was a cheap trick,' Doran said, with a smile of his own. 'Needs must I'm afraid. It's been a tough few days and to be honest, I just don't want to be fighting with my best friend any more.'

Zander mulled this over, his eyes distant. 'Yeah, me neither.'

'I'm sorry,' Doran said, the words lifting what felt like a great weight from his chest. 'You were right. I don't understand what it must have been like for you in that house all those years. I shouldn't have asked you to go back.'

Zander let out a heavy sigh. 'I'm sorry too. You just wanted to get us home and let your mum know you were all right. I was being selfish. I just couldn't face going back.'

'I know.'

'It's just…' Zander began before searching for the right words. He stared into the beam of moonlight. 'We had the world at our fingertips and I didn't want it to end. To return to reality, to that house. To return to the village where nothing happens.'

'Yeah,' Doran murmured. He knew the very feeling.

'And I shouldn't have said what I said about your dad,' Zander continued, a similar weight seeming to lift from him as well. 'That wasn't fair. I was just angry and wasn't thinking.'

'I know. So was I,' Doran said. 'But you're right in a way. I don't get it. I can't.'

'Yeah, well, my situation isn't exactly normal. I would hope if your dad were around, he'd be a damn sight better than mine.' He was still staring at the glimmer of light on the floor, the same light illuminating the pain on his face. After a moment, a tear escaped from his eye. 'You know, part of me wishes that he yelled at me – hit me even. At least that would've been something. At least that would've meant him showing some kind of emotion towards me. Instead, I got a dad who didn't even care enough to do that. I got nothing.' He finally tore his gaze from the moonlight, looking at Doran with a helpless smile. 'How messed up is that?'

Doran didn't quite know how to respond. So instead he stood, wandered across the cellar, and plonked himself at Zander's side. Both boys stared ahead, neither daring nor able to look at the other.

'You know, he might not get you, but there are people in your life who do. Maybe for some, your family isn't who you're born to, it's who you choose. There are people who realise how brilliant you are.' Doran paused, slapping Zander on the knee. 'Infuriating, sure, but brilliant.'

They each let out a rueful laugh, Zander wiping his cheeks with his sleeve. 'Who would that be then?' he asked through the wet chuckles.

'No idea, best get looking,' Doran said, grinning.

Zander gave him a gentle nudge, Doran nudged him back, and both finally broke out in radiant smiles.

This quickly turned to embarrassment and both boys looked away, cheeks flushed. Doran's mouth seemed to open of its own accord and mutter something along the lines of, 'Yes, very good, yes.' But truthfully, he wasn't sure what he had said.

'Where did you go?' Zander asked after a moment. 'When we split up?'

Doran's whole body went rigid. For the tiniest of moments, it had just been him and Zander, talking. He had forgotten all about that other world, filled with lethal warriors, secret societies and devious doctors.

'About that...'

And he recounted his time with the Vigils, with Mr Bishop

and within the mansion's walls. Zander gaped throughout the story, only closing his mouth to make odd humming noises.

'I don't believe it,' he said when Doran had finished. He let out a low whistle. 'Mr Bishop... Well, I suppose it's always the quiet ones. And he stayed there?'

'He seemed confident he'd be found innocent.'

'And this Tobias Blue person. Do you think he's going to try and come after you again?'

'Probably. I don't think anywhere in time will be safe, but the present definitely isn't. Not until I get more control of these powers. At least then I may stand a chance of defending myself.'

'Well between this secret society, that suited man and the badass samurai woman, you've become quite popular.'

Doran ruffled his hair. 'Tell me about it.'

'For now, though,' Zander said, scanning the cellar. 'We need a plan. How do we get out of this one then?'

'Not sure,' Doran said. 'It's not quite the same as trying to sneak out of Mrs Donoghue's class while she naps.'

'She really has a problem.'

'Yup.'

The small door above screeched opened again and they both fell silent.

'Actually,' came the voice of Sir Richard as he stomped down the stairs, 'patience was never a virtue I was blessed with. I think I'll take one of you now.'

One of his soldiers emerged from behind him and unlocked the cell door. He grabbed Doran, who writhed and kicked, but to no avail.

'Let him go!' Zander yelled, charging at the guard.

The guard, whose neck was as thick as Zander's entire body, simply raised an arm and shoved him backwards, his other arm still wrapped around Doran. 'I'll be fine,' Doran assured Zander and he stopped struggling. There was no point in his friend getting hurt further in a vain attempt to save him.

The cellar door swung shut and he was hauled up the stairs and out into the only other room in the building. There was a small, battered stool alone in the centre of the room. Doran was dumped on top of it and he glowered at the guard, who simply returned his disdain with a conceited smile. The guard sauntered away, leaving only Doran and Sir Richard.

No one spoke for several increasingly unsettling seconds.

Stay calm. Stay in control.

'Tell me, where exactly do you come from?' Sir Richard said in a self-assured voice.

'Jedburgh, sir,' Doran replied, taking care to keep his tone as polite as possible.

'Ah, then can you tell me, who is the highest-ranking member of the community in this town?' Sir Richard asked, a cocky glint in his eye. Doran had no answer for him, causing the cold eyes to widen in triumph. 'Liar,' he said. 'Can you perhaps tell me what your family name is?'

'McDowall,' Doran said, saying the first name that came into his head. 'My name is Kieran McDowall.'

'Liar,' Sir Richard said again, apparently not even feeling the need to probe this assertion further.

'I'm sensing a pattern here,' Doran said before he could stop himself. But this was not some teacher he had cheekily spoken back to. Sir Richard drew his sword and held the sharp end of the blade under Doran's chin. He crossed his eyes to look down at the shining silver. 'My apologies, *sir*. That was rude of me.'

Sir Richard didn't lower his sword, though a smile passed over his lips. 'Let's not continue with this charade, shall we?' he said. 'You are not some Jedburgh peasant boy, and to be truthful, I have no interest in whether or not you crossed paths with our fleeing friend on that moor.'

This time Sir Richard lowered his sword, making a show of putting it down on the table.

'Then what do you want?' Doran asked, his mouth dry.

'Do not mistake me, it is my duty to my king to quell any leakage of information from our camp,' Sir Richard began, meandering back and forth. He came to a stop before Doran, bending down until their eyes met. 'I killed that slave and I can always torture your uninteresting friend to make sure nothing was passed on to you. How *you* can help me, is to tell me who you really are and, more notably, how you came to be here in this time?'

'I don't know what—' Doran started but Sir Richard raised a gloved hand and slapped him across his face.

It was as though it had happened to someone else; as if his brain had put up a brick wall to prevent him from comprehending what had just happened. He wiggled his jaw, a delayed twinge of pain quickly fading.

'I believe I said enough of the charade, boy,' Sir Richard said. 'To make myself plainer I will say this; you will tell me what I want to know, or I will drag your friend in here in your place and torture him in front of you until he screams.' He smiled, but only with the lower half of his face. His eyes remained cruel. 'But as I said, I care little for finding out that information – only a sense of duty would make me wish for it. I could very easily say you both knew nothing and allow you to leave this place. As long as you give me what I want.'

Doran glared at him. He might have endured as best he could any physical torture Sir Richard had thrown at him, but threatening Zander was something else, and the knight knew it. 'What do you want to know?' Doran asked through gritted teeth.

Sir Richard let out a contented bark and thumped him on the shoulder. 'We share the same mark, you and I,' he said. 'What my grandfather called the *"teine uaine"*.' Sir Richard swooped down in front of him, Doran almost tasting his rotten breath. 'But based on your strange garments, you are not from this time or even a time close to this one. Therefore, I ask you, who are you? And before you answer, please remember your friend and understand that I will know if you are lying to me.'

Doran's eyes narrowed. 'My name is Doran West,' he said, forcing the words through his lips. 'I come from Scotland, only around seven hundred years in the future.'

Sir Richard took a step back and jerked upright, looking at Doran as though he had just informed him of a loved one's passing. '*What* did you say your name was?'

Doran frowned. What had he said? 'Doran West.'

'That's not possible,' Sir Richard said. 'How? How did you do it?' he asked, breathless.

'What?'

Sir Richard sprang forward and shook him as though trying to dislodge the information. 'How?' he bellowed. 'How did you travel so far?'

'It was an accident,' Doran said, terrified. 'I didn't mean to. I lost control.'

The shaking stopped and Sir Richard gave him a searching look, scouring every inch of his face for any hint of a lie. No hint came, and he appeared satisfied. 'It's not possible,' he said softly to himself, finally taking his foul breath out of Doran's personal space. 'You are a West?'

'Yes...'

'Then that means you are my direct descendant,' Sir Richard said. 'And if you can travel so far then that means...the curse is broken. How? How did you break it?'

'What curse?' Doran said. 'I don't know anything about any curse?'

Sir Richard looked as if he wanted to charge at him again but instead gave him another searching look. 'I may have the "*teine uaine*" but I do not possess the travelling ability that you appear to have. My grandfather also told me of the West family curse. We wielded great power centuries ago but were betrayed and robbed of our abilities. All that remains is an inconsistent inheritance of the remnants of these abilities. For example, I can have visions of the future – only glimpses, shadows – but more often than not they become a reality. It has been rather advantageous in many ways throughout my life. There have also been times when I have inexplicably woken up days after I went to sleep, or found myself miles away from where I had just been. I have no control over this ability and neither did my grandfather, while my father possessed no trace of these powers. But now, here you are, a West with the ability to travel great distances. Tell me, tell me how this is possible.'

'I-I don't know,' Doran stammered. 'I just...can. I don't know about any curse. All I know is my dad could do it and so can I.'

'And you can control this ability?'

'No, I...' Doran began before he allowed his voice to trail off. His eyes betrayed him and flitted to his trouser pocket.

Sir Richard lunged towards him and stuffed his calloused hand into the pocket, pulling out the schematic of the watch's design. Doran tried to grab it back but the knight slapped him across the face again, much harder than the first time.

The pain was intense but Doran sat up straight, determined not to let Sir Richard see that he had hurt him.

'What is this?' Sir Richard asked, examining the diagram as though he'd been handed a treasure map.

'It's a schematic; nothing more.'

'A...*scee-ma-tic*?'

'It's a picture of a potential way to control our abilities.'

'A weapon?' Sir Richard asked with a hungry glint in his eye.

'Depends on your perspective.'

Sir Richard pressed the diagram so hard he nearly pushed his finger through it. 'And you've built this...this...'

'Watch.'

'You have built this watch?' Sir Richard asked, surveying him.

'Yes,' Doran said. 'But I lost it on my journey here.'

'How convenient.'

'You said you would know if I was lying,' Doran said. 'Am I?'

'No...' Sir Richard said. 'No, I do not believe you are. But you can build another one?'

Doran could tell there was more to that question than met the eye. He took a moment before he answered, considering his predicament and what might happen to Zander if he gave the wrong response. 'Yes.'

This was true of course. He could. But what Sir Richard did not need to know was that there was nothing in this time period that would allow him to.

Sir Richard nodded. 'Well then, you will build this watch for me – now.'

'Now?'

'You can think of a better time?'

Doran thought quickly. 'The process takes a great deal of energy from me. I will need to rest. Can I begin tomorrow morning?'

'You will begin now,' Sir Richard said, as if commanding one of his soldiers.

'Respectfully, sir, I do not wish to be so exhausted that I make a mistake. What if the device does not work correctly and injures either of us?'

Sir Richard's eyes became slits. He paused, weighing up what Doran had said. His eagerness and hunger for what Doran could offer him had evidently corrupted his self-proclaimed ability to distinguish truth from lies, as he nodded once again. 'Very well,' he said, albeit with great reluctance. 'You will begin in the morning. We will start by making a list of any materials and tools you will need. And the day you finish, you will teach me how to use this *"device"* you speak of and all you know, so that I can finally regain the power that was stolen from my family.' His tone became even more threatening. 'I will also remind you that any attempt to deceive me or my soldiers will result in the instant removal of one of your friend's limbs. Have I made myself plain?'

'Very plain.'

Sir Richard glared with the deepest distrust for a moment, but it appeared his desire once again outweighed his sense, and he ordered that Doran be taken back to the cellar.

Doran was dragged from the room and thrown like a sack of potatoes to land beside Zander, who grabbed him and checked for any sign of injury. Doran waited patiently for the guard to leave before engaging. 'I'm fine, I'm OK.'

'What happened?'

'I was right; he's like me,' Doran said. 'He's my ancestor. But he's different somehow. His powers have been suppressed or diluted, or something. And he wants me to help him get stronger.'

'*Great*,' Zander said. 'So, he didn't want to know about Edward dying?'

Doran shushed him, checking the door before continuing. 'No,' he whispered. 'But our escape just got a little harder… He has one of the schematics for the watch now.'

'But what use is that to him? Can we not just leave it?'

Doran shook his head. 'Can't risk it. Who knows what someone seeing that in this time could change? It just takes one person to understand even a fragment of it in the next seven hundred years and we've altered history.'

'Fair point,' Zander said. 'So…what's the plan?'

After a few hours of discussing various schemes and plans of escape, the boys fell asleep at opposite ends of the cellar. Doran lay huddled on the chilly floor, tossing and turning. In his mind, he was back in the woods. He was running. The man in the suit was chasing him. He was going to catch him. He couldn't jump. He couldn't get away. The man was getting closer and closer. A long-fingered, skeletal hand reached out, inches from grabbing his shoulder.

Doran sat up with a start, panting as though he actually had been fleeing through the woods. He jerked his head around, scanning his surroundings. He was back in the cellar. It was just a dream.

He was about to lie back down when something he saw out of the corner of his eye caught his attention. He spun around to see the very man who had been haunting his dreams sitting on a wooden stool on the other side of the metal bars. His pale face had a smile stretched across it, his green eyes watching Doran with a singular focus.

'Hello, Doran,' he said.

19

THE SUITED MAN

He was there. How was he there? Doran's eyes flitted in the direction of Zander.

'Best not to wake him,' the suited man said. 'I would prefer to keep this to just the two of us.' His voice was smooth and precise, every word carefully chosen and delivered. He crossed his legs and smoothed down his trousers with the long, bony hands which had been plaguing Doran's nightmare only moments before.

He smiled again, though somehow this put Doran even less at ease.

Doran had yet to find his voice, so instead decided to analyse the man before him. For that's what he was, wasn't he? He wasn't some spectre or monster; simply a man. So why did Doran feel so haunted by him?

The longer he looked, the clearer the answer became. The

suited man also remained silent, apparently content to wait for Doran to make the next move. He just sat there, staring at him, perfectly relaxed. The green eyes didn't move or display any urgency. But it was more than that. The closest parallel Doran could think of was of a lion, patiently lying in the grasslands, waiting for an antelope to run by.

He had two prominent scars, the first starting at his chin and running down his neck, spoiling an otherwise flawless raven-black beard. The beard looked as if it had been chiselled rather than grown, like someone had wrapped a shadowy mask around his jaw and mouth.

The second pencil-thin scar also disrupted the man's face, separating his left eyebrow into two and finishing underneath the eye itself.

His hair was combed backwards into a dark brown quiff, sprinkled with grey. He looked in his early forties but, truthfully, Doran found his age hard to pinpoint. It was as though his features had been cobbled together, each part stolen from a different period in someone's life.

However, the most intriguing thing was the man's skin – a ghostly white with green veins faintly visible, most prominently on his neck.

'How did you get in here?' Doran asked, the question erupting from his mouth, surprising even himself.

The suited man chuckled. 'Of course that's your first question. Not who I am. Not why I am following you. No, no. Of course. You're like me. You have a desire to understand how things work.'

Doran's brow furrowed. 'Who are you?'

The suited man raised a long, skeletal index finger and wagged it, tutting. 'That's two questions. Which one would you like me to answer first?'

He was enjoying himself, Doran could tell. 'Who are you?' he repeated, keeping his voice as even as possible.

'I've had many names,' the suited man said with a wave of his hand. 'You can call me Samael.'

'Samael?'

'Yes. Your second question?'

It was as if he were playing a game, only Doran was unsure what the rules were. 'How did you get in here?'

'Oh, that part is easy,' Samael said, clasping his hands together and resting them on his knee as though about to launch into an amusing anecdote. 'I'm not really here.'

'Am I still dreaming?'

'No, you are quite awake, and rest assured I'm quite real.'

He was deliberately withholding the information Doran wanted, goading him into keeping the conversation going. 'Then how?'

'I'm projecting my consciousness across time,' Samael said, talking out of the side of his hand as if it were some big secret.

'What does that mean?' Doran asked, deciding to comply with Samael's apparent desire to be questioned. 'Wait, does that mean you're like me?'

'Very much like you, dear boy,' Samael said. 'Although I'm the only person on Earth who can do this particular trick,' he added with a wink.

'But you're a Traveller? Like me?'

'Yes, I can travel in time,' Samael said. 'However, an accident a long time ago made me unable to control it. It gave me certain gifts such as this one, but also provided a few hindrances which have been most unwelcome.'

'What happened?' Doran asked, now greatly intrigued by what Samael was saying.

'That is a story for another time I think,' Samael said. 'I cannot project for very long and there are matters we need to discuss.'

'I'm listening,' Doran said, trying to show a degree of confidence.

Samael appeared to find this amusing, smirking at Doran like he was a puppy who had not quite found his bark yet. 'I have come to warn you, Doran West.'

'Warn me? About what?'

'Someone is coming for you. Who means to destroy you.' He paused at Doran's expression. 'No, not me. I trust your assessment of me wasn't based purely on my appearance. Were you never taught not to judge a book by its cover?'

Doran pondered Samael's accusation. Had he been? It was true; whenever he had seen Samael, he had bolted in the opposite direction. This was their first conversation, yet in his head, he already regarded Samael as someone not to be trusted. But had this been completely his fault?

'The man in the woods,' Doran said. 'The man in the woods. He told me to run.'

For the first time, Samael's face transformed. The mechanical smile was wiped away and a shadow spread across his face. This statement had been unexpected, as if Doran had improvised in the middle of an otherwise scripted dialogue. 'What man?' he asked. His voice was calm but his eyes were wild.

'I-I don't know. He just appeared and gave me this watch and then keeled over.'

Samael's eyes widened ever so slightly. 'I see,' he said. Then, as quickly as if someone had flicked a switch, his unsettling composure returned. 'We are running out of time. The woman you met, who prevented me from reaching you in Florence – her name is Léonie Devereux. She is a member of the Eternalisium, around two decades from your present.'

'She's from the future?'

'In her time the Eternalisium is a corrupt organisation that serves a heartless dictator known as the Magistair.'

Doran thought of what Malloch had said. Did that mean Tobias' power grab would be successful? In the future, would the doctor rule the Eternalisium with an iron fist?

'The Society bends and shapes time to its will,' Samael continued. 'No matter the consequences, no matter the ripple effects. I've been fighting the Eternalisium for years, gaining support slowly, but I still have nowhere near the power to defeat them. That is, until you.'

'Me?'

'You are a West. Your family lineage has a certain *mythology* around it. The most powerful of all Travellers. Wests possess a greater command of time than any others with the gift.'

'I don't understand—' Doran began, but Samael held up a hand to stop him.

'I know this must be a lot to take in, believe me.' He was smiling again, though this time Doran almost thought it seemed *kind*. There was an affection in his eyes that Doran hadn't been expecting to see.

Suddenly, his face and then his whole body started to become less tangible, shifting to a spectral state. 'I must go now. I'm growing weak. I will find you, I promise. In the meantime, you must do everything you can to stay away from Léonie Devereux. She is second only to the Magistair himself and she wants you dead or under their control. Either way, it doesn't matter to them. Stay safe. Doran. Stay hidden, until I can get to you.'

Samael began to fade faster. 'What do I do? How do I get out of here?' Doran asked, leaping to his feet.

'Trust your abilities. They are coming to you, albeit slowly. You can use them. You are a West. Time is yours to command.'

Samael faded into nothingness, leaving Doran with a few answers – but even more questions.

20

THE HANGING

Morning broke, a finger of sunlight invading the cellar. Zander moved from side to side, then sat up with a start. 'Don't go, Jodie; we can make it work!'

He scanned the room in a daze until he saw Doran. For a moment, Doran forgot what had transpired during the night and smirked. 'You dreaming about that actress again?'

'Shut up,' Zander said, his cheeks going pink. He rubbed his eyes, orienting himself. 'Ah yes, still in the penthouse suite I see.'

'Room service is on its way.'

'As long as they get my eggs right, I won't complain.' Zander stood and stretched as though about to go for a morning run. With a wince, he clasped his lower back. 'I now appear to have the body of an eighty-year-old.'

'Rough sleeping will do that.'

'I'll say. This will be reflected in my review,' Zander said in a pompous voice, strutting towards the bars. He clasped them, trying to peer through the gap under the door above, but failed to see anything. Dejected, he came to help Doran to his feet. 'You look awful. Did you sleep at all?'

Doran glanced at the sunlight, pretending he was looking for warmth. 'Not really.'

'I don't blame you,' Zander said slowly, and he arched an eyebrow. 'Although, please tell me you've used the time to think of a way out of here?'

'Not a plan exactly, just a thought.' He hadn't decided whether to tell Zander about Samael just yet. He was still getting his head around their conversation himself.

It was very hard in such a long friendship to hide things from one another and Doran could tell Zander was suspicious. But after narrowing his eyes for a moment he seemed to push past it – for now. 'And what is the chance of success for this thought?'

'Little to none,' Doran said with the ghost of a smile.

'Our usual odds then,' Zander said, wheeling Doran around to face the bars. 'Better get to it though. I just heard footsteps.'

'Get him to come in here.'

'What?'

'Just do it.'

Sure enough, an English soldier came trudging down the stairs, already dressed in full chainmail and with a scowl on his face. He had a stocky build, resembling a caveman more than a knight.

'You know, it must be hard wearing that stuff all day every day,' Zander said to the soldier, nodding to his armour. 'Especially with the added weight of such a huge, melon-sized head.'

The soldier's flattened nostrils flared. 'What did you say?'

'I don't think they have melons yet,' Doran murmured out of

the corner of his mouth.

'I think he got the picture,' Zander murmured back. When he spoke to the soldier again, he mimicked his voice and accent. 'I said, your face looks like it should be guarding the bell tower of a cathedral.'

He turned to Doran as though asking for approval. He got a sarcastic thumbs up.

Nevertheless, Zander's words had an impact. The soldier grabbed the keys from his belt and furiously looked for the right one, thrusting it into the lock. He swung the bars open and stomped towards Zander.

'Eh – Doran? You mind telling me what that thought was now?' Zander said, his voice a full octave higher than usual.

Doran raised his hand and closed his eyes as if he was trying to stop the soldier by peaceful protest. He reached out as he'd done so instinctively in that alleyway. He could feel it. He could feel time itself. It was all there before him. Waves and ripples, with beams of light shooting off in multiple directions. His own personal Aurora Borealis. He became connected to it and then in a calm, authoritative voice he simply said, 'Stop.'

The waves and ripples froze, the lights pausing in their journey. Doran prised his eyes open one at a time, scared of what he was about to see.

The soldier was inches away from an alarmed Zander. Doran observed them as if they were an oil painting in a gallery, revelling in the stillness.

Slowly, as if trying not to wake him, he unsheathed the man's blade and struck him hard on the back of the head with the handle. Malloch would be proud.

The man remained motionless, but the impact had been made. Doran clutched the sword and closed his eyes again, seeing time once more. He needed it to begin again. He willed it so.

The waves, ripples and lights all exploded into life like meteorites flying across the night sky. Doran heard a *crunch* and opened his eyes to see the soldier lying on top of Zander, unconscious, his large cheek and open mouth pressed against Zander's face.

Doran felt giddy. 'It worked.'

'*Fantastic,*' Zander said. 'Now, could you please get this lump of lard off me?'

Doran lugged the man off Zander, leaving him lying on his back. He was still breathing, his well-fed stomach rising and falling.

'OK. Let's go,' Doran said.

The two boys scurried out of the cellar, grabbing the soldier's keys along the way and locking the sleeping giant inside.

They crept silently up the stairs, hovering behind the door.

'What now?' Zander whispered.

'Now we play one of your old favourite games,' Doran whispered back, handing Zander the sword.

Zander glanced at the sword. 'Crazy man and hostage?'

'Crazy man and hostage.'

Zander beamed as though Doran had surprised him with the most thoughtful gift in the world. He mouthed a countdown from three and kicked in the door, pulling Doran through by his collar.

The sword hovered in front of Doran's throat. 'Nobody move!' Zander yelled at Sir Richard's soldiers, who up to this point had been standing around the table, midway through a conversation.

At the boys' sudden entrance, they all moved into formation, drawing their swords. Sir Richard rose from a stool, seemingly underwhelmed by Zander's dramatic entrance. Doran's eyes flitted to the table; the schematic was still there.

'Stay back!' Zander carried on, brandishing the sword and alternating between pointing it at the soldiers and at Doran's neck. 'Stay back, or I swear I'll cut his throat!'

The soldiers looked at Sir Richard, uneasy. Their commander's eyes were fixed on the scene before him. 'Keep your weapons ready,' he said to his soldiers. 'The Scots attempt to fool us. I am curious as to how they got the better of Sir David. I thought he was more skilled than that.'

Zander shook Doran by the collar like a rag doll. 'I cut him, just like I'll cut this one.'

'You have no intention of doing any such thing.'

'Want to wager on that?' Zander shouted, his eyes manic, the sword closer than ever to Doran's throat. 'I want out of here and I don't care how I do it!'

'So, you will take your friend as your prisoner?' Sir Richard said, raising an eyebrow.

'This is no friend of mine,' Zander spat, glaring at Doran as if he would indeed like nothing better than to slice his head from his neck. 'He lied to me and got me stuck here! He's nothing more than an incompetent, arrogant, fool!'

'Easy,' Doran muttered out of the corner of his mouth.

'Sorry, just trying to sell it,' Zander muttered back before addressing Sir Richard again. 'And unless you want his entrails all over the floor, you will do as I say.' He thrust the sword towards Doran's throat, stopping just before the point of the blade touched his skin.

Doran felt the end of the sword tickle the few faint facial hairs he possessed. 'Please, Sir Richard, he's serious! He hasn't forgiven me for taking us here and losing the watch. He'll do it; he's lost his mind.'

Zander shook him again. 'I'd be glad to do it. I've nothing left to lose. Come anywhere near and he dies.'

Sir Richard's mouth curled. He had become far less composed and a glimmer of worry invaded his expression. Zander's acting was clearly swaying him and he was weighing up his options. Glaring at Zander, he raised his hand. His soldiers looked perplexed for a moment before sheathing their swords and stepping aside.

Zander pushed Doran forwards, pointing the sword at his back. 'OK, I need all of you to stand right against that wall.' He brandished the sword briefly towards one of the walls. 'You too, handsome,' he added to Sir Richard.

Even though his murderous gaze was directed at Zander, Doran still felt the full blast of the flaming fury in Sir Richard's eyes. Nevertheless, he complied with Zander's order, prompting the others to do the same.

'Facing the wall if you don't mind,' Zander said, prodding Doran in the back for effect.

They all obeyed again, facing the wall. Zander grabbed Doran and stood behind him, his free arm wrapped around his chest and the sword across his throat. The pair edged forwards, Doran grabbing the schematic as they passed the table.

Zander pushed him through the door, addressing the soldiers and Sir Richard one final time. 'And if I see anyone following, he'll be dead before you can reach us.'

And, like a thespian exiting the stage after a satisfying performance, he left, slamming the door behind them.

With no time to celebrate, the boys broke into a run as soon as they were outside, Zander dropping the sword, which was slowing him down.

As they neared the town boundary, Zander shot out an arm

and both boys skidded in the dirt. 'Wait a second, wait a second. I have to know. In the cellar…*how* did we escape exactly?'

Doran paused before answering. 'I stopped time.'

Zander blinked numerous times. 'All right then; just checking,' he said, apparently taking the information in his stride and moving swiftly on. 'OK, let's get out of town and out of sight, then you try your best to jump us out of here. Not got much choice now,' he added. 'We need to go before they catch us or we do any real damage. Even I'm not going to be careless about this particular time in our country's history.'

Zander then ran on again, but Doran remained still. Zander was almost out of the town before he noticed and raced back.

'Doran – Doran – we've got to go.'

'What if we've already changed history?' Doran said, the words distant, as if someone else were saying them.

'What? What are you talking about?'

'That man… That man, Finlay Robertson, who we met on the way into town. He said if it hadn't been for us, he would have made it to Jedburgh in time. What if he was meant to get there, to survive and pass on the message? What if now Robert the Bruce doesn't find out about Edward until it's too late? What if this information does lead to a revival of the war which leads to Scotland's victory?'

'We can't know that. What if he was always caught and it never mattered anyway?'

'I can't explain it, I just have this *feeling* that things aren't right.'

'A feeling? Just how many new powers haven't you told me about?'

Doran thought back to what Tobias had said. Did he indeed have all this untapped potential, waiting to be awakened? What exactly was he capable of?

Zander's incredulous expression snapped him from his reverie. 'Don't look at me like that,' he said. 'Plus, are you willing to take that chance? What if there's no Scotland to go back to?'

His words seemed to have swayed Zander, who was now biting his bottom lip. 'So, what are you saying?'

'I'm saying we deliver the message ourselves.'

Zander scoffed until he saw Doran's grave expression. 'You aren't kidding, are you?'

Doran shook his head. 'We've got to do this.'

'But we have no phones, no map. Do we even know where to go?'

'Annandale – that's what Finlay said. That's where Bruce must be.'

Zander appeared unable to stop his head from nodding, his eyes glazed over. 'This is madness.'

'No arguments from me,' Doran said. 'But we have no choice.'

Zander paced around for a moment, glancing at him every few steps. At first, he was disbelieving, then sceptical, until finally, he shook his head at the sky with a smile. 'Onto the next adventure then.'

Once they had resigned themselves to their quest, Doran realised their chances of finding Annandale would be slim without a map. Unfortunately, their best chance of finding one would be in the town of Jedburgh. They would have to be careful this time not to draw attention to themselves.

They slipped quietly back in among the huts of the town. It had been a full hour since their escape, but the town seemed dead. Unlike the previous day, there were no passers-by around to ogle at their strange attire. They could have been parading down the main track through the town singing Taylor Swift songs seven centuries too early and no one would have witnessed them.

Suddenly a sharp scream sliced through the air, followed by the yells of a crowd.

Curious, they ran towards the hubbub, coming to a stop in the shadows behind an open square.

A crowd of irate townspeople were gathered in front of a large tree with a rope hung over its thickest branch. At the end of the rope, dangling in the light breeze, was a noose. Under the tree, it appeared a small wooden platform had been constructed, resembling a stage. Doran felt sickened that this was considered a centrepiece of the town.

In front of the 'stage' were the English soldiers who had apprehended Doran and Zander, including the one Doran had knocked unconscious. He had a foul expression and was clutching his recovered sword as if he were looking for any excuse to use it. On the platform itself was Sir Richard West, standing before his audience. Beside him was a trembling girl, no older than Doran himself, her face freshly bruised. It seemed Sir Richard had no intention of chasing them. He appeared to have another method of flushing them out.

'Now, I will give each of you a choice,' Sir Richard called out to the crowd. 'You can either continue to harbour these prisoners or you can give them up. They are enemies of your king and anyone who helped them escape, or is hiding them now, will be charged alongside them as traitors.'

There were cries from the townspeople, protesting their innocence and imploring Sir Richard to let the girl go. Tears were now streaming down her face and she flinched whenever Sir Richard moved. He grabbed her by the back of the neck and thrust her towards the swinging rope. Her chilling scream echoed through the air again and Doran held his breath. This time it was joined by shrieks from the crowd.

'What do we do?' Zander asked Doran in a hushed voice.

He didn't answer, staring at the frightened girl. What could they do? He didn't have the control to stop this many soldiers at once. But this was their fault. The girl was going to die because of them.

'Doran?'

He couldn't move. The noose was placed around the girl's neck. She was going to die. She was going to die right there in front of him and he couldn't so much as take one step forwards.

'Stop!'

Doran snapped out of his daze. Zander had emerged from the shadows, standing tall before the crowd.

'Let her go. It's me you want,' Zander continued, striding through the crowd towards the stage. The townsfolk parted and he stood before Sir Richard, staring up at him, defiant.

'And where is my descendant?' Sir Richard asked with a thin smile.

'Gone,' Zander said. 'He ran the moment we got out. You won't catch him now.'

'And yet you stayed?'

Zander smirked. 'What can I say? Guess I'm the stupid one.'

'Indeed,' Sir Richard said, confirmation that he had been fooled dawning on his face. His expression grew dark, but he sneered. 'Let us hope he hasn't gone too far… Take him.'

The soldiers seized Zander, who wrestled against them as he was hauled on to the stage. The girl was cast back into the crowd to her grateful parents, who enveloped her. The girl's father glared murderously at Sir Richard.

Zander was put into the noose in her place and Sir Richard

addressed the crowd once more, though his words were meant for Doran and Doran alone.

'I know you are here!' he yelled. 'I know what you are! Now is your chance to prove it. Save your friend.'

The townspeople appeared both horrified and confused. Doran tried to step forward but couldn't seem to move out from the shadows. Closing his eyes, he raised his hand, willing his newfound ability to emerge once again.

Darkness. No lights, no feeling. Just darkness. He couldn't do it. It wasn't working.

He opened his eyes to see Sir Richard waiting, looking increasingly impatient. With a leer, he turned to Zander. 'It appears he has abandoned you after all. Any final words?'

Doran could see the fear in Zander's eyes. But this soon shifted to a purposeful expression as he stared out at the crowd before him. 'My countrymen!' he projected, so that all could hear him. 'I am a humble Scottish farmer, like many of you. This man…' he pointed to his captor, '…Sir Richard West, aims to pillage and loot our great town, leaving it bare, leaving us penniless and destitute. All in the name of King Edward. I am but a thorn in his side and he hangs me. What will he do to any of you who may defy him, simply trying to live your life in peace? We shouldn't have to live in fear. We shouldn't have to live in a land where Edward is our king. He cares nothing for Scotland. Only for the riches it can bring him. It is time for us to rise up once more. Wallace was but the beginning. We must continue the fight he started. We must fight until the last man, until our last breath, until the day Scotland is free!'

The crowd who had been murmuring in agreement throughout Zander's speech gave a loud cheer. Spurred on, Zander continued.

'I know Scotland will one day be free. I have seen it. Free to rule as we see fit. For our people, by our people. It isn't perfect; nothing ever is. But at least the imperfection belongs to us! I ask that you begin that journey once again, here, today. Will you stand with me? Will you stand with Scotland?'

The crowd gave an almighty roar and Zander turned to Sir Richard with a devilish twinkle in his eye. 'How was that?'

Sir Richard's face had turned scarlet. It was hard to hear over the noise of the crowd, but Doran saw Sir Richard's lips form the words, 'Do it.'

The soldier whom Doran had thumped moved readily towards the base of the tree and untied the rope. With a yank, he pulled hard and tightened the noose around Zander's neck, hoisting him from the stage and into the air.

21

LÉONIE DEVEREUX

Screams and yells erupted as Zander's feet left the ground.

Doran remained hidden, trembling. *Come on, Doran. Move. Move!*

His friend was dying, right in front of him, and he couldn't stop it. *Just put one foot in front of the other. Do it. Now!*

His left foot edged forward and he was about to emerge from the shadows when he felt a hand on his shoulder. He spun around to see the woman he now knew as Léonie Devereux, her red hair gleaming in the sun. She raised her hand and began turning it anti-clockwise. Doran turned and stared at the scene before them: the entire crowd, Zander, the soldiers and Sir Richard were all moving backwards, just as the suited man in Florence had done. They kept rewinding until Zander was once again on the ground, safe for the time being.

Léonie's arm dropped and she swore under her breath,

panting. Doran could see her nose was bleeding.

'I know you are here!' Sir Richard's voice bellowed. 'I know what you are! Now is your chance to prove it. Save your friend.'

He was calling for Doran once more. Then Zander's booming voice filled his ears for the second time as his friend launched into his rousing speech. It was all happening again. Zander was about to be strung up by his neck at any moment. Léonie now seemed like she might faint from exhaustion, no longer in a fit state to repeat her heroics. It was all down to Doran, and in his mind's eye he could still see only a black sky – no trace of those gleaming meteorites flying across it.

Léonie met his gaze and seemed to understand. 'You can do this,' she said. 'It's too much for me to rewind at once. You've got to stop time.'

'I tried. I can't.'

'You have to. Your friend is about to die if you don't,' Léonie said, grasping his shoulders and shoving him out into the light. 'You're Doran bloody West – now stop time!' she yelled directly in his ear.

Once again it was instinctual. Doran raised his hand and the word filled his entire body. *STOP!*

The scene jerked to a halt, as did Léonie. Zander was frozen in his triumphant smirk while Sir Richard was midway through a scowl.

Doran wove his way through the crowd to the stage. Removing the noose from Zander's neck, he beheld the irate statues of the Jedburgh townspeople – all of whom had a lethal gaze directed at the English soldiers. With what felt like a great effort, Doran took a deep breath and mouthed the word, 'Start.'

Jedburgh erupted again, followed by a few gasps and screams of shock at Doran's sudden appearance on stage.

Everything happened at once. Sir Richard drew his sword and the father of the girl Zander had saved let out a shrill battle cry. Like a swarm of locusts, the townspeople stormed forward, enveloping the English soldiers. Doran and Zander leapt down from the stage into the horde in the hope of crowd-surfing to safety. With a squelch, their feet sank into the churned-up mud, then they made their way gradually against the tide of the mob to its outer edge, back to where Léonie was waiting.

Breathing in the clear air, they glanced back to see Sir Richard and his soldiers cornered, yelling at the locals and slashing at anyone who came too close.

'Nice speech.'

'Pretty sure I stole most of that from *Braveheart*.'

'Let's get clear of the locals,' Léonie said, ushering the boys to follow her.

Doran could see Sir Richard had started to disappear beneath the swarm, an animalistic look in his eyes. Perhaps Léonie wasn't a bad option at that particular moment.

She bounded out in front, not stopping until they reached the edge of town. 'OK, no sign of anyone. Trap us out of here, Doran.'

She might as well have been speaking Italian. In fact, Raffaello's ramblings in Florence would have made more sense.

'What are you waiting for? Let's go. Come on.'

'I don't know what you're talking about.'

Léonie stared at him like he had made a bad joke. 'You need to jump us all out of here.'

'Why can't you?' Zander asked.

'I'm not a Trapper...' Léonie said, as if it was the most obvious thing in the world. 'I can't take pedestrians along for the ride,' she added, directing her remark at Zander.

'Rude,' Zander said to Doran.

'I can't. I don't have control yet,' Doran said.

She gave him a searching look and her face drained of colour. She cried out in frustration. 'I knew I'd got it wrong. I knew you seemed too young. Do you even know who I am?'

Doran thought back to what Samael had said, deciding to keep his cards close to his chest. In truth, he supposed he shouldn't know who she was. He shook his head, keeping his face as inscrutable as possible.

'I've really messed up this time,' Léonie said, pacing back and forth. 'Who knows what this could do to the timeline?'

'We hear you there,' Zander said.

Léonie stopped. 'What do you mean?'

'We think we've already screwed things up during our little jaunt to Jedburgh,' Zander said.

Léonie glared at Doran. 'Is this true?'

Doran had a very similar feeling to when his mum chastised him. He checked on his muddy shoelaces for a moment. 'We may have, *inadvertently*, stopped an important message getting to Robert the Bruce.'

'How important?'

'Like Scotland-losing-the-war important,' Zander said.

Léonie stared at them. Her stoic expression slowly began to crack, and she sniggered. This evolved into a full-blown laugh which, while settling Doran slightly, also confused him. 'What's so funny?'

Léonie waved her hand. 'I'm sorry,' she said through the giggles. 'It's just great to see you mess up like this. *The* Doran West.'

'Not sure I'm finding it as funny.'

Léonie managed to regain her composure. 'You're right. I'm

sorry,' she said. She kept a straight face for barely a second, unable to contain the laughter which erupted from her mouth.

Zander leaned across. 'I like her.'

Doran ignored him. 'Look, I don't know who you think I am. But it would be good if you could tell us who *you* are and what is going on.' It was his turn to become his mother.

Léonie's laughter died and there was a reverence in her gaze that he didn't quite understand. Now her expression clearly showed that she was looking at someone she knew. 'You're right. This must all be very confusing for you,' she said. 'My name is Léonie Devereux and I'm not sure what else I can tell you. This is all wrong. You don't know me yet. For now, let's focus on fixing your inaccuracy.'

Zander stepped forward. 'A man named Finlay Robertson had a message about King Edward for Robert the Bruce. We held him up and he must have been killed by Sir Richard on his way into town. We have to go to Annandale and deliver the message ourselves.'

Léonie considered this then turned away from them, shielding something. The boys peered around her to see she had pulled out a thin, flat device that resembled a phone. It looked like a sheet of glass, glinting in the sunlight.

She gave it a few frantic taps and a holographic image appeared on what Doran now realised was a screen. Léonie swiped through various options until she eventually found what she was looking for. She analysed whatever was in front of her and attached the screen to a leather strap on her wrist. The screen made a bizarre whirring sound, like an ineffectual power drill, and collapsed in on itself to half its size. To Doran, it looked as if Léonie was now wearing a high-tech smart watch. 'OK, you were right,' she said. 'Whatever you did has created an inaccuracy. I knew I felt a little off when I landed here.'

'What was that thing?' Doran asked, the device momentarily the only thing in existence to him.

'You'll find out,' Léonie said. 'Better get to it though. Annandale is about a three-day hike from here, given the terrain.'

'Her watch looks better than yours' Zander muttered to Doran.

Léonie appeared distracted by something in the sky, like someone checking for rain. 'Let's go while we still can. We don't want the timeline setting on us.'

'Setting?' Doran said.

'When a change is made to the timeline, it has a ripple effect,' Léonie explained, though her tone was that of a teacher who wished to move onto their next point, rather than be asked yet another question. 'That change isn't permanent at first as time adjusts to the new reality. So, as long as you can rectify what's happened before the new reality sets, you can put things back to the way they should be. If we can get to Bruce soon and deliver the message by the intended date, then everything will be fine.'

Doran thought of his mum, alone in a future where he was missing, presumed dead. Had this reality set? Was he already too late? He had to believe otherwise. He had to believe there was still time to fix his first mistake.

'Why can't you just zap us all there and deliver the message right now?' Zander asked. 'Given the state I'm still in, that would be my preferred choice over a three-day hike.'

Léonie raised a thin eyebrow at him then looked to Doran for help in explaining the reason to this apparent fool. She then seemed to remember Doran shared the same ignorance and sighed. 'I'm not a Trapper, remember? I can only go myself, and let's face it, someone who looks like me wouldn't get very far in this time, let alone be believed by a nobleman.' She turned to Doran. 'Are you sure you can't take us?'

'Not since the watch got lo-' Zander began but Doran elbowed him hard in his ribs. 'Ow!' he moaned. 'Still delicate, remember?'

Léonie gave them a shrewd look. 'You have the watch? Well then surely you can take us after all?' It appeared he hadn't quietened Zander quickly enough.

Doran's shoes twisted in the dirt. 'I...eh...lost it in London in the future.'

Léonie didn't appear to know what to say. She bit her lip, clearly crestfallen. 'OK – one more inaccuracy to deal with. First, let's fix this one, then we can work out how to get the watch back.' She flicked a hand in his general direction. 'For now, I guess we have to go the long way around.'

And with that, she began to trudge up the first of the many hills lining up into the distance, following a man-made path.

'So...do we follow her?' Zander asked. 'I take it causing me further injury wasn't an unprovoked attack?' he added, rubbing his ribs.

'Not got much choice.'

Zander smiled, though it might have been a wince as, after giving Doran an encouraging tap on his shoulder, he limped after Léonie, braving the first steady incline.

Doran wasn't as quick to follow, dwelling on what he'd been told in the cellar. Was Léonie there to hurt him – or worse: indoctrinate him into being part of the Eternalisium? It certainly didn't seem that way at present. She *appeared* to be on his side, but then again, so did everyone. The Eternalisium, Samael, and now Léonie. They couldn't all be on 'Team Doran'. Someone had to be lying, especially with Samael claiming to be the Eternalisium's nemesis. But if what Samael had said was true and Léonie served this Magistair then she couldn't possibly be Doran's ally. Especially if the 'heartless dictator' was indeed a future Tobias Blue.

Nevertheless, she definitely seemed to know him – and about the watch. But how? He would have to try to find out. In any case, it would be nice to have a samurai sword-wielding time warrior on their side as they ventured through the fourteenth-century Scottish wilderness. After a final glance back to Jedburgh, with the cries of the townsfolk still in the air, Doran followed Zander into the unknown.

They had been hiking for what felt like a week. Doran's trainers had soon been soaked through by the marshland, each miserable squelch making him long for the invention of concrete. Zander was faring no better, his injuries getting worse. His limp grew steadily more pronounced. Yet, despite his outward appearance, his spirits didn't seem to have been dampened. In fact, out of the three, he was the most cheerful; cracking jokes and interjecting sarcastic comments as often as he could.

Léonie's sense of humour didn't appear to have made the journey, her neutral expression as immovable as the hills they trekked across. She had threatened to show Zander the sharp end of her sword if he didn't stop talking on two occasions that day already.

He hadn't taken any notice.

'Where'd you get the sword from?' he had asked, his fifth question in the past ten minutes.

Doran thought he heard Léonie growl. 'It's called a Katana. It was given to me. Now can you *please* just shut up?' She marched faster in an attempt to get out of earshot.

'Who gave you it?' Zander asked, a little louder, to be sure she could still hear him.

Léonie spun around with a ferocity in her eyes that stopped both boys in their tracks. Doran thought he saw her eyes flit in his direction for the briefest of moments, though it could just have been tiredness playing tricks on him.

Léonie took a few precise steps back towards Zander. 'You know, you remind me of a boy I trained with.'

'Handsome, was he?' Zander said, tossing his hair back.

A darkness passed across Léonie's eyes. 'He was…until I got my hands on him.'

Zander looked like he had just taken a large gulp of water. He became notably quieter after this exchange.

As they neared the end of the first day, the trio came to a forest. Léonie revealed that cutting through it would shave off a few precious hours from their journey; any chance of shortening their trek like music to the boys' ears.

After a couple of hours of plodding through the trees, the light began to fade and they settled down for a night sleeping under the stars. It appeared Léonie was prepared for any and all scenarios. From her utility belt, she pulled out a lighter, creating a fire using the dried leaves and broken pieces of wood to hand.

'I don't suppose you've got a sleeping bag in that belt of yours?' Zander asked. 'I wouldn't say no to a hypoallergenic pillow either. My nose would thank you greatly.'

Léonie closed her eyes and tilted her head to the sky as though seeking strength from a higher power. 'Is he always like this?' she asked Doran.

'Exclusively.'

'How have you not murdered him in his sleep yet?'

Zander swung his arm around Doran and smiled toothily. 'I'm slightly concerned she means that,' he muttered to Doran, while maintaining a jovial expression for Léonie's benefit. He gave a high-pitched laugh, trying to maintain the illusion they were all friends, and tapped Doran a little too hard on the shoulder. Then, without another word, he trotted away, as though scared so much as to snap a twig, and sat on a nearby log, murmuring to himself.

Doran, who had found all this deeply entertaining, watched him go and was about to placate Léonie when something caught his eye. To his surprise, she was also observing Zander, a hint of a smile on her face.

'That's why,' Doran said. Her attention snapped back to him, her mouth uncurling. 'He's annoying as hell, but he grows on you. Underneath all the clowning around there's a decent person who'd do anything for you. He's a good friend. Those are hard to come by and worth hanging on to. I don't know where I'd be or who I'd be without him, to be honest.'

Léonie stared at him like he was an oddity of nature she had never seen before. The gaze lasted a little too long and, to Doran, it felt like she was inspecting his very soul. She was trying to work him out, and it seemed she didn't have an answer yet.

'What?' he asked, after a few seconds of uncomfortable silence.

'Nothing,' she murmured. 'You're just…' she began but trailed off, instead reverting to her initial response. 'Nothing…'

She trudged away, removing the sword from her back like a jaded warrior after a long battle and settling against a large tree. Once comfortable, she pressed the side of the device on her wrist and Doran heard another clicking sound. The transparent screen expanded into its original rectangular shape and popped off the leather strap. In the blink of an eye, her hand jerked up, caught the screen, and stuffed it into her jacket pocket.

Doran couldn't recall ever meeting anyone quite like her, watching her as though she was a character on his favourite television show. His experiences of people were limited, to say the least. Linntean wasn't exactly a melting pot.

All three were facing each other around the fire but conversation didn't happen. Zander soon lay down and dropped off to sleep, first ensuring his head was still facing towards Léonie.

Doran sat warming his hands by the fire, gazing at the flames which crackled and danced before him. After a while, he chanced a few glances in Léonie's direction. She was still awake and seemed to have no intention of sleeping.

He had to know more. He couldn't continue to journey with this mysterious woman without understanding her intentions. He had to take a chance and find out what he could.

'I know about the Eternalisium,' he blurted rather than stated.

Léonie's eyes narrowed. 'OK?'

'A couple of days ago, I was taken by two Vigils. They took me to the Eternalisium and Tobias Blue tried to get me to join. I escaped.'

'So that makes you sixteen,' Léonie said. 'Wow, I really did mess up.'

'I also know about you,' Doran pressed on.

This revelation seemed to dumbfound Léonie. 'How is that possible? You can't know me yet; you're too young.'

'A man, a man in a suit. He came to me while I was locked in that cellar and told me everything. He told me about the fate of the Eternalisium, about the Magistair, about you. He said in the future it's an evil organisation that wants to control time and shape history for their own purposes. And that you want me dead or to recruit me to your ranks.'

Léonie had become very still throughout his rant, her face impassive. 'Did this man have a name?'

Doran detected a hint of fear in her voice for the first time. 'He said his name was Samael.'

Léonie winced, though appeared to have been expecting as much. 'So he found you,' she said, more to herself than to him.

'Who is he?'

'An enemy from your future,' Léonie said, and her voice now regained its conviction. 'A terrorist, a mass murderer, hell-bent on destroying us all – and everything the Eternalisium has built.'

'He seems to have a very similar view of your Magistair.'

'Everyone is the hero of their own story.'

'Including your Magistair?'

Léonie's cheeks flushed. 'The Magistair is a good man, far better than some who came before him. You think the Eternalisium becomes an evil organisation in the future? In your time it already is, and it was long before you set foot inside it. The Magistair revolutionised the Society. Do you know that even as recently as your present, women weren't allowed to be out on missions? They were confined within the walls of the Society with the older, learned men and students, deemed too *delicate* for any other work. The Magistair changed all that; there is far more equality now. He also transformed how the Society operated. We became more involved in protecting those in need, rather than having these powers and sitting idly by as mere observers.'

That certainly didn't sound like Tobias. Then again, if Léonie was his second-in-command, as Samael had said, then she would deem the good doctor as this great saviour.

Doran bit his cheek and studied her. He had got her riled, and with that, she had become far more forthcoming. He pressed on, taking advantage of her lapse in concentration. 'Who is the Magistair?'

'I've already said too much. You shouldn't know any of this yet. The records clearly state you don't join until your eighteenth birthday.'

Doran sat up. 'What do you mean? You mean I *join* the Eternalisium?'

She sighed. For a moment, there was silence, as she seemed to be having an internal argument, weighing up her options. Appearing to come to a decision, she leaned forward. 'I guess I've already messed with the timeline – might as well destroy it completely. Needs must.' She paused, gathering her thoughts. 'After the last Magistair died, no one took his place. The Society sort of…stood still, operating on autopilot almost; directionless. He had been in charge for far longer than any other before him, out of necessity more than anything else. They said he was a kind man once, but steadfast in his views. It had been a hundred years of very little progression, as I said before. For nearly seventy years the Society waited for someone, with various high-ranking members acting as stewards until the heir to the leadership came of age.'

'Why so long?'

'The person who should have replaced him never did. They say he shunned the Eternalisium completely – wanted no part of it.'

Doran thought for a moment. Where had he heard that before? 'Couldn't someone else have taken over?'

Léonie frowned as though this question was troublesome. 'The Eternalisium is ancient. No one knows for sure when exactly it was founded. It would take too long to go through its history. But there was a crisis, a long time ago, and since then there has been one rule that remains to this day. Only a particular type of Traveller can be Magistair. Someone powerful, who possesses multiple abilities. There has only ever been one family line who has such power…'

Doran took in a few shaky breaths. 'Who is the Magistair?'

Léonie met his gaze, the weight of the information etched into her face. 'You are,' she said.

For a moment, Doran thought he might faint as the two words repeated over and over inside his head. It couldn't be true. He couldn't be the dictator Samael had spoken of with such contempt.

'Or at least…you will be…some day.'

A question managed to find its way to the forefront of his mind. 'If I'm the Magistair…does that mean *I* sent you?'

Léonie looked away for a moment. 'No,' she said with an air of guilt. 'I came alone.'

'Why?'

'A person shouldn't know their fate.'

Doran scoffed. 'It's a bit late for that.'

Léonie looked for a moment as if she might hit him but instead she gave a deep sigh towards the forest floor. Whether this was to quell her anger at his remark or out of begrudging acceptance, he was momentarily unsure.

'You're right,' she said. 'In my present, you've gone; disappeared. No one knows where or why. The last time I saw you, you were in your study, sheets of equations, books and drawings scattered all over the place. You kept muttering, "The watch is the key. The watch is the key…" I didn't know what you were talking about. And the next day you were gone. I tried to travel back along your personal timeline to work out what happened, but I must have got one of your stories mixed up in my head, overshot, and found you too early. Before you joined the Eternalisium or became the Magistair. Trouble is, with Samael back and regaining his following, we need Doran West more than ever.'

'What does Samael want?'

'To put an end to the Eternalisium. To you. All he wants is chaos and destruction. He came close before, but you beat him. The battle is legendary. Professor Harlequin references it all the time in her lectures. We all thought he was gone for good but he's regaining his momentum and for some reason is targeting you here. Now.'

'Why?'

'Only he knows,' Léonie said. 'I don't think anyone can understand what goes on in that twisted mind of his. I guess you're lucky I got things so wrong and ended up in Florence after all.'

Doran didn't answer. Nothing about any of this seemed 'lucky'. His head was spinning with all the new information. He now had two conflicting narratives battling in his mind. He didn't know which he preferred. Both seemed alien to him. Was he destined to be an evil dictator; or to spend the next twenty years reforming an organisation he had no interest in being part of before inevitably disappearing? He wanted neither option. A mere week ago, he was dreaming of his escape from Linntean to go to university. He would do his degree and live his life in the city, the world at his fingertips. A life. An ordinary life, full of possibility and unknown challenges. But that was all gone now. The dream had died the moment Léonie had told him his fate.

He found his thoughts turning to his father. The man who had vanished trying to achieve the same normality Doran now craved. A question was burning on the end of his tongue, desperate to escape his lips. 'What do you know about the Wests?'

Léonie gave him a searching look. 'Only what's in the records,' she said, taking her time. 'And the bits and pieces you've let slip over the years.'

Doran held his breath, favouring silence over risking a wrong word in response.

'As I said, the last Magistair died with no one to succeed him. His son possessed no abilities and became a bit of a pariah within the Society's walls. What they used to call an outlier. One day he left, vowing never to return. The Magistair was heartbroken of course. Some say that's what started his breakdown. The records that remain show his son moved to a village in Ireland and married a local woman. After that, there isn't much else until he had a son of his own named Arlen.'

'My dad,' Doran said, still barely daring to breathe.

'Yes,' Léonie said. 'Once the Magistair died, his son inherited the West family's land in Scotland. Shortly after, they moved there. When your father came of age, all we know is that he rejected the Eternalisium, as I said, leaving it without a Magistair until—'

'Until me.'

'Exactly.'

So that's why Tobias had wanted him. Malloch had said Tobias wanted to seize control of the Eternalisium, which meant Doran was the only thing standing in his way. Which made his destiny…what? To make a triumphant return to the Eternalisium and battle Tobias for the title of Magistair? He was starting to understand why his dad hadn't wanted any part of this.

'So, you don't know anything else about him? About what happened to him?' Doran asked, hope evaporating.

'No. I'm sorry, I don't. There's nothing in the records after that. And you aren't very forthcoming about your past, even with me.'

Doran gulped away the lump in his throat, switching his focus to the dancing flames. Perhaps his dad hadn't escaped his fate after all. Surely if he was out there, lost in time, there would be some sign, some indication of his whereabouts? Wouldn't the Eternalisium have wanted to find and rescue the man who could be their next Magistair? Maybe his mum had been right. Maybe the likelihood was that Arlen West was dead, killed in the attempt to free himself and Doran from their gifts and the obligations that came with them.

As the fire began to dwindle, Léonie excused herself to find more wood. Doran sat alone, sure of one thing. It was clear in his mind. He wasn't some great warrior or leader, nor did he want to be. As far as he was concerned, Tobias was welcome to the job. Let the doctor battle with Samael and preserve the *sacred timeline*. Right now, all Doran was concerned with was sorting this mess he had made and going home. He would succeed where his father had failed. What he had been told wouldn't be his fate any more. Time could be rewritten. It had to be. Doran would make sure of that.

22

BORDER REIVERS

Doran… Doran… DORAN!

Doran woke with a start. The crisp, hushed voice of Samael rang inside his head. The suited man had plagued his dreams again, reaching out for him with that ghostly hand.

It wasn't until his eyes came into focus that he saw something shiny and metallic inches from his nose.

A burly man stood before him, with long salt-and-pepper hair, and cold, pale blue eyes beneath a protruding brow. In his arms was a crossbow, steady, and pointed at Doran.

Doran craned his neck to see that Zander also had a crossbow pointed in his face, while Léonie was giving a murderous glare to the third assailant, who was standing over her. He was pressing her Katana against her chest, admiring the blade with curiosity.

Doran's aggressor had a cruel smile partly visible through his bushy beard. 'Sorry to wake you all,' he said in a voice like gravel. It complemented his appearance well. 'How lucky we are to have stumbled upon such interesting folk,' he added to his accomplices. The two other men gave a hearty laugh. 'May I ask where you are headed?'

No one answered, and the man's smile vanished as though wiped away.

'Kill the girl,' he said with a casual wave of his hand.

'Stop!' Doran yelled. 'We'll tell you – just leave her alone.'

'A fellow Scot!' the man said, with what Doran could tell was fake joviality. 'Though, clearly not from this far south. So, tell me, fellow Scot, what is your name and what is your business here?'

Doran didn't see the point in lying, taking a chance on the man's allegiance. 'My name is Doran West. We have an important message for Robert the Bruce. We are heading to Annandale to deliver it to him.'

'Not a clan name I've heard of,' the man said. 'Pleased to make your acquaintance, Doran West. My name is Gordon Hume. A message to Bruce, you say? And what message is that?'

'I'll tell you if you tell your men to stop aiming their weapons at my friends.'

Hume chuckled, the noise a hair's breadth from a cough. 'I don't believe you are in any position to make demands, lad,' he said. 'How about, if you don't tell me, I start by removing the fair-haired one's fingers?'

Zander's face turned chalk-white and he balled his hands into fists as if trying to hide his fingers from Hume. Doran tried to convey some kind of reassurance in his glance but imagined his complexion probably also had a spectral quality to it.

Léonie's face, on the other hand, seemed to have sucked the colour from her hair. Her rage-filled eyes were still fixed on the man brandishing her sword, as though he had grabbed part of her body without permission.

'We have important information about King Edward. It could turn the tide of the war back in our favour.'

Hume stared at him and the three men burst out laughing. He had apparently said something of childish amusement. Lowering his crossbow, Hume slumped onto a nearby log. He rested the weapon across his lap, finger still itching in front of the trigger. 'Turn the war back in our favour again, huh?' he said with a snigger. 'And where will that end? More dead? More land changing hands? More families watching their crops, their livelihoods, burned before their eyes?'

'Don't you want Scotland to be free?' Doran interrupted with a boldness that surprised even him.

Hume sighed and shot him a look that was all too familiar. It was how every adult and teacher in his life looked at people his age; like they just didn't understand yet how the world works. 'To be honest with you, lad, I don't care. Edward ruling…some nobleman fool like Bruce… They're all the same. This war, this fight for freedom, has destroyed the land I once called home. The people of the Borders have suffered more than any other. Our lands are the first to be hit by any oncoming or reclaiming force. Well, there are a fair few of us now who have finally said enough is enough. We are going to take matters into our own hands. Our allegiance is only to the people of the Borders. To our kin. Scottish, English – it doesn't matter. We will take from anyone to serve our purpose and *survive*.'

'And that includes us.'

Hume's eyes twinkled. 'Yes, lad. And based on your strange garments and your bonnie lass's weaponry, I believe we are having a very good start to our day. You can all leave with your lives, as long as you part with your possessions willingly.'

For a moment, Doran was glad the watch was lost in the future – better there than in the possession of this thief, where it could do real damage to the timeline.

The other two men stuffed their stubby fingers into Zander and Léonie's pockets. Doran could tell Léonie was calculating all the different ways she could slay the man poking around in her jacket. She glanced at him, giving a signal that he only partially understood, but her will was so strong that the message made it through.

'Shame too,' Hume mused. 'We were in Annandale, raiding, just the other day. No sign of any Bruce.'

'So, where is he?' Doran asked, making sure Hume was only looking at him.

'I may have heard rumours. I couldn't possibly say.'

Doran's eyes flitted to Léonie, who clearly shared the same thought. The man who had been searching her pulled out her device. He raised the sheet of glass to the sunlight, peering at it as though it were a precious gemstone. He was opening his mouth to call over to Hume when Léonie sprang into action.

In one movement, she grasped the handle of the crossbow attached to his belt, kicking his legs from under him. Like a chopped tree, the man fell, and Léonie yanked the crossbow, bringing it into her possession. She aimed it at the man holding Zander hostage and before he even had a chance to turn around, she fired, and the arrow sank into his back with a *thump*.

She dropped the crossbow and grabbed the Katana, which was now lying on the leaves. Becoming a fearsome executioner, she raised the sword above her head and plunged the blade into the man lying at her feet, ending him.

As she turned her attention to Hume, he also switched focus, turning his body away from Doran and pointing his crossbow at her.

Doran seized his chance. As Hume's finger began to squeeze the trigger, Doran kicked him hard in the back. He stumbled forward, thrown off balance, and Léonie punched him in the face. There was an almighty thud as Hume crumpled onto a pile of leaves, out cold.

Doran, Zander and Léonie all loomed over him. Léonie grinned. 'Thanks for the assist.'

'Why didn't you just use your powers?' Doran asked.

She gave a derisive snort. 'I don't need my powers to deal with the likes of them.'

'I think I'm in love,' Zander said. 'And also, still quite scared. It's all very confusing.'

Léonie sheathed her sword and inspected one of the dead bodies. 'Reivers, they must be,' she murmured to herself.

'What's a Reiver?' Zander asked.

'Depends on your perspective,' Léonie said. 'Some would call them bandits or raiders, but I don't think Mr Hume would see it that way. You heard his reasons. They operate in this area from around now until the seventeenth century.' She scanned the forest. 'They'll have horses. We can cover ground faster now.' She wandered back over to Hume. 'And this one can lead us to Robert the Bruce.'

At these words, Hume moaned as though prematurely woken from a dreamless sleep and Léonie knelt beside him. She roughly tugged his head up from the ground by his hair to whisper in his ear, 'I'm nobody's *bonnie lass*,' before letting go and allowing Hume's hairy head to bounce off the ground once again. Apparently satisfied that the non-consensual handling of her weapon had now been fully avenged, she rose and nodded to Doran and Zander. 'Get him up.'

23

THE FUTURE
KING OF SCOTS

Once Hume was back on his feet, Léonie announced that she
wanted a private word with him, so Doran and Zander found
themselves despatched to take care of the newly acquired horses.
They soon became aware that Hume was on the receiving end of
some more painful treatment.

Several agonised shrieks later, Léonie and Hume emerged
from the trees, he with a distant, disturbed look in his eye and
she with a destination – and the dead men's tunics, which she
flung at Doran and Zander; evidently their new disguise.

'Dumfries,' she said simply, and she mounted the large,
speckled grey horse Doran was holding. Rummaging around in
the leather bag attached to her saddle, she found some rope and
chucked it back to Zander, who tied Hume to the back of one

of the horses. Doran thought the Reiver might struggle or voice some form of protest but he remained meek. Whatever it was that Léonie had done to him, his broad frame seemed to have shrunk.

It had been a while since Doran had been on a horse, though every child in Linntean was given riding lessons as part of the primary school curriculum. As he mounted the muscular black stallion, he tried to remember the techniques he'd been taught all those years ago. His new mode of transport was a little reluctant at first but gradually yielded to his cajoling.

Zander was having a wonderful time. He had always been a confident rider, keeping up his lessons well into his teens. At Hume's refusal to answer when he had asked the horses' names, he had taken it upon himself to dub his brown and white steed 'Hamish'.

'Can you trap animals as well as people?' he called ahead to Doran and Léonie as the little party set off, Zander at the rear, and Hume plodding along behind him.

'No!' Léonie called back.

'Are you just saying that 'cause you don't want me to keep Hamish?'

There was no answer, so Doran chimed in. 'You're not keeping the horse.'

'You're becoming as boring as her,' Zander said, a little too loud, and he hid himself behind Hamish's mane. But once Léonie's gaze had left him, Doran heard Zander give the horse a hearty pat and whisper in its ear, 'Don't worry Hamish. You're part of the gang now.'

The riding party carried on towards Dumfries, which they would reach by sunset now that their four-legged friends were doing most of the hard work for them – apart from Hume, of course. Even the torture he had endured at the hands of Léonie seemed to trouble him less than being attached to Zander's horse. Zander delighted in annoying and provoking him throughout the long ride. Hume remained stony-faced and quiet, though clearly quietly brimming with wrath.

Léonie had moved further ahead and Doran gained on her until they were riding side by side. She ignored his presence for a while until he saw her brow furrow and she finally spoke. 'You want to know more.'

'Wouldn't you?'

She sighed and gathered herself, as if this conversation was going to require a great deal of energy. The horses filled the silence, pressing their hooves down on the grassy ground, completely in sync.

'I'm not sure what else I can tell you, other than what you already know.'

'That can't be all you know. Samael said you're my second-in-command. You must—'

Léonie interrupted with a scoff. 'I must know more about you?' she said. 'Yeah, well, you aren't exactly the most open of people.'

She turned away and Doran could tell he had struck a nerve. 'I just don't understand what makes me join the Eternalisium,' he said. 'Right now, I can't think of anything worse. And yet you say in just over a year I sign on the dotted line.'

'That's what the records say.'

'And what if I decide not to?'

Léonie yanked on her reins and the horse halted. Doran followed suit, though his horse gave a snort that sounded almost scornful. 'What do you mean?'

'What if I just…decide not to?'

She stared at him as if he had gone mad. 'You're the Magistair – you're Doran West. You can't just—'

'What if I don't want to be *Doran West?*' he said, bristling. 'What if I just want to live a normal life? Get a regular job, pay a mortgage I can't afford – all of it.'

'It doesn't work like that,' Léonie said, shaking her head, and Doran's cheeks burned. Yet another adult was treating him like an alien who had just landed on the planet. He was sixteen years old. He did have some idea of how the world worked.

'Why not?'

'Because like it or not, you *are* Doran West,' Léonie said, snapping as though he were a petulant child. 'Your destiny is a fixed point. You have to become the Magistair and change everything. Otherwise, who knows what will happen? Do you have any idea how many lives we've protected since you took over? How much good you've done? Like it or not, you matter, Doran. And I'm afraid there are too many people relying on you becoming the man you're supposed to be.'

'I didn't ask for this,' Doran said, the prickling in his cheeks spreading all over his face now. 'I'm just a kid from a tiny village. A kid whose mum is seven hundred years away with no idea what happened to her son. And as soon as we fix this mess I made, then you can be damn sure I'm going back to make sure she's OK.'

Léonie was once again staring at him as though unable to comprehend his existence. But he saw her pull herself together as she sat up straighter in the saddle. 'I will do everything I can to help you get out of this place and back to your own time. You and your friend shouldn't be here. But you have to understand that even if we succeed, one day soon you will have to leave your old life behind...' She glanced back at Zander, who was in an animated one-sided discussion with the despondent Hume. '...

Him and your mum.'

'Time can be rewritten; the future isn't here yet,' Doran said. *Right?* he added to himself.

'Not all things, not always,' Léonie said, and he noticed a sadness in her eyes. 'Some things just *have to be*, otherwise, the whole universe will crumble around us. Paradoxes, rips in time, end-of-the-world-level threats. That is what the Eternalisium does. We keep things the way they should be, changing events for the better only when we can.'

'How do you know? You killed two men back there. How do you know their deaths won't be like stepping on a butterfly and lead to the end of the world?'

'Travellers all have this kind of sixth sense,' Léonie said. 'It's something you learn to develop and grow. You get a sort of… *feeling* when things aren't right. No feeling means no negative consequences from your actions. Think of time like the ocean. If you throw a couple of sticks into the water, not much will change. Sure, there'll be ripples, but the water will remain basically untouched and reach the same destination it always would. The problem is when you change the flow completely or make waves. That's what you did in Jedburgh – created a wave that we now have to stop from reaching the shore.

Doran thought back to the odd sensation he had had in Jedburgh; how convinced he'd been that he and Zander had to get the message to Robert the Bruce. And on the rooftop in Florence, he had fixated on the handlebars and pedals. They had felt odd to him, like they didn't belong. Had this unknown ability kicked in then too? 'Nice explanation.'

'Thanks. It's yours,' Léonie said, her eyes lingering on him. 'Mastering that instinct isn't easy. Seers are the best at it.'

'Seers?'

'It's what we call those of us who can interpret time itself. Seers can intuitively know the right course of action and what should and should not be.'

So that explains Malloch, Doran thought. *He must be a Seer.*

'They're always a bit weird though – tend to stick with their own,' Léonie continued. 'Not the first on the dance floor at a party, if you catch my meaning.'

Doran did catch her meaning, and he remembered the odd group of people in cream-coloured robes who had been sitting in a meditative circle. 'What are the other variations?'

'There are five disciplines of study,' Léonie said. 'Winders, like me. Stoppers, Rushers, Trappers and Seers.'

Doran could fill in the blanks for four of the five. 'What are Rushers?'

'Time accelerators,' Léonie said, and her face contorted as though an unpleasant smell had wafted into her nostrils. 'Essentially the opposite of a Winder. They can do many things, but most of the time they use their powers to show off and make it look like they've got super-speed.'

It was at this moment that Zander caught up with them, still chattering away in his one-sided conversation with Hume. Doran smiled to himself: Zander would definitely be a Rusher if he were a Traveller.

Hume poked his ashen face out from behind the rear end of Zander's horse. 'For the love of God, could one of you please tie me to the back of a different horse?'

Doran and Léonie both ignored his pleas and resumed their ride, trotting off in front again and leaving Zander sitting upon Hamish as though there were no place he would rather be.

'Now, where was I?' Doran heard him ponder to himself. 'Ah yes, now I still think when all this is done, that I'll have a chance with Georgia Mackay. I feel older from this whole experience – more mature, you know?'

The sun had begun to set when their destination came within sight. Its reddish light painted Dumfries and its narrow streets as though they were awash with blood. The riding party brought its horses to a stop on a ridge overlooking the town. Léonie glared back at Hume, whose legs were now as wobbly as those of a newborn fawn. He swayed perilously, clinging onto the rope for support.

'You say Bruce is in this town?'

'Yes,' Hume said with a wheeze. 'In the tavern. The locals told us he's not left it for days.'

'That's where we start then,' Léonie said to the boys before rounding her horse on Hume. 'If your information is correct then we will maybe, just maybe, let you be on your way. But if you are lying and taking us in completely the wrong direction so your brethren can ambush us, then mark my words, you'll think what I did to you in the woods was a kindness.'

'You have my word. I have no kin here.'

'Let's hope for the sake of your fingernails you're telling the truth.'

Doran and Zander glanced at each other. Doran was not sure if he trusted Léonie yet. Her methods seemed unduly harsh. Though she was under his future self's command, wasn't she? Didn't that make her methods *his*? He shuddered at the thought, as the horses trotted on down the hill and into Dumfries.

The first thing Doran noticed was the smell. The putrid stench of animal manure offended his nostrils and left a foul taste in the mouth. The streets were full of drunken men staggering along, yelling incoherently. Doran thought back to

London and the surprisingly similar sights he had seen there. The crowds of people seemed to sway in the chilly wind as they shambled along. Even in seven hundred years, it appeared some things never changed.

When they found the tavern where Bruce was reputed to be, they dismounted and tied their horses to the wooden post outside. Zander gave Hamish an affectionate rub and untied Hume. As he did so, the Reiver's body suddenly drooped and Zander tried to pull him upright.

'Watch him,' Léonie called. But it was too late.

Hume, using the last of his strength, had grabbed Zander, throwing a brawny arm around his neck.

Léonie reached for her sword, but Hume gave her a warning look. 'Best not, lassie,' he said. 'Not unless you think you can cut me down before I snap the lad's neck?'

Doran held up his hand to Léonie. She stared at it, transfixed for a moment, and her face and hair once again became a similar shade. Her hand slid off the hilt of her blade.

'That's better,' growled Hume. 'Now, I've given you what you wanted. It's time I be on my way.'

Doran shrugged. 'Feel free. Just let him go and you can leave.'

'I don't think so,' Hume said, his eyes flitting to Léonie. 'The moment I release my grip she will slice me up like mutton. No, I think I will be taking the lad with me – just to ensure my safety, mind.'

Hume hauled Zander backwards, his eyes daring either Doran or Léonie to try anything.

Doran realised he urgently needed to act.

He was about to raise his hand to freeze time when a group of horsemen came charging down the road, their English flag flapping wildly in the wind. *It can't be*, Doran thought. *He can't have found us.* But his fears were short-lived. As soon as the soldiers came into view, it was clear he didn't recognise any of them. None were part of the troop under Sir Richard West's command.

Léonie had also spotted the oncoming force. She inspected Doran's tunic like a fussing mother. 'Flip your badge around,' she whispered in his ear.

It was an odd request, but he complied. His hand drifted to the badge on his tunic and he found that it could be turned over; there was a completely different family crest embroidered on the reverse side.

After changing his own, he tried to convey the same message visually to Zander, who, once he realised what was afoot, with the sleight of hand of a magician, brushed his badge and flipped it over so it once again matched Doran's.

'Why did we do that?' Doran murmured to Léonie.

'Just trust me,' Léonie said. 'Pretend you're loyal to the English.'

'What?'

'Just do it.'

'What is this scene before me?' the lead soldier cried out as the English troop approached.

'We were transporting a prisoner, my lord,' Doran replied, in what may have been the worst English accent ever spoken.

Zander, despite the situation, nearly choked attempting to suppress a laugh before stepping in to help their cause. 'Help me, my lord. He has overpowered me,' he called to the soldiers, in a voice that was not only distinctly southern English but also sounded very much era-appropriate.

The English turned their weapons towards Hume, who backed away from them, using Zander as a shield.

'Release him!' the lead soldier shouted.

Hume ignored him, continuing to haul Zander backwards. He was so focused on the English soldiers that he didn't realise he was now beside the hind legs of Hamish. At his close approach, the horse suddenly whinnied and kicked out hard, striking him in the ribs.

A sharp *crack* filled the air and the Reiver cried out as his body contorted. He crumpled to the ground, dragging Zander with him.

The soldiers leapt from their horses, drawing their swords. Zander elbowed Hume in what appeared to be a homage to Hamish as he broke free from the man's grasp and moved over to stand by Doran and Léonie. The Reiver was writhing on the ground, clutching his side, as five longswords were pointed at his face.

'That, my lord, is the notorious Reiver, Gordon Hume,' Doran said, half giving up on the accent now. 'We caught him raiding a nearby town and have been trying to bring him before our king – King Edward's – men. We would see justice done.'

Doran could tell Zander was giving him an approving nod at his improvisational skills, but he ignored him, keeping his eyes on the lead soldier.

The soldier peered at their tunics for a moment and then nodded. 'Very well. My deepest thanks to you both,' he said, ignoring Léonie. 'We have been after this one for a long time,' he added, looking down at Hume. 'For your troubles.' The soldier unclipped a small money pouch from his belt and threw it in their direction.

The trio watched as Hume was led off, stumbling after the English soldiers.

'Well…we gave him another horse,' Léonie said, with the ghost of a smirk.

'Was that a joke?' Zander asked her, before giving Doran's arm a series of taps. 'I think that was a joke.'

Léonie rolled her eyes and strolled towards the tavern.

'She's starting to like me,' Zander said, puffing out his chest.

'Yes, you'll be married within the week. Come on.'

Doran scooped up the small bag of coins and walked towards the tavern, hearing Zander hobble back to Hamish and give the horse a grateful pat. 'Well done, boy.'

Inside the tavern, they saw Léonie talking to what Doran imagined must be the fourteenth-century equivalent of a bartender.

He watched as the man pointed across the room at a broad-shouldered man slumped over his tankard, yet making the odd slurred remark to the apparent amusement of his fellows, whose guffaws were hearty.

Was *this* really Robert the Bruce? Was this the man who would set Scotland on the path to freedom? He looked more like a tramp than a future king, with his unkempt mane of reddish-brown hair and matching wild beard.

Doran watched Léonie's eyes lock onto her target as she began to march towards him. He and Zander scurried forwards, intercepting her. 'What's the plan here, She-Hulk?' asked Zander. 'Sorry,' he added, when he saw Léonie's glare. 'I forgot – you probably have no idea who that is.'

Léonie tutted. 'I know who that is. We still have superhero films in the future.'

'Really?' Zander said, fascinated. 'What Phase are they in now? Did Iron-Man ever come back?' He was about to continue when Doran threw him a sharp look. 'Sorry, yes; bigger picture.'

'How does this usually work, though?' Doran asked Léonie. Her eyes were still locked onto Robert, who was finishing the contents of his tankard as though expecting to find a prize at the bottom.

'There's not a handbook if that's what you mean,' she said. 'You're trained to use your gut.'

Doran raised an eyebrow. 'And does that mean always charging in all guns blazing?'

Léonie grimaced at him. 'Ugh, you sound just like…well, just like *you*.'

Zander looked at the two of them. 'What does that mean?'

'Nothing,' Doran and Léonie said in unison.

'Surely this requires a well-thought-out approach,' Doran continued.

Léonie's lips were pursed so tight they had started to lose their colour. 'And I suppose you have a plan?'

'We have to get him on his own,' Doran said, staring at the crowd of men gathered around Robert, still hanging on his every word.

'I can take care of that,' Léonie said.

'He has to trust us. He won't do that if you go slicing and dicing all his drinking buddies.'

'Can we just get on with what you want to do so we can all go home?' Léonie said, her tone venomous.

Doran was perplexed by her sudden change in attitude. What had he said to make her like that? He turned his attention to the job in hand, looking back towards Robert the Bruce. And his companions. They were passing small pebbles around to one another, having placed a stack of gold coins in the middle of the table. An idea came to him. 'I say we go over there and place a couple of bets,' he said, suddenly confident and assured as he marched towards the table.

'Good evening,' he announced to Robert and the others. As

one, they stared at him, the shock of their harsh gaze momentarily striking him dumb. 'Do you have room for one more player?'

They all laughed, and Robert spoke, his voice strong and commanding despite his sozzled state. 'Come back when you have some hair on your chest, lad.'

The men chortled again, some pounding their tankards on the table in the general hilarity. Doran simply smiled, pulled out the small bag of coins given to him by the English soldiers and threw it onto the table with a thud. The bag spilt, revealing some of the gold within.

'Will that put some hair on my chest?'

Robert and his men stared at the bag of gold then back at Doran as though their coexistence was completely absurd. 'Where did you get that amount of coin?' Robert asked.

Doran's eyes twinkled. 'From the last bunch of balding, grey-haired men who were brave enough to let me play.'

There was a moment of heavy silence. Doran feared he might have gone too far. Then, all at once, the men erupted with laughter again.

Robert roared and slapped the table with such force Doran was afraid the tankards might tip over. 'I like this lad. Come on then; sit, sit; you can join after this game.'

Doran perched himself on a seat on the edge of the table. The man beside him, who was still chuckling, gave him a toothless grin and a hearty slap on the back with a large, hairy hand. Doran felt the wind leave him for a moment but tried his best not to show it.

The game itself seemed relatively simple. It only took Doran two rounds to work out how to play. Each man was given eight pebbles. They would put one gold coin in the centre of the table as a wager. The pebbles were shielded by the back of one hand

and the men covered a chosen number with their free hand. After around ten seconds, the men would drag the free hand towards them, keeping everything hidden. Each man would reveal the content of their shielding hand one by one. The man who had the most pebbles would win, provided no other player shared that number. For example, in the first round Doran watched, two men revealed they had seven pebbles, meaning that another man, who had chosen five, took that round's winnings.

After the third round, Doran was allowed to play, and was handed eight small shiny pebbles. He placed them neatly in a row in front of him, causing some of the men to titter with laughter again.

Doran placed the first gold coin from his sack in the middle of the table, along with the other coins in the game. The players all began shielding and taking away pebbles while casting suspicious looks around the table. Doran quickly pretended to choose his pebbles and as soon as he could see that all the other players had done the same, he closed his eyes, reaching out in his mind, trying to picture what he had seen when he and Zander had been trapped in the cellar. If he was to be *Doran West*, he had better start acting the part. He had to command time.

STOP. Doran opened his eyes tentatively. The scene was frozen, the men mid-way through chortling or taking a drink. He stood and moved around the table, quickly lifting each man's hand to check their pebbles. Three of the men had picked five. Two had picked six. Robert had picked seven and the other two, four. No one had gone for the full eight. Doran returned to his seat, pulled his hand back with nothing underneath it and then closed his eyes again, focusing.

START. The stillness ceased and Doran opened his eyes. Each player in turn then wagered more coins. Doran did his best to look nonchalant.

When all were done, they revealed their hands. The men groaned or laughed at one another for picking an identical number. Gradually they realised who had won. A few glowered at him while others let out a congratulatory yell at his apparent beginners' luck. Robert was one of these people, chuckling to himself and taking a swig from his tankard.

Playing in this less-than-honest way, Doran steadily won more and more of the men's gold. He took care to ensure that Robert also won a few rounds, even if he looked a little surprised when the number of pebbles under his hand wasn't what he had originally put there. Gradually, players began to drop out of the game, some in good spirits, others less so. Eventually, only Robert and Doran remained facing each other. A crowd of onlookers had gathered to watch the unfolding spectacle, Zander and Léonie among them.

As Doran slowly amassed the remainder of Robert's coins, he grew less amiable. He was trying to maintain a cool façade, but Doran could see that he was seething. Finally, Robert threw in the last of his gold. Doran also threw in all of his coins. Robert raised an eyebrow at him.

'What are you doing, lad?' he asked. 'I cannot match you.'

Doran sat back and shrugged, 'Why don't you also wager your horse and armour?'

Robert scoffed. 'My horse is a stallion bred for war. My armour is the finest in the land. Even your large amount of coin will not cover that.'

'Then I will also throw in our horses and provisions,' Doran said, refusing to look at Zander, whom he knew was horrified.

Robert ogled him for a moment then grinned. He slammed the table with his fist. 'Aye! You're on!' he said in his booming voice and gave a throaty chuckle. The spectators cheered.

In the merriment, Doran flashed a quick look to Léonie and Zander, silently asking them to trust him. He took his hand away, revealing five pebbles. Robert stared at it, then let out a triumphant yell, showing he had seven. The crowd joined him and Robert stood, outstretching a hand to Doran and nearly lifting him off his feet.

'Best man I have ever played,' Robert called to everyone, embracing Doran and giving him a hearty thump on the back. Using both forearms, he dragged the pile of gleaming coins towards him.

As the crowd continued to chatter, Doran took his chance. 'Shall we go and inspect your winnings?'

Robert seemed so jubilant that he saw nothing suspicious about Doran's suggestion. He nodded, saying, 'Aye!', then threw a pile of coins at the owner of the tavern, inviting everyone to get a fresh drink.

Finally they went outside to find the horses. Hamish was delighted to see Zander again, greeting him like an overgrown Labrador.

'Fine beasts you've got here, lad,' Robert said, patting the black stallion Doran had been riding. 'I almost feel bad about taking them from you.'

'About that,' Doran began before falling to his knees and looking up at Robert. He felt this was the only way a future king would take him seriously. 'My lord, I have brought you out here under false pretences. We are here to deliver a message to you. A sensitive message that we couldn't pass on in public.'

Robert's eyes darted to each of them, as if expecting someone to make an attempt on his life. No attack came and he fixed his gaze on Doran. When he spoke, his voice seemed strained, a far cry from the commanding roar he had displayed in the tavern. 'On your feet, lad,' he said. 'And there'll be no need for titles. I have no lands any more. The Comyns and Edward saw to that.'

He made a move to return to the safety of the tavern but Léonie and, more warily, Zander stepped in front of him. 'Just listen. Please just listen to what I have to say,' Doran said.

Robert ignored him, still staring at those who were blocking his path. 'I have no desire to fight a woman or a laddie who looks like he's never held a sword in his life. Step aside the both of you.'

'Yeah? You wouldn't last five seconds with *this* woman,' Léonie said, stepping forwards and getting so close to Robert's face that their noses almost touched.

Doran rose to his feet. 'Léonie, that's enough,' he said, emulating Robert.

She didn't take her eyes off Robert but acknowledged she had heard him. 'Yes, *Magistair*.'

Her tone and her choice of title stung Doran. He had no idea what had caused the sudden animosity between them. She retreated to Zander's side and Doran addressed Robert again. 'We have information that could turn the war back in our favour.'

'War? There is no *war*. We lost. It is done.'

'It doesn't have to be,' Doran said, moving closer. 'Scotland can still be free.'

Robert waved a hand. 'You are young and foolhardy, clinging to hope. I fought Edward last time and look what it cost me. I have nothing now. No lands, no titles. I was married to a woman whose family are allied with Edward.'

'But you're still alive,' Doran said. 'You can still lead the people to victory.'

Robert shook his head. 'Wallace was the one they wanted. He was the fire of this rebellion.'

'Wallace is gone,' Doran said, with a finality that appeared to startle Robert. 'Scotland needs a new man to follow. And believe me, Robert the Bruce, you are that man.'

'How can you know that?'

Doran bit his lip. 'Because I believe in you,' he said. 'I believe in Robert the Bruce.'

Robert appeared stunned into silence. He stared at Doran, frowning then, uttering a deep sigh, he sat down on a tree stump, refusing to look at any of them. 'Aye, well, I think you might be the only one… I am done trying.'

'Where's a spider when you need one?' Zander muttered.

'What was that?' Robert asked, glancing at him with a mystified expression.

'Nothing,' Zander answered quickly.

Doran walked forwards and knelt in front of Robert. He looked into his eyes and for a moment he no longer saw the great Robert the Bruce; the man from the history books; the man whose statue was displayed on the cover of every tourist magazine and whose name was synonymous with the country of Scotland itself. Before him was simply a human being who had lost his faith and sense of purpose. He wasn't the man he was meant to be yet and Doran felt an overwhelming desire to help him get there.

'Listen to me very carefully, Robert,' he said.

Robert looked at him as though hearing him for the first time. Despite all the waiving of titles, it was clearly odd for someone to call him solely by his first name. 'Edward is dying. A servant boy in his camp by the name of Finlay of clan Robertson escaped to try to get this message to you. He was prepared to die for this message, for you – and he did. And I am certain others in this country would do the same. Like it or not, Robert, you have a destiny ahead of you. You are the man who is going to unite this country once more and drive the English forces from it. Edward will be gone soon and his son will take over. You can beat him, Robert. You *will* beat him. You will go down in history as the greatest and most renowned King that Scotland will ever know. But you need to embrace who you really are.'

Doran gave a brief sideways glance to Léonie, whose face had softened.

Robert had fallen silent. He took a few slow breaths, not taking his eyes off Doran, apparently trying to feel out whether his intentions were true. The silence seemed to bind the two of them and their eyes remained locked onto each other until a song cut suddenly through the cold air.

'O Flower of Scotland,
When will we see,
Your like again,
That fought and died for,
Your wee bit Hill and Glen,
And stood against him,
'Gainst Who
Proud Edward's army,
W—'

'Zander!' Doran interrupted, horrified.

Zander gaped as though the song had possessed him and he was unaware he had become so carried away. Still compelled to finish, he continued, but meekly and under his breath.

'And sent him homeward,
Tae think again…'

As the song died, the silence returned. Léonie's hand was beginning to drift towards Zander's throat when there came a sniff. Robert the Bruce was sitting with his head in his hands. 'That...' he began, choking on his words, '...that was the most beautiful thing I have ever heard. Did you write that, lad?'

'No, I think it was a guy called Roy—' Zander said without thinking. Léonie elbowed him hard in his ribs.

'Well, you tell this Roy he has just written the words to this rebellion,' Robert said, rising to his feet once more. 'We will stand against him and send him homeward!'

Doran, Léonie and Zander gave these words a rousing cheer, though Léonie was simultaneously miming a finger slicing her throat for Zander to see.

'The rebellion begins anew tonight!' Robert roared, marching back towards the tavern. After a few steps, he paused, turning back to the three youths. 'Will you join me?'

'We've done our part, Robert; now you do yours. It's time for us to go home,' Doran said.

'I wish you safe travels then,' Robert replied, bowing ever so slightly. 'I will never forget what you've done for me tonight. Scotland will never forget it either.'

And with that he entered the tavern, the future king of Scotland vanishing from sight.

As soon as they were alone, Doran and Léonie turned on Zander, who was unable to keep the proud smile from his face.

'What?' he asked.

24

THE MOON OF THE MOOR

Doran, Zander and Léonie sat huddled around a fire on the outskirts of Dumfries. They had found a small clearing, where they had set up camp. Or rather, Léonie had set up camp while the two boys stood and watched.

It hadn't taken long for Doran to forgive Zander. The slightest of smirks from his friend and the boys were rolling around with laughter on the grass, clutching their stomachs. Léonie had folded her arms in her teacherly manner, determined to be unimpressed. Yet Doran could have sworn he saw the corners of her mouth twitch.

'You two certainly seem pleased with yourselves.'

'We just saved Scotland,' Doran said, the hysterics combined with the sense of accomplishment making him light-headed. It was certainly the happiest he had felt since the whole adventure had begun.

'With style,' Zander chimed in.

'May I remind you both that we still have another mess to clear up,' Léonie said. 'We still need to get back to the future and retrieve the watch. So don't celebrate just yet.'

It was clear to Doran that she was fighting the urge to enjoy the moment with them. 'Come on, bask in the glory, will you?'

She stared, seemingly horrified by the mere suggestion. 'I don't get it,' she muttered to herself. 'I just don't get how you can be the same person.'

'What is she talking about?' Zander asked, his giggles subsiding.

Doran groaned. 'In the future I become some humourless, hardnosed idiot.' Registering the look of alarm on Léonie's face, he explained, 'He's my best friend; I'm not keeping this from him. If I have to do this you can be damn sure I'm not doing it without him.'

Zander looked confused. 'Can either of you explain what's going on?'

Doran bowed his head to Léonie but she was unmoved by his chivalry. 'Fine,' she said through gritted teeth. 'I come from a secret society known as the Eternalisium. Our job is to fight anomalies in time and keep the world safe. Doran, in the future, is our leader.'

'And I'm a bit of a git apparently,' Doran added.

'It's not easy being in charge,' Léonie began, though it seemed like a pre-programmed response. 'But yeah, you can be sometimes,' she said, her cheeks turning pink.

'So why are you here?' Zander asked her.

'I've disappeared in the future and she was trying to investigate,' Doran said.

'Right, of course; makes complete sense,' Zander said. 'So...

what are you going to do?'

'I've made my decision,' Doran said. 'You were right,' he added to Léonie. 'I can't run from who I am any more than Robert could. But I can change what kind of Magistair I become. You have my word; I will do everything I can to be better than the Doran you know.'

She blinked; her expression frozen. Doran thought for a moment that she might even cry, which struck him as the most dumbfounding of all the bizarre things to have happened to him on their adventures thus far.

'I need a walk,' Léonie announced, as she started to trudge away towards the open moor.

Zander watched her go. 'What's with her?'

Doran didn't answer. Suddenly compelled to follow her, he jumped up and set off after her.

'I'll just stay here then, shall I?' Zander called after him.

Doran caught up with Léonie at the top of a small hill in what was predominantly a flat stretch of land. It went on for as far as the eye could see, the moonlight giving the ground a blue-green hue. Doran thought of the loch back home, which he had so wished never to see again barely a week ago. What he wouldn't give now to look upon it – even for a second.

Léonie was staring up at the moon as though she were in deep conversation with it. Doran stood quietly beside her, waiting patiently for her reverie to end.

'It's one of the few things that's always there, no matter where you go,' she said, the moon's image reflecting in her pupils. 'You know you used that fact to help me when I first came to the Eternalisium. I was terrible at grounding myself. I'd always end up in some random place, miles away from the target location. One time I jumped to the edge of Mount Etna! It got so bad that

I became terrified ever to travel again. But one night you took me to a place not unlike this, actually, and told me to stare up at the moon. You said to focus on where it was in the sky and focus on nothing else but that image in my mind. That the moon was a constant and could not change. I should feel safe underneath it and let it guide me. I travelled and ended up two feet from where I'd just been standing.'

Léonie finally turned to face Doran, a sad smile on her face. 'You're not all bad you know,' she said, wiping away a tear. 'You're just…' The rest of the sentence seemed impossible to speak and she tittered. But there was no trace of happiness in the sound. 'Well, that's just it, isn't it? I don't know.'

As she made to leave, Doran touched her arm. His fingers barely brushed against the leather of her jacket but she stopped and stared at his hand, transfixed.

'I am going to try to be better.'

Léonie gave another sad smile and her face sagged as if she hadn't slept for days. 'Tonight you displayed the qualities of the Doran West I know,' she said. 'The good *and* the bad. Perhaps that's why I was so angry with you. I could see him in you for the first time. So maybe you will – maybe you will be better… Or maybe the you I know also made that same vow all those years ago.'

His hand slipped from her arm as she strode away once more. 'Find your anchor,' she said after a few steps. 'It's the only way we're all going to get out of here.'

And with that she left, leaving Doran alone under the cool gaze of the moon.

Doran stood motionless on the same hilltop for at least half an hour, reflecting on Léonie's words. He had seen enough time-travel movies to understand the logic in what she had told him. It all depended on which theory of the universe he subscribed to. Did he have the control to change his fate, the free will to make his own choices? Or was time itself the one in control? Was everything preordained and he simply had the illusion of control? Was he destined, no matter what he did, to become the distant, lonesome man of Léonie's present?

That can't be true, he told himself. He alone would decide what kind of man he would be. And perhaps with Léonie's presence, time had already changed. She had said it herself; she was worried that she had damaged things by meeting him at this point in his life. Maybe the flow of the river Léonie had talked about was already altered. He had to believe that.

Feeling a little more settled in himself, he became more aware of his surroundings. The stillness and the deep silence of the night around him were intense. Gradually they penetrated his inner realm, bringing him to a state of calm stillness in which he began to see the bigger picture with a little more clarity. He was finally able to start to appreciate his astonishing new reality. The whole impossible adventure had felt like a dream so far, as he had hopped from one crisis to the next. Now the reality of it all was just beginning to sink in, but he was still no clearer about why he had been sent on this path.

The identity of the man who had given him the fob watch plagued his mind. Was *he* Doran's father? And if he wasn't, then who was he? Why had he chosen him?

Doran elected not to journey too far down that road. He knew its destination would bring hope, which created the possibility of pain. For now, he needed to focus on getting himself and Zander out of the fourteenth century, finding the watch and returning to their own time. The stabilisers were off. It was time for him to find his anchor.

As he continued to gaze at the moon, a thought struck him. Could it be that his future self had imparted that wisdom about the moon to Léonie because it was what had worked for him? It was worth a try. He committed the image of the moon in the sky to his memory and closed his eyes. He planned to move only to the other side of the hilltop. Picturing the place in his mind, he imagined himself looking up at the moon in that spot and felt his body being whisked away.

He landed heavily, crashing somewhat to the ground, but at least perhaps he had landed in the right place and time this time?

It was still night-time, though it seemed a little earlier than before. He was also nowhere near the hilltop he had started from, which he could now see in the distance. Wearily and cursing out his frustration along the way, he trudged back to where he had started.

As he drew near, he saw a figure standing on the hilltop. He was about to run back to the camp to warn the others when his jaw dropped in recognition of the figure. It was *him*. He could see himself standing on the hilltop, staring up at the moonlit sky.

It was an odd sensation, being in two places at once. It didn't quite feel real, as if he were having some kind of lucid dream.

A familiar ringing sound cut the air. It was a noise he hadn't heard since the night in the woods. He clasped his head and sank to his knees, ready to cry out in anguish. But, as quickly as it had come, the pain vanished. When he looked up his other self had gone.

His faculties returned to normal and the headache he had been feeling eased off as he rubbed his forehead. As he rubbed, realisation slowly dawned on him. If that sensation happened when the same Traveller was in two places at the same point in time, then that could mean…

He walked back towards the campsite, engaged in his reflections. As he drew near, the sound of voices interrupted his train of thought. Curious, he moved soundlessly towards them, keeping to the cover of the surrounding trees.

After a few moments, he saw Léonie, back at the campsite, with Zander sitting across from her, staring intently at her.

'You all right?' he heard Zander say.

'Fine,' Léonie answered.

'You seem it.'

Léonie glared at him but then seemed to soften, saying, 'You wouldn't understand.'

'Try me.'

'Why? So you can make some dumb joke?'

'I'm only allowed one?' Zander asked with a smirk.

Léonie started to head towards the forest and Doran tucked himself tighter in behind his tree.

'You're right. I'm sorry,' Zander said, and Léonie froze, apparently shocked by the apology. Zander gave her a kind smile. 'I make jokes. It helps. Always has. We all have our fronts. You have your whole badass thing going on. Not letting anyone get close. I get that.'

Léonie still seemed unable to move. She was staring at Zander as though she had never seen him before. 'I don't know what you mean.'

'Look, my mum walked out on me and my dad when I was eight. My dad then decided the best course of action was to shut down and try to drink his body weight in whisky every night. I started playing up at school a bit, trying to make everyone laugh. I don't know – maybe I was trying to get his attention. Never worked of course.' He paused, giving Léonie a knowing look. 'I'm not stupid. I see the way you look at him. It's the same way I look at my dad.'

'He's not my father,' Léonie said, her words cutting through the air with such force she may as well have swung her Katana.

'No…no of course he's not,' Zander said. 'All I'm saying is I understand what having an absentee dad is like. Doran may not be your father but he must have been pretty damn close.'

Léonie finally seemed to find her feet and glided across to a small mound of grass near Zander. She perched there, staring at him with a hint of suspicion. 'Why do you care?'

'Shouldn't I?'

'You don't know me.'

Zander smiled. 'I'd like to. If you let me. Would it be so wrong for us to become friends?'

'Goes against every instinct in my body.'

'Now who's the one making jokes?'

The tiniest laugh escaped Léonie's lips. She gave Zander one last searching look as if to see if his intentions were true and let out a sigh. 'I never knew my dad. My mum didn't speak about him much and when she did it was usually followed by a swear word. I had no idea about the Eternalisium or my powers until I was fifteen. That's when…that's when Doran turned up on my doorstep. And suddenly everything seemed to make sense. Why I'd always felt a little different. He made me feel just that bit less…'

'Alone…' Zander and Léonie said together.

Zander's eyes twinkled. 'Of all the things I've heard about this almighty leader of yours tonight; that's the first story where him being Doran makes sense. At eight he did the same thing for me. It's who he is.'

'I thought so,' Léonie murmured. 'So why did he leave?'

'I don't know. But we can help you find out. If you let us.'

Léonie bit her lip and glanced up at the night sky for a moment. 'You know, this is the longest I've gone without wanting to stab you.'

'A new personal best. Fantastic,' Zander said. 'Does this mean we are in fact friends now?'

'Must we?'

'I'm afraid so.'

Léonie beamed at him. It completely transformed her face, and for a moment Doran caught a glimpse of the human being hiding behind the blade. 'You know, Doran was right about you,' she said. 'You're the most annoying individual I've ever met, but you're a good person. I could use a friend like that.'

'What did Doran say exactly?'

'I'm paraphrasing,' Léonie said with a grin. 'You mean a great deal to him.'

Zander seemed to grow a few inches, pulling his shoulders back. 'He means a great deal to me too. So you also have my word that as long as I'm around he won't forget about that kid who helped a sad boy miss his mum a little less.'

Doran wiped away a hot prickle in his eyes with his sleeve and took a step back from the tree. Trying to make it look as if he'd just arrived, he emerged from his hiding place. He didn't fancy telling either of them that he'd overheard their conversation.

Léonie greeted him: 'You had any epiphanies yet?'

Doran stared at her for a moment, unsure how to respond. 'Getting there,' he said, as evenly as he could.

'Good,' Léonie said. 'Now, I'm going to jump and get us some food. Some *proper* food. We may be stuck here but I refuse to eat food from a time before toilets. Doran, you keep practising. I'll be back in a flash.'

She disappeared and the gust of air nearly knocked Doran off balance. He steadied himself and stared at the space she had been standing in.

Zander called Hamish and the steed came trotting over. As the horse nestled its face into his side, Zander noticed Doran's silence. 'What's up with you?'

'Nothing,' Doran said, a little too quickly.

'You sure?'

'Yeah,' Doran said. 'Listen, while she's away I need to tell you something – and this may sound mental—'

'I think I'm acclimatised but do go on.'

'When I was practising on that moor over there, I saw myself.'

'You what?'

'I tried to jump but I ended up travelling back to a little after Léonie left me up on the hill. And when I saw myself, I felt like my head was going to explode, just like I did when that man in the woods gave me the fob watch.'

For a moment it seemed like Zander's face was on some kind of delay, until his eyes widened. 'You don't mean—'

'Yup,' Doran said. 'What if the man who gave me the watch was *me*? The me that Léonie knows, the one who disappeared. She told me that the day before future me vanished he was rambling about the watch being the key. What if that's what he – I – meant? That I needed to go back and give myself the watch.'

'B-but,' Zander said, his face ashen. 'But he…*died*,' he said, the final word like a horrid secret.

'Maybe,' Doran said, though his methodical tone did not match the twisting knot in his stomach. 'But we never found the body. We don't actually know what happened.'

'Still,' Zander said, now looking like he was about to be sick. 'If it is your destiny to become this "Magibear" or whatever, then one day you could be that man.'

Doran gulped. It was an odd sensation. Although they were potentially talking about him it didn't feel that way. It was more as if they were talking about a stranger; as though what they were discussing had happened to someone else. But if the man who had given him the fob watch was indeed a future version of himself, then did that mean that night in the forest was not just in his past, but also his future?

'Yeah,' Doran said, shuddering. 'And if I didn't meet my sticky end that night, what happened to me? Where did I go? And why did I give myself the watch in the first place?'

'I don't know, mate,' Zander said. 'But we're going to find out. Should we tell Léonie?'

'Not until we're sure. I don't want to get her hopes up.'

Both boys let out a yelp as Léonie reappeared with a flash beside them. She surveyed them both as she dumped a large rucksack and three sleeping bags onto the grass. 'All right?'

'Yeah, great,' Zander said, taking a shaky breath. 'I think you frightened Hamish though.'

The horse let out a snort.

'Uh-huh,' Léonie said, smirking. She emptied the rucksack to reveal treats, only some of which Doran recognised, and sandwiches that looked freshly made. She unclipped something from the bottom of the bag and threw it at Zander. The small projectile bounced off his face and landed at his feet.

'There's your pillow,' she said.

Zander's face shone, totally unconcerned by the blow. 'I think that sense of humour is coming along nicely.'

Doran feigned a small chuckle but his heart wasn't in it as the trio tucked into their futuristic feast. Every so often, he would chance a glance at Léonie and his mind drifted back to the conversation he had overheard. Despite what she had said, was his future self really the closest thing she had known to a father? The idea seemed so foreign to him. He couldn't even begin to imagine being a dad to anyone. He didn't exactly have a model to base his brand of fatherhood on.

Maybe that's the point, he thought. Whatever relationship he and Léonie might have in the future, it was certainly complex. From Léonie's description of the Magistair, he didn't exactly sound like dad of the year. But he had his mum's example to follow. How could he have strayed so far from what had made her such a good parent? At this point, Doran realised just how bizarre his train of thought was becoming and promptly excused himself, heading for his sleeping bag.

All his complex questions about his future churned away in his mind late into the night, keeping him awake until his body just couldn't delay sleep any longer.

25

THE COMMON

Bursts of electric-green light flashed around the lobby of the mansion. Like a frenetically timed lights display, members of the Eternalisium arrived in clusters and trickles and bustled their way into the grand lecture theatre.

The raked circular space was divided into five adjoining pods. At the front of each pod was the embossed symbol of one of the five disciplines. Those entering in groups split from one another, as they climbed the steps to sit where they belonged. Those already seated surveyed the room expectantly.

Ianto hovered by the entrance, scanning every face that entered. Holborn, Davies, even Oakland. They were all present. Every fully qualified member of the Society had turned up to hear what Tobias had to say.

Across the theatre from Ianto was a small room, usually used as a holding area by the speaker, or for a lecturer to make a swift exit and avoid any troublesome questions. Ianto imagined Tobias would probably use this room to make a dramatic entrance. He decided to make a detour on the way to his seat.

Sure enough, when he entered the room, Tobias was there, staring up at the portrait of an older man with a mighty moustache.

'It seems like a lifetime ago that he roamed these halls,' Tobias murmured.

For a moment Ianto was unsure whether Tobias was talking to him or to himself but the doctor swivelled round to face him, revealing a self-satisfied smile.

'Indeed,' Ianto said. Tobias Blue was the only man he knew who could make small talk unnerving. 'I was just a student when he died.'

'As was I,' Tobias said. 'I only met him once. Nearing one hundred years old but he still had an air of...*power* about him. The last Magistair...'

'Until now.'

Tobias' lips stretched again into a thin smile. 'What can I do for you, Professor Everie?'

'You called a Common?'

'I did.'

'May I ask why?'

Tobias arched an eyebrow, quite amused. 'As the leader of this Society—'

'Acting leader,' Ianto said before he could stop himself. He drew breath, ready for an attack.

It didn't come. In fact, Tobias seemed unusually calm, an aura of triumph surrounding him. 'Braver having seen your saviour are we?'

Ianto bit his tongue.

'I imagine the news I'm about to share with the rest of the Common will come as quite a shock to you,' Tobias said. He paused to moisten his lips, apparently wishing to savour the next sentence as it left his mouth. 'So, I'd like you to hear it from me first. The boy has gone.'

Ianto stared. 'What?'

'Young Doran wasn't quite as inexperienced as we expected. Well, he is a West after all. He surprised Malloch and Crum and escaped. The Seers are now unable to locate him.'

'I don't understand,' Ianto said, wringing his hands. 'He left?'

'Clearly he takes after his father and grandfather. He has chosen to become an outlier.'

'No,' Ianto said, his voice shaking. 'No, no; he can't have understood. We have to find him and make him see—'

Tobias raised a hand and Ianto fell silent. 'The boy has made his choice. Now we must make ours.'

Ianto felt a prickly heat wash over his face. 'What does that mean?'

'The Society has been without a Magistair for too long. The boy was our last hope. We must begin the process of devising a new form of leadership. It is the only way the Eternalisium will finally be able to move forward once again.'

A bead of sweat ran down Ianto's back. 'You…you planned this somehow, didn't you? You wanted Doran to escape.'

The air of triumph finally made sense. Tobias stood up and slithered towards Ianto. 'People tend to behave exactly as you expect them to. Now take your seat. The Common is about to begin.'

He slid past Ianto and out into the lecture theatre while the professor stood, frozen. It was over. The boy had abandoned them. Only when Tobias' voice boomed out to the crowd, did Ianto shuffle to his seat, taking his place beside the other Winders.

'Fellow Travellers,' Tobias began, throwing open his arms as if to embrace the entire room. 'Thank you for making the journey here. I only wish it were under better circumstances. I'm afraid I have grave news... Doran West...has gone.'

Murmuring rippled around the lecture theatre. Tobias waited, allowing it to complete its circuit before he spoke again.

'He left last night, assaulting two Vigils in the process.'

An older man from the Stopper tribe with shoulder-length silver hair leapt to his feet. 'This cannot be. I saw the boy myself mere hours before. He was taking a tour of the grounds. Tobias, explain yourself.'

More murmuring reverberated around the room, and Ianto was aware that members of the Common would now be saying very different things depending on who they were sitting next to. He looked from the old Stopper to Tobias, who seemed quite unperturbed by the interruption. Ianto supposed he would have been expecting a little pushback to the news that the Magistair had deserted them.

'You are welcome to interrogate the two Vigils in question but you can see their injuries for yourself.' Tobias gestured to Crum and Malloch. Malloch tilted his head to reveal a lump that had bubbled under his crewcut. Crum's cut nose and two black eyes were plain to see.

Could Doran have done this?

'I, however, have a better idea,' Tobias continued, and Ianto mopped his brow. 'Why not question the last person to see the Magistair?'

Crum and Malloch moved as one out of the lecture hall and returned moments later dragging Ewan Bishop. Ianto could hear the sound of his own heart thumping in his ears. *Not Ewan. Not Ewan.*

Bishop was forced onto his knees beside Tobias. Ianto watched as his former student's eyes searched the room looking for him. Ianto could feel his terror. He longed to take the young man's place, but he couldn't. Their work was bigger than either of them. The Common would decide Bishop's fate.

Tobias paced around the kneeling defendant. 'Ewan Bishop. You have been brought forth before the Common as a result of your actions during the rescue of Doran West.'

Rescue? Ha, Ianto thought.

'You knowingly interfered with official Eternalisium affairs and tried to prevent Vigils Crum and Malloch from bringing the boy in safely. Do you deny these accusations?'

'I do not,' Bishop said.

'Your task,' Tobias carried on as if the answer were inconsequential, 'was to monitor Doran West, posing as his teacher and to alert the Society when any sign of manifestation occurred. Is this correct?'

'Yes.'

'Did you alert any Eternalisium member upon learning that the boy had travelled in time?'

Bishop's eyes flitted to Ianto. 'No.'

'Why not?'

'I wanted to bring the boy in myself. I wanted to protect him.'

'Protect him?' And Tobias paraded in front of the crowd. 'What on earth does the boy need protecting from?'

Bishop glared at Tobias. Ianto held his breath. Would the young man remain tactful? This was Tobias' domain. He would have prepared a well thought-out response to any accusation. They had no proof of Tobias' plot against Doran and the snake knew it.

'I merely thought the use of Vigils was a little excessive and that it would be better to try to convince the boy to come with me. As per my original directive. After all, I know him, know what he's like.'

Ianto let out the small puff of air he had been retaining. *That's right, my boy, keep to the facts.*

'You were over-zealous and thought you could correct your error of losing him in the first place,' Tobias said. 'Nothing more.'

'That's not true,' Bishop retorted and Ianto saw the fire in his eyes.

'Tell us about last night,' Tobias ploughed on. 'Did Doran West come to you before he left?'

The whole room waited. 'Yes,' Bishop said and the room erupted.

Tobias held up his hand and a look of delight flickered across his face when the crowd quietened.

'What did the boy say?' Tobias said, drawing closer to Bishop. 'And I will remind you that to be caught lying to the Common is grounds for immediate exile.'

Ianto leaned forward in his seat – and he wasn't alone. The silver-haired Stopper looked ready to fall off his chair.

'He asked me to come with him. I refused. He ran off before I had a chance to convince him to stay. That was the last I saw of him.'

The entire lecture theatre filled with outraged chatter. In the cacophony of voices, Bishop gave Ianto one final pleading glance. Ianto tried his hardest to respond with what he hoped was an understanding smile. Sometimes the smart choice was to know when you're beaten and live to fight another day. He only hoped Tobias would show some mercy for Bishop's cooperation.

'You showed loyalty to the Eternalisium,' Tobias said. 'It is only fair I point this out. You could have chosen exile and gone with him but you did not.' He paused and the crowd seemed to freeze with him. Ianto couldn't help but marvel at the way Tobias could command a room. Had he been born an ordinary man, he imagined Tobias could have been prime minister. 'Nevertheless, you have broken serious Society laws and risked the exposure of our existence in your attempt to correct your mistakes. This cannot go unpunished. I'm afraid I have no choice but to propose exile.'

Bishop closed his eyes as the murmuring returned. Ianto picked up snippets of the conversations around him. The vote was going to be close.

'Those in favour of exile?' Tobias asked the Common.

Ianto tried to count every hand. Half? Maybe less. Or was he simply remaining hopeful?

'And those in favour of clearing the defendant?'

He hadn't imagined it. Ianto counted again and was convinced that over half of the hands were now in the air. Tobias blinked, once. Whatever he was feeling, he was hiding it behind his performance. 'Very well. The defendant is cleared. Though I propose a reassignment from internal Eternalisium work in favour of a role outside the Society. This will be decided at a future date.'

Crum and Malloch pulled Bishop to his feet. He shrugged them off and stood proudly before the Common. Ianto didn't know if he would have had the strength to do what the young man did next. Bishop brushed himself down and climbed the steps to join his fellow Stoppers. All of them picked a different point in the room to stare at.

'Now to the matter of Doran West,' Tobias said, resuming

as if Bishop had simply vanished into thin air. 'You have heard testimony that the young Magistair has rejected the Society. A third generation of the family West has shunned us.'

A few murmurs of agreement spread around the circle above Tobias. Others hissed their disapproval at his audacity.

'I say this with no pleasure. I too had hoped that our wait was finally over. That our Magistair would take his rightful place. But no. Travellers…we are at a crossroads in our history. And for me the path is clear. We cannot wait any longer. What next? Must we now wait for Doran West to perhaps have children and hope they might be more receptive?'

Ianto heard a few people around him say, 'No.' Not only in the Winders section of the theatre.

'We have to act!' Tobias said, working to keep the crowd with him. 'We have to be bold. We have to take our society back! A fairer society, with an elected Magistair. Not a child; not someone simply born to be in charge; not someone who shirks their responsibilities and abandons their people. It is time for a different Magistair. One who will listen to its members and act in conjunction with the Common.'

'Yes!' came a few louder voices from opposite Ianto. One Rusher was on her feet.

'I propose change. I propose progression. The Eternalisium must move forward. I have served you humbly as your acting leader this past decade, as did my predecessors before me. We have guarded the Eternalisium with all we have and I give you everything still. I can help us devise our path into the future. Will you let me? Will you let me lead you out of the shadow of the Wests and into a brighter future?'

A round of applause echoed around the theatre. Not all were clapping, though. Some were casting a shrewd eye over the doctor. Ianto committed each of their faces to memory and was surprised to find the young Vigil Malloch in this company. Perhaps all was not lost just yet. There were those still willing to defy Dr Blue's 'cure' for the Society. He couldn't give up. Doran West remained their only hope. The cries from the members notwithstanding, the boy was the only one capable of cultivating the support to stop Tobias' power grab. Despite what the good doctor had said, there was nothing fair or progressive about an Eternalisium under his control.

Ianto surveyed Tobias, who was standing, arms outstretched, absorbing every cry of support as if it were sustaining his very existence.

As the yells thundered around the lecture theatre, a single thought grew stronger within Ianto's mind. It may cost him his freedom or even his life, but the professor vowed to find Doran West again and bring him back where he belonged.

26

FIRE AND ICE

'I am trying!' Doran yelled, standing out in the open moor, one hand resting on the black stallion. A whinny echoed across the heath.

'Not hard enough!' Léonie replied, matching him.

'Can I make a suggestion?' Zander said.

'NO!' the other two bellowed.

It had been two weeks since their first night on the outskirts of Dumfries. The campsite had gradually become more modern as the days passed. Léonie popped back and forward, sourcing more items to help them survive. The future boasted many helpful products. The best was a pop-up tent that could expand to fit all three of them, then become the size of a sheet of paper when not in use. They made sure to be well hidden during the night and packed everything away during the day.

By day fifteen, tensions were beginning to run high.

In the first week, Doran had pretty much mastered teleportation and could travel in space on his own. Controlling the date or time he jumped to was still an issue. There was also no hope at this point of taking anyone with him. Léonie managed to snare various squirrels and birds for him to practise with. He disappeared holding the animal and reappeared empty-handed, having no idea where it had gone. His best attempt was when he jumped five minutes into the future and arrived holding a *predominantly* intact squirrel, its bushy tail nowhere to be found and the rodent staring at him with an indignant glint in its eye.

Two weeks in, Doran had begun to feel he was actually getting worse. The previous day, he had wasted the whole morning by jumping five hours into the future to find Léonie and Zander sitting, heads in hands, by the fire.

'You have to stay calm,' Léonie reminded him. 'Without the watch, you have nothing to calm your mind. The more adrenaline you have, the less control you have. You must be centred. Grounded.'

Doran's cheeks burned. 'Then perhaps you should stop yelling at me. It's hard enough trying to be calm to jump myself. You try not worrying about taking another living thing with you.'

'Why don't you just jump forward to your time on your own, build a new watch and come back?' Léonie asked for the fourth time that week.

'I told you, no,' Doran said. 'I'm not risking a big jump where I could end up anywhere, get hurt, and not make it back for Zander. Plus, I had a head start before. Building a watch from scratch is a little more complicated.'

'Then you've got to concentrate.'

'Oh yeah, thanks. I'll try that,' Doran said. 'Why can't you go get one of your Trapper friends to come and help us?'

Léonie exhaled with such force that for a moment Doran thought it was his horse again. 'I've told you. It doesn't work like that. They're all away on missions or stationed at a particular time. And may I remind you, I'm not supposed to be here.' She gave the bright blue sky above a despairing shake of the head. 'Was I really this annoying when I was learning?' she asked the heavens.

'I hope I was a better teacher than you.'

Léonie scoffed. 'Oh, well I'm sorry I'm not the *great Doran West*. I'll just go get him, shall I? 'Cause he sure ain't here!'

Like a jaded married couple, they glared at each other and turned away, arms folded. Zander shook his head and wandered off, apparently leaving them to it. They sat in painful silence for a while until eventually, Léonie glanced over at Doran. 'Sorry,' she murmured, the word barely audible.

'Yeah, me too,' Doran said, just as quietly. 'I'm just tired.'

'I know. And you're right, I'm not much of a teacher. To tell you the truth I'm barely out of training myself. Only got my sword a year ago.'

Doran frowned, reminding her of his ignorance.

'Something else you brought to the Society,' she explained. 'We didn't have watches before you came. That was your invention. One of your many inventions. Before that, students just sort of got on with it. Not all survived, according to the records. But your watch made the early days of learning safe. After you complete your training, you get your watch melted down and turned into a weapon of your choice. I chose this.' She pulled out the Katana from the sheath on her back and revealed a small opening in the hilt. Doran could see a thin strip that seemed familiar. He pulled the schematic for the watch out of his pocket and looked closely at the sensor beneath the watch's button. Sure enough, there it was – the same thin strip. When building the watch, he had likened it to fingerprint technology.

'Why keep that specific part of the watch?'

'You made it so each watch is unique and only works for that person's DNA. When you choose your weapon it's sort of a ceremonial gesture. That this is your weapon and is a part of you.'

Doran nodded slowly. The DNA sensor had been his father's design. But why had his dad built the watch that way? So only he or Doran could use it? That made some sense, as his dad's initial objective had been to help control both their abilities. But why had Doran's future self kept this feature not only for himself but for other members of the Society also?

Doran caught himself wringing his hands and stuffed them into his pockets, along with the schematic. 'So what I'm trying to do *is* unsafe then?'

'Yeah.'

'Super.'

Doran stared out at the open moor and felt the most peculiar sensation. It was as if someone had dropped an idea into his head. He wasn't sure where the notion had come from but he suddenly felt compelled to take a stroll.

'I need a walk to clear my head before we try again…'

Correct, came a voice from the same part of his brain the idea had sprung from. This was exactly what he needed. Without another word, he set off, leaving Léonie staring blankly ahead.

Doran had been walking for about twenty minutes when his feet seemed to dig into the ground of their own accord. He felt a tingle as though someone was gently blowing on the back of his neck. He turned sharply but there was no one there – just the open, desolate moor. Yet he had a distinct feeling that he was being watched. He was just about to resume his stroll when he saw a man – standing some way off in a dark suit, which, Doran observed, had a bottle-green tinge when seen by light of day.

Samael.

Doran's first instinct was to turn and run back towards Léonie and the campsite. But the suited man's stillness gave him pause. Samael was just standing there, arms behind his back, polished shoes firmly together, and a contented smile on his face. He appeared to be expecting Doran to go to him. So, dismissing his better judgment, Doran started to walk over to him. Only when he had come close enough to take in the minutest details of Samael's face – the scars accentuated by the bright sunlight – did he stop, feeling the inhuman, electric-green eyes fixed upon him.

'Hello, Doran,' Samael said in the same crisp, measured voice Doran remembered from the night in the cellar.

'What are you doing here?'

Samael smirked. 'Formalities at an end I see,' he said. 'It appears someone has been listening to Miss Devereux's tales about me.'

'How you're my enemy from the future and a murderer, you mean?' Doran said, keeping his voice as strong as he could.

'I'm sure – in her eyes – I am,' Samael said, as though the accusation was nothing more than a playground insult. 'It is hardest for those who are indoctrinated to see the truth. Dictators always create their own narratives. The Magistair has made me the villain of his story – quite expertly I might add. I do not blame Miss Devereux for her perception of me.'

Doran's eyes narrowed. 'Did you know? Did you know who I really am?'

'Did I know that you will grow into the greatest evil this world has ever known? Yes.'

'Then why didn't you just kill me?'

Samael inspected him for a moment with his dark pupils. 'Our fates are intertwined, Doran West,' he said. 'Without you, there is no me. To kill you here and now would mean to murder myself as well.'

'Wouldn't that be worth it? I thought a crusader like yourself would be willing to give his life for the greater good?' Doran asked, though he wasn't sure what had brought on this sudden death wish. Why was he goading Samael to kill him?

Quite unexpectedly, Samael smiled again. 'Perhaps it's because I don't want to kill you,' he said, and a hint of sadness seemed to file down the sharp edges of his face. 'There has been enough bloodshed in this war of ours. We have both lost much. What I'm offering you is a chance to undo all of that. I do not want to sacrifice myself by killing you, but I am willing to do it by changing you.'

'What does that mean?'

'It means I want to help,' Samael said. 'I want to help you become a better man. I want to turn you into a person who will do good in this world, not seize more and more power until it consumes them.'

Doran stared. Samael wanted to *help* him. 'And why should I trust you?'

'Because I'm the only one, other than yourself, who actually wants you to change,' Samael said. 'Your friends don't want you to. Miss Devereux, despite what she might say, doesn't want you to. She wants Doran West back. She wants her Magistair back, to stop the evil man from the fairy tales she was told.' He spread his hands theatrically, indicating himself. 'Can you honestly say you trust she has your best interests at heart?'

'But why?' Doran asked, wearing his scepticism on his sleeve. 'If we're enemies, why would you want to help me? Why not just let Tobias Blue take control?'

'Do you want him to take control?' Samael asked, and for the first time, he appeared intrigued.

Doran deliberated for a moment. 'I thought I did,' he said. 'I thought he was welcome to the job. But now I'm not so sure.'

'Heavy is the head that wears the crown,' Samael said, and he gave a sarcastic bow.

'You didn't answer my question. Why do you want to help me?'

Samael's neutral expression changed, as it had done briefly the last time he and Doran conversed. There was a caring quality to his eyes again. 'I come from a time where you *are* the Magistair, as does young Miss Devereux. You may have the luxury of debate on the matter but I do not. And frankly, I don't want to see you become that man.'

'And how do I know you aren't doing this just to seize power for yourself, exactly like Tobias?'

Samael seemed to find this amusing. 'Tobias Blue is an authoritarian politician posing as an academic. My motivations are…more personal.' His gaze wandered above Doran's head; distant. 'I have no interest in power. It's why I shunned the Eternalisium all those years ago. It has pained me to see what it's done to you, my boy. That it has made us enemies. That is not something I would ever have wanted.' His eyes flitted back to him. 'Despite it all, despite everything you will one day do as the Magistair, I still care about you.'

Not for the first time, Samael's words snared Doran's thought process, pulling it in an unexpected direction. What he was currently thinking was madness. It couldn't be true. 'Who are you?'

Samael stared at him and when he spoke his voice was surprisingly soft. 'Come with me.'

Doran blinked and glanced back in the direction of the campsite.

'They'll be fine,' Samael assured him. 'I will guide you and make sure you get back with the knowledge to take your friend home.'

His tone was confusingly comforting now. Doran was unsure how to react. Every instinct screamed at him to turn and run; run back to Léonie and protect Zander. Yet Samael did not appear interested in hurting either of them. The only thing he appeared to be interested in was speaking to Doran himself. But did Doran really believe that Samael was there to help? Either way, the same inexplicable pull that had dragged him out on his stroll and made him approach Samael seemed to arise again. It felt as though an invisible rope had been tied around his waist, preventing him from leaving this man. Whether that rope was being controlled by Samael or by himself he was unsure.

'What do I do?'

Samael's lips stretched across his face into a smile. 'Once again, I am projecting across time. I will move to another time period and I want you to follow me.'

'How?' Doran could barely travel through time on his own, let alone follow a set of coordinates.

'You can do it,' Samael said, with what bordered on an encouraging tone. 'When I tell you to, I want you to reach out towards me and follow where I go. You will understand when you see it.'

'But I—'

'Now,' Samael said, cutting off Doran's protest.

He immediately began to fade. Doran reached out his hand to where Samael had been standing, closing his eyes. His mind burst into life; flashes of light pinging in infinite directions; the shooting stars were back. One playful spark burned brighter than the others – a blinding sun at the centre of a sparkling solar system. Doran pictured himself moving towards it, trying to catch it. It danced around until, eventually, he visualised his hand closing around it. A flash of white light enveloped him, and they vanished.

BOOM! An explosion knocked Doran off his feet. Ringing filled his ears. Everything seemed out of focus. He looked up to see the blurry image of Samael staring down at him. With a sharp snap, the world became clear again. Doran was lying in the dirt, gunfire flying overhead and bombs dropping unrelentingly around him. Horrified, he looked up at Samael, who, to add to his horror, was smiling. He was standing over Doran, arms still clasped behind his back, perfectly at ease. Doran thought he might even have seen a bullet fly through the man, leaving him intact but punching a small hole in a wooden beam behind him.

'What's going on?' Doran yelled.

'This is World War One, the Battle of Verdun, nineteen sixteen,' Samael called back over the noise of the assault above.

Doran recoiled as a mound of earth rained down on top of him. He could taste the ash in the air, and spat out a clod of dirt. '*Ugh*. Why have you brought us here?'

'For your first lesson,' Samael said, his voice not unlike Mr Bishop's when regaling his class with fun facts. 'This battle was the longest and one of the costliest of the entire war. You are currently experiencing the opening ten-hour bombardment.'

There was another explosion, this time just a few feet from where Doran was sitting. Instinctively, he crawled through the dirt to press his body against a wall of mud in front of him. It dawned on him that he was in a trench. It felt as if he was sitting in a pathway created by the body of a giant snake, the narrow corridor stretching out on either side of him and winding out of sight. Wiping the mud from his face, he stared at Samael accusingly, wishing he could test the man's intangibility with a handy firearm. '*Why* have you brought us here?'

Samael bent down into a squat, his thin legs jutting out in front of him. 'I told you,' he said, his voice still measured and calm. 'You are here for your first lesson.'

Doran snarled. 'This doesn't seem like a good place for a first lesson!'

'On the contrary, my boy, it is the perfect place. Primarily, you have to learn to remain calm in a pressured situation. Otherwise, you'll be jumping every time you get the slightest bit afraid. You don't want to end up in Pompeii the next time you see a spider in the bath, do you?'

Doran didn't find the attempt at levity appropriate. He glowered at Samael, who appeared quite amused with himself. He stood and beckoned Doran to join him with a long, skeletal finger.

Doran let out a high-pitched laugh. The suited man had to be mad. 'No thanks. I'm good down here.'

'You'll be fine; trust me.'

'Trust you? You've taken me to a war zone!'

'Feel free to jump out of here,' Samael said, as though it was *he* who was being difficult. 'Oh. Wait. You have no control. That's why we're here.'

Doran glared as Samael pointed to an ownerless helmet lying

in the dirt. 'Wear that if it makes you feel better.'

Doran picked up the black steel helmet and pushed his finger through a bullet-shaped hole at the front. He poked his finger through the gap, waving the hunk of metal at Samael, unconvinced.

Despite this, Samael simply raised an eyebrow at him as though, once again, it was Doran who was being unreasonable. 'By all means, stay cowering down there. But he's running out of time.'

Samael was surveying what Doran assumed was the open battlefield. Cautiously, Doran got to his feet. He spotted a rat hiding in plain sight in the dank mud near the bottom of the trench, and felt a keen desire to trade places with it; a thought he had never dreamed would cross his mind. Grudgingly, he placed the helmet on his head and edged himself up to peer out at the battlefield.

Lying in a small crater in front of him he could see a young man, though to call him a man may have been a stretch. He seemed around the same age as Doran himself. Sprawled on his back, he was clutching his bleeding leg and wailing in agony.

Samael stared at the fallen soldier as a scientist might look upon a mouse in a maze. 'His name is Jonas Beckmann from the small town of Miltenberg, Germany. And right now, his fate hangs in the balance. In two minutes, another French bomb will hit that crater and kill him. Unless you get to him first and save him. If you do, he will survive this war, get sent home a hero, marry his childhood sweetheart Anja, have two children, and die at the ripe old age of eighty-three.'

Doran's eyes were fixed on the screaming figure of Jonas. 'How do you know all this?'

Samael didn't face him, still gazing at Jonas analytically.

'Another side effect of my *condition*. I see…everything.' There was a haunted look in his eyes that remained as he finally turned to Doran again. 'Save him,' he said, as simply as if he were asking to be handed something.

'W-what? I—'

'Save him or he will die. He only has a minute left now.'

'I can't,' Doran insisted automatically, his mind racing. He had no hope of concentrating enough to have the control he needed. He looked at the soldier's uniform and remembered what Samael had said. 'Plus, he's a German. They were the enemy.'

Samael gave him a smile that vanished as quickly as it had appeared. It seemed he had been expecting this question. 'And there is your real first lesson,' he said. 'Does it matter? The world is not split into good and evil. History has a way of making conflicts such as this black and white. The brave Allied Powers against their tyrannical enemy. But young Jonas out there didn't start this war. He is merely a pawn on the chessboard, an expendable loss in a general's plans. A general who, I might add, is nowhere to be found on this battlefield. Jonas isn't a villain or a monster. He is simply a man. A boy, even. A boy who was asked to fight for a cause he most likely doesn't understand or believe in. I can't save him. No one else can. Only you. So, I ask you, Doran, does he deserve to die?'

Doran's chest rose and fell as he stared into Samael's impossible, electric-green eyes. Chaos rained down all around as they stood, locked onto each other. Events were unfolding. But the outcome was still unwritten.

Suddenly quitting all further thought, Doran leapt up over the top of the trench, flung both hands in front of him and yelled at the top of his lungs, 'STOP!'

A ball of lightning burst from him, creating a shockwave that covered every inch of the battlefield. The world of fire and death froze before his eyes. Soldiers were either midway through falling or charging in opposite directions. Bullets hung in the air, and in the distance Doran could see an explosion suspended in its early stages. The level of destruction was like nothing he had ever seen. He couldn't comprehend how one day the world would look any different, how it could possibly have recovered from this.

He walked towards the still cowering figure of Jonas, whose face was stuck midway through a scream of pain. As Doran neared, his legs seemed to bend of their own accord and the world momentarily turned black. A blink later, his vision was restored but his hands had become clammy and he felt a strong urge to lie down.

A pressure began to build inside his head, as if his brain were trying to squeeze itself through his eye sockets. He dropped to his knees, wiping his nose to see blood smeared across the side of his hand. He couldn't hold time still much longer. He could feel its desire, its need to start again. This wasn't the same as London or the Jedburgh cellar. This was an entire battlefield, and not only that, a key point in history. He had stopped too much. The pressure in his head was becoming unbearable. His vision was blurring. He had no choice.

START!

The noise of the gunfire and yells erupted once more and Doran felt a tremendous sense of release. He had moved himself so that he was right beside Jonas, who had stopped screaming in favour of bewilderment at Doran's sudden presence. Doran stared at Samael, who had poked his head over the top of the trench, smiling in a way that might have been proud, might have been cruel. Samael then glanced at the sky, before looking back at Doran, turning his head expectantly.

Doran understood the gesture: he was running out of time. In seconds, a bomb would hit the crater, killing both him and Jonas. There was no time to drag Jonas to the safety of the trench and Doran knew he was too weak to stop time again. There was only one thing to do, and from Samael's gleeful expression, Doran could tell that was what his new teacher had planned all along. He grabbed Jonas by the shirt and closed his eyes. There was a flash as the bomb hit the crater, and the world exploded around them.

Doran crashed against the trench wall again. He felt Jonas's shirt still clasped in his hand. Thinking of the tail-less squirrel, he braced himself and turned slowly, hoping to see an intact Jonas beside him. The young soldier was there, whole, and looking thoroughly dumbfounded by his sudden miraculous return to the trench. Doran glanced up to see Samael beaming at him.

He did not reciprocate.

'Lesson one complete. Well done,' Samael said. 'Ready for round two?'

He immediately began to fade again. Doran released Jonas, reaching out to follow the suited man, just as before. The German helmet blew off his head, landing in the dirt where he had first found it.

As Samael was fading, he smiled at the thunderstruck Jonas, gave him a courteous nod, and in fluent German said, 'You are welcome, Jonas. Do say hello to Anja and the children for me.'

And with that, both he and Doran vanished, leaving Jonas alone in the trench, staring wildly into the space where Samael had been.

The sound of traffic was deafening. The air was smothering. For his second lesson, Samael appeared to have chosen a place Doran's senses recognised. 'London?'

He was standing next to Samael on the edge of an empty street between two large buildings, late at night. There was nothing ahead of them, only a blackness which seemed to come closer the longer his gaze lingered.

A cackle echoed out from that darkness, soon joined by others.

Samael, seemingly unperturbed by the shadow's unpleasant laughter, strolled towards it.

Despite an unmistakable feeling of impending doom, Doran followed.

Samael was waiting patiently up ahead, as though Doran was lagging behind on a Sunday afternoon stroll. When he caught up, he found Samael contemplating an extremely dilapidated warehouse. At first sight it looked totally abandoned but then Doran noticed a light coming from the inside.

'Why have you brought me to the location of a low-budget horror film?' Doran asked.

To his surprise, Samael actually laughed. It was an odd sound – mechanical, as if he'd read a manual on how to do it. 'For your second lesson. Tell me, do you recognise them?'

Doran was about to say 'who?' when he saw a group of youths in tracksuits swaggering towards the entrance of the warehouse. So this was who had been making the cackling noises Doran had attributed to some spectre of the shadows. The one leading the way was examining something silver, which winked at Doran in the moonlight.

'My watch,' Doran said. 'Are those the guys who attacked Zander?'

'The very same.'

'They nearly killed him.'

'And now they also have your watch. An inaccuracy is brewing. The watch shouldn't be here, especially in the possession of that upstanding member of the community.'

'So, what do we do?'

'We?'

'Well, yes.'

'You are a slow learner, aren't you?' Samael leant closer. 'I'm not really here, remember. Unless you want me to pretend to be a ghost and scare them?'

'OK...' Doran said. 'Then what do you want me to do?'

'You just froze an entire battlefield in time and saved a man's life. Surely you can take care of a few skinny boys in tracksuits?'

Doran stared. 'That doesn't mean I suddenly know kung fu.'

'Why would you need that?' Samael said, and he wandered in the direction of the warehouse. 'You can stop time,' he called back at Doran. 'You can be in and out before they even know you were there.'

Still brimming with mistrust, Doran followed Samael to the gap in the building where the door should have been.

The first thing he heard was a garbled shriek. He peered inside the building. Graffiti lined the walls and pillars. He saw its chaotic forms and colours dimly reflected in puddles on the open warehouse floor. Gradually surveying the shadowy scene before him he spotted a teenage boy, a couple of years his junior, tied to a rickety old chair. There was a gag tied around his small face. The resignation and exhaustion apparent in his demeanour suggested he had been there for many hours.

The gang of young men had gathered around the boy. The leader was still clutching Doran's watch in one hand as he spoke roughly to his hostage.

'Where is it?'

One of the youths pulled the gag down the boy's face and he gasped for air. 'I don't know. Please, please, just let me go.'

'We told your mum if she didn't pay up we'd be taking a finger every day until we got our money.'

'She doesn't have it. She doesn't have it.' The small boy's eyes shone with terror. 'Please! Please don't do this!'

A couple of the gang members delivered a few careless blows to the boy, who squealed out in pain and despair. The rag was stuffed back into his mouth and one of the youths pulled out a large knife while another grasped his hand to hold it still.

Doran noticed Samael watching the scene with the same analytical stare with which he had watched the plight of Jonas. 'What do I do?'

Samael blinked. 'Stop them,' he said, as though wondering why Doran even needed to ask. 'Use your power. Command time.'

Doran glared at him. *Easy as that, was it?* He raised his hand and closed his eyes, reaching out for the light show. But just as at Zander's hanging, he saw nothing at all.

The muffled yells of the boy grew more frantic. Doran saw that the knife was being raised.

'Time's running out, Doran,' Samael observed.

'I'm trying. It's not working.' Doran shut his eyes again. Where were the lights? He couldn't feel anything.

'Don't tell me you wasted all your energy in Verdun?'

The boy was struggling with all he had but his hand was being held still ready to receive the knife.

Doran ran his fingers through his hair. *Come on. Stop. STOP!* The blade was moving.

A bloodcurdling scream echoed around the warehouse.

'What a shame,' Samael said, clucking. 'Well, who needs all those fingers anyway?'

Doran was shaking in horror. *Why hadn't it worked?*

'These thugs are having quite a night,' Samael said, carrying on as if seeing this sort of violence were an everyday occurrence. 'First, they almost kill your friend; then they steal your watch; now they've maimed a teenager. I wonder what mischief they'll get up to next?'

There was an ugly outburst of heartless laughter and whoops mixed with the agonised wails of the boy. Doran felt a burning, violent hatred consume him. *Why should they keep getting away with it? They hurt Zander. They were going to keep hurting this boy. What if their next victim was the kid's mum?*

He may not have had the energy to stop time but there was one other skill he had almost mastered during his training with Léonie. He closed his eyes and disappeared in a storm of lightning. Reappearing on the first floor of the warehouse he noticed an old paint can and gave it a swift kick down towards the unpleasant scene below. It skimmed one of the youths before hitting the floor with a resounding *clang*.

The laughter stopped.

'What was that?' growled the gang leader.

Doran vanished again, reappearing on the other side of the warehouse, where he knocked over a forgotten broom, which then fell earthwards. He allowed just enough time for the gang members to see him disappearing when they looked up to see where the broom had come from.

'Who's there?' one of the youths called out. His voice was shaky.

Good, Doran thought.

He teleported to the warehouse floor, keeping to the shadows.

Then he spoke, his voice echoing eerily across the dingy space. 'You shouldn't be here.' All heads turned towards where the voice had come from. A moment later, he was on the other side of the building. 'I don't like visitors,' he boomed out.

A white-faced youth spoke: 'Yo, bruv. Something not right is going on in here.'

'Someone's playing games,' another chimed in.

'Who are you?' the leader yelled across the space.

Doran was back on the first floor. It was time for the big finish. 'Your reckoning,' he cried as he leapt from the first floor.

The frightened gang were shrieking and cowering together. Doran vanished in mid-air again, then reappeared behind the leader and shouted right into his ear: 'BOO!'

The youth fell back, collapsing in a heap. His cronies squealed in terror as they fled. Doran watched them go. He almost wished Zander had been there to see his performance.

'Feeling powerful?' a crisp voice came from across the warehouse.

He could see Samael's eyes shining across the dimly lit warehouse.

Doran noticed his lungs heaving. He couldn't seem to make them stop. 'They deserved it.'

'Did they now?'

'Yes.' *That was true, right?*

'Well, you've saved the day. Why don't you retrieve your watch and untie the boy you've rescued?'

Doran glared. Samael was clearly trying to make some sort of point. What was the lesson? He'd demonstrated his travelling abilities; he'd made sure the boy was not further hurt. Not only that, he had given those thugs a taste of their own medicine. Perhaps they would think twice before their next crime.

Doran wandered over to the unconscious figure on the floor and prised the fob watch from his hand. The cool metal rested on his palm once again, imparting a sense of security that he hadn't realised how much he'd been missing. His breathing slowed and his chest settled. The inaccuracy was fixed.

He then went over to the whimpering boy, and started to untie him from the chair. The boy let out a piercing shriek through his gag.

'Hey, hey. It's all right. It's OK. I'm not going to hurt you.'

But the boy continued to yell wildly.

'I'm not going to hurt you, I promise,' Doran said, holding up his hands. Slowly, with the boy still whimpering, he undid all the knots and removed the gag.

As soon as he was freed, the boy leapt up from the chair and fell. Doran moved to help him up but he yelled and kicked out. Scooping up his severed finger, he ran from the warehouse as though his life depended on it.

Doran stared after him, frozen. How the boy had looked at him… He couldn't even begin to comprehend it. All he knew was that it made him sick to his stomach.

Filled with distress about what had just happened, Doran finally looked over towards Samael. 'Let's continue the lesson,' Samael said, and he snapped his fingers.

The first thing Doran felt was a blast of freezing air on his face. Stirring, as though shaken awake, he realised he was lying flat on his back, covered in snow. His arms already felt as if they belonged to someone else but he fought the numbness to push himself up and onto his feet.

Snowflakes whirled all around him, blinding him, covering him, freezing him. He hugged himself tightly but his stringy arms were a far cry from a warm, padded jacket.

'SAMAEL!' he called, looking around himself frantically.

No one answered. Even if they had, Doran wasn't sure he would have been able to hear. Why had Samael brought him into a blizzard? And where on earth was he now?

He pulled the watch out from his pocket. He had his stabilisers back. He didn't need the suited man any more. He could just jump back to Zander and Léonie in Dumfries and boycott the rest of the twisted lessons Samael had planned for him. But when he looked at the watch, he saw the hands had frozen, and when he rested his shaking thumb on the button, no green light appeared. It seemed the watch was also suffering from the blizzard conditions.

He would have to risk jumping without it. He closed his eyes in readiness but he couldn't concentrate at all; he could only shake wildly; his body was fighting to survive. It could not support him to use his powers in such a state.

'SAMAEL!' he bellowed. 'Samael, where are you?'

Hopeless and clueless, there was nothing to do but trudge through the snow, keeping moving, though aiming nowhere other than to put the wind at his back. After just a few yards, he stumbled upon what at first looked like a pile of small, purple cushions. It took a moment to realise that it was a little girl in a violet snowsuit. She was lying curled up in a ball, and shivering as fiercely as he was. He bent down and placed a hand on her shoulder, but she recoiled at his touch, opening her blue eyes wide in alarm. Doran raised both his hands to show he meant no harm, smiling as best he could through chattering teeth.

'It's all right,' he said. 'My name is Doran. What's yours?'

'L-Laura,' the girl stammered. She spoke with what Doran believed to be an American accent. She couldn't have been more than five or six.

'OK, Laura,' Doran said, trying to remember how primary school teachers had spoken to him whenever he'd been upset. 'I need you to help me. Can you tell me where we are?'

'St. Sauveur,' Laura said.

Doran was no clearer. 'Where is that? Which country?' Would a five-year-old know which part of the world she lived in?

She stared at him as if he had dung on his face. 'Canada,' she said, as though it was the most obvious thing in the world. The fact that she was now helping a very stupid person seemed to settle her. 'Why do you talk funny?'

'I'm from Scotland,' Doran said.

Laura shivered. Both of them were getting colder by the second. Doran could see the girl's eyelids growing heavier. She rubbed them with a mittened hand. 'Do you know where Scotland is?' He had to keep her awake.

She shook her head and yawned. Doran reached out and pulled her to her feet, bending low to talk to her and put her hood up and wrap the scarf she was wearing more tightly around her neck. 'Laura, how did you end up all the way out here?'

'We were in the car and Daddy hit a tree. They were all sleeping so I went to get help.'

Doran took a deep breath, his heart sinking. 'That was very brave, Laura. Now, I want you to come with me, if that's OK? We need to find a way out of here.'

She nodded, so he picked her up and put her on his shoulders, wondering where on earth they should go. The snow still fell thickly all around them, enclosing them into a blind white world. At least she was better prepared for the weather than he was, he thought, as he felt her small gloved hands grab his head, and they set off.

Doran chatted to Laura about any subject he could think of to try to keep them both from sleeping as they trudged along. He tried repeatedly to see if his powers would work, but his body refused to cooperate. All of it was focused on keeping him alive.

Eventually, he felt his legs buckle. He staggered, causing Laura to grasp his head more tightly. 'It's all right,' he assured her.

But it wasn't.

He felt his legs go from under him and they both fell into the snow. Doran brought her in front of him and wrapped himself around her. He had to keep her warm. The cold would have to take *him* first. He saw Laura's eyes begin to close and he could feel his own growing heavy. Finally, on his last desperate glance out into the whiteness, he caught sight of something. The blurry outline of a man in a suit stood before him, his hands clasped behind his back, seemingly quite unaware of the frozen wasteland surrounding him.

'Help us,' Doran said, his voice barely above a whisper. Samael did nothing, simply standing there, motionless. Even through the snow, Doran could see that his face was quite expressionless; no trace of emotion played upon it. 'Help us!' he tried again, all his remaining energy now focused on yelling for help until he was hoarse – until he could no longer make any sound at all.

He saw Samael fade away and an inner darkness soon began to take hold. It called to him with a devilish lullaby. With what he felt would surely be his dying moments he hugged Laura tighter, struggling to keep her awake with tales of Scotland and the Loch Ness monster.

Her blinks grew longer and longer. Doran tapped his own cheeks. He had to keep his eyes open too. He looked down and realised Laura's eyes were now closed and peaceful, as though he had just read her favourite bedtime story. *Not this*, he thought.

Not her. It should be me.

'Come on, Laura,' he moaned desperately, shaking her and tapping her cheek. 'I've more stories for you. *Come on, wake up.*'

A bark broke through the thick white silence of the storm. Then came yelling. Doran's heart leapt. 'Here!' he called out in what sounded like a primal scream. 'She's over here! Help her!'

The sliver of remaining energy left his body, carried off by his final word. The darkness cheered.

The next thing Doran knew he was being carried. He awoke with a start to find himself wrapped in a warm, silver blanket as though about to be shoved into an oversized oven; a stretcher his baking tray. He could see that he was being carried towards a truck by men in military gear. One of the soldiers looked down and saw he was awake. 'Il est réveillé,' he said. *He is awake.*

'Laura!' Doran said, trying unsuccessfully to sit up. 'Is she—'

'She's fine,' the other soldier said, switching to English. 'She's sitting in the truck. Quite the chatty little thing. You're a real hero, you know, kid. She didn't have long left. Though you should dress better for the occasion next time.' The soldiers chuckled and lay him down at the back of the truck. 'Sit tight, kid. We'll be back in a minute.'

'Her family – did you find them?' Doran called after them.

'They're all right,' one of the soldiers said. 'A bit the worse for wear, but they'll pull through. Nice accent by the way. I'm a quarter Irish myself.'

The soldiers walked off and Samael suddenly materialised at Doran's side, his face still vacant, lacking any sign of feeling.

'Where were you?' Doran said, wishing he was strong enough to reach out and throttle that veiny neck. 'What kind of sick game was that?'

'*That* was your second lesson,' Samael said, completely indifferent to Doran's tone. 'Perhaps the most important of anything I am trying to teach you.'

'Oh yeah, and what's that?'

'That you are more than just your powers. They don't define you or make you a hero.' He sighed. 'Something your future self would do well to remember.'

He began to fade again; a sign Doran should follow him once more. Doran stared at him in disbelief. 'I'm not going anywhere else with you.'

'I see,' Samael said, his face finally showing signs of life again. 'Well then, stay. I hear Montreal is lovely at this time of year. But it will take your body a while to get well enough to travel on your own again in these conditions, even with the watch. Meanwhile, you'll have to explain to your soldier friends how a scantily clad boy from Scotland ended up in the Canadian wilderness.'

With a glower, Doran raised his arm towards Samael's ethereal form and both disappeared in a flash of light.

27

HOMECOMING

Drowned in blackness, Doran raised his hand in front of his face, searching for himself and only finding the faintest trace of skin. He glanced up to see Samael's glowing eyes, shining through the dark. The eyes drew closer.

'When was that?' Doran asked.

'St. Sauveur, Canada, during the ice storms of nineteen ninety-eight. An awful time. Parts of the country were without power for weeks. People and livestock succumbed to the cold. Eventually, the military had to get involved.'

'Was she all right?'

It seemed to take Samael a moment to realise what he meant. 'Ah, yes, little Laura. Yes, she grows up to be a schoolteacher and raises golden retrievers. She lives a fulfilled life.' Samael's eyes burned and there was a new kind of sternness there. 'And the reason she gets to do that is because of you. Doran West. Not the all-powerful Magistair. *You* saved her.'

Doran met his solemn gaze, searching in its depths for an answer to the question Samael had refused to entertain before they had begun their journey together. He still couldn't bring himself to ask it out loud. He knew what he believed the answer to be; what he – strangely – hoped it would be. But he wasn't sure he was ready to be told otherwise just yet. If his question remained unanswered, it could still be true.

'So, where are we now?' Doran said instead, breaking eye contact.

Samael smiled. 'Neither here nor there,' he said. 'Follow me.'

He glided out of sight. 'That's not an answer,' Doran said, as he heard the sound of a door closing.

Standing up, he found the door, hovering in the darkness, connected to nothing. Frowning, he reached for the handle only to find his hand pass through it. He tried again, and again.

'Samael?' Doran called. 'What is this?'

Samael's voice echoed around him. 'For your next lesson, we can only be spectres. I have unlocked the pathway for you, but you must pass through.'

'You want me to project? I thought you said you were the only one who could do it?'

'With my help, you can. Now concentrate. Grasp the handle.'

Doran reached for it again and his hand slipped through.

'*Concentrate*,' Samuel's voice echoed around him. 'Let nothing exist apart from the handle. Imagine pushing it down and swinging the door open.'

Doran glared at the handle, blocking out all the thoughts swimming around in his head. The wood of the door faded into the shadows, only the gleam of the handle remaining. He took a deep breath and pushed.

The darkness dissolved and he found himself standing in a place he knew. Every hair on his body stood on end. He couldn't believe it. It couldn't be real. After weeks lost in time, he was home.

Careering into the living room, he saw his mum sitting in her armchair, a glazed look on her face. She looked exhausted, with dark bags under her eyes and chalk-white skin.

'Mum!' he cried. 'Mum. I'm back.'

She didn't move or show any sign that she had heard him. For a moment, Doran wondered if she was frozen in time, but then the doorbell rang.

Kate West blinked as if the sound had brought her to life. She pushed herself out of her seat and traipsed towards the front door.

Along the way, Doran reached out to grab her arm. 'Mum, stop. It's me.' But just as it had with the door handle, his hand passed through her.

'She can't hear you.'

Doran turned to see Samael surveying him.

'You're still a projection,' he continued. 'This is my domain. I alone control who can be seen.'

'Then let her see me.'

'No.'

Doran's face hardened. 'Why not?'

'This isn't like Jonas or Laura,' Samael said. 'This is your personal timeline. To affect it could create a paradox.'

'Then why bring me here?' Doran said, his temper rising. 'Is this some kind of punishment? Another game? Why bring me here at all if I can't speak to her?'

Samael didn't answer, nodding instead towards the front door. Doran wheeled around to see his mum letting in two men. For the second time, he was surprised to see Mr Bishop somewhere he had no right to be. Behind him was the sweaty, tweed-suited Professor Everie from the Eternalisium. Why on earth were they there? And more to the point, why did his mum look as if she had been expecting them?

Doran followed them back into the living room, where Mr Bishop and Professor Everie sat together on the sofa. Both wore the same melancholic expression and waited patiently for Kate to lower herself into her chair. Every muscle in her body was shaking.

'Thank you for agreeing to see us,' Professor Everie said.

'I've run out of options,' Kate replied. While her voice was quiet, it felt like a symphony to Doran's ears. It had seemed an eternity since he'd heard her voice.

'As far as we know he's safe,' Mr Bishop said. 'I tried to stop him from leaving but I couldn't get through to him. I'm sorry.'

'I'm sorry he was at that infernal place to begin with,' Kate said, her voice regaining some of its usual strength. She glared at Mr Bishop. 'And don't get me started about the fact that you're one of them. You failed to mention that at parents' evening.'

'I believed I was keeping your son safe, Mrs West.'

'And why is that your job?' Kate said. 'I'm his mother. I'm the one who's meant to…to…' But she couldn't finish. Instead, her face fell into her hands and she let out a series of sobs. Doran ached to run over to her, to hug her, to let her know he was all right. He glared at Samael, ready to lambast him for not allowing this. But to his surprise, Samael seemed almost as upset as he was. He appeared to be finding the events before him difficult to watch, unable to lock his usually unwavering stare onto the event.

'I can't imagine what you're going through,' Professor Everie said, and Doran's attention snapped back to his mother. 'But you have to understand we were only trying to do what was best for

Doran.'

'What's best for your precious society you mean,' Kate said, fighting back more tears. 'He's just a boy. He's not your messiah – and neither was Arlen.'

'Mrs West,' Mr Bishop said, raising a soothing hand. 'Make no mistake; we are aware of how much you have lost already. What happened to your husband was a tragedy. But if Doran isn't found and helped to control his abilities, he will be in danger of meeting the same fate as his father.'

Kate shook her head. 'Except it's not that simple, is it? He wouldn't just be a student; he would be your new leader. Arlen explained everything to me. Why is it so important that a West be in charge?'

A good question, Mum, Doran thought.

'Because the alternative is something this world cannot allow,' Professor Everie said. 'The power vacuum is demanding to be filled. Tobias Blue is seizing control and I doubt his hunger will stop with the Eternalisium. We have yet to discover what he's planning, but rest assured it will not bode well for the Society – or for the world. Doran is the only one with the lineage to sway the turning tide. The West name still means a lot to a number of members. If we can find him and bring him back to the Eternalisium, we can still stop Tobias. It won't be easy but I know it is the right thing to do.'

'You can't ask me to give up my only son to your cause.'

'Your son is already involved,' Mr Bishop said. 'Tobias has seen to that. This isn't over. We believe he engineered Doran's escape to discredit him and highlight his rejection of the Eternalisium. But he won't stop there. Tobias can't allow a West to be running around. One day, when he feels the time is right, he will have Doran taken care of.'

Kate took a moment to process what Mr Bishop had said. The glazed look she'd had before returned. 'I've been thinking a lot about our last conversation. I was upset, and I let my own fear take over. That was wrong. I know that now. He's not my little boy any more. I've been trying to fight it but I shouldn't have.' She looked at both men, her face determined. 'Find him. But when you do, you must give him a choice. That's more than I did. I should have told him everything long before now, and I'll regret that I didn't for the rest of my life. So, promise me. To hell with his family name or Tobias' plans. Promise me that if you do find him, you'll give him a choice.'

Mr Bishop and Professor Everie glanced at each other, nodded in solemn agreement, and then vanished.

Doran rubbed away a ghostly tear and turned to see Samael staring at him. 'Thank you.'

'You're welcome,' Samael said. 'Though there is a lesson here. I want you to remember your mother's words very carefully. There's always a choice, Doran. Don't let the desire of men like Bishop and Everie corrupt you. They, like Miss Devereux, want you to become their saviour. Their Magistair. Just be sure that if you do take up the mantle, it is *your* choice.'

Samael reached out a hand to usher him away but Doran shook his head. 'Not yet.'

He wandered across to his mum, who was still once again. He wanted to hold her hand but settled for kneeling before her. 'I wish you could hear me. I wish you could see I'm all right. But I still want you to know that none of this is your fault. You were just trying to protect me. I chose to rebuild the watch. I chose to test my powers. And I'm so sorry about what my leaving has done to you. What it will do to you. But I swear, I'm coming back. I'm doing everything I can to get back to you.'

Kate blinked and stared just above his head. Had she somehow heard him?

'It's time to go,' Samael said from the doorway.

Doran nodded, his gaze not leaving his mother until a flash of white light came between them.

Doran found himself slumped against something solid in a darkened room, Samael sitting next to him. If he closed his eyes, he could still see his mum's face, the image fading the more he tried to find it.

'Quite the day out,' Samael said, breaking Doran's connection. 'First, I would like to take a moment to see how much you've learned thus far.' He spoke like a teacher providing feedback.

Doran raised an eyebrow. 'You mean, other than how to survive near-death experiences?'

Samael let out that mechanical cackle again. 'Well, on that front, you are certainly excelling,' he said, smiling. 'My apologies for the harsh nature of my...curriculum. Nevertheless, the first two lessons were necessary for helping you to understand.'

'Understand what?'

'Well, that is what I hope you can tell me.'

Samael stretched his legs out in front of him, crossing them and resting his hands on his lap. Once again, he appeared in no rush, waiting patiently for Doran to engage with his questions.

Doran pondered his next words carefully. Once ready, he looked at Samael, who was inspecting his fingernails with great interest. 'That I shouldn't see the world in absolutes of good versus evil and that I'm more than just my powers.'

'Elaborate,' Samael said, giving every syllable great importance and still inspecting his fingernails.

'That people have both light and darkness inside them,

including me, including you even, and I have to remember that. Also, that I should know my powers don't automatically make me good or a hero. I have to decide to be that person and use my powers *for* good.'

Samael finally ceased his scrutiny and responded to Doran's analysis with a proud smile. 'Very well put. Our crash course seems to have been effective. It pains me it had to happen this way and I wasn't able to spend more time with you.'

Doran's heart thumped just as it had done before leaping over the top of the trench. However, a very different kind of bravery was required now. The question was once again on the tip of his tongue. He was now willing himself to ask it, shouting at himself to just do it. He opened his mouth but Samael, unaware of his internal struggle, continued.

'Of course, that was only half of what I wanted you to glean from this quality time together. I was also trying to teach you how to use your powers. So tell me, have you worked it out yet?'

'Worked what out?'

'Your anchor!' Samael said, as though it were the most obvious thing in the world. 'Surely you must have an idea now? There is one thing that has linked every single occasion where you have managed to have a degree of control over your abilities. Further, it was displayed prominently in your heroics with Jonas and Laura.'

Doran tried to think back to each time he had used his powers successfully. He thought of the recent example of Jonas, of jumping with Zander to Florence, stopping time in the alleyway and in Jedburgh. 'I… I was trying to help.'

'Precisely,' Samael said. 'Your anchor is your overwhelming desire to help people. It is what will aid you in your quest to manage that staggering potential of yours. And when you do, believe me, you will be quite extraordinary. Your only failing is when you reach such dizzying heights, you neglect to remember the one thing that grounded you in the first place. And in so doing, you forget who you are.'

Doran blinked at him. It was an odd feeling. Samael knew more about his life than he did. A perfect stranger from Doran's perspective. Then again, he supposed Samael was no different from Léonie in that sense. But there was something in the way Samael spoke which made him surer than ever that there was a connection between the two of them. Perhaps he'd had it twisted, presuming the person who had given him the fob watch to be someone special to him and believing his warnings about the nightmarish suited man. There was a familiarity to Samael that Doran was finding harder and harder to deny. This was a man who was counselling him, knew him in a way – Doran finally dared to believe – that only a father could.

The thought seemed to swirl around in his mind, destroying every other musing in its path. He stared at Samael, who was returning his gaze with a sombre smile.

Suddenly, an alarm blared from outside the darkened room in which Doran and Samael were sitting. A red flashing light illumined the small, square chamber.

'What's happening?' Doran said, the alarm growing louder and the red light shining brighter.

'Oh, that would be a signal that someone is finally coming for me,' Samael said, as though Doran had asked him the time.

Doran's head jerked to the thick steel door in front of them and then back to Samael.

'But...' Doran began, before pausing, confused. 'But you're not really here. I thought you were projecting. Why would they be coming for you?'

Samael's lips stretched up one side of his face as though half of his mouth hadn't received the memo to smile. 'I *was* projecting,' he said. 'However, I can assure you, right now I am quite real. This…' – he gestured to their surroundings –'…is my prison cell. The one you put me in a decade ago.'

Doran's brain was struggling to keep up. 'But—'

'I'm afraid our final lesson will have to wait. Though rest assured – it will come,' Samael said, his green eyes more alive than Doran had ever seen them.

'But Léonie said you had returned? That you were already rising to power?'

'The only person who ever knew I was here was you,' Samael said, his voice still very measured. 'In fact, the cell is designed so that only you and I are permitted inside. I have spent ten years breaking down the defences and shields you engineered to contain me, slowly regaining my powers. Miss Devereux's information regarding my return comes only from me spreading rumours by projecting myself to strategic points in time. And now that your future self has inexplicably vanished, I feel we have reached the perfect moment.'

'For what?'

Samael reached out and, with a now solid hand, clasped his bony fingers on Doran's shoulder. 'Today is the day I escape.'

Doran sat up with a start, panting as if he had just run for miles. It was dusk and he was sitting in the long grass of the now-familiar open moor of fourteenth-century Dumfries. He reached up to where Samael's hand had been, still feeling the fierce grip on his shoulder. He looked around, his eyes wild, half expecting to see the suited man beside him. His mind raced.

His dad was alive. It had to be him. And he had just escaped.

28

THE EMPTY HOUSE

Doran bounded back across the moor and into the clearing containing the campsite. Both Léonie and Zander sprang to their feet, ready to fight whatever he was running away from at such speed.

'What is it? What's wrong?' Léonie said.

Doran skidded to a stop and clasped his knees, panting. 'Sam…Samael,' he said, struggling to get the words out. 'S-Samael…escaped.'

'What?' Léonie and Zander said in unison, though the intention behind their shared question was quite different. Zander looked positively bemused, and while Léonie shared some of his confusion, she also had an unmistakable look of fear in her eyes.

'Samael has escaped,' Doran repeated, this time more fluidly, getting his breath back.

'Who's Samael?' Zander asked, giving Hamish a calming pat on the side.

Doran glanced at him then at Léonie, who gave him a warning look and a swift shake of her head. Should he tell Zander what he suspected? That his dad was alive and appeared to be, at least to the outside world, his impending foe?

'The man who's been chasing me,' Doran said simply, unwilling to say any more in Léonie's presence. Did she know the truth? Had she been keeping this from him?

Before Zander could ask a follow-up question, Léonie cut in. 'What do you mean, he's escaped? We already know this. The Eternalisium in my time has been tracking him for months.'

'You only think you have,' Doran said, his expression grave. 'He's been projecting until now. Today – I mean, today for him – is the day he actually gets out of his cell.'

Léonie looked aghast now, and Doran could see she was shaking. 'How do you know all this?'

'Because…' he began, but his voice trailed off. Once again, Léonie was doing a very accurate impression of his mum. 'Because he came to me, on the moor, and… Well, he asked me to follow him.'

'And you went with him?' Léonie's voice was trembling with fury. 'Do you have any idea of the danger you just put yourself in? Anything could have happened. He could have killed you.'

'I don't think he wants to kill me,' Doran said, trying to keep his voice as calm as possible in the hope of quelling Léonie's rage.

This did not happen. In fact, she seemed to be getting angrier by the second. Her cheeks were once again as red as her hair and she was staring at him as though she couldn't possibly have heard him correctly. 'And how on earth can you presume to know what that lunatic wants?' she yelled. 'You have no idea what he's done.

The misery he's caused. He will not stop until he has eradicated any threat to his rise to power.'

'I don't think—' Doran tried again but Léonie cut across him.

'You don't think? *You* don't think?' She was now pacing and rubbing her temples. 'I *told* you. He wants you out of the way. He wants to get to you before you're strong enough to stop him. And you…' She stopped pacing and shook her head in disbelief before carrying on. 'You just…*followed* him?'

'Look, I was desperate. All right? He said he could teach me how to get us all out of here.' This was partly true, but Doran neglected to mention the irresistible curiosity he felt while in Samael's presence. He reached into his pocket and pulled out the watch. 'He also helped me get this back.'

'How did you—' Zander began.

'It doesn't matter,' Doran said. 'The point is, he helped me. He even took me home to see my mum.'

'He did what?' Zander said. 'Did you talk to her?'

'I was just a projection,' Doran said. 'I was there but she couldn't see or hear me,' he added, seeing Zander's confused expression.

'How convenient,' Léonie muttered.

Doran glared at her. 'He also helped me see the Eternalisium for what it is.'

'And what is that supposed to mean?'

'That it's filled with liars and people with their own agendas who would bother a worried mother just to get what they want.'

'The Eternalisium isn't like that.'

'No?'

'Maybe in your time. But the Eternalisium I know is nothing like that. I've told you.'

Samael's voice rang inside Doran's head. '…*she wants her*

Magistair back…'

'Really?' Doran said, his own cheeks flushed now. Who was Léonie to stand here and judge him? 'Since you've got here, all you've wanted to do is get me ready to fight off this great evil. Your Eternalisium doesn't seem much different to me.'

'Doran, easy,' Zander said. 'Léonie's been trying to help us.'

Doran tore his gaze away from Léonie, who, for the first time looked genuinely hurt by his words. Zander was staring at him, an eyebrow raised, which he interpreted as, 'Are you all right?'

Doran sighed. *What are you doing?* he thought. 'I'm sorry,' he said to Léonie. 'I know you have.'

She acknowledged his apology with a nod but then seemed to lose herself in thought. 'Florence…'

'What?' Both boys said.

'Florence,' she said again. 'When I faced off against Samael, he dodged all my attacks. He had the upper hand but he never landed a blow on me. He didn't even try.'

'Is that like him?' Zander said.

'No. Not according to the records, anyway. He was known for being an expert fighter who showed no mercy in combat.'

'So why didn't he hit you?'

Doran and Léonie shared a look and both sets of eyes widened. 'Because he didn't want you to know he was projecting,' Doran said.

Léonie nodded. 'You're right. He's been fooling the Eternalisium all this time, trying to throw us off the scent. But why?'

'I don't know,' Doran said. 'But we have to find him. Fast.'

'And how do we do that?' Zander said.

'We have to work out what he wants,' Doran said, now pacing back and forth. 'Why now? He's been leaving a false trail all this time, so why bring me to that cell? Why not allow everyone to keep believing his lies?'

Léonie frowned. 'You,' she said, the word barely escaping her lips. Doran froze. 'He wants you. You'd be the only thing he would come out of the shadows for.'

Doran considered this. If Samael was his father, there was one place he would go.

'He'd go home. To...' His eyes widened. 'Clear the campsite. I think I know where he's going.'

'Wait. What? How?' Léonie said.

'Just do it,' Doran said. 'We need to go. Now.'

Zander grabbed his arm. 'Hate to interrupt,' he said. 'But what about me? Am I to live the rest of my days as Robert the Bruce's serving boy?'

'I can take you,' Doran assured him, and to both Léonie and Zander's surprise, he stuffed the watch into his pocket.

'You can?' Zander asked.

'I can do it,' Doran said. 'Stabilisers have to come off sometime, right?' he added to Léonie.

They quickly cleared the campsite and stood together in a circle. 'Now, you have to have contact with both of us to ensure you take everyone where you're going,' Léonie explained.

'And Hamish,' Zander said, giving him a pleading look.

'Fine. And Hamish,' Doran said. There was no time to argue the point.

Zander beamed at him. 'And where are we going?'

'Home. To Linntean.'

'Why would he go there?'

'I'll explain later,' Doran said. 'I'm going to aim for the day after we left.' He gave Zander a searching look. 'This isn't your fight. I can drop you back in London first. You don't have to go back.'

'And miss all the fun? You're joking, right?'

The pair shared a moment and Doran hoped his face conveyed just how much this offer meant to him.

He allowed both of them to clutch his left hand and placed his right on Hamish's side. His eyes closed and he reached through the array of lights to find where he wanted to go. Opening one eye, he saw sparks igniting around them. It was working. He forced both eyes shut again and concentrated, focused on their destination and the contact of those around him. They all disappeared with a flash, no trace of their presence left in the woods.

The two apple trees in front of the West family home rustled. Their branches clawed at the air and a whirlpool of leaves swept across the lawn.

A flash of light illuminated the house momentarily before it sank back into darkness. Doran hurried up the garden path, rummaging around in his pockets for his keys. *Where were they?* He hammered on the front door. 'Mum! Mum, it's me!'

There was no reply. Blackness hung over the house. Not a trace of light inside. He had expected a lamp to flicker on and the front door to swing open, revealing his weeping, relieved mother. Neither occurred.

'What's going on? Why are we here?' Léonie called after him.

'She's not in. She must be working,' Doran said, not entertaining her question. He had to believe this to be the case. If Samael had come, he hoped that he, Doran, had got there first to warn his mum. He was afraid of what the shock might do to her.

Doran cupped his hands around his eyes and peered in

through the living room window. Nothing. *She's at work – that's all*, he tried to tell himself. *Maybe the back door will have been left open.*

He charged around to the rear of the house and slammed his hand down on the handle, daring it to be locked. He would break the door down if he had to. But brute force proved unnecessary, as the handle gave a familiar click and moved willingly with his hand.

'Mum?' Doran called, careering into the kitchen so fast that he didn't notice a large cobweb blocking his passage. He collided with it and, with a yell of disgust, clawed it from his face as he stared at the kitchen. It was as though he had stepped into a haunted house, the cobweb he had disturbed a mere amuse-bouche. The entire room was coated with dust that had clearly not been touched in many months, the kitchen countertops lost under a thin sheet of filth.

'We heard you yell,' came Léonie's voice as she and Zander caught up with Doran.'What's…' Her voice trailed off as she too took in the surroundings.

'Blimey,' Zander said. 'It's like Spider-Man had a nervous breakdown in here.'

Doran ignored them, as he hurried to inspect the rest of the house. When he reached the living room he saw the furniture was shrouded by large white sheets.

His stomach twisted into ever-tightening knots. Both bedrooms were equally shut down.

As he re-emerged from his mum's vacant room, he glanced at the front door. The letterbox was vomiting a pile of unopened letters, overdue bills and leaflets scattered across the floor.

What year was this? Doran had aimed to jump to the day after he and Zander had supposedly vanished, hoping to prevent his mum's police appeal from ever happening. That was definitely not where they had ended up.

'Did you get the right date?' Zander asked, as if reading his thoughts. 'Are we in the past?'

'No, we're not in the past,' Doran murmured, gesturing to a picture of him and his mother on the wall. The photograph had been taken recently, as he remembered his mum complaining that she didn't have any current pictures of the two of them.

'So this is what…the future then?' Zander asked. "Cause when we left, your house didn't look like this.'

Léonie checked her watch. 'We're a year off,' she said. 'A year on from your present.'

With a yell, Doran grabbed a dusty lampshade and flung it against the wall. Zander cowered as if he had been shot at. Even Léonie flinched. But Doran didn't care. He had got it wrong again! Who was he kidding, trying to do it all without the watch? He had failed.

'A year!' he bellowed. 'A *year!*'

'Doran, stop,' Léonie said firmly.

'She thinks we've been gone a year,' Doran said, grasping the back of his head. 'We have to try again,' he added, his voice close to being hysterical. He ran towards Zander and Léonie, arms outstretched.

'No,' Léonie said, raising her hand.

Doran halted – out of shock more than because of her command. 'What do you mean, no?'

'We have to work out what's happened,' Léonie said, her tone the complete antithesis of his. 'There could be clues here.'

'I know what's happened. My mum has gone.'

'Yes, but *why* has she gone?'

Zander, who had been unusually still until this point, finally seemed able to interject. 'She's right, mate,' he said, though he didn't look at Doran. 'Think about it – why would your mum ever leave this place?'

Doran felt like finding another lamp. Were they not listening? 'Maybe because I broke her heart by leaving?' he yelled. 'You saw that police appeal.'

'She would never leave here,' Zander said, grasping Doran by the shoulders as if about to shake sense into him. 'Think about it. She never left when your dad disappeared. She could have done. I'm sure it would have been easier to just pack up and leave the memory of this place. But she didn't. I think she still hoped that one day, despite all the odds, he would return. Even if she never admitted it. And that same strength and resolve wouldn't leave her now. Especially not when it comes to you. She would wait. I would bet my life on that.'

Doran stared at him, fighting back the stinging tears that were brimming. Zander was right. His mum wouldn't leave. Not unless she was forced to.

But then, where was she?

Had Samael managed to get to her already? There was nothing left to lose now; he had to tell Zander and Léonie what he suspected.

'I think…' he began, but he required a breath to finish the sentence. 'I think Samael is my father.'

Saying it out loud made it seem preposterous. But neither Zander nor Léonie laughed – or even cracked a smile. Instead, they both appeared deeply concerned.

'What?' Léonie asked tonelessly.

'Samael is my father,' Doran repeated, this time with more conviction; uncertainty and absurdity evaporating. 'That is why he's so obsessed with me and refuses to kill me. And as soon as he escaped, I thought he would come here. Back to our home. To my mum.'

'Are you serious?' Zander asked, horrified. 'The same guy who's been chasing us?'

Léonie backed away, shaking her head. She put her hand over her mouth, turning her back on them. Doran thought he even heard a sniff.

'Léonie…?' he asked nervously.

Léonie turned back, her eyes pink, but she refused to acknowledge she had just shed a tear. 'Come on, let's go outside and plan our next move.'

She hurried out into the front garden, clearly eager to get out of the house. Doran exchanged a quizzical look with Zander, who was equally bemused, and the pair followed her out.

Léonie was standing next to Hamish, whom Zander had tied to one of the apple trees. To both boys' surprise, she was petting him. Her hand was lost in his mane and she was staring wide-eyed into space. Whatever she was pondering seemed to be taking her a while to sort through and she gave a slight start when Doran spoke.

'What is it?'

'Nothing,' Léonie said. Her voice contained an odd quiver. 'I just want to find Samael. That's all.'

'We will,' Zander said. 'We just need a plan.' He turned to Doran. 'But first – do you mind explaining how on earth this guy can be your dead dad?'

Doran sank his teeth into his cheek. How could he explain what he suspected? Would Zander think him mad – or worse, respond to his theory with pity? 'My mum told me before all this started that there was a chance my dad could still be out there. She never knew for sure if his experiment killed him or if he simply got lost in time. And Samael said that an accident long ago made him unable to control his powers. But it's not just that. When he was teaching me… When I was with him… I don't know. I just…know it's him.'

Zander nodded. He looked concerned, but he appeared to believe him.

'Listen, I'm sorry I didn't say anything before. I wasn't sure whether…you know…with everything that's going on with you—'

'That I wouldn't want to hear about anything dad-related?' Zander helped, his lips curling into a grimace.

'Yeah. I mean we'd made up and I didn't want to—'

Zander raised his hand. 'It's all right. I get it. You've told me now and I want to help. Whatever you need, I've got your back.'

With a speed that would have made a Rusher proud, Doran hauled Zander to him, embracing him with a squeeze. 'Thanks mate.'

Zander chuckled. 'Anytime.'

The boys parted to see Léonie staring at them, appalled.

Doran sighed. 'I know this must seem insane,' he said. 'Just promise me when we find him, you'll give me a chance to talk to him first.'

Léonie seemed incapable of speaking. She could only give a swift nod. *What was wrong with her?* Doran wasn't sure, but he did know one thing: from the shock on her face, she had been telling the truth that night by the campfire. She didn't know anything about his father.

He was about to offer more words of reassurance when he noticed the sun poking out from behind the mountains in the distance. It was a new day.

His sense of time had been completely warped by all he had

been through. It felt as though he'd been drifting along aimlessly, relying purely on instinct to tell him how much time had passed. He believed it had been around a month since the night in the Linntean woods when it all began, and a strange feeling came over him. He wasn't sure how he knew, but it suddenly seemed very clear to him.

'It's my birthday,' he murmured, more to himself than to Zander or Léonie.

'What?' Zander said.

'Your internal clock is kicking in,' Léonie said, though her voice still seemed distant. 'Every Traveller has it. It's how we stay anchored to our biological age. Otherwise, we wouldn't have a clue, with all the jumping around.'

Doran closed his eyes and felt the warmth of the morning sun brushing his skin, The sun's rays felt like a long-sought-after hug, and for a moment he thought of his mum. Had it really been a month? Had it really been so long since they'd had a meal together, or simply sat in each other's company and watched TV?

'Seventeen,' Doran said, opening his eyes. 'One year left before...'

He had a year before destiny claimed that his story within the Eternalisium would begin. Would he spend that year there? Back home, with his mum and Zander? Or was that already somebody else's life now? Léonie's words from their ride to Dumfries entered his thoughts: *One day soon you will have to leave your old life behind... Him and your mum.*

'We're running out of time,' he said. 'We've got to find my parents.'

'Doran,' Léonie said, her hand dropping from Hamish's mane. 'Doran, there's something I've got to tell you.'

A blinding white light suddenly flashed in front of them, its blaze momentarily filling the sky. For a brief instant Doran thought the sun had somehow shot itself upwards into the sky. Gradually the brilliance appeared to settle some metres in front of where the trio stood.

From out of the centre of the light, a slender figure slowly began to emerge, gradually growing larger as it walked towards them, as if approaching through a tunnel of light.

'What the hell is that?' Zander asked, in awe.

It was Samael, and Doran found himself once again inexplicably drawn to him.

'Doran,' Samael said, sounding quite different from how he had sounded before – full of panic and concern. 'You must come with me. It's your mother. Something terrible is about to happen.'

Doran stumbled towards him. 'What?'

'You have to come with me, now. Only the two of us together can stop it,' Samael said, extending his hand.

Without hesitation, Doran continued towards Samael, only halting when he heard Léonie. 'Stop!' she yelled. 'Don't do it. You can't trust him!'

Doran looked back towards her. Her obvious angst caused him to hesitate momentarily, but he snapped himself out of it. 'He's not the man you think he is,' he said, trying to appeal to her. 'He knows what's happened to my mum – I've got to go with him.'

He glanced at Zander, who seemed frozen in terror. The boys locked eyes momentarily and Doran felt Zander understood as he continued to walk towards Samael, joining him and then disappearing with him into the blinding light.

29

THE LION AND THE DOE

Doran landed in a crumpled heap on wet dewy grass. He picked himself up to see Samael already standing at the end of what looked like a ridge, hands clasped behind his back. Doran walked over to stand at his side. They appeared to be on a small wooded hilltop, with a winding, single-track road visible below.

'Where are we? Why have you brought us here?' Doran asked, wondering where Samael's urgency had gone. He appeared to be quite calm now, as if he were waiting patiently for a bus to come along.

'I thought you would have recognised this place?' Samael asked, not taking his eyes off the road.

Doran looked around. 'We're in the Linntean woods, near Garnaith's Path, just on the edge of the village. But why are we here? What's this got to do with my mum?'

Samael finally turned to him, his expression grave. 'I searched across time for you and your mother and this moment kept plaguing my thoughts. The events are unclear, but I believe something awful is about to happen.'

'What moment? When exactly are we?'

'We are three weeks after you first left Linntean,' Samael said, his eyes flitting to the road as he spoke.

'How do you know when I first left Linntean?'

'As I said, I've been searching for you both for a while.'

'Why couldn't we have gone back to just after I left?'

Samael didn't answer him, his eyes fixed on the road once more. At the point in time Samael had taken him to, Doran would have been missing for several weeks; the police appeal would already have happened. A wave of guilt washed over him. He was still too late. 'What do we do?'

Samael continued to ignore him. For a while, nothing happened, and Doran started to wonder if they were in the right place. He kept glancing at Samael. Was now the right time to ask? Whatever might be about to happen, he had to know. 'Samael...' he began. How should he phrase it? 'There's something I've been meaning to ask you—'

But before he could finish the question, he noticed Samael's eyes widening. 'It's coming,' he murmured. 'Events are unfolding now.'

Doran stared at him, stunned into silence as he began to be aware of the sound of a car in the distance. His attention returned to the road and he saw a dark-blue Renault Clio careering around the bend below. His mum's car.

He watched, numbly, as the car seemed to veer almost lazily to the left, then flip over onto its roof before sliding a few metres more. Doran couldn't move, couldn't think. It was almost dark, but he could just make out the now unconscious figure of his mum upside-down behind the steering wheel. Returning to his senses, he cried shrilly and was about to charge forward down the hill when...

BOOM!

The car ignited, fire instantaneously bursting out to engulf every inch of the vehicle. Doran fell to his knees, staring wide-eyed at the flames. This couldn't be real. It had to be a trick, another test. It couldn't be real. It just couldn't.

Coming to his senses again, he sprang to his feet, ready to dive headfirst into burning wreckage, ready to pull his mum out with his bare hands.

Samael's voice cut through the air. 'Stop. There's nothing you can do for her now.'

'I have to try!' Doran yelled, his voice cracking.

'She's gone,' Samael said. 'But we can still save her.'

Doran looked up at him. Samael's pale face was resolute and his eyes unblinking. 'How?'

'Together,' Samael said. 'But first, you have to free me.'

Doran buried his hands into his hair. 'But you're already free. You broke out after you took me to your cell.'

'I said that was the day I was going to escape,' Samael said. 'And this is how.'

'What are you talking about?'

'I'm still in my cell,' Samael said, reaching out with a ghostly hand and moving it through Doran's arm. He wasn't solid; he was still projecting. 'But this is how and why I escape. Doran, you have to listen to me very carefully. We can still save your mother, but you need to do exactly as I say.'

Doran nodded hurriedly.

'You have to send me the fob watch. I can use it. It will work for me. Trap it to my cell on the day I took you there. Remember that moment and feel the time stream to get it exactly right. Once I escape, I will use it to finally control my jumps and come here. Then, together, we can stop this whole event from happening.'

Doran hovered, staring wildly, unsure whether to rush to his mother or to place his hopes in Samael. 'How?'

'We can do it,' Samael assured him. 'Together, we can. Trust me. Now send me the watch.'

Doran looked deep into the eyes he had once considered heartless. Now they shone at him, beseeching him.

He pulled the fob watch from his pocket and placed his hand over it. Closing his eyes, he focused on the cell, the sound of the alarm blaring and Samael sitting against the cold, steel wall. He uncovered his hand to see the watch had vanished and looked up to find himself alone. The projection of Samael had gone. He willed Samael to return, every second he waited feeling like an eternity.

When the storm of light did come, it was not the slim, suited figure he saw striding towards him, but Léonie, red hair flashing in the evening light as she ran.

'Tell me you didn't do it,' she said, panting. 'Where is he? Tell me you didn't.'

Doran stared at her, completely thrown by her presence. Where was Samael? Why wasn't he there yet?

Léonie grabbed his hands, then searched his pockets. When she found nothing, she let out a cry of anguish and held her head in her hands. She then noticed the flames, and looked in horror at the scene before them. 'What's going on?'

'My mum,' Doran said, his voice now hoarse. 'My mum – she was in that car and…and it crashed. Samael said we could fix it.'

Léonie looked more and more distressed as he spoke. On instinct, she moved forwards to face the wreckage, outstretching her hand and turning it, just as she had done during Zander's hanging. She let out a howl of pain and fell to her knees, clutching her head. Doran rushed over to her. 'Fixed...point. I can't,' she said. Her failed attempt to rewind time seemed to have drained all the energy from her body.

She stood up, pacing up and down in intense anguish. 'No, no, no,' she cried, grasping her head again. 'This wasn't supposed to happen. This wasn't supposed to happen. He said... He promised me...'

Doran stood, watching her. A slow, terrible realisation began to grow in him.

'Léonie...' he said. 'What are you talking about?' Then another thought struck him. 'And how did you find me? How did you know where to jump to?'

Her entire body seized up. She didn't look at him. It seemed she couldn't face him. 'I'm sorry. I'm so sorry,' she whispered.

The appalling connections continued to form in Doran's mind and his face grew dark. 'What have you done?'

She was crying now. 'N-no one w-was s-supposed to get hurt. We were only s-supposed to get you to release him,' she said through the sobs.

'We? You...you were working with him? All this time? *Why?*'

She nodded, covering her mouth as though about to be sick. 'You don't understand what you were like,' she said. 'The real you – the future you, I mean. You were so distant, so detached, from all of us...from me. You pushed us all away. Then you just disappeared.' She finally brought herself to look at him, but only for her next few words. 'And I hated you for it.'

The words stung, more than Doran would have expected. He didn't reply; he couldn't yet.

Léonie continued. 'When you left...the Society was in ruins;

no one knew what to do… And Samael… Samael – he came to me; projected. He was so understanding. He seemed to know exactly how I was feeling. And gradually, over time, I would speak to him more and more.'

She looked at him again, this time with a bit more fire in her glistening eyes. 'He was *there* for me. In a way you never were. He was everything you should have been. He told me that he had seen the error of his ways and that all he wanted now was to undo all of the terrible things he'd done. He said he wanted to go back and try to help you. He wanted to turn you into a better Magistair and prevent the first war from ever happening. You had gone. We needed Doran West back – a better Doran West. So I joined him. And together we hatched a plan to get him released so he could finally be free and we could change things for the better. We would find you before you joined the Eternalisium, or became the Magistair, and between the two of us, convince you to send him the watch. Only Doran West could enter the cell or use his powers there.'

'I thought…' Doran began but was still struggling to find the words. '…I thought you were helping me.'

Léonie gulped as a few more tears fell to the ground. 'I believed I was. Just not in the way you thought,' she said. 'We staged the fight in Florence. Then I was to find you in Jedburgh and keep you there and away from the Eternalisium in your present. I'd start training you but hold back enough for you to become frustrated. Samael would offer to train you instead and you'd learn from him rather than from the Eternalisium. Then maybe you would allow him to mould you into a better Magistair. But…' She paused, the wreckage below illuminating the horror in her eyes. '*This*. He never told me he was planning *this*.'

There was a rumbling of thunder above them. The evening

clouds had turned a dark green, darkening the sky into an early dusk. The rumbling grew louder and closer.

Léonie gasped. 'He's done it. He's escaped…'

CRACK! An electric-green lightning bolt flashed downwards from the dark clouds, striking the ground near where they stood, throwing them backwards. From where he lay on the ground, Doran saw Samael emerge from the light, fob watch in hand. He casually dusted his shoulder with his free hand before fixing Doran with his predatory green eyes, just as he had done on the night in the Jedburgh cellar. A sickening smirk spread across his face – the very image of crooked triumph. Then he turned away from Doran and wafted his hands gently, feeling the cold night air upon his skin. Closing his eyes, he took a long, deep breath, clearly revelling in every second of it. After a long moment of absorption, he spoke: 'It's good to be back.'

'You lied to me!' Léonie bellowed, springing up and charging at Samael.

She had barely drawn her Katana blade before the suited man, moving at what seemed like super-speed, had his hands around her throat. The Katana blade fell to the floor and he raised her off the ground, her feet dangling and her hands clawing at his.

No trace of emotion shaded his face as he stared into her eyes. It was very clear to Doran that despite what Léonie might have believed, he felt absolutely nothing for her. 'Don't embarrass yourself, you silly little girl.' His arm jerked, a lightning storm at his fingertips, and Léonie flew through the air. Her body collided with a tree and Doran heard a sickening snap as he saw her slump to the ground. She was still breathing, but her right arm was obviously broken.

The cold green eyes fell upon Doran once more. 'On your feet, Doran West.'

Doran's arms trembled as he pushed himself up. 'Save her,' he said, gesturing a heavy arm towards the wreckage of his mum's car. 'Please.'

Samael smirked again. When he smiled in that way he barely looked human at all. 'I'm afraid I can't do that.'

Tears pestered Doran's eyes. How could he have been so stupid? 'Why not?'

'Oh – many reasons,' Samael said, clasping his hands behind his back again and pacing back and forth, the caged animal released. 'First and foremost, I am simply enjoying seeing you suffer so.'

The rage was too much. Doran roared and charged, just as Léonie had done. It was as though a match had been lit inside his head and suddenly everything had become clear. Instead of picturing random sparks, he could now see a series of whirlpools. They lay before him, each one able to take him somewhere different. He focused all his efforts on teleporting himself to a position behind Samael. His best chance would be to take him by surprise. One of the whirlpools in his mind began to swirl faster and shine brighter with more frequent lightning. He imagined himself diving headfirst into the swirling abyss, allowing his body to be swept away by the current.

As his mind swam with the inner current, his body leapt from the ground, soaring into the air, fists ready. He felt a familiar tingle and a rush of air before he vanished.

With a flash, he reappeared behind Samael, still in mid-leap and swinging his fist back in an attempt to strike Samael in the back of the head.

But Samael was ready for him.

Dazzling electric-green eyes shone at him out of the darkness. Samael had somehow already turned to face Doran, hand outstretched.

It took Doran a second to realise that he was no longer soaring through the air towards his target. He felt suddenly paralysed. It dawned on him that Samael must have stopped him in mid-air – apparently without anything else being frozen in time.

Doran stared again into those cold, green eyes and, to his astonishment, he thought he saw disappointment there. 'Try again when you're a better match for me,' he heard Samael say, before he slammed the heel of his hand into Doran's sternum.

Doran flew backwards, smacking into the ground. He rolled through the wet grass before finishing in a crumpled heap, coughing and spluttering, trying to catch his breath.

'But I'm so sorry, where are my manners?' Samael oozed, smacking his forehead as if he had forgotten something important. 'You were going to ask me something. Go on… Say it,' he said quietly.

Doran could not speak. When no response came, Samael bellowed: 'SAY IT!'

The words rang out around the hilltop. Doran recoiled in terror at Samael's frenzied state, chilled to the core by the inhumanity in his wild, staring eyes.

A tear rolled down Doran's cheek. He knew exactly what Samael was referring to. He had been wanting to ask him something. Something to which, only a few minutes earlier, he would have longed to hear a 'yes' in reply. Now the thought of that being the answer made him sick with horror. But, yes, he had to know the answer.

'Are…are you my father?' he croaked through the tears.

Samael let out a callous laugh. It was perhaps the cruellest sound Doran had ever heard. 'No,' he answered. 'But I had you going there for a while, didn't I?' he added with a wink.

He's enjoying this, Doran thought, sickened.

'No, out of the two of us, it is you who does the creating here,' Samael continued cryptically. He began to pace again. 'I needed a way of escaping. It took a long time for me to work out a way in which to do so without causing the universe to implode.' He paused to flash Doran a dark look. 'But I had ample thinking time, thanks to you.' He resumed his leisurely pacing. 'So I lied. I'm good at that, you see; making people believe what I want them to. You and Miss Devereux were both far too easy to manipulate.'

Doran's eyes fell on Léonie, who seemed to be regaining consciousness. He continued to look at her until eventually she looked in his direction. As Samael started to talk about her, Doran could see her weeping, but she kept her eyes locked onto Doran's.

'You see, both yourself and Miss Devereux are similar in many ways. Yet there is one weakness you share above all others – your incessant desire for a father figure. I was more than happy to oblige. Your future self had failed Miss Devereux in that regard and it was all too easy for me to give her what she wanted, and slowly bend her to my will. It does appear she was beginning to realise something was amiss. A shame she didn't put up much of a fight. I have missed a good battle.'

Léonie continued to weep but somehow Doran found himself unable to feel any pity for her. Rage and grief were all he could feel. His mother was dead and Léonie had had a hand in it, whether or not she had been conscious of it. He returned her remorseful gaze with a cold stare that made it clear he could not forgive her so readily.

She blinked as the unspoken message was received and closed her eyes. When she opened them again, Doran saw an intense rage in them, that was clearly reserved only for Samael. The suited man seemed quite oblivious, now kneeling, and running his hands through the long grass. Every physical sensation seemed to thrill him and he closed his eyes, apparently enjoying the fresh air once again.

Doran watched as Léonie began hovering her hand over her broken arm as though her fingers were an X-Ray machine. She was biting her lip in an apparent attempt to stop herself from screaming. It was as if the arm had a mind of its own as it began to convulse and jerk horribly. She was rewinding her injury.

As she worked, she continued to glare at Samael with murderous ferocity, although he, still with his back to her, had yet to realise that she had awoken.

Léonie used her eyes to indicate to Doran that he should keep Samael talking until she was fully healed. And for all that he felt no desire ever to see her again, he realised that their only chance against Samael would be to work together, so he rose slowly to his feet, ignoring the pain that seemed to have spread to every corner of his body.

Samael's eyes opened and he surveyed Doran, seeming vaguely impressed, but clearly delighting in his discomfort. He got to his feet, facing Doran with an unpleasant grin.

'But I don't understand,' Doran said, eyeing the watch that was now clasped in Samael's hand. 'I thought the watch was linked to my DNA? If you're not my father then how can you use it?'

Samael simply smirked at him, looking as if this secret was some delicious morsel of food that grew tastier the longer he held it inside his mouth.

'Why have you done this?' Doran asked instead, giving a pleading look towards the flaming wreckage of his mum's car.

'Because I loathe you,' Samael said, his voice dripping with venom. 'While this is only the beginning for you, we have been at war across centuries, you and I. And trust me, Doran West, this is nothing more than you deserve.'

'But why my mum?' Why did you have to kill her? She's done nothing to you.'

Samael looked affronted by this remark, placing his hand on his chest as though outraged by Doran's rudeness. '*Kill* your mother?' he said, gesturing to the blazing car below. 'I didn't *kill* your mother. No, no, no. That was you, Doran.'

'Me?'

'Your mother was always destined to die on this day, in this accident. The reason? She was so tired from working those long hours to support you, and so sleeplessly worried about your whereabouts, that she fell asleep at the wheel and crashed her car.'

Doran gave a furious shake of his head. 'No! That's not true!' Though part of him already knew it was.

Samael smirked that horrendous smirk again. 'You know it is. *I* haven't done anything. I simply allowed events to take place as they were supposed to.'

'But you knew it was going to happen!' Doran yelled. 'You – *we* – could have stopped it. We could have changed things!'

Samael's cruel laugh returned, but then he looked at Doran as no one had ever done before. The intensity of the hatred in Samael's stare felt so much like a physical assault, he actually had to take a step backwards.

'The irony is delicious,' Samael commented. He spoke evenly and lightly but it was clear to Doran that he was suppressing his true feelings of contempt to keep their force out of his voice. 'And now we finally come to your last lesson. I have given you a taste – just a taste – of what it is like to have events take place which you are now powerless to prevent. You see, you are part of events now. To go back and change things would create a paradox that would tear a hole through the middle of this universe. You cannot change what you have physically seen – only avert things in the moment, or repair inaccuracies. Your mother is dead. And there is nothing you can do about it.'

The inevitability of what Doran had already suspected hit him. 'Why teach me this?' he asked. 'Why?'

'Revenge,' Samael said, and Doran thought perhaps he saw just the hint of a tear forming in the cold green eyes. 'Justice,' he hissed. 'Very simply: an eye for an eye. You see, one day, Doran West, you will have a choice between your precious principles and what is right. You choose to do nothing and, as a result, you allow innocent people to die.'

Doran processed every word individually before asking: 'Who are you?'

'You'll find out soon,' Samael said, as the suggestion of emotion disappeared and the manic gleefulness returned. 'Oh I do hope it's me who gets to tell you. I never did know, you see.' He then checked the fob watch as if looking at the time. 'Oh my, it's getting late. Lots to do, people to see – you know how it is when you've been away for a while. I'll be seeing you soon I'm sure, Doran West. Thank you for the watch. It should finally give me the control I need to enact my plans.' And with a terrible grin, he outstretched his arm, brandishing the watch.

Whoosh.

A sharp blade swung out from the shadows behind Samael, the smooth metal glistening in the moonlight. With a scream of fury, Léonie lunged forwards and brought the blade down on Samael's wrist.

There was a deafening shriek of agony and Doran watched, stunned, as both the watch and the hand Samael had been holding it in, fell to the ground with a soft thud.

'Bet you didn't see that coming,' Léonie said, and booted Samael in the stomach.

What happened next happened as if it were in slow motion. Samael stumbled backwards, clutching his severed wrist. Doran and Léonie glanced at each other and nodded before charging as one towards their injured foe.

Samael leapt upwards, still clutching his wrist and contorting his body into a spinning kick. The blow was aimed at Léonie's hands, and Samael's wingtip shoes collided with the hilt of the Katana, dislodging it from her grip. The sword flew behind her and landed out of reach a few metres away, implanting itself in the ground.

Léonie instinctively began to turn her hand in an attempt to call the sword back to her. But Samael was too quick. As soon as he had landed, he performed another deft spin, this time on the ground, with the grace of a figure skater. The move tripped Léonie and she fell flat on her back.

As she fell, Doran swung his fist in Samael's direction but he blocked it lazily and shoved him backwards. Doran ran at him again, swinging his arms in every direction he could think of. Quantity over quality seemed to be his only option.

The system appeared to work initially, as he managed to land a couple of blows on Samael's torso and wounded arm, but they did not make any real impact and the suited man then kicked downwards hard at Doran's shin.

Before he could even clock the pain, Samael swung at him with an uppercut, his fist brimming with lightning. The bony ball of flesh rammed into Doran's chin, lifting him clean off his feet and landing him flat on his back again. Stunned and hurting, he nonetheless struggled to pull himself together enough to go to Léonie's aid.

She and Samael were now in full combat. Unlike their fight in Florence, this was real. And it appeared to Doran like a fight to the death.

The pair seemed quite evenly matched in hand-to-hand combat, with Léonie possibly having the edge – and a full complement of hands. For a while she parried most of his blows, but the balance of power changed immediately when the electric-green of Samael's eyes began to flash.

He began rushing around her, darting at impossible speed and landing a series of ferocious blows. She couldn't keep up, trying desperately to raise her hand in an attempt to slow him down. But he was unrelenting, hammering her head, torso, legs and arms in random succession. He became so fast that his entire body looked as if it was vibrating.

Finally, he ceased his assault, and Léonie collapsed in a heap on the ground. Samael surveyed her wilted figure for a moment and gave a callous, satisfied chuckle. 'That was more like it,' he said, stretching his arms as if he had just finished a fun workout.

Before Doran could so much as blink, Samael had flown across to the Katana in a storm of sparks, instantly returning to stand over Léonie, keeping the sword's sharp point suspended inches above her body. He examined the blade then peered down at her. She panted up at him, defiant, her face bloody.

'What do you think?' Samael said. He was still looking at Léonie, but Doran could tell the question was directed at him. 'An eye for an eye?' he asked with a malevolent twinkle.

He raised the sword and swung it towards Léonie's hand.

'STOP!' Doran bellowed, commanding the scene before him.

It was like the after-effect of an explosion as a rush of air flew from him. The gust sailed towards Samael and swept over him and Léonie, rustling the trees behind them.

Samael, who had closed his eyes, opened them, cautious, seemingly surprised for the first time. His initially vacant look shifted into a triumphant smile as he gave a genial wave to Doran with his bloodied stump.

'You've failed again, *Magistair*,' he said, and jerked his hand upwards in an attempt to have another swing with the sword.

But the sword didn't move. Samael tried again, this time with more force, but it remained motionless.

Slowly, one finger at a time, he released the sword from his grip. Even when he had fully let go, the sword didn't fall; it remained frozen in mid-air.

Samael turned his head, glaring at Doran. 'It appears I was too good a teacher,' he said with a leer, and he charged, lightning erupting all around him again.

In the split second before Samael hurtled towards him, Doran had realised something. Samael *needed* the watch. Yes, he could use the other Traveller abilities he seemed to possess, but he had said it himself; his jumps were unpredictable because of a long-ago accident. Therefore, he couldn't risk jumping without the watch. Doran had one advantage over Samael: he could jump and Samael couldn't.

The whirlpools swam before him once more. The tingle spread through his body and sparks flew off him. Before Samael could reach him, he was gone.

Doran jumped, again and again, surrounding Samael like a one-man army. Each time he jumped he landed a sharp blow, disappearing before the suited man could retaliate. Each strike felt like a small victory, his opponent growing weaker and more infuriated with every hit.

For Doran, it felt as though he was stepping through a series of doors, sliding between openings at different points around Samael. The rush was like nothing he had ever experienced.

But the euphoric feeling vanished as soon as he remembered what Samael had done. He jumped faster, striking harder. Too late, he realised his body was growing hotter with every jump, and that his head had begun to throb.

It only took one sloppy jump for Samael to seize his chance. He barged into Doran before he could disappear again, knocking him to the ground.

Doran had presumed that the throbbing and the heat emanating from him would stop as soon he was no longer using his abilities. But he still felt as though his insides were burning.

Samael loomed over him, sneering. 'Looks like you're not quite up to it yet after all.'

Sweat poured from Doran. He might as well have been in the unbearable heat of the flaming wreckage below. Electric-green sparks erupted from him, growing more frequent until they covered every inch of him. The pressure was building in his head. He couldn't survive much longer in such a state. He had to rid himself of that feeling; he had to rid himself of the overwhelming weight.

The last thing Doran saw before it happened was Samael's sneer. A sneer that turned into a comprehending grimace.

BOOM! An explosion of green lightning blasted outwards away from him, colliding with anything in its path.

Samael was propelled backwards, bearing the brunt of the explosion. He flipped in the air and landed in a heap on the dewy grass.

The feeling of release was so great that Doran could have

fallen asleep right there on the hill. But it wasn't over yet. He stood, just in time to see Samael staggering to his feet.

The bottle-green suit was charred and there were new cuts and burns adorning his already scarred face. Just for a moment, Doran thought he glimpsed a begrudging reverence in Samael's cold stare, but his usual casual indifference soon returned, as he clasped his hand and stump behind his back as if about to take an evening stroll.

For a moment, they simply beamed intense hatred at one another. But then Samael's lips stretched into a thin smile and he raised his eyebrows playfully.

Doran wondered for a second what on earth was so funny but then, to his horror, he saw Samael reveal the arm that still had a hand attached to it. In it, he was clutching both the watch and his severed hand. Doran cursed himself. How had he missed Samael picking them up? With a triumphant wink, Samael pressed the button and was gone.

In the heavy silence that fell over the hilltop. Doran stood alone, swaying on the spot. With a jolt, he remembered Léonie and hobbled over to her. She was in a sorry state but she was still alive.

'Did we get him?' she asked, wheezing.

Doran answered with a solemn shake of the head.

With a mournful sigh, Léonie outstretched a gnarled hand. 'You mind?'

Doran helped her up and grabbed the sword which was still frozen in mid-air. It came unstuck at his touch and he sheathed the blade behind Léonie's back.

Léonie surveyed the battlefield, inspecting the scorch marks caused by Doran's outburst. 'You put up a good fight then?'

He didn't answer her, the silence conveying everything he felt.

Léonie nodded, understanding, and attempted to stand on her own. For a moment, the pair said nothing, both staring ahead.

'I know I don't deserve your forgiveness,' she began, her voice breaking. 'But you know what the worst part of all this is? It came to me that night on the moor. If this always happened… if we've changed nothing after all…then that means you always knew that one day I'd travel back here and betray you. And you still took me in and trained me…'

She couldn't hold the tears back any longer. Doran fought the urge to look at her, maintaining his stare into the distance.

'I don't know what I do to earn your forgiveness one day – or if I even do,' she said. She was still sobbing but a resoluteness had entered her voice now. 'But I'm going to do everything in my power to put things right. I promise, I will find you – the future you – and failing that, I will stop that lying murderer Samael myself if I have to.'

Doran felt her hand graze his shoulder, her touch like a dagger through his heart.

'Goodbye, Doran,' she whispered. Sparks erupted around her and she vanished.

It took Doran a while to bring himself to look at the blaze still raging at the bottom of the hill. It wasn't until the sirens began to blare in the distance that he snapped out of his daze. He sat on a small boulder at the edge of the hill and watched as an ambulance, police cars and a fire engine all appeared and crowded around his mum's car. He watched the blaze die down under the pressure of the water. He watched them load the ambulance with a stretcher and drive off out of sight. He watched as the road was cordoned and the wreckage of the car towed away. Eventually, the road sank into darkness again – the cones and tape the only indication of the world-shattering event which had taken place there.

'A terrible night indeed,' a solemn voice came from behind him.

Doran turned on his boulder, ready to fight again. Had Samael or Léonie returned?

Professor Everie stood before him, wearing a pristine tweed suit and looking thoroughly out of place in the great outdoors. Next to him was Mr Bishop, who looked devastated. Under his arm, he gripped a small book.

'As soon as we knew, we came at once,' Mr Bishop said. 'We had to find you.'

30

THE WEST RESTORATION FRONT

'Why are you here?' Doran asked.

'We've been searching for you ever since you left the mansion,' Mr Bishop said. 'And then we learned of this event taking place.'

Doran glared at them both. They were talking as if his mother's death was some prearranged meeting spot.

'We are deeply sorry for your loss,' Professor Everie said. 'If there is anything—'

'Why are you here?' Doran repeated, weary of all well-wishing.

Professor Everie dabbed his forehead with a soggy handkerchief. Mr Bishop attempted to move closer but Doran's hard stare held him back.

'We understand our timing is far from ideal,' Mr Bishop said.

'But we must speak with you,' Professor Everie carried on.

'The fate of the Eternalisium hangs in the balance.'

If Doran wasn't ready to drop from exhaustion he would have screamed. 'I don't… Do you think I… I don't *care* about the bloody Eternalisium! I had my orientation, I learned everything I needed to. I know about my destiny. I know about the Magistair. And I want no part in any of it.'

Professor Everie and Mr Bishop looked for a moment as if it had been *they* who had just lost a close family member. But Doran had no time for either of them. How dare they come there? How dare they invade this deeply private moment?

'Your father felt the same way,' Professor Everie said. 'Please don't make the same mistake as he did.'

Doran's jaw clenched. 'Mistake?'

'Your father shunned his duty. He shunned his destiny. And right now, the Society is paying the price for it.'

Doran would have liked nothing better than to grab the book Mr Bishop was still clutching and whack them both hard in the stomach with it. 'I don't care,' he said.

'You should,' Mr Bishop said. 'Tobias has been slowly taking control of the Eternalisium for nearly a decade, and now he has finally made his move. I cannot express to you how devastating his leadership could be for the Society – and for the world.'

'Then stop him,' Doran said. 'You can't be the only ones who feel this way. Surely there are those in the Society who can help?'

The two men glanced at one another. 'Tobias is an incredibly powerful individual with a strong family line. However, even he cannot compete with a West. That is why we are here. We are here on behalf of The West Restoration Front…'

'The what?'

'The West Restoration Front,' Professor Everie repeated. 'We are a secret faction that has risen up in recent years within the

Society. We aim to return the Eternalisium to the old ways. We want the true Magistair back on the throne.'

'I don't want any throne!'

'My apologies – a poor choice of word,' Professor Everie said, though he did look as if he were fighting the urge to bow. 'What I mean to say is that we need a leader. The Eternalisium needs a leader. Tobias will ruin us. He will ruin everything we have built. We need a West back in charge. It's the only way. We need *you*, Doran.'

'Don't make the same mistake your father did,' Mr Bishop added. 'His choices only led to a terrible accident. He died trying to achieve an impossible task. You cannot rid yourself of these abilities. But *we* can help you learn how to truly control them. We can keep you safe. And in return, you can keep the Society and the world safe.'

'I know what the Eternalisium is like now,' Doran said. 'It has no hand in keeping the world safe.'

Mr Bishop's knuckles turned white as he gripped the spine of the book. 'Then change it! You are the Magistair. The Society will follow you in whatever direction you want to take it. I know it will.'

Doran raised an eyebrow. 'And what about Tobias?'

'Tobias wanted you gone to discredit you. He engineered your escape,' Professor Everie said. 'But rest assured this will not be the last you hear from him. As soon as he assumes control, he will formally make you an enemy of the Eternalisium and hunt you down. The only way to keep yourself safe is for you to face him head-on. Come with us. We can hatch a plan together. We can take him down piece by piece, for you to take your rightful place as Magistair.'

Doran felt sick. 'I don't want this,' he said. Why couldn't he just go home? Why couldn't he be allowed to grieve?

'And that's exactly why it should be you,' Mr Bishop said, and tossed the book to him.

Doran snatched it out of the air and saw the words: *Ancient Myths of the Pictish People by Oswald MacAlpine* written on the cover in gold letters.

'We stopped by your house on the way here,' Mr Bishop said. 'I gave you that book to help you understand where you come from. You have a destiny, Doran. I'm sorry, I truly am. And you have my word, if there was any other way, we would have found it by now. You are our only hope. I understand all this must be very overwhelming. But I am begging you. We are begging you. Come and lead us into a better future.'

Doran stared at the man who a matter of weeks ago had simply been an over-eager teacher. Back when his life had been normal. A life that now belonged to someone else. But what kind of life would he have now? What would he choose?

The word escaped Doran's lips before he was even aware of it. 'No,' he whispered, feeling the last of his energy ebb away.

'I'm sorry?'

'I said no. Tell Tobias you couldn't find me. Tell him I'm lost in time. Tell him whatever you like. But I disappear, tonight.'

Before Professor Everie or Mr Bishop could open their mouths in protest, Doran had taken one final glance at the now empty road that had caused so much suffering. It was time to leave Linntean behind for good. There was nothing left for him there. He thought of his house, the cobwebs and the empty sensation he had felt when he had wandered through it. He thought of Zander and prayed that he was still where he had left him. The grass rustled as Doran departed from the hilltop, leaving a devastated Professor Everie and Mr Bishop in his wake.

31

THE SHOW MUST GO ON

Doran slipped between the growing number of people fighting to get in line for the latest film in town. He managed to push himself beyond the queue for the ticket booth and looked up to see a billboard showing two familiar faces.

MGM Presents
Alexander DiCaprio
in
The Birth of Zorro
featuring Hamish the Horse as Tornado

He stared up at the smouldering expression of Zander, who was holding his sword aloft astride Hamish. Dressed all in black, with a matching eye mask and hat, he really did embody the role of the swashbuckling vigilante.

With a final glance at a group of young women who were staring at Zander's giant face and whispering excitedly, Doran extricated himself from the crowd and strode on down the street. The large white letters of HOLLYWOODLAND stood on a hilltop in the distance. Every few steps he would scratch the leg of his trousers, cursing the irritating clothing of the era he was in. He never thought he would miss his old school uniform, but just then he would have killed for a ten-second raid of Mrs Hunter's lost-property box.

He rounded the corner and crossed the street to a garage where two large hairy men were already working away on a sleek black car that, while looking old to Doran's eyes, had only just come off the production line.

'You're late, Bruce,' the older of the two men said to Doran in a West Coast drawl. 'We got the nineteen twenty-five Model T in today and I told you to be on time.'

'Go easy on Robert,' the younger man said. He had a wheezing, gruff voice that could only come from years of smoking unfiltered cigarettes. 'He was probably out late last night hanging out with all his actor pals.'

Doran's ears went pink. 'My apologies Mr Harper; won't happen again,' he said to the older of the two men. His mouth curled as he glanced at the junior mechanic. 'Try not to touch anything important till I get back, Fred. Wouldn't want you exerting yourself.'

Fred simply grunted at him before getting back to work on the car. As Doran took his overalls down from the peg, he heard a loud clang followed by a yell. 'Dammit Freddy. Be careful, will you? That headlamp is worth more than your year's wages!' Mr Harper shouted, and a grin flashed across Doran's face as he started to get changed.

After a long day, and suppressing the keen desire to invent electric car windows a few decades too early, Doran trudged the long mile home. He passed Zander's billboard once again, which was now lit up and shining among all the other bright lights of the boulevard.

Doran's walk home was his least favourite part of the day. There was too much silence, too much thinking time. At work, despite the company, he was relatively content, busying himself by tinkering away with the automobiles. But at night he had nothing to distract him – smartphones, or even MP3 players, a far-off thought. While he could probably have found an ingenious way to make a 1920s alternative, both he and Zander had agreed to live without modern comforts. Neither fancied trying to explain their existence in a time before television.

So Doran found himself alone in his thoughts, each night worse than the last. His internal body clock was telling him that almost a year had passed since the night he had returned to Linntean. This also meant his eighteenth birthday was fast approaching. The first after his mum's death – and the day destiny insisted he join the Eternalisium. However, Doran had no intention of granting destiny's wishes. He had made that perfectly clear on the hilltop that night. How could he be expected to become the Magistair that would one day train the very person he knew would betray him? How could he look her in the eye after what had happened? No. Doran had cut all ties to his fate. He had returned to Zander and insisted that he choose a place for them to hide. Hide from Samael, the Eternalisium, Tobias and anyone else who knew the name Doran West. So Zander had chosen Los Angeles in the Roaring Twenties. The birth of cinema. They changed their names and began a new life.

No one in the city cared about their past as long as they could work.

Doran became Robert Bruce, a mechanic. Zander, on the other hand, found it difficult to remain in the shadows. He turned up one day on the MGM Film Studio lot, Hamish in tow, pretending to be a horseman. A quick demonstration, and he had the job – as did Hamish. They began work as the stunt double on *The Birth of Zorro*, the origin story of the fabled masked hero.

The production, by all accounts, hadn't run smoothly. The original choice for Zorro, an actor named Douglas Fairbanks who, according to Zander, was a 'big deal', had to drop out due to a scheduling conflict. He was then replaced by some young upstart who, rumour had it, had been given the job due to his wealthy father's deep pockets.

The new lead actor hadn't proved too popular with members of the cast and crew, treating everyone like dirt on his boot. Hamish was equally unimpressed, and hadn't taken too kindly to the young man's rough nature. On the third day of filming, the horse happened to kick out a stray leg and the actor was badly injured. Onlookers and Zander insisted it had been the star's fault rather than Hamish's.

With thousands of pounds already spent, as well as the actor's medical bills, the studio was facing a terrible decision. They needed to find yet another new lead actor who would work for peanuts – and fast – or lose a great deal of money by halting production. Zander was more than happy to demonstrate his ability and, rather reluctantly, the studio had found its latest star. Production was stopped for a month while Zander was given a crash course in swordfighting and all the tools necessary to be a daring hero. Now, nine months later, Alexander DiCaprio and

Hamish were about to make their silver-screen debut, and Los Angeles was abuzz with anticipation.

Doran hadn't been too happy when he had found out about Zander's stage name. But apparently, according to the studio executives, 'Zander Munro wouldn't do,' as 'Who'd pay to see a movie with a star named Munro?' So Zander had panicked and blurted out the first actor's surname he could think of and the producers had liked it so much that he couldn't change it.

While Doran had initially been reluctant about his friend becoming a famous star of classic cinema, he had eventually come around to the idea. Firstly due to the incessant pleading from Zander but secondly, he saw it as a chance to show time and destiny what he thought of them. He would allow this change to take place. It was only a small change after all. It wasn't hurting anybody. Unless you counted the actor who was still lying in a hospital bed. But he had deserved it, right? Zander had come home from work on his first two days seething at how the actor was treating Hamish. 'No respect,' he spat. 'He's whipping Hamish within an inch of his life!'

Exactly. He didn't deserve whatever career he was meant to have anyway. Doran hadn't even heard of him. So he had decided to take the risk and hope the Eternalisium would pay no attention to such an innocuous anomaly. That had been until the voices started.

'Doran,' came a rippling, echoing voice, as he was walking home one evening.

Doran covered his ears, though he knew it would be no use. The voice never came from the outside world. It was in his head.

'Doran,' it said again, louder.

Doran broke into a run, trying desperately to shut out the voices. If he could just get home. If he could just get to Zander...

'*DORAN!*' It was the loudest the voice had been. Other voices joined it, filling his head. He stumbled and dropped to his knees, pulling at his hair and letting out a silent scream.

Then suddenly the voices stopped and a quietness fell over the street. Yet he felt the hairs on the back of his neck stand on end, and he looked up to see the slight frame of the Seer who had eyed him so keenly at the Eternalisium. She towered over him, her long neck stretching out of her cream-coloured robes. Her dark brown eyes inspected him and the glint of the *teine uaine* shone in the moonlight. 'Destiny calls, Doran West.'

And as suddenly as she had appeared, she vanished again.

That was new, he thought. A bead of sweat ran down his forehead and he brushed it away, rising to his feet.

'I'M NOT COMING!' he thundered to the heavens. He wouldn't let them win. He refused. *He* would decide his fate.

Doran hurried on, back to his apartment, hearing no more voices. He finally shut the front door behind him and rested against it for a moment, breathing a deep sigh of relief. He had made it. He was home.

It was a very basic living space, with an open-plan kitchen and two armchairs and beds taking up most of the room. The only hidden part of the flat was the toilet, sink and bath, which were crammed into a corner. A small coffee table sat in the middle of the main room which had playing cards scattered across it – one of the few sources of entertainment. It had been quite an adjustment at first for two teenagers who had grown up encircled by technology to adjust to having no screens in their home. For the first two months, they were worried they would die of boredom.

Nevertheless, they had persevered and grown accustomed to their humble surroundings, occupying their time with games, reading and, in the case of Zander, working on his first screenplay. Doran had become the story's chief editor, kindly reminding his friend of any pieces from future pop culture that he might be unconsciously – or consciously – stealing.

Zander was where he always was when Doran arrived home, asleep in his armchair after a ten-hour day of filming. Over the past year, Zander had gone through a growth spurt, and was now the same height as Doran. He also seemed to have grown into his looks, flaunting a chiselled jawline and high cheekbones. All he had needed was a professional taming of his curls by an MGM make-up artist and the movie-star transformation was complete.

Doran sat beside him and nudged him awake. Stirring, he returned a drowsy smile.

'Out like a light again, was I?' he asked, yawning.

'Hamish still working you hard?' Doran said. He tried to make his tone jovial, but he failed. While the voices were silent, he never felt they were truly gone – merely sleeping. He could still feel them, ready to erupt at any moment.

'Rough day?'

Doran averted his gaze. 'Just the usual. Fred being Fred at work.' He had made the decision not to tell Zander about the voices. Zander would only blame himself for his actions having allowed the Eternalisium to find them.

Zander clearly didn't believe him but seemed to decide to allow the conversation to move on. 'I had to do a fight scene all on Hamish today,' he said, his voice now showing signs of life. 'He was loving it. That horse is a born performer.'

'Wonder where he got that from.'

Zander grinned. 'He likes his new stable – you should see it. Best of the best.'

There was a pregnant pause and Doran could tell Zander was working up the courage to ask him something. 'You know the head of props said he was looking for a new mechanical expert for rigging the practical effects. I could put in a good word for you if you like?'

'Thanks,' Doran said. 'But I'm fine where I am.'

'Oh, come on,' Zander said, shifting in his seat. 'It would be so cool – me and you working together. Beats slogging away with the two meatheads all day.'

'I don't mind it really,' Doran said. 'It keeps me occupied, keeps my hands busy. You always say there's such a lot of downtime on a film set.'

'That's just for us lowly actors,' Zander said. 'The crew is always doing something. You'd be kept plenty busy. Plus, you'd get to make things again. Create fun toys and explosions for me to ride away from heroically.'

He struck a pose and Doran snorted. 'Maybe,' he said. 'I'll think about it.'

'Awesome,' Zander said, grinning again and sitting back in his chair. After a moment, the grin fell away and his eyes slid out of focus. 'Can't believe we've been here nearly a year…' His voice trailed off and he shot Doran an apologetic look.

'It's fine.'

Zander motioned in his direction and knocked a half-filled glass from the table. It shattered and both of them glanced at the shards.

'I'll get it,' Zander said, moving into the kitchen and finding a dustpan and brush. He swept up the fragments and then stared at them. 'I saw your hand twitch,' he murmured, not looking at Doran.

'But I didn't do anything.'

'But did you want to?'

Doran flapped his arms. 'It's not like I'm trying to quit smoking. I'm trying to suppress…instinct.'

'I know, I know,' Zander said, disposing of the broken glass. 'I'm only saying because you asked me to keep an eye on you—'

'And make sure I don't use my powers. Yes, I know,' Doran said, jumping to his feet and pacing back and forth. 'I don't *want* to use them.'

'I know—'

'Will you stop saying you know?' Doran roared and Zander flinched. 'You don't. You're not the one whose powers have caused nothing but pain and misery. You're not the one whose powers caused his mum…' Doran stopped, hot tears stinging in his eyes.

Zander let out a long sigh. 'You're right. I'm sorry,' he said. 'This must be a difficult time for you. Do you want to talk about it?'

Doran shook his head, willing the tears back into their ducts.

'You haven't talked… Not since that first night when you collapsed in front of me holding that book,' Zander said, fumbling for the words and gesturing to the copy of *Ancient Myths of the Pictish People*, which was lying squint on the top section of the bookshelf. It was clear he was unsure how to progress the conversation.

'Talking wouldn't help.'

'It might,' Zander said. 'Look, I'm here whenever you need me. You would do the same for me. In fact, you already did.'

'Thanks.'

Zander nodded in acknowledgement. He looked ready to sit back down but seemed compelled to say something. 'I'm sorry this happened to you. But listen to me very carefully. What happened that night wasn't your fault.'

'But it was,' Doran said. He took a moment's pause, finding his voice before carrying on. 'My mum died because of who I am. She died because I have these powers. Because I went off gallivanting without any warning. She *knew*. She tried to tell me how dangerous all this was, but I wouldn't listen. I rebuilt the watch and we went off on our merry adventure.'

'That journey started with an accident. You know that. If you hadn't jumped us to Florence, we both would've fallen to the bottom of that ravine.'

'I still put us up on that cliff edge. That was me.' Everything Doran had been thinking was pouring out of his mouth now. Perhaps it was the upcoming anniversary of that fateful night in the woods, or perhaps it was purely because he hadn't spoken of any of this since he had jumped to get Zander straight after it all happened, but everything was coming out in a stream of consciousness. 'I can't use these powers again. Not when they're the reason she's gone. Not if they can't do anything to save her.'

'Doran, I can't imagine what you're going through,' Zander said. He grabbed him by the shoulders and squeezed. 'But you have to stop blaming yourself. Otherwise, you're never going to be able to move on. I know it's not the same, but when my mum left, I can't tell you how many nights I'd lie awake thinking that somehow, I was the reason she'd gone. And if you can't let that feeling go, it will tear you apart.'

Doran gave him a searching look. 'It's not the same,' he said, his face sagging. 'It *is* my fault. I got it wrong. I trusted the wrong people. If I hadn't been so naïve and stupid, maybe I could have worked it out. Maybe I could have saved her.'

He shrugged Zander off and turned his back on him. Rage bloomed inside him as he thought of Samael, Léonie and his own stupidity for falling for their plan. Zander was wrong; it *was* his fault.

'DORAN!' The echoing voice that had plagued his walk home reverberated in his head once more.

Doran covered his ears again and moaned. 'Not now, not now.'

'What's wrong?' Zander asked.

'DORAN!' The echoing voice was louder and the other voices joined the taunting again.

'Stop it, stop it,' Doran pleaded through gritted teeth.

'What's happening?' he heard Zander call through the voices.

Then the unmistakable silky-smooth voice of the Seer echoed on its own. 'Destiny calls, Doran West.'

'SHUT UP!' Doran bellowed, flailing his arms as if attempting to strike a blow upon his tormentors.

'Doran!' he heard Zander call again. 'You need to stop!'

Doran spun around, not realising what Zander truly meant until he saw the look of fear on his friend's face. He wasn't looking at him, but at the electric-green sparks which had started to surround him.

He was losing control. Suppressing his powers for nearly a year had caused him to regress. The grief and anger pinned down all sense. It felt just like it had done before – the inevitability that he was about to jump. Doran stared back at Zander, sharing his fear now. 'I'm sorry,' he said, before pushing his friend backwards to safety.

Doran was engulfed by the storm and he disappeared, with no idea of his next destination.

32

THE BEGINNING

Doran landed, panting, on snowy grass. A wave of fury crashed over him and he hammered the snow with his fists.

Once he had tired himself out, he looked up to see a very familiar set of surroundings. The West family home lay before him. He was in his front garden. When exactly, he did not know.

He trudged through the thick, white blanket, creating a track of footsteps to the front door where the path should be. Closing his eyes, he teleported a further two metres across the threshold and into the house.

His eyes remained fastened shut. He knew where he was, he could feel the front doormat beneath his still snow-covered shoes. Yet a voice in his head seemed to be warning him against looking, as if to do so meant certain, unimaginable torture. Slowly, one eye at a time, he forced himself to brave the pain.

It was clear the house had been unoccupied for several

months, just as it had been the last time he had visited. Dust and cobwebs lay in every corner and crevice. Doran squinted at his feet to see unopened letters and flyers surrounding him. He edged through the hallway, placing one foot in front of the other as though scared the floor might fall from under him. The rooms of the house seemed to be repelling him, his eyes unable to bear the sight of them for more than a second. To see his mum's favourite chair vacant, or the remnants of her last day still laid out awaiting her return. He eventually made it to the kitchen, where he stopped. Something wasn't right.

The table was completely clear – a sheet of dust undisturbed apart from at the very centre, where an emerald-green coin sat expectantly. As Doran approached, he saw the familiar pentagon-shaped crest of the Eternalisium. It was embossed on the front of the coin in an audacious gold, which winked at him in the gloom of the cold kitchen. Reaching out, his hand trembling, he plucked the coin from the table. Particles of dust sprang to life, shimmering in the moonlight.

Below the coin was a note, written on a business card embossed with 'Professor Ianto Everie' in gold lettering. Covering this, in black ink was the message, 'If you change your mind.'

Doran was about to put the coin back on the table when he looked up to see movement outside the window. Was it Tobias or the Vigils? Had they come for him? Or had Professor Everie or Mr Bishop only just placed the coin, moments before his arrival?

He opened the back door and stepped out into the snow once more. What he saw was not an intruder but a scruffy, one-antlered stag, hovering nervously in the shadows. Momentarily disturbed by Doran's sudden appearance, he soon settled again and stood as though posing for a photograph.

'Rufus?' Doran murmured, the breath of the word hanging in front of his face in the icy air.

The stag remained still, prompting Doran to stuff the coin in his pocket, turn on the spot and go back into the house. He found himself opening a cupboard, searching for the boxes of cereal. He wasn't sure why he was doing it but there he was, taking out a box of dusty cornflakes and returning to the back garden.

Rufus was still there in the same spot, as motionless as a painting. Doran poured the cereal into his hand and reached out towards the stag's mouth. It took a few breathless seconds, but Rufus eventually turned his head and began munching on the still crunchy flakes. Doran let out a soft giggle at the tickling sensation on his hand, reaching for more flakes and allowing Rufus to continue eating. After a while, the stag stopped, content with the meal he had been given. Doran put the box on the ground and very cautiously, he slowly began to stroke the deer's neck and side. After revelling for a moment at being this close to such an animal, he noticed the stag's black, beady eyes, which were not on him, but on the house. Doran followed their gaze, then looked back at Rufus, his brow furrowed. With a sigh that seemed like his last breath, he nodded.

'Yeah,' he whispered. 'I miss her too.'

He felt the hot tears prickling his eyes. Unable to stop himself any longer, he began to sob. It was the first time he had allowed himself to do so properly. The tears streamed down his cheeks, dripping onto the snow. He sniffed, and stroked the stag as a weeping child might pat its stuffed animal.

'You know, the worst part is she never got to hear how sorry I was,' he said. 'For leaving, for what I said – the last thing she heard me say to her...' He sniffed again. 'And that I'll never get to tell her she was the best mum that anyone could ever have asked for. She raised me, all on her own, and I wish I had told her how amazing and strong I thought she was.'

The tears continued to fall. But with them came a new sense of purpose. Doran pulled the coin out of his pocket and stared at the crest once more. His mind drifted back to something Tobias had said during his tour. *'We can teach you things you have barely dreamed of. What you have discovered so far will only be the beginning. You are capable of so much more.'* He then heard the memory of Léonie echoing in his head. *'They still whisper about what he was capable of. He was so old and had learned more than any Magistair before him...'* Finally, the words of Samael plagued his thoughts. *'You are a West. Time is yours to command...' 'The most powerful of all...'*

'This is why I do it,' Doran murmured, his eyes widening. His grip tightened around the coin, the emblem burrowing into his palm, and he looked up into Rufus' beady eyes. 'It's the only way to save her.'

His arm dropped from the stag's side and he shut his eyes, leaving Linntean behind.

Down the hidden lane near Greenwich Park in London, Doran appeared before the forgotten mansion that sits invisible to most who pass by. It was the eve of his eighteenth birthday. The sun was setting, giving the world a pinkish tinge, the remaining light highlighting the arched entrance gate. This was not the Eternalisium from which Léonie had journeyed – the one he had built in his image. This was when destiny had decreed his story within the mansion's walls would begin. A new era. A new leader.

The door of the mansion opened to reveal a beaming Professor

Everie. As Doran crossed over the threshold, the professor gave
a slight bow.

'Welcome, Magistair.'

And the emerald-green doors swung shut behind them.

ACKNOWLEDGEMENTS

I was always the kid in the class who rushed through their work to be the first finished. This novel finally taught that eager kid that getting anything right takes time. Also, that it's OK to ask for help sometimes.

To my family and friends, thank you for your unwavering support and encouragement throughout this process. To those who listened to my ramblings, and who read early ideas and drafts, your help is something I will never forget. A special thanks must go to Anni, the first Doran West fan. Doubts are natural when working on something like this so I thank her for believing in this story on the days I did not.

To Miles Hawksley at DGA. You were the first person to cast a professional eye over this novel. Your feedback was kind, fair and gave me the confidence to keep going.

Finally, I would like to thank everyone at Lightning Books for giving Doran's story a home and for their invaluable guidance in helping it reach its potential.

If you have enjoyed *The Rebel of Time*, do please help us spread the word – by putting a review online; by posting something on social media; or in the old-fashioned way by simply telling your friends or family about it.

Book publishing is a very competitive business these days, in a saturated market, and small independent publishers such as ourselves are often crowded out by the big houses. Support from readers like you can make all the difference to a book's success.

Many thanks.

Dan Hiscocks
Publisher
Lightning Books

CRAIG ANDREW MOONEY is a Scottish writer, actor and producer, originally from Dundee. His first taste of writing came at a young age when he was tasked with devising his Primary 5 assembly. The play focused on his class's history topic all about Robert the Bruce and the Wars of Scottish Independence. The time period always stayed with Craig and now, nearly twenty-five years later, he has revisited it in his debut novel, *The Rebel of Time*, a time-travelling adventure where the protagonists find themselves meeting Scotland's most famous king.